Keeper's Secrets

The Final Keeper Trilogy

Book Two

Chronicles from Alku

Recommended Reading Order

The Final Keeper Trilogy
Keeper's Reign - Book 1
Keeper's Secrets - Book 2

First Published by Eliza's Imaginary Adventures LLC 2024

Copyright © 2024 by Eliza Leone

ISBN: 979-8-9893984-5-4

Contents

Foreword

"Always second-guess me. Always watch for signs of weakness and corruption because if you notice it, others will notice, and they will come running to try and slip into those cracks and destroy everything."

It's been less than a year since I was finally convinced to publish Keeper's Reign, and it feels like it was only yesterday. That's probably due to the amount of caffeine and hours I've spent in front of my Steam Deck and iPad in the last ten months. (Yes, I write on a Steam Deck. Don't judge.) At this point, I see red spelling squiggles in my sleep.

All that aside, my love for Alku and its residents hasn't dulled, only grown. I still cry when they are in pain, laugh when they say something witty, and scream when they are being dense. But they are mine, and I love them and feel honored that I can share their stories with you.

Keeper's Secrets is the second part in The Final Keeper Trilogy and where you'll see Onnie and the others begin to come into their own. They have many more stories to share and lessons to learn as they navigate the changing world around them. But darkness is moving, and by choice or fate, they are directly in its path.
Stay with me, and we'll see how bright they glow.

From my world to yours,
Eliza

For those who feel required to wear a book jacket that disguises the words beneath it.

I hope one day you and I can wear the one that reflects the truth of what lies within.

Pronunciation Guide

Warning!
This page contains possible spoilers!

Names:

Eliza Leone : e-lie-za lee-o-knee

Onnie Moore : on-ee more

Abbot Moore : ab-ot more

Danella Vansand : dan-ella van-sand

Maldwyn : maald-win

Xayn Ellwood : z-ay-n l-wood

Elaric : e-lar-ick

Kushima : caw-she-ma

Sove : so-vuh

Athan : ah-thahn

Locations:

Alku : al-coo

Tiefen Hool : tee-fen who-oo-l

Nisi Dakry : nye-sigh dack-ry

Species / Races:

Sanguiste : sang-whist

Paranam : para-nam

Transmogromorph : trans-mog-row-morph

Atarga : ah-tar-guh

Qondo : con-doe

Nymph : nim-pfh

Mechanite : meh-caw-night

Zwerkalt : zwer-cult

Ceirnes : see-sins

Items:

Custos regni : cus-toes wren-ee

The story so far...

October 2021, a young woman named Onnie moves to a quaint town nestled in the forested mountains of the Pacific Northwest called Alku. Her Grandfather requested that she inherit his bookshop, and when she arrives, she finds he is sicker than she thought, and a mysterious woman named Rebecca is running things in his place.

Over the next few weeks, Onnie learns to care for the bookshop and how to run it effectively. Her days are filled with happy tourists, dinner at her grandfather's, and her nights watching the clock until she can return to the shop. She meets many residents of Alku, including Dany, a spirited chameleon of a woman who doesn't give Onnie the option of not being her friend.

One stormy afternoon, the local PE teacher, Gabriel, braves the rain to ask Onnie for help in finding a book he's desperate to obtain. They spend hours searching, and when they've given up and taken a break from the dust and paper cuts, Onnie finds a book matching the description under the front counter. When both she and Gabriel touch the book simultaneously, they feel a tingle of electricity and then are thrown backward.

Onnie learns she's not just inheriting a bookshop but has also been chosen by the entity that is the world's knowledge archive to become the next Keeper or protector of said knowledge. Gabriel has been chosen to be her Guardian and watch over her, and she finds out that they are emotionally connected via glowing strands called the Bond.

Gabriel begins to train Onnie in self-defense, but during one session, a pain sears through them both, bringing them to their knees. Onnie astral projects herself into the bookshop and finds it's been broken into and vandalized. After checking in person the state of it, Mal, her cat, appears in her arms, unconscious, able to talk, and with bad news. The damage done to the shop was too much for the weakened Keeper, and her grandfather was killed in the attack.

The morning after the break-in, Onnie learns the truth and sees the attacker and chases after him into the woods, but he disappears from within her grasp, and she's left with more questions than answers.

While Gabriel and Mal finalize the funeral arrangements, Onnie moves into her grandfather's home, inviting Gabriel to join her and Mal. On the day of the funeral, Onnie is met with a group of people from around the world who traveled to pay their respects to the fallen Keeper and witness the Transference of power between him and Onnie, the new Keeper.

Onnie is shocked and betrayed when Gabriel stabs her in the heart as part of the ceremony, and she finds herself in the void, the plane where the Bond resides. They complete the ritual and return to their bodies, and the transfer is complete. Then Onnie feels an icy feeling, but now she's more powerful and able to freeze the sulking man in black in place to confront him. After shocking all in attendance with the use of powers she should not possess, Onnie sends the man in black, Mal and Gabriel, to the bookshop to interrogate him further.

After a chaotic start to a new life in Alku, Onnie finally feels like she's found the place she belongs, and when a soft, feminine voice agrees in her mind, Onnie knows her new life has only begun.

Keeper's Secrets

The Final Keeper Trilogy
Book 2

Chapter 1: Pest Control

March 2022 - Alku | Onnie Moore

The chilled morning air made Onnie shiver as the dew-covered moss she knelt on in the forest outside of Alku began to seep into her jeans. Everything around her was still as if it held its breath and tried to be as unintrusive as possible. The leaves didn't sway, no birds or bugs were above her, and the songs of the frogs and crickets were silent. It felt unsettling, but considering everything was trying to help by staying out of their way, Onnie appreciated it and tried to ignore the eeriness.

Onnie withdrew from her physical surroundings and closed her eyes as she slipped entirely into her mind. All around her were strands of colors, vibrant and pulsing at different brightness and patterns atop endless black. She'd entered the void and was observing the Bonds that connected everything in the world.

Currently, there were two she was most interested in, and both originated from within her chest. She followed a purple thread to her best friend, Dany, and a red one to Gabe, Dany's brother and Onnie's Guardian and boyfriend. Both of them were chasing after another one of their enemy's pawns and carefully leading the roach, as they'd begun to call them, to a prearranged point within the trees.

He's headed your way, Dany, Gabe said mentally along the Bond.

Got it! Dany answered quickly. *I'll herd him toward Wayward Clearing. Are you ready for us, Onnie?*

I am.

After seeing their progress for herself, Onnie was confident she was ready for the creep. This latest pawn was more dumb than the last if he allowed himself to be railroaded so easily. He should be easy to dispatch and easier still to pick through his memories for any information they could use.

Don't get cocky, Cat. Remember the last one. Gabe chided after having felt her emotions shift along their Bond from alert and focused to bored and apathetic.

Onnie rubbed her upper arm, and the sharp pain of a healing wound brought her focus back to the present and her arrogance back in check.

I remember.

Their last assailant, a small, spry woman with dull brown eyes and sandy blonde hair, had been more cunning than they initially thought. When the three of them had made some assumptions about the roach, they'd been wrong, and she'd got too close to Onnie. Even though it hurt and she'd felt stupid, the slice along her arm was a good reminder. It reinforced her need to be stronger, faster, and more focused. There was an entire town full of people counting on her, and she couldn't afford to make mistakes.

Onnie dropped her hand and resumed tracking their group's progress through the trees and wild berry bushes. With her eyes still closed, she tried to use Dany and Gabe's Bonds to triangulate where their quarry was, but it wasn't as precise as Onnie would have liked.

Where is he now? Onnie asked with a frown on her lips.

He's headed your way, directly in front of me. About three minutes out. Dany cursed, and the annoyance in her tone of voice, mental or not, was pissed off. *I swear, Onnie, if this dude runs through one more muddy river, I will kill him before we get to the clearing.*

I told you not to wear good clothes today.

Onnie smiled as she teased the woman who typically looked ready for the runway, not a runaway, and today was no exception. Her brightly colored hair may have been braided, and her pants were certainly leather, but Dany really could make anything look stunning.

I didn't think that meant my shirt too! I wore combat boots and leather pants. For goodness sake, what more do you want from me?

Shut up, Dany, and focus! Gabe snapped. *He's too far left. At this rate, he'll miss the clearing.*

I can fix that. Onnie followed Dany's Bond to where she'd estimated the roach was, and then Onnie projected an image of herself in his probable path. She waited, and when the greasy-haired man burst through the shrubs and saw her, he let out a yelp and then turned and ran in a different direction.

He's back on course now, Onnie said with an eye roll at the predictable pawn.

Thanks, Onnie, Dany replied, out of breath, even mentally. *Al...most...there....*

Onnie returned her mind to her body and got to her feet, her palm raised, ready to freeze the man in place once he ran right into their trap. Less than a minute later, he exploded into the clearing at a full sprint, his Bond dull and lifeless. She quickly captured the thread and opened her eyes, and when the man's eyes met hers, fear flashed across his face. He only had a split second to whimper before Onnie closed her palm, pulling on his Bond and freezing him in place.

Other than a slight bit of slack to allow his body to continue functioning and the capability to move his eyes, he was nearly entirely immobile. His eyes quickly darted around the trees wildly, looking for an escape, and when Onnie lowered her hand and met his stare, she saw raw fear in his eyes.

"You know who I am," she stated. "Look left for yes, right for no."

They were always defiant initially, and this roach was no different when he predictably looked up.

"Do not make me ask you again," Onnie walked closer to him, and when she was five feet away, she stopped, "or I will hand you over to my friends when we are finished."

That seemed to get his attention, and while none of them were true, there seemed to be some misconceptions about her within the roach's ranks. It didn't matter. She could use them to her advantage. When his eyes widened even further, her stomach dropped, but she continued nonetheless.

"Oh, you've heard of them. My Guardian and our allies do not play as nicely as I do." Onnie tilted her head to the side, "Oh, I hear them now…" she smiled at him. "Don't you?"

He quickly flicked his eyes left.

She was relieved it hadn't taken long to gain his cooperation, but she still hated being feared.

"Oh, good. You're learning."

She heard when Gabe and Dany entered the clearing from opposite sides and came to stand behind her. Their presence calmed her nerves and reminded her why she'd needed to toughen up and shuck her people-pleaser attitude in the first place. To protect them and others.

They'd run this routine too many times to count at this point, and even without turning to look, Onnie knew what the two people behind her were doing.

Gabe stood with his arms crossed, his brooding expression making his six-and-a-half-foot, broad frame even more intimidating. Dany feigned boredom, likely examining one of her fingernails.

Onnie returned her focus to the man she held frozen before her.

"Just in time, too. Why don't we try that first question again? You know who I am, correct?"

The roach looked left for a few heartbeats before looking back at her.

"Good. Then you know what has happened to those who have come before you."

After another few seconds of looking left, Onnie could see the sweat that had begun to bead on his brow despite the cold March chill.

"Were you sent here to kill me?"

He hesitated for a few seconds, but then his eyes looked left, then to the right.

"Interesting...." Onnie said, pacing out of his view, his body still frozen mid-stride.

Dany and Gabe stayed where they were, hands on hips and arms crossed, respectively.

"Are you working alone?" Onnie asked but looked at Gabe to provide the answer instead of the roach since she couldn't see his eyes from where she was.

Gabe shook his head, his brown hair brushing along his forehead as he relayed to her that the man hadn't answered at all.

"Hmm.... Let me rephrase. Do you know of other active pawns?"

"Right," said Gabe, relaying the response.

"Fair enough," Onnie patted the man on the shoulder twice from her position behind him. "I can't fault you for what you do not know." She circled back to stand in front of him and smiled over her shoulder to Dany. "He's been so helpful. Don't you think? Should I let him speak?"

Dany twirled her toe in the moss and leaves, cleaning off some of the mud from her boot. "He wasn't very helpful to my wardrobe, but if you think he'll cooperate, then sure," she shrugged. "Go for it."

Gabe rolled his eyes at his sister's horrible acting, and Onnie genuinely laughed at the pair.

"How about a compromise?" Onnie told the pawn, "If I let you speak, will you apologize to Dany for making her run through all that mud?"

The man looked confused, but after a moment, his eyes went to the left.

"Great! It's settled then!" Onnie said with a touch of false enthusiasm in her voice.

She removed the binding from around his head, and the man inhaled a deep breath on reflex before coughing and sputtering.

"I am sorry. I know it's difficult to breathe when bound, but we didn't know if we could trust one another yet, so I had to be sure."

Per their depressingly well-practiced script, it was Gabe's turn. He stepped forward and leaned his full six and a half-foot frame toward the man, his face looming over him and casting a shadow. The Guardian's voice was lower than usual and nearly a growl.

"You do remember the conditions of our trust, I presume."

The roach gulped loudly before looking past Gabe and over at Dany and then lowered his eyes slightly. "I am sorry for dirtying your boots."

Dany smiled and waved him off. "Oh, it wasn't your fault, silly pawn, but thank you anyway."

While Dany was truly a genuine and good person, her current over-the-top, sugary-sweet character was a stereotype, and it drastically conflicted with Gabe's tough and twitchy one. All of that was expected and planned in their charade, but Onnie was always amused watching them play such exaggerated versions of themselves.

"That wasn't what I meant," Gabe stated. "The truth continues, and so does your life, and then maybe your freedom. Understood?"

The man's head moved up and down emphatically. "Yes, Sir."

"Well, now that we've gotten that part out of the way," Onnie said, swapping places with Gabe again as he returned to stand beside Dany to brood once more, "I'd like to talk about your boss."

"I don't know much, really," the man shook his head vigorously. "He doesn't tell me anything. Only what I need to know."

Onnie smirked. "Ah, so which is it? He tells you nothing, or he tells you what you need to know?"

The man's eyes widened, and he shook his head, sputtering as he tried to walk back his admission.

"Make me believe you," Onnie said, crossing her arms. "Tell me everything you *do* know."

"I-I—" he stuttered.

Dany stepped forward and past Onnie, stopping a step closer to the roach than Onnie was.

"What's your name?"

"Ah…Maurice."

"Nice to meet you, Maurice. It's a shame you're working for the rogue guardian. You look like a smart man. You know my friends over there?" she pointed over her shoulder with her thumb. "You've seen what the Keeper can do," she leaned in closer to whisper. "This is just a taste of her power, though, trust me. That said, she will treat you fairly if you cooperate with us." Then she stepped back and gestured to Gabe. "Him, on the other hand, her Guardian, he will not hesitate to kill you. So, if you want my advice, tell us what we want to know, and then you can be on your way."

"You'll never let me go. You're going to kill me."

Dany tsked at him. "Maybe, but you can make that much easier on yourself and far less likely."

Gabe grunted, "Let's get this over with. Stop coddling him and let me take him to the shop. I will rip out his thoughts, get what we need, and then ship his heart back to his boss in a box."

Maurice paled, and what parts of him weren't frozen by Onnie began to shake, and his teeth chattered slightly.

"See what I mean," Dany continued. If you answer the Keeper's questions, we will dispose of you quickly and painlessly, and you'll be free from whatever deal you made with the rogue."

Maurice's expression was filled with terror, his eyes so wide that there was more white than iris.

"He'll find me in the afterlife. He'll bring me back. He'll torture me."

"It won't be worse than what I'll do to you," Gabe sneered. "I promise you that."

The pawn's voice was frantic, and his grip on his emotions was near to breaking. Maurice had turned out just like the other roaches in the end, and Onnie knew they wouldn't get any more from him the civilized way.

"Alright, enough of this," Onnie said exasperatedly as she pulled a small vial filled with a deep purple fluid from her pocket. She flicked the hinged top back with practiced skill and swallowed the tablespoon of liquid. Then she closed her eyes and pressed her thumb inside her palm against the flawlessly clear quartz stone set into a ring she had flipped the wrong way around. As the potion coated her throat and the stone began to hum slightly under her touch, Onnie saw the ring's Bond flash brighter. She used the potion's power boost and the ring's channeling assistance as she reached for Maurice's Bond.

"Please, no! Not my little girl!" Maurice begged on his knees.

A robed figure projected an image of a small child, no older than seven, into his palm. She was bound by rope, gagged with a dirty piece of fabric, and surrounded by darkness filled with the sounds of monsters.

"Do what I want, and your little girl will have another chance at life. Fail me, and you will not live long enough to regret what I will do to her once I'm rid of you."

"Anything, anything!"

The man Onnie had come to understand was Jakob, must have been pleased because even within another person's memory, he made her shiver as evil radiated off of him in waves.

"He has your daughter," Onnie said aloud, her eyes still shut.

"Yes," Maurice sobbed.

"Then we have an understanding, you and I." Jakob began pacing the stone floor in front of Maurice's kneeling form. "You will follow the Keeper and her pet Guardian. You will report back to me with what you learn of their habits, their plans, and anyone they come in contact with."

Maurice looked up, eyes puffy and red, tears streaming down his cheeks. He nodded once at the rogue guardian before him. "In return, you'll free my daughter?"

The hooded figure nodded, "I promise I will release the poor soul."

Onnie withdrew from the memory and looked Maurice in the eyes. It was understandable why he'd fallen for the false hope Jakob had given him. Clearly, the man was an Outsider and not familiar with their world of magic. That didn't make his and the little girl's needless pain any less, though, for the two of them or Onnie, who had to relive it and would now carry the memory with her.

"I am sorry for your loss," she said with genuine regret.

Maurice's brow creased in confusion, and he began to look rapidly between the three of them. "What loss? What are you talking about? I have done everything he's asked of me. My daughter will be safe."

Onnie shook her head, her vision slightly blurred, while Dany became suddenly very interested in a twig beneath her boot.

Gabe stepped forward. "If Jakob had your daughter, she is already dead. That...or something worse."

"No!" Maurice said as he began to struggle against Onnie's hold. "She's fine! He gave me his word."

Onnie shook her head, a tear rolling down her cheek for the cruelty that stole a child's life too early. "He gave you his word he'd release her *soul,*" she said quietly, "and we will make sure he did, but your daughter is gone. What he did to her is irreversible, and she was likely gone before the two of you even spoke."

Maurice stilled, went silent for a few heartbeats, and then let out a wailing cry filled with enough rage and fury that Dany jumped. Onnie stepped back and joined her, grabbing her hand and providing them both with a bit of comfort.

I hate this part, Onnie said to Dany along their Bond.

Dany nodded and stepped forward, her arm trailing a bit behind her as it still held Onnie's. "Maurice, I promise I will do all I can to find your daughter's soul and return it to the angels."

Onnie knew what was coming, but seeing the tears stream from the pawn's eyes, his flesh red and blotchy, and his breathing erratic from his struggling, she wished she hadn't been right. It never got easier to see them, once innocent, so broken.

"It's your fault he did what he did! You stupid bitch!" The roach snarled at Onnie.

Gabe stepped past her and Dany and, in an instant, had the struggling man's jaw between his fingers.

"The Keeper had nothing to do with your daughter's death, and the Head Sister just offered to see her at peace."

The man jerked his chin free from Gabe's grasp and spat on the floor at his feet in response.

"We're done here." Gabe turned to look at the two women still behind him. "See yourselves out. I will finish this up."

Onnie swallowed roughly, "Wait."

She let go of Dany's hand and strode past Gabe and around to Maurice's back. "I am sorry, truly, but we tried to reason with you."

After she hesitated for a fraction of a second, knowing what was coming and wishing there was any other way, she gripped his neck and closed her eyes, clawing through his consciousness. She wove her way past his memories, through his dreams, and along the Bond to his glowing soul. With one firm snap, she severed his processing mind from his body and detached his soul.

When she opened her eyes, she knew they glowed ice blue from the amount of power and emotion she had expended.

Maurice now stared straight ahead at Gabe and Dany, muttering incoherently to himself. His body remained conscious, but his mind was gone. The man was now closer to brain-dead than living.

A zombie.

And she'd made him that way.

"It's done," Onnie said, releasing her hand from his neck while she dropped her hold over his Bond, unfreezing him. With a soft thud, he fell to his knees on the moss.

Onnie turned and left the clearing, never looking back.

Onnie had only made it a few hundred yards before Dany and Gabe were at her sides, each grabbing one of her hands and leaving her with her silence.

She watched the trees go by as they walked, strong and tall in their long lives. They stood unyielding to even the harshest of storms. Perhaps they lost a few branches here and there, but they always grew back stronger.

It made her wish people were more like trees. Except no one stood their ground for what they believed in anymore. Everyone was too scared. Scared of what others would think or do or how they could lose something if they did the perceived 'wrong' thing. People didn't live their lives for karma. They lived each day to get through it and then die. All while they prayed that the afterlife would take mercy on them and that the grass would be greener on the literal, other side.

Maurice had been no different. When faced with a moral choice, his daughter or the life of a woman he'd never met, he chose the former. Onnie couldn't even imagine being given that choice, but Maurice had made it easily. How was an Outsider to know that by choosing to save the life of one, he was condemning many more to death and hardship than he understood? Not that it mattered. His choice didn't save his little girl in the end. Now, the father was essentially dead, just like his child.

She'd done that, and it wasn't the first time. What room did she have to judge his moral choices?

"Cat, I know what you're thinking," Gabe said with a gentle squeeze of her hand in his. "What you did was far more merciful than what my father would have done."

"His soul has found peace, Onnie, and I'll inform the angels so that someday, so will his daughter's. If you hadn't done what you did, you know dear old Dad would have destroyed his soul."

"I know it's hard," Gabe kissed the back of her hand, "but we're with you."

"I know," she lied. They weren't, and they didn't even realize it. She stopped walking and tried to plaster a calm expression on her face. "Do you mind if I walk alone for a while?"

They exchanged glances over her head, and Onnie clenched her jaw to prevent herself from snapping at them for treating her like china. Again.

"Not far, just a ways behind you. I just need to think," she added, releasing both of their hands.

Dany nodded and hugged her before looping her arm around her brother's and leading him forward.

Onnie fell in step behind them, though not too far, and she could still hear them whispering about how they thought she was persevering and how it wasn't fair for her to deal with all of this. She appreciated their concern and continued walking and listening to them, but really wished they'd talked along the Bond instead of verbally. Hearing their pity made her want to scream into the void.

They were right, though, and it wasn't fair.

It wasn't fair that they were all forced to deal with these horrors, especially Dany. Gabe was her Guardian, and that job came with its fair share of destruction and deception, even if most Keepers lived calm and carefree lives. Keepers were supposed to spend their days learning and documenting the world around them. Maybe they would step in to settle an occasional grievance or moderate a dispute, but none had ever been in any situation like their current one.

Dany had found a book explaining the history pertaining to Warrior Keepers from the past, of which, there were only a few. Onnie was one of only three Keepers in history whose powers were not solely focused on learning but also on protecting defensively *and* offensively. Historically, Keepers were passive, gentle creatures, but even the other two Warrior Keepers had never had to do anything close to what Onnie had done in the last few months. It was becoming increasingly clear that the nightmare she was stuck in was different, and it was changing her.

Onnie's attention was drawn back to the two ahead of her when she heard Dany mumble, "I can't imagine what she sees in their minds."

"I can, and I would do it for her if I could," Gabe said, and Onnie felt his sorrow trickle down their Bond before he pulled it back. "She has nightmares."

"I would have been surprised if she didn't," Dany sighed. "At least we're getting better. That time was…easier," Dany said with hesitation.

"I'm not sure that's a good thing," Gabe muttered.

"I know. Just once, I wish they would listen to us. I genuinely do want to help them."

Dany's voice was heavy with anguish, and Onnie knew her morally good best friend was also suffering more than she let on to others.

"You were laying the good cop on a little thick, Dany," Gabe grinned.

"Hey, it's Onnie's job to awe them, yours to make them wet themselves, and mine to make them feel hope, and I think I have been doing a damn good job. Thank you very much, you big oaf."

Gabe wrapped his arm around Dany and pulled her to him, ruffling her hair. "You did fine."

"I know," Dany beamed. "So did you, Mr. Dark and Brooding. 'I will rip out your thoughts and then ship your heart back to your boss in a box,' where did you get that from?"

"I didn't get it from anywhere. I would have done it if we knew where to send the box."

"Ew," Dany shivered. "I'm glad you're on our side."

"I always will be," he kissed the top of her head. "Would you report this one to Dillon?"

"Sure, I can stop by the police station on my way to the library."

Gabe looked over his shoulder at Onnie, who was mainly looking at the sidewalk beneath her feet as they walked. "Cat, you're quiet."

"I'm fine," she answered crisply. She glanced up to see them look at each other again, concern shown plainly in their eyes and along Gabe's Bond.

It was Dany who broke first. "Well, I have to go into the library. I'll catch you both later?" She turned, heading down a gravel path that branched towards the east side of Alku. "Coffee this afternoon?" she called back to Onnie.

"Sure. I'll meet you there," Onnie said with another faked, happy smile.

"Love you!" Dany called out before heading on her way.

Gabe slowed his strides and waited for Onnie to catch up before he pulled her into his arms and held her tightly.

"I hate this," he whispered over the top of her head.

"I know," she nodded against his sternum.

"I wish I could do that part for you."

"I know."

He kissed the top of her head, and she softly squeezed him around his waist in return.

"I have to go to class. Will you be alright?"

"I'll be fine. I'm going to the shop." Onnie stepped back and smiled as best she could. "Check in on Mal. Maybe make him inspect that box I got in yesterday with all those German books."

Gabe smiled, "Make the fuzzball earn his keep. I'll stop by this afternoon, and maybe I can walk you to coffee?" He bent to kiss her cheek, and she nodded.

"Sure. Have a good day. Teach those kids good stuff."

He beamed, his love for his job and students making him practically glow.

"It's basketball inside the gym today. They'll be very happy."

Onnie smiled genuinely for the first time since they'd left the house earlier that day, and then they turned and went their separate ways.

Chapter 2: Darkness Within

March 2022 - Alku | Onnie Moore

Onnie had only been puttering around the shop for a few hours before she gave up. Her mind was all over the place, and if she let it wander, she'd find herself back in Wayward Clearing and the situation from earlier that morning. So, she'd tried distracting herself but that hadn't worked either. She'd already balanced the sales log twice, having had to redo it once she noticed none of her counts added up. When she switched to studying about the magical world, she'd read the same page four times before groaning and setting it aside and admitting defeat.

Onnie whined into the empty shop from where she leaned on the front counter. Her forehead was pillowed on her arms, face buried under her loose black hair.

Hey, Mal?

What's up? Mal replied telepathically along their Bond before the Russian Blue feline appeared beside her arm on the marble counter in the shop. His fur was glossy, he was licking his lips, and he had probably been in the middle of a bath.

"Hey, I'm gonna head home early. Just wanted to give you a heads up." She stood up and stretched her shoulders out before she proceeded with the shop's closing routine. She could feel Mal watching her with his intelligent yellow eyes, but she ignored him. Instead, Onnie turned off the kettle, washed the tea set, and extinguished the vanilla-scented incense in the front window before sliding the stained glass window, depicting an owl, closed.

"You don't have to tell me when you're leaving. What's up, Onnie?"

She felt Mal's concern subtly push along their Bond, contradicting his relaxed and playful tone.

"No reason," Onnie said, turning off the gas look-a-like lamps along the central aisle with a sharp click as she walked by them.

"Onnie…." Mal said in a mix between a growl and a purr.

"I'm fine," she reassured, approaching the counter and tapping his nose with her fingertip. "Just a little tired from this morning. I think I'm going to head home and take a bath."

Mal playfully swatted away her finger and narrowed his eyes at her. "Fine, but you call me if you need me."

"Of course." Onnie smiled, then scooped the feline into her arms and snuggled her nose down into his fur before she mimicked his purring.

"Did you want me to stay here?" Mal asked when she put him back down on top of the counter.

"Would you mind? Just for a few hours." She pulled her coat on, grabbed her bag from the back room, and slung it over her shoulder.

"No big," Mal said with a cat grin. "I can understand the desire for a private bath."

She gently tugged on one of his ears as she passed him and headed for the front door, stepping around a few neatly stacked piles of books. "Thanks, Mal. I won't be too long."

"Do what you need to."

Onnie pulled open the door and glanced back over her shoulder. "Oh, I left you a tea in Abbot's study."

Mal licked his lips, "Thanks, girl. Later!"

She closed the door behind her and heard the soft thud of Mal jumping off the counter. Then, the shop's lock clicked into place without her needing to pull her keys from her bag.

Onnie rested her palm on the green wooden door and softly ran her fingertips over the word, *Abbot's* engraved into it. The warmth of the shop radiated through her palm, which helped calm her frantic mind. It felt like the shop was trying to tell her everything would be okay, and for a few moments, Onnie believed it.

"I'll be fine," Onnie whispered. "I just need to…be alone for a bit."

There was a feeling of understanding along her Bond with the shop, and Onnie smiled and turned to face the cobblestone street. She inhaled a deep breath of the fresh, cold air and began her walk toward her Grandfather's old home, where she now lived with Gabe and Mal. Gabe would be at the school for a few more hours, and with Mal at the shop, Onnie had the house to herself, and she didn't plan on wasting the opportunity.

Onnie glanced at her phone and mentally calculated how long she had before she was supposed to meet Dany for coffee but then internally groaned at having to lie to her best friend again. She tried justifying to herself that she wasn't lying to the others when she told them she'd be fine. She *would* be fine. She didn't have a choice. Too many people relied on her, but just for this afternoon, Onnie wanted not to be fine, even if it was only for a few hours.

She carefully put walls between her Bond and everyone else in her mind and shut them out. All of them would come running if they felt her release the hold she had been keeping on her emotions. Everyone only wanted to help, and she knew that, but she needed to do this by herself. No matter how wonderful they were or how much Onnie loved them.

As she lazily wandered the streets toward her lake house, she smiled at the blooming flowers around her. Even though it was winter, when nature should be sleeping, Alku and its residents enjoyed an extra touch of beauty. Flowers blossomed, animals roamed freely through the green spaces around town without fear, and the contrast between what should be and what was never ceased to amaze her. Alku was indeed a magical place, and she was still ashamed she'd not realized it for so long when she'd first moved to the town.

Alku was a bastion for peace, and a lot of that safety weighed heavily on her shoulders. Everything from those flowers that woke during the winter when they shouldn't, to the various magical races that lived in harmony. All of them were under her protection.

Keepers were magnets for magic, drawing people to them and the home of the archive. Unfortunately, they drew all shades of morality. Because of that, the current Keeper and their Guardian assisted with the wards and protection of the town. While Onnie provided magical coverage, Gabe was the muscle to back it up. They took their responsibility very seriously, and not just because they were Keeper and Guardian, but because Alku was their home, and they loved the people in it.

In a standard Keeper's lifetime, there wasn't often anything historical or dramatic that they needed to be involved with. Except, Onnie drew evil to her like seagulls flock to bread on a beach. Her power made her an appealing target for those wanting to take it from her. Like Jakob, Abbot's former Guardian, and Gabe and Dany's father. Only he'd abandoned his duty and gone rogue. He was not the first in history, but certainly the worst since nearly the creation of the Keepers.

But it wasn't just the ill-intentioned; even the occasional stupid magical teenager tried to prove themselves to their friends by testing their strength against her own. Onnie was the equivalent of the creepy house at the end of the block, and all the brave kids challenged their friends to run up and touch the porch. Most of it was good fun, and she didn't mind, but it was exhausting, even if she wasn't bored.

When Onnie glanced up and saw her home at the end of the road ahead of her in a straight, unimpeded line, she closed her eyes. As she walked, she reached out to the city's wards. She'd only recently learned that if she knew where to look, she was able to see their Bonds, too, and they glowed just like everything else around her. The only difference was they were significantly more complex and made up of various colors. All woven into each other thanks to all of the different power sources and protections fueling them.

Similar to when she interacted with another person's Bond, Onnie pulled on the large bundle that was the wards, checking for slack or holes. When nothing shifted, she concluded everything was fine and pulled herself back to her body, opening her eyes just as she arrived at her driveway, her small Jetta parked in the right spot.

With a quick skip, Onnie took the small path beneath a dormant jasmine vine and up the few steps to the front door, where she swiftly unlocked it, stepped inside, and shut it behind her. Warmth enveloped her from every direction, and she leaned against the wall and sighed. Her Grandfather and Rebecca were gone, but their essence would never leave their former house, and every day, it wrapped Onnie in its arms and welcomed her home.

She slid her bag from her shoulder onto a nearby bench with a quiet thunk before pulling off her coat and placing it on a hook nearby. Then she pulled off her boots, hat, and scarf, putting them all in their places.

Onnie hummed softly as she walked through the house that had hardly changed from when her grandfather had been alive. They hadn't had much time or energy to replace the antique furniture but the three of them didn't mind. She made her way directly into the bathroom connected to her bedroom, where she immediately turned on the taps and began filling the expansive bathtub. A small glass jar sat on the side of the bath filled with a milky-colored liquid, and she uncorked it and poured a few tablespoons into the water. It immediately started to foam, and the soft scent of roses and vanilla tickled her nose.

She shed her clothes and slipped into the warm water before it was halfway finished filling the tub, the silky smooth water massaging her bare skin as it continued to undulate around her. She sank her body into the warmth up to her collarbones, closed her eyes, and carefully freed the tension and emotions she'd locked away within herself for the last few months. The water rippled from the intangible release of energy, and she heard the glass in the windows and shower door vibrate slightly. Thankfully, the house was warded, so none of what she'd just freed would escape. Not that it was harmful, but it wasn't something she wanted to spoil the world with.

With her eyes still closed, Onnie turned off the taps by pulling on the faint Bond of the knobs and waited until the slow dripping stopped, leaving her in a quiet room. She focused her mind and soon saw only a black void with strands of light flowing all around her. The Bond. They pulsed and glowed softly, a rainbow of colors.

The Bonds that connected her to her friends glowed brighter than the rest. Gabe's red one, Mal's yellow, and the thread that ran to the shop, which shimmered and shifted like the inside of an abalone shell. The Bond she'd strengthened temporarily with Dany was nearby, and her purple one also glowed a bit brighter than the others around her.

Onnie found her own Bond and looked at the glowing bundle more closely until she could see the individual threads and discern each one's unique brightness level and strength. What she was doing, she was pretty sure, should have been impossible from all of her research on Keepers and the Bond. Yet here she was, doing it anyway.

She carefully searched through the threads until she found the darkest one of them all. It was the only thread within her Bond that was a deeper green, nearly black, color. Thankfully, it wasn't noticeable among the others when wound into the whole. If Gabe or Mal found it, she'd have quite a bit of explaining to do, and she would do pretty much anything to avoid that conversation. Thankfully, she was confident that neither of them could see the Bond in that much detail.

She tugged gently on the dark thread, separated it from the others, and pulled a section towards her like a rope attached to an anchor. A small bundle of glowing orb-like objects was attached to the darkest portion, and she quickly counted them.

One, two, four, ten, twelve. Okay, all here.

She mentally sighed and stared at the orbs.

With every roach they dispatched after the first few, Onnie had been severing their souls from their bodies in an attempt to free them from the rogue's control. Gabe, Dany, and Mal assumed at the point she severed one, she released it for the angels of death, the species of beings who ferry souls to the afterlife, to collect. Except she'd tried that.

Once.

Two days later, that same roach, now with an unsettling stare and the subtle smell of foul, had tried to complete their mission for a second time.

Onnie had found the abomination's soul was again in their body, but fused in a way to their Bond that made Onnie's hair stand on end for nearly a day after she'd seen it. As with their first encounter, she removed their soul, this time damaging it due to the heinous magic that had replaced it within them. Then, she watched as she let go of the soul and saw it begin to return to the rogue a second time.

Onnie hadn't had much time to consider the consequences nor discuss anything with the others, but she had quickly retrieved it and decided, from then on, that she'd keep them safe until after the rogue guardian was removed from the equation.

Now, right before she severed a roach's soul, she pulled her own darkened Bond thread free and wrapped it around the soul's essence. Then, when she was ready, the thread would rebound like a rubber band and pull the soul into hiding with the others, and so far, no one else had noticed or asked what she'd done differently.

Onnie searched for the most recent addition to her growing collection and separated it from the others. Once her mental projection came in contact with the essence directly, she heard the voice of a young girl reverberate around the void.

"But Dad, why can't I go? I've never been to the zoo before. Daniel's Mom will be there."

Onnie knew what was coming next, and as expected, she heard a familiar voice.

"I'm sorry, but not today. Maybe next time."

It was the voice of the roach—no, Maurice. The man from that morning, as he replied to his daughter.

"Fine!" The young girl shouted at him, and Onnie could feel the girl's anger as she walked away from her father in the memory.

Maurice sighed, his guilt emanating from him in soft pulses. *"I'm sorry, baby, but we just don't have the money,"* he whispered.

Onnie felt his struggle between granting his daughter's desire and knowing they couldn't spend what was practically their last dollar on anything other than food or her school tuition.

Before Onnie could see or hear more, the memory shifted. They always did.

At some point, Jakob had undoubtedly realized that Onnie was doing something to keep the souls from returning to him, and he'd begun leaving a sort of insurance policy within his roaches. If Onnie spent too much time looking through their memories or tried to use them to learn information about him, she would trigger it.

A dark fog began to wrap around the orb, encircling it like a python and trying to choke out the remaining light that shone from within it. Then, the darkness began clouding her mind and making her ears ring. Onnie quickly but carefully replaced the orb with the others and re-hid them within her Bond, ensuring they were safe, secure, and, most importantly, undetectable.

When she'd finished and was confident no one would find them, she began the slow mental walk back to her body, which was now shivering in frigid bath water.

Onnie barely cracked her eyes open and blinked at the contrast in light from within the void and the room around her. Once acclimated, she opened them fully and saw that the bathroom's white walls had a soft blue tint, and she confirmed in the mirror that her eyes were the source. They always glowed blue when she tapped into a large amount of power, focus, or emotion, and checking on the souls she carried required all three.

Outside the window, it looked like the sun was setting, and she pulled herself from the water and quickly wrapped up in a towel.

She groaned, her body stiffer after the bath than before it.

"Sitting in the same position for multiple hours will do that to you, I guess."

She examined her extremely pruney toes and fingers before cleaning up and getting dressed.

It was easy for her to lose track of time when she was that deeply meditating, but it still caught her off guard. It almost felt like she'd blacked out and woken up in a new place without any recollection of how she'd gotten there.

When she was dried and dressed, she wandered into her grandfather's library, lit a fire in the fireplace, and went to the kitchen to make a cup of Keeper's tea.

As the kettle warmed up, Onnie checked her cell phone and smiled sadly at the message from one of her older brothers, Tyler. They had been texting about nothing important all day, and the benign interaction had been a double-bladed knife of joy and loneliness. She responded to his message and then pulled up her group one with Xayn and Elsi.

Another roach today. Xayn, I have the empty bottle and will swap it with you tomorrow. Oh, and Elsi the slight modification you made to the ring's setting was perfect. The Bond's magnification was more stable and able to stay active the entire duration of the potion's effects. Thank you again, both of you.

As she hit send on the message, the electric kettle beeped.

She poured herself a steaming mug of the purple-tinted tea and then returned to settle into a pile of pillows and a warm blanket before the fireplace in the library. As Onnie sipped her tea, she began pulling all the energy she'd released prior to her bath back into herself. By the time she had finished, her skin was coated in a thin layer of cold sweat, and she felt physically ill. The darkness that tainted the souls she carried settled back within her and she hated the feeling of it.

After a few minutes of controlled breathing to settle her stomach, Onnie finished the remainder of her tea and set aside the mug. Then she curled further into the blankets and the soft bed she'd made on the floor and closed her eyes.

Onnie carefully lowered her mental walls and was thankful no one noticed her disappearance for a few hours, or they'd decided not to mention it. She was exhausted and drained, and her mood began to turn even more foul as she wondered if she'd ever be free of Jakob, his roaches, and protecting the souls of those who had tried to harm her and her friends.

I'm finished with my bath. I think I'm gonna nap, she told Mal. Then she put aside thoughts of the dim thread within her Bond and the twelve secrets it hid.

Onnie shut her eyes, and when she felt the warmth along her Bond from her family, she wrapped it around herself, just like her blankets, and drifted off into a deep sleep.

Chapter 3: Transmogromorphs

March 2022 - Alku | Onnie Moore

A soft tingling pricked the back of Onnie's neck, making her smile and look up from the weathered book she was reading at the shop's front counter.

The door opened, and Dany's teacher voice drifted into the quiet bookshop.

"Alright, everyone, don't forget to use your inside voices. We don't want to make Miss Onnie sad, do we?"

"I sure don't!"

"Nooo…."

"Naw, aw."

The little ones all said in rumbling, high-pitched voices.

As a group of Alku's finest kindergartners filed into the space, Onnie closed her book and went to lean on the front of the counter and wait for them. All of them were dressed in hats, coats, and scarves, making them look like a small army of tiny skiers and utterly adorable as they waddled around in circles.

Dany stepped inside last and closed the door before removing her winter coat and hanging it on the coat rack. "Remember, you can take off your jackets, but make sure to hold on to them."

"Yes, Miss Dany," the chorus of little voices said as they began struggling with their bulky winter gear, turning to help their friends and then be helped in return.

Onnie watched the adorable chaos cyclone as it aimed itself in her direction.

Dany tapped a young boy on the nose with her finger, who now held a puffy bundle in his tiny arms. "Come on, Eric, you lead the way."

Eric fist-pumped the air and whooped, nearly dropping his jacket in his excitement. "Yes!" He skipped past Dany, down the center aisle, and towards where Onnie stood waiting for them. "Onnie, Onnie!" Eric said, cheering at her and altogether abandoning his inside voice.

"Hello, Eric!" Onnie beamed and squatted to his level, giving him a high five. "You've grown at least two inches since I've seen you last!" She held up two fingers, and Eric's eyes widened.

"I have?"

Onnie giggled and nodded her head. "You have. Either that or I've shrunk!" That earned her a chuckle from the entire group of kids, and she stood before waving at them. "Hi, everyone. Welcome back to Abbot's. Ready for story time?"

"Yay!" the kids cheered in unison.

"Okay, how about you follow Mal into the reading room? Miss Dany and I will be right behind you."

When the children saw a cat slink around the counter and begin weaving around one of the young girl's legs, they all giggled.

"I guess you're the leader today, Jenny. Follow Mal and help get everyone settled, okay?" Onnie said to prod them all along.

"Okay!" a little blonde in overalls said with a quick pat on Mal's head.

Onnie nodded once at Mal, and he led the gaggle of children deeper into the back of the shop.

Don't be long, you two, Mal said to both Dany and Onnie along the Bond. *You know what happened last time.*

I told Dany they weren't allowed gum in the store anymore, Onnie replied with a smirk to Dany. *You'll be fine.*

Mal growled in their minds as the last kid's back rounded a bookshelf and slipped out of the two women's sight.

"It was just a little gum, and he liked the attention," Dany said before bracing herself on the counter and jumping up to sit on it.

"I know. Marie felt so bad I'm willing to bet he'll be snuggled up in her lap during the entire story today."

"Pet whore," Dany said with a shake of her head and a grin.

"Completely."

"How are you doing?" Dany asked carefully.

"Fine."

Dany glared at her, but Onnie ignored it.

"Onnie, yesterday was difficult on all of us, you more than any of us. How are you really?"

Onnie sighed. "I'm okay, I promise. I just needed some time. I'm sorry I ditched you for coffee. I took a bath and a nap."

"It's fine, and you'll make it up to me. Besides, that sounds better than coffee," Dany teased.

Onnie grinned, "Of course, whatever you want." She'd expect the request for a s'mores date or dinner at the Day Night Cafe to come within the week.

Dany beamed like the children, "So, what's today's story?"

Onnie walked over to a thin shelf of colorful leather-bound books on the rare book side of the shop and pulled one with a deep emerald spine from the top. "I'm thinking transmogromorphs. We haven't taught them about them yet."

"Shape-shifters?" Dany said with raised eyebrows. "That's a bit more...fantastical than you normally teach."

Onnie shrugged. "Magic comes in many forms, and if we can teach the little ones the capabilities of a shifter, they'll be better off for it. Besides, it's not fantastical," Onnie said, rolling her eyes. "They are real after all, even if rare."

"True that."

"Besides," Onnie said, smiling at the ceiling, "she created the reading grove for the kids to learn and keep them safe. The more the little ones visit, the more they'll remember they have a place to hide if they ever need it."

Dany sighed before she slid from the counter and walked over to the door behind it. "Sucks that you're right. Both of you," she frowned at the spot Onnie had been looking at above them. "Well, you head back. I'll grab you some water."

"Thanks, make it a tea. The kettle's on and should be done in a few minutes. Tin's by the serving tray."

"Got it," Dany said from the back room. "Now you get in there and save poor Mal from too many snuggles!"

Onnie chortled and made her way a few shelves back into the modern half of the shop. Then, she looked down at the carpeting beneath her feet and followed a path of small embroidered leaves. The whimsical pattern led her twisting and turning between shelves full of stories. The further she walked, the more extensive and more detailed the foliage became until it switched from embroidery to being quilted.

If anyone other than herself, the children, or a few trusted people had tried to find the reading room, they would have wandered for many minutes before becoming frustrated. Those not trusted would stray from the correct trail, become lost, and eventually end up in the front of the shop again. There was only one way to find the shop's children's section: by following the path only seen by those with pure intentions and a need.

A warmth in her chest made Onnie smile.

"I know you would not lead me astray," she told the shop.

The Book Nook, now renamed Abbot's for short, had grown more powerful and intelligent over the past three months, and together, she and Onnie were learning to protect themselves. And their friends. The reading grove for the children was an example of that.

The leaves beneath Onnie's feet became a mixture of loose and stitched to the quilted moss floor as they became substantially more dense. Turning the last corner, she found herself in a fabric replica of the tree circle, Wayward Clearing, from the forest just outside Alku. The kids were all lounging on oversized pillows in the shape of giant leaves, rocks, and flowers. Mal was, sure enough, curled up in Marie's lap, purring with his eyes closed.

Predictable, Onnie said to Dany. *Exactly where we thought he'd be.*

Shocker, Dany replied with a giggle.

The octagonal room was encircled by fabric trees, with branches that reached the two-story ceiling and wove together before erupting in various quilted leaves that would change with the season. The quilted ground had a slight give to it, and since the last time Onnie read to Alku's youngest residents, flowers had sprouted from tiny tufts of cotton grass.

"Look, Onnie!" Eric said, running over and holding out a delicate golden poppy made of fabric to her. "I found you a flower!"

"Thank you, Eric, that's very sweet of you."

He blushed when she took it from him and tucked it behind her ear. Then, he quickly scurried off to rejoin his friends, who had gathered some loose flowers around where they sat while they waited for her.

Mal yawned from his petting place, and Onnie threw him a sideways smile. "Shall we get started, guys?"

They were a rowdy bunch today and cheered once again as Onnie made her way to the stool shaped like a large stump among the trees. She sat down and folded open the emerald book with a creak of the spine and dust fluttering up into the air.

"Everybody ready?" she asked.

Nearly a dozen heads nodded at her in reply.

Onnie cleared her throat and began to read.

"Once upon a time, there was a naughty little princess named Esme. She was fair and beautiful, but all of her people feared her, for she was a wicked, wicked girl. She liked to pull the wings off of butterflies, yell at her servant girls, and would often scream and shout at her mother and father.

One day, her mother, the Queen, came to talk to the Princess. She told Princess Esme that another little girl was coming to live in the castle with them and that the two girls were to be sisters.

This made the Princess really angry. Esme didn't want a sister. She wanted to be the center of attention, eat all the sweets from the kitchen, and be given all the presents. She threw her hairbrush and stomped her feet, but the Queen would not change her mind and left the Princess there to pout."

From her peripheral vision, Onnie saw when Marie raised her hand and Mal raised one eyelid.

"Miss Onnie?" the little girl asked in a quiet voice.

"Yes, Marie?"

"Um… Why didn't the Princess's Mommy give her a timeout?"

Onnie smiled at the naivety of one so young. "Because Marie, sometimes people are naughty, and it doesn't matter what their Mom does, they can't change that, no matter how many timeouts they are given."

Marie's little eyebrows knit together, and Mal gently nudged her tiny fingers with his nose. She resumed petting him, and he winked at Onnie to continue.

"When the foster girl arrived at the castle a few weeks later, parties and festivals welcomed her. Much to the Princess's anger, everyone who met the new girl quickly loved her. Princess Esme's hatred grew as the days went on, and she began trying to hurt the young girl meant to be her sister."

"That's mean," Eric interrupted and crossed his arms dramatically. Onnie smiled but continued.

"But the young foster girl was gentle, ignored Princess Esme, and did not retaliate. Since coming to the castle, the foster girl had made many friends, and though the two little girls did not act as sisters should, she was happy.

One day, the foster girl wandered to a nearby village, and the Princess secretly followed her. Esme watched the girl but quickly became bored, and when she did, the Princess decided to pick up a stone and throw it at the girl."

"Ah!" A gasp rang out from the audience of little ones just as Dany entered the circle between the trees, her eyebrow raised in questioning. She carried the tray over to Onnie and sat it on the floor beside her before going to stand behind the children.

"As if by magic, the stone missed the foster girl, landing at her feet with a soft thud. The Princess was furious and began to shout at the girl she'd grown to hate.

"How did you do that?" Esme demanded, but the foster girl had no reply, for she hadn't done it.

As Princess Esme continued to shout, an old man in long grey robes stepped from the shadows and interrupted the Princess.

"My Lady, you have committed a grave deed. For no ruler should strike her subjects."

The Princess snarled and spat back at him, "What would you know, old man?" Then she knelt and picked up another stone, throwing it again at the foster girl. Only this time, once it left her hand and sped through the air, Princess Esme was suddenly the one in the rock's path, and it bounced off of her own shoulder. She cried out and turned around to look at the older man, only to find him in front of her now instead of behind.

"I tried to warn you, child," he sighed.

The Princess wasn't listening to him though, for standing before her was...herself."

Marie raised her hand again, "Yes, Marie?" Onnie asked.

"Where did the foster girl go?"

"Good question, Marie," Onnie smiled but continued.

"The Princess looked at her feet and saw she wore unfamiliar clothes. Instead of her soft and comfortable fabrics, she wore an itchy shirt and skirt like her maids."

Marie's eyes widened, and she smiled, "Oh cooool!"

Dany snorted and sat beside the girl, scratching Mal once under the chin.

"It is cool," Onnie said before finishing the story.

"The Princess was confused and scared, but the old man did not care.

"I warned you, Princess," he scolded. "Now you suffer the consequences. You will live your life in the shoes of another. A young girl, one less fortunate than you, and with no power to change her situation. While the foster princess will rule your people as they deserve to be ruled and save the kingdom from your betrayal and violence."

The foster girl, who now wore the face of Princess Esme, looked down at her hands in wonder when the man turned to look at her.

"You, my dear foster princess, will always have a choice. To aid you in your duty, you may choose any form you wish to take and need never settle."

The foster princess's eyes widened. "I can change what I look like?"

The old man smiled slightly, amused at the young girl's spirit. "Indeed."

"What about me?" Princess Esme shouted.

The old man ignored her anger and shouting. "You cannot. You will live out your life as you are now."

Esme realized she was trapped in a commoner's body and stomped away from the old man and the foster girl. When she returned to the castle, Esme tried to explain what had happened to her mother and father, and when the foster girl returned, she agreed that Esme was telling the truth. The King and Queen believed the two girls but could do nothing to reverse the spell.

From that day forward, Esme lived as a maid within the castle, never able to rule her people, while the Foster Princess went on to lead the kingdom into a time of peace and happiness.

She often altered what she looked like and walked among her people, but no matter who she looked like, the Foster Princess never changed. She was always kind, caring, and nurturing, just as a leader should be."

Onnie closed the book and lifted her tea from the tray on the floor beside her.

"The end."

"Yay!" The children cheered and then began to talk and giggle amongst themselves about the story they'd just heard.

"Does anyone know what the moral of the story is?" Onnie asked after a few minutes of watching them discuss it. Most of the little foreheads crinkled up in thought, when no one spoke up, she answered for them. "Never judge a book by its cover. Book jackets can be swapped, and you never know what stories are hiding underneath."

All of the little ones grinned and nodded their heads in unison.

Onnie sipped her tea and watched some of the youngest citizens of Alku talk and laugh before her. They were carefree, silly, and full of possibility—impressionable blank slates.

She drained her tea, refilled her small china teacup, and watched them a little longer.

They're so innocent, Onnie said to Dany, who snorted in response.

You say that because you only see them for an hour a week.

Onnie smiled and shrugged at her best friend, still seated across the room. *True, but either way. We need to make sure they're kept safe.*

We will, Onnie. Dany nodded to her across the heads of the children, who had no idea they were being spoken about.

They sat and let the children talk to each other and pet Mal. Some wandered around the clearing for a while, playing with the fabric flowers and fallen leaves. A few picked books off of shelves and read them in pairs, and one little boy curled up for a nap behind the stuffed stump Onnie was sitting on.

Eventually, their hour was up, and Dany ruffled Marie's hair and got to her feet. "Alright, kiddos, I think it's time we say goodbye to Miss Onnie for this week."

"Awwwww…" the room moaned.

"Do we have to?" Eric asked with puppy dog eyes and a pouty lip.

Onnie gave him a high-five and helped him to his feet. "Yup, you know the deal, buddy."

Dany went to wake the napping child as all the kids rushed to Onnie in one tangled mass of limbs for a group hug. She thanked each and every one of them for coming to see her, and then Mal led the youngsters back to the shop's main room.

"Onnie?" Dany asked tentatively as Onnie picked up the tea tray to return it to the front room. "How much of that tea have you been drinking?"

Onnie paused briefly before smiling at her best friend and continuing after the children. "What I need to. Don't worry, Dany. I'm being careful."

"Does Gabe know how much you're drinking?"

"Of course. Stop worrying. We're fine," Onnie said up at the shop's glossy wooden beams. "She's stronger than ever. I'm stronger than ever, and as long as I continue to get even stronger, everyone will be safe."

Dany reached out and rested her palm on Onnie's forearm. "Onnie, we *are* safe. Right now, I'm more worried about you."

Onnie nodded and walked away, and when the children came into view, she smiled wide. "You guys have a great week, okay?"

"We will!" They lilted in unison, their uncoordinated little bodies struggling with their coats as they began their transformation into little marshmallow children.

Onnie didn't miss the worried glance Dany gave Mal when they passed each other, but they said nothing. At least not verbally. Onnie set the tea tray on the front counter and rested against it and out of the way.

"Come on, kiddos, we've got a bit of a walk ahead of us." Dany ushered them to the door and pulled her coat on. "Say thank you to Miss Onnie now."

"Thank you, Miss Onnie," the little voices sang.

She waved to them as they left the shop and frowned when the door closed after the last one.

"Come on, Mal, spit it out. Why are you frowning at me?"

"I'm a cat. We don't frown."

"You do," Onnie stated before pouring another cup of tea.

"That's why I'm frowning," he jumped up on to the counter and pointed his paw at her cup.

Onnie lowered her teacup into the saucer with a clatter. "We've talked about this. Drop it," she snapped. With that, she turned and left Mal at the front counter, taking her tea and heading into her Grandfather's study.

She entered the room tucked away in a back corner of the bookshop that Abbot used to call his. Onnie carefully sat her tea on the heavy wooden desk and then walked around the back of the couch to flop into it. She closed her eyes and rubbed them gently with her fingertips.

Mal's warmth flowed along their Bond before he jumped onto her lap and bonked her chin with his head. He didn't say anything, just curled up and purred in her lap.

Onnie's anger and frustration evaporated, and she scratched the top of his head. "Do you feel it coming, Mal?"

"Hmm?" he said between purrs.

"The...darkness. Something evil is coming."

Mal stopped his purring and pulled Onnie's hand down with his paws. "What are you saying, Onnie? Did you see something?"

She shook her head, "Thankfully, not psychic. It's just a feeling."

"Trust it, Onnie. Besides, if you're feeling something malicious, we need to be ready for it. All of us."

"I know," she closed her eyes again and rested her head back. "That's why I want you to lay off about the tea. Strengthening my Bond with the shop will only help us. "

After a few moments of silence, Mal spoke again. "Onnie, why did you pick today's story?"

"Oh," Onnie opened her eyes and stared at the ceiling. "I don't know. I just felt like I should."

A soft humming rippled through her Bond, and she followed it back to the shop. "Did you want me to read that story to the kids?" Onnie asked the space around her.

The humming grew louder and more insistent before it stopped altogether. A few seconds after stopping, Onnie felt a faint tickling at the back of her neck, indicating someone was entering the shop.

"Customer?" Mal asked, jumping off of her lap so she could stand.

Onnie closed her eyes and looked for the newcomer's Bond. When she saw one shimmering oddly, she shook her head and left the study.

No...I don't think so. He's nothing I've ever seen before.

She quickened her pace and put shields around her mind to separate her Bond from the others as she entered the main room of the bookshop. Her manipulation of the Bond was still new, and she refused to let anyone get hurt because she was attacked due to not being careful enough. Instead, she temporarily cut herself off from the others, essentially building a wall of power between them.

In the center aisle stood a short man, thin and lean, his body made of odd proportions. He had short brown hair and sharp features and wore a business suit that made him look simultaneously like a young guy and an older man at the same time.

"Can I help you?" she asked, taking her place behind the counter with a friendly smile plastered on her face.

As he approached, the stranger smiled, but the air around his body seemed to shimmer. When Onnie looked a little closer, it was like his body was flickering on and off at a rapid rate.

He stopped when he reached the counter and placed both palms on the glossy marble. "I am hoping you can. I am looking for a book."

The wavering stilled slightly with the man's lack of movement, and his body visually solidified.

"Then I think you've come to the right place," Onnie said with friendly sass.

He smiled again before pacing away from the counter, the flickering restarting. "I am looking for a book of maps."

"Maps?"

He stopped and pulled his cell phone from his pocket before holding it up and shrugging. "Yes, sometimes I really hate technology."

She narrowed her gaze but nodded and led him to the modern books section. "I can understand that. I'm not very good with technology either. What location are you looking for?"

"Alku and the surrounding cities," the stranger said as he bent over to read the spines on the books on the nearest shelf to him.

Onnie hesitated for a split second but felt her Bond with the shop warm slightly. The man's talk of moving to Alku shouldn't be possible for an Outsider, but thanks to the unnatural flickering his body was still doing, he was likely to be part of the magical world, and she relaxed a little. If he were a danger to Alku, the wards wouldn't have let him in, so for now, she would humor the stranger.

"Here's one," she said, pulling a folded pamphlet from the shelf and passing it to him.

His eyes widened when he took it, and he unfolded it. "This is just what I need. Thank you."

Onnie nodded, led the way back to the counter, and started to ring up his purchase.

"What brings you to Alku, Mr...." she trailed off as she read the name from his credit card, "Elaric Rickson."

He walked over to a shelf of faded scrolls and casually examined them as he answered. "Opportunity for change. New horizons, all that."

"So, you're thinking of moving to Alku, then?"

"I hope to be. I am going to spend some time driving around the place. Scope out the *dark* underbelly of Alku, the local *sanctuaries,* all that. You know how it goes."

He punctuated the words 'dark' and 'sanctuaries' before slipping into a fake smile and walking over to sign the credit card slip. Then he picked up his map.

"Thanks for the help."

He winked before turning his back on her and walking out of the shop, the door clattering shut behind his jittery form.

"Mal, get out here," Onnie said as she pulled her cell phone from under the counter out of habit.

"As if I wasn't already here," he said, jumping up to sit beside the register. "Did that dude just say sanctuary?"

"Yes, he did. Tell Gabe that Dany's coming for dinner." Onnie said, dialing Dany.

No one just moves to Alku. There were wards and spells in place to prevent Outsiders from overstaying their welcome. Even if the stranger was part of their world, it was still extremely rare for Alku's population to increase by outside methods.

Dany answered on the first ring. "What happened?"

"Sorry, I didn't mean to shut you out, but I had an unexpected visitor in the shop. Come over for dinner."

Dany didn't hesitate, "Of course, who were they?"

"Not a who—a what. I'm pretty sure I know why I read that book to the kids today." Onnie looked at Mal, who cocked his head to the side. "I think I just met my first transmogromorph."

She grinned from ear to ear as Mal's eyes widened, and Dany gasped.

Chapter 4: Unexpected Visitors

March 2022 - Alku | Onnie Moore

"Maldwyn, I swear, if you don't get your paws out of the cream sauce, I will shave you bald!" Dany said, shaking a spoon at the feline, who was halfway in the stock pot on the stove, his tail swishing in the air without a care.

He pulled himself from the pot and licked his whiskers with loud smacking sounds.

"Watch it, Mal. She'll do it," Gabe said with a chuckle. "She shaved my beard off in my sleep once."

"You looked like a mountain man." Dany retorted before swatting Mal with the spoon, only to have him expertly dodge out of the way and jump down to the floor out of the spoon's range.

"Kind of like now?" Onnie added, looking up from the book she currently had her nose in at the dining room table.

Gabe rubbed his beard, and it made a loud scritchy sound. "It was a cold winter. You try chasing around school kids in the snow and tell me an extra layer of warmth isn't warranted."

Mal jumped onto Gabe's lap, the counter, and then the man's shoulder before gently running his claws through his bushy beard hair.

"I'm with the girls. You need a shave, man."

Gabe gave Mal a sidelong glare, flicking his fingers at him. "Be careful. I may side with them and lend them the razor."

Mal bumped his head against Gabe's temple and purred.

"Suck up," Onnie muttered with a smile as she added the book back to the stack on the kitchen table.

Mal jumped from his perch on Gabe to over on the table and sat on the placemat next to Onnie. "You know you're my favorite."

"I better be," Onnie said, scratching under his chin. "Now focus and help me."

"What's up, buttercup?" Mal said, lying down and peering at the books.

"Transmogromorphs," Onnie stated.

"You're worried about the guy from the bookshop today," Mal said without question in his voice.

"You're sure you met a transmogromorph?" Dany said, jumping up and down a little bit. "Abbot used to talk about them."

"We've never met one," Gabe added. "Abbot said he knew a few, but they rarely ventured too close to Alku."

"Why?" Onnie asked, flipping through a yellowed tome.

"I don't think there was a specific reason. They just didn't." Gabe pulled out a chair and joined her at the table, sliding an emerald book closer to himself and opening the front cover. "This is the origin story of transmogromorphs."

"I know. I read it to the kids today."

Gabe looked from her to Mal and back again.

"I know what you're thinking, Gabe, and I have no idea why I read it to them. I just had a feeling it would be a good choice for today."

"The kids loved it. Besides," Dany said, plating the fragrant pasta into dishes for all of them, "it wouldn't hurt to educate them on all types of magic users. That's why we started story day in the first place, wasn't it?"

Onnie nodded. "Exactly, but normally, I just pick what sounds fun. Today, the shop….” she paused momentarily, “Or something else wanted me to read this story specifically.”

“And you did exactly what *it* wanted you to do,” Gabe frowned.

Mal took pity on her, reached out a paw, and tapped the open page in front of Onnie, diverting the conversation away from the lecture Gabe was no doubt planning.

“Is this what you saw?”

The book had an illustration of one human-looking form converging with another, their outlines overlapping and becoming fuzzy.

“Kind of. That looks like they are blending into one. What I saw was like they were…fighting.” Onnie passed the book over to Gabe to see.

Dany carried over two plates, passed one to Onnie, and looked over Gabe’s shoulder. “Is that?”

Mal nodded, “A soul-manipulation ritual.”

“They have to steal another’s soul?” Onnie asked with a curled lip, all too aware of what playing with souls entailed.

“Not steal, just…copy,” Gabe corrected. “The transmogromorph lineage grants them the ability to shape change at will, but to activate the power, they need something to build off of. I’m not quite sure how they copy it, though.”

“There’s not much written about them, and most of it conflicts,” Mal said. “Much like Onnie, they seem to need to come in contact with the person’s soul, and as the saying goes, ‘the eyes are the window to the soul.’ Once they have the blueprint, they can change into it whenever they want.”

“And what of the person whose soul they copied?” Onnie asked.

“They aren’t harmed,” Gabe answered. “As far as we know. They can be a little disoriented at first, but it sounds like that’s more because a stranger is standing in front of them, and their own face is staring into their eyes.” Gabe chuffed, “After that, they live out the rest of their life in their original body. None the wiser that there is a copy, or husk, of them elsewhere in the world being used by the transmogromorph."

Onnie shivered, "Disturbing."

"There are much worse out there than them. What they do doesn't harm the person." Gabe shrugged at Onnie's glare. "It all depends on how well they accept the momentary discomfort or bury the memory."

Dany added over her shoulder, "There's even some evidence that some transmogromorphs will erase the person's memories of the interaction, making it even less disruptive."

"Interesting. I wonder how," Onnie said.

"No idea. Could be a myth for all we know."

Gabe shrugged. "Besides, transmogromorphs are generally good people. Thanks to their bloodline from the foster princess, they're not inherently evil beings."

"Good and evil are not decisions made by blood," Onnie said firmly.

Mal smiled his toothy cat grin, "In this case, it is."

Dany interrupted before Onnie could comment. "It's still freaky." Dany returned to the stove for her and Mal's dinner plates. "Do you think he's sticking around, Onnie?"

Onnie closed the books and set them aside so they could eat. "Oh yes. He bought a map of Alku and our neighboring cities."

Gabe raised an eyebrow.

"He's looking to invest in real estate," Onnie finished before putting a bite of the creamy pasta in her mouth.

"Oh, goody!" Dany said, her voice thick with sarcasm. "Another freak to add to the watch list with dear old Dad." She plopped into her chair with a huff and passed Mal a small dish of fried bacon.

"What, no cream sauce?" he complained.

"You're not supposed to have the dairy, Mal," Dany chided.

He pouted and looked at Onnie, who rolled her eyes and then used the Bond to pull a dollop of sauce from the pot across the room and plopped it into his bowl, where it landed with a resounding splat.

"Thanks, Onnie!" he cheered, quickly lapping it up before Dany could take it away.

"Push over," Dany grumbled, to which Onnie shrugged.

"It's not like it actually hurts him. If it did, I wouldn't let him eat half the stuff he does."

"Thank the gods for that," Mal said, a pasta noodle hanging halfway out of his mouth.

Onnie looked over to where Gabe was chewing thoughtfully, his brow creased and his eyes downcast.

After a few moments, he swallowed and looked up. "Did he seem to know who you were, Cat?"

She shrugged, "I would assume he knew the bookshop and could piece together who I was."

Onnie felt the shop gently tug at their Bond as it tried to get her attention. She closed her eyes, followed the bright thread to the heart of the shop, and projected herself within its walls.

Are you alright? Onnie asked the shop telepathically, even though she knew it couldn't reply.

Mal relocated from the house to beside her astral form, and they walked over to the shop door, where someone softly knocked on it.

Be careful, Onnie, Mal said from beside her.

Onnie rolled her eyes. *What? Do you think the bad guys suddenly knock?*

No, but the transmogromorph might. It's better to be safe than sorry.

Onnie made her astral form invisible and then shifted through the wall beside the front door, where she saw her friend and local nymph, Mrs. Radcliff, the town florist. Onnie smiled and projected her voice into the older woman's mind.

Hello, Mrs. Radcliff.

The woman jumped and clutched her heart. "Onnie, you rascal, you scared me half to death. Where are you, child?"

Onnie smiled. *I'm sorry. I didn't mean to frighten you, but I figured if I magically appeared behind you, that would have been worse.*

Mrs. Radcliff nodded her head, "Yes, yes, I supposed it would have. I just stopped by to bring you a new batch of tea and a little something special I cooked up for you."

Oh, that's very sweet of you. I can let you in, and you can leave it on the counter if you'd like. Onnie unlocked the shop door and turned on the lamps along the center aisle. *Go in, and I'll join you once we close the door.*

Mrs. Radcliff opened the heavy wooden door, and Onnie followed her inside. After the shop closed the door, Onnie returned to her visible astral form.

Hello, Onnie grinned, her incorporeal hands clasped in front of her.

"You're still in my head, dear," Mrs. Radcliff said with a smile.

I know, I'm not physically here. Is this okay? Onnie led her friend to the counter.

"Yes, of course. How are you both here and somewhere else?" Mrs. Radcliff asked as she unpacked the small gardening basket on the counter. She pulled out a few jars of Keeper's tea and a mason jar of a special blend Onnie asked her to create.

Your teas are helping. Your garden is pure magic.

"Oh, tosh," Mrs. Radcliff said with a wave. "You flatter me, dearie. Besides, most of this comes from Yvonne and Xayn's garden. But do be careful, will you? I know Abbot was never as strong as you are, but I still worry you may hurt yourself."

Onnie rested her palm on Mrs. Radcliff's hand even though neither woman felt it. *Thank you for caring. I am fine, but I appreciate you looking out for me.*

Mrs. Radcliff's eyes glistened. "It's my honor, both as Abbot's friend and as a servant to the Keeper."

Now, it was Onnie's turn to wave the older woman away. *Stop that. You are no servant. You are a friend whom I trust and care about.*

Mrs. Radcliff smiled and pulled out a small white box from the bottom of her basket. "Here's the last of it, dear. It's a batch of my mother's shortbread. I hope you like them."

I'm sure I'll love them! Thank you, Mrs. Radcliff. I will come in tomorrow and have them with one of your delectable teas for breakfast. I'm sure they'll taste excellent with the tea you made for Dany, too.

"Good to hear. Well, I best be going, and I'm sure you'll want to get back," she paused and tapped her chin with a wrinkled finger. "I suppose you never left, did you?"

Onnie smiled and shook her head. *Thank you again.*

Mrs. Radcliff waved and quickly left the shop. Once she was gone, Onnie locked the door again and turned out the lights before she returned to her body.

"Where'd you go, Cat?" Gabe asked when she opened her eyes.

"Mrs. Radcliff stopped by the shop. I let her in, and we chatted for a few minutes. Mal—" Onnie looked over to where the feline had been sitting on the table before she left, and his space was empty.

"He left when you did," Dany said between mouthfuls.

"He didn't come back?" Onnie asked.

Gabe shook his head.

A loud knock, followed by the doorbell, rang through the house, and all three of them froze, mouths mid-chew or wide open.

"Another visitor?" Dany asked. "My, you are popular today."

"Onnie..." Gabe growled in warning. "Call Mal."

Onnie stood from the table and called to Mal with her mind as she walked to the front door, but he neither replied nor appeared.

Be careful, Cat, Gabe warned.

Duh, she said back with a smile over her shoulder.

When she reached the door, she peered through the peephole and into the handsome face of a sizable, dark-skinned man. She put her defensive shields up in her mind and opened the door a few feet.

"Can I help you?"

The man smiled and slipped his hands into the pockets of his leather jacket, "I sure hope you can, Keeper."

Onnie narrowed her gaze but did not move. "What is your business with me?"

"I am looking for allies, and what better ally than that of a Keeper?"

She opened her mouth to speak, but Gabe pulled the door from her grip to open it wider.

"You have not answered the lady's question, stranger."

"Might we continue this conversation inside?" he asked with a slight shiver, so obviously faked that Onnie rolled her eyes.

"Give me your name, and you may enter," Onnie said before Gabe could immediately say no.

The stranger sighed and rubbed a hand over his shaved head, "You already have my name. It's Elaric."

Onnie stepped back and bumped into Gabe as she froze the stranger in place on her stoop with a well-practiced tug on his Bond. "Why would a shifter, who's already lied to me once, show up on my doorstep and expect me to let him in?"

The sharpness in her voice startled Gabe and drew Dany into the room at a run.

"Cat," Gabe said as he tensed behind her. Their Bond flooded with his anger and distrust.

Onnie ignored them all and spoke directly to the man via his Bond. *Don't push me. Just tell me why you're here, and if you're one of his pawns, I'll make this quick.*

The stranger seemed unperturbed by her mental intrusion and slightly impressed. *I am here to help, as I said before. If you unfreeze me, we can talk, and I'll answer anything you want.*

Onnie narrowed her eyes at him, "How do I know your words are true?"

You'll have to trust me. Abbot did.

The second Onnie heard Abbot's name, her control lapsed, and Elaric inhaled a deep breath before she recomposed herself and entirely dropped her control over him.

"You knew Abbot?"

"I did. He was an irreplaceable friend." Elaric looked around the street behind him, "Please, may we continue this inside?"

She paused only a second before stepping aside and letting him enter. Much to her surprise, Mal skipped in behind him. "Mal?"

"Hi'ya Onnie, hurry up and let us in. My whiskers are freezing off out here." Mal quickly trotted past her and Gabe and looked up at Elaric. "Come on, Dany made dinner. Want a plate?" The feline led a smiling Elaric into the kitchen.

Dany looked from Gabe to Onnie and back again. "Um…did we just make a new friend?"

Onnie chuckled and closed the front door. "No, I think we made an old one."

"Cat, I don't like this," Gabe said, grabbing her forearm to stop her from walking away. "What do we know of this man?"

"Nothing. But if Mal knows him, I believe Elaric when he says he knew Abbot." She quickly kissed Gabe's cheek and said softly, "Come on, aren't you the least bit curious?"

The entirety of Gabe's body language changed from active protector to one of a child sharing secrets. His eyes glittered, and he grinned like a boy with a present.

"A transmogromorph!" he whispered excitedly.

Dany had apparently been waiting for their decision, and with both Onnie and Gabe's acceptance, she whooped and headed for the kitchen as fast as her heeled boots would carry her.

"I get the first question!" she shouted over her shoulder.

Keep your guard up, just in case, Onnie warned everyone. A rush of warmth bounced back to her down their Bonds in agreement, and she heard Dany's voice lilt out from the kitchen.

"Would you like some pasta?" she offered.

"The cream sauce is amazing," Mal added as Onnie and Gabe entered the kitchen.

Elaric looked at Onnie, who rolled her eyes in response. "You don't need to ask me. Besides, it would be horribly rude for us to continue dinner in front of you."

Elaric smiled and then inclined his head to Dany. "I would love some pasta, thank you." He took a free seat at the kitchen table, "It smells wonderful."

"Thank you," Dany said, setting a steaming bowl before him and handing him a fork while everyone returned to their seats.

They each managed a mouthful before Gabe interrupted the happy chewing noises.

"Not to be rude," Gabe started, "but who are you?"

"Gabriel…" Dany and Onnie bemoaned together.

Elaric raised his hand, "It's okay. It's a valid question." He lowered his fork and wiped his mouth with his napkin. "My name is Elaric Rickson. I was a friend of Abbot's for many, many years, and before he passed, I received a letter from Rebecca about the new Keeper."

The entire table looked at Mal, who stopped eating mid-noodle slurp. "What? I'm not Rebecca. Do I look like that old woman to you?"

Dany pulled the small bowl of cream sauce away from him and held it out of the feline's reach while Onnie spoke. "Mal. Don't play dumb with us. You know what Rebecca knew. How many letters were sent out?"

Mal gulped, "A few."

"Maldwyn…" Onnie growled out.

He hissed and stared into her eyes. *Don't take that tone with me, Onnie. I didn't keep anything from you. Rebecca did. We are not the same person.*

You're right, but you still could have told me. Instead, here we are, caught unaware with a stranger on our doorstep.

You can trust him, Onnie. The shop and I were talking while you were with Elanor. He's who he says he is. She's known him for years.

"I never did get used to Abbot and Rebecca talking like that to one another," Elaric remarked.

"Like what?" Onnie said, blinking as she ended her conversation with Mal.

"In their minds." He smiled at the shock she must have had on her face. "I told you I knew them. I used to tease Abbot that having a conversation where no one could eavesdrop was rude."

Dany snorted, "I bet he laughed at that."

"He did." Elaric smile was filled with sadness and regret as he twirled his pasta on his fork. "I miss the old coot."

"We all do," Dany said quietly, and the group ate for a few minutes without conversation.

When her plate was nearly empty, Onnie lowered her fork and sat back in her chair. "Elaric. I think it's time you told us what the letter said and why you're here."

"Sure," he nodded. "Most of the letter was between him and me, but he did mention his granddaughter was the new Keeper. He said you were very young and with excellent potential."

Onnie shifted uncomfortably in her chair and felt the back of her neck heat.

"He said you were a Keeper of great power and that with the help of Mal and your Guardian, you would face more evil than the last ten generations of Keepers combined."

Dany shifted in her chair this time, and Gabe clenched his fists.

"So, he knew all this was coming," Onnie stated flatly.

Elaric sighed, "Yes, and I think that's why he sent the letter."

Onnie's eyes flicked to Gabe, whose anger was no longer only flowing along their Bond but being expressed visibly in his stiff posture. She wasn't the only one to notice, as Dany and Elaric looked at him, too.

"Calm yourself, Guardian," Elaric said. "Your anger won't help her, and I am not your enemy."

Gabe slammed his fist on the table, and the plates rattled loudly. "What would you know about my anger? Were you here the last few months when the three of us had to hunt down the army of roaches thrown at us?"

"Will your anger help you find them faster?"

"Without my anger, I would not be able to let Onnie rip the souls from their bodies!"

"Guardian!" Onnie snapped and stood from the table, her chair falling over on the floor with a crash. "Enough," she growled lowly.

Her hands were shaking, and her face was flushed, but most importantly, she knew her eyes were glowing blue.

"Elaric. Mal." Onnie addressed them while not looking away from Gabriel. "Please, come join me in the other room where we can continue our discussion over tea."

"Sure," Elaric said, carrying his and Mal's plates to the sink.

She turned to Dany, and her eyes softened. "Dany, feel free to join them while I start the tea."

Dany picked up the rest of the dirty plates and shook her head. "Nope. Go with them. I'll brew."

Thank you, Onnie said with a nod before she looked at her Guardian.

"Gabriel. Assist Dany with cleaning the kitchen and then go for a run. I'll see you in an hour."

"Cat—" He started to argue, but she shot him a look that quieted him instantly. "Fine." He stood and collected the dirty cups.

Onnie nodded at Elaric to follow her, and her hands still visibly shook as she passed him, and it was enough that she knew it didn't go unnoticed. "Dany, please call me when the water is ready for tea."

Dany waved her off, and Onnie heard Elaric thank her for dinner.

Onnie scooped up Mal from the table and ran her fingers along his back, more to calm herself than to make him purr. She stopped in the kitchen doorway to let Elaric pass, and she watched as he navigated the house without hesitation and settled into the chair one over from the fireplace. Were Abbot alive, Elaric would have sat next to him. She set Mal down on the couch opposite Elaric and busied herself, lighting a fire in the stone fireplace.

"I am sorry for earlier. None of us are doing well with the chaos and deception circling us lately," she said softly.

"Understandable," Elaric nodded. "I didn't mean to bring more deception to your door."

"Then why did you come to the shop under false pretenses this afternoon?"

"You've made an assumption," Elaric smirked. "Either way, forgive me for that. I had to make sure you were who I thought you were. Also, that I wasn't already too late." He paused and rubbed the back of his neck, "Besides, I have to protect myself also."

"From us?" Onnie asked, affronted.

"No," he shook his head. "If I am to be useful to you and your friends, then our enemy can't see any of my typical forms."

Onnie looked sidelong at him.

"Oh," he froze. "I assumed you knew the history of transmogromorphs."

"I know the lore." Onnie chuckled, and Elaric cocked his head at her, the amusement in her voice obviously not matching the statement. "I happened to have read the creation history of your kind to a young group of kiddos this afternoon."

"The group of children Dany brought from the library?"

Mal snickered quietly, and Onnie laughed lightheartedly. "I'm praying you are who you say you are, Elaric, for if you're not, we are in trouble. You would be a difficult roach to defeat."

Elaric grinned. "My kind is naturally good, so you don't need to worry about me being evil. A gift from my ancestor, the foster queen."

"So I've been told. Explain that to me. How are morals passed via blood?" Onnie said, settling into the couch and pulling Mal onto her lap.

"You've read the story. The foster queen was awarded her rule because of her pure heart. Her children and lineage have all been blessed with her abilities and pure heart up until now."

Onnie frowned and stroked the top of Mal's head. "What about free will?"

Elaric laughed. "We still have free will. Think of it this way. If given two choices, one good and one bad, we would metaphorically only see the good one. Basically, it doesn't even occur to us to aid evil."

"Interesting," Onnie said, her brows creasing as she contemplated what she'd just learned. In the other room, she heard the back door open and close as Gabe went for his run. She saw Dany entering the living room with a tray of tea paraphernalia. "Oh, thank you, Dany. I would have come and gotten it."

"It's alright, and I'm finished. May I join you?" Dany set the tray on the coffee table.

"Of course," Onnie said, scooting Mal off her lap and reaching for her tin of tea. While Onnie made her and Mal's tea, Dany fixed one for herself and Elaric.

"Thanks, girl," Mal said when Onnie placed a shallow bowl of Keeper's tea on the end of the table for him.

She nodded with a smile, picked up a cookie, and settled back into the couch. "Alright. So why are you here, Elaric?" Onnie swirled a biscuit into her teacup. "You said you wanted to help us. Why?"

"Because Abbot was a dear friend of mine, and it's the right thing to do."

"But why is it the right thing to do?" Onnie smirked over her cup. She knew she was testing him, but without a deeper understanding of transmogromorphs, she wanted to be careful. "Everyone thinks their perspective is righteous. How do you know that our side is the *good* side?"

Elaric didn't answer immediately. Instead, he stared into his tea in silent contemplation. After a few minutes, in which Dany finished making her tea and curled up on the couch next to Onnie, he finally looked up.

"I guess I don't know. My first instinct is to tell you that my gut tells me you're good, and thanks to my lineage, my gut is never wrong, but that feels like a cop-out. Then I think about the history of Keepers and how they are a beacon for good and a figure of protection for all. Going off of that, I wouldn't even need my gut, but that would be relying on the past and being blind to the future, which is just as bad. That's when things change, and evil can take root." He paused again. "But then I remember Abbot, and he was my friend. More than that, he was chosen family to me. He was kind and true and cared about all the creatures in our world, even the undeserving ones."

Elaric paused and met Onnie's eyes. "The one thing I can tell you without hesitation is that he would never let anyone take up the Keeper's mantle that was not fit to wear it in a caring and just way. If he and the shop chose you to lead us, then I trust that and will follow you as he wanted."

Onnie nodded and smiled softly before breaking their eye contact. She stared at the framed photo on the mantle of her and her Grandfather when he'd come to California for her high school graduation. It was the only picture she had with him.

"Abbot would most definitely not pass me his legacy if I was not fit to have it. You are right about that. I admire your faith in him, and in time, I hope to have the same level of respect between us, but please, do one thing for me, if nothing else."

She turned to look at him once more, "Always second-guess me. Always watch for signs of weakness and corruption because if you notice it, others will notice, and they will come running to try and slip into those cracks and destroy everything."

Elaric's eyes filled with pride, and he raised his teacup with a nod. "I can do that." He sipped his tea before adding, "You truly are a powerful Keeper, Onnie. In more ways than I expected."

Onnie blushed and cleared her throat. "Alright, enough of that. Tell me about yourself, Elaric. You seem to know much about me. I think it's your turn."

Elaric chuckled. "Fair enough. You know my real name, and you've now seen my true form," he indicated to himself with a gesture.

"Is that why you don't flicker tonight?" Onnie interjected.

Elaric smirked at her, "You saw that?"

She nodded.

"Yes, that's why I don't flicker. This is my base form."

"What was the flicker?" Dany asked.

"It is the waring of magic and nature. My base form tries to push through the one I have taken on, and they clash. I can reduce the clashing with more concentration and familiarity with my chosen form."

"So, if you spend months in the form of someone's nan, you

would need to exert less energy with it over time, and it wouldn't flicker?" said Dany, connecting the dots.

"Yup. The form I used when I met you, Onnie, was one I was not as used to wearing. No human would have seen anything. Most races of magic wouldn't either, but apparently with your strength, you could see something going on."

"Would I have seen it?" Dany asked.

"Oh, I'm sorry," Onnie said, shaking her head. "I didn't really do introductions, did I?" She scratched Mal behind his ears, "This is Maldwyn, or Mal for short. Though I believe you already know each other."

Elaric nodded, and Mal raised his little paw to wave.

"Gabriel is my Guardian and…the rogue guardian's son."

Elaric hissed, "That can't be fun."

"It's not," Dany said sternly.

"And this…" Onnie squeezed Dany's hand gently. "Dany is Gabriel's sister, Alku's managing librarian, and the Head Sister of Light."

Dany inclined her head, "It's nice to meet another friend of Abbot. He was like a father to Gabe and me."

"He was a great man," Elaric responded solemnly.

"He was," Onnie added with a sad smile.

The group sat in silence for a few minutes. Each lost in their memory and thoughts of Abbot while a fire roared in the hearth, and their hands were warmed by their teacups.

Mal eventually stretched his spine, all four paws splayed and claws extended. He stood up and bumped his forehead against Onnie before blinking out of sight. Elaric raised an eyebrow at the cat's sudden disappearance but said nothing.

Onnie shrugged. "Unlike Rebecca, Mal has much more autonomy and gives me space. Where Rebecca rarely left Grandfather's side, Mal won't hesitate to appear and disappear when needed, so distance isn't an issue."

"I see," Elaric said quietly. "You're right. I don't think I saw Rebecca do that more than once or twice in all the time I knew her."

Onnie nodded and closed her eyes as she sipped her tea and focused on the warmth from the fire. Her Bond with Gabe pulsed in her mind, and she sent him feelings of calm and peace. She felt when Gabe realized she was in his mind, and he probably slowed to a light jog as he shifted his focus to her.

I'm sorry I yelled at you.

I'm sorry I said what I did. I had no right to tell him that.

She sent him more warmth along their Bond and felt him push his love back. *Come home soon. Elaric is who he says he is, and we five need to have a conversation.*

Be there soon, Gabe said before drawing away from her mind.

Onnie opened her eyes and told Dany. "He's fine and on his way home from his run."

"Okay, good."

Elaric hesitated, "Ah...."

"You want to know what Gabe meant about ripping souls out," Onnie said without hesitation. She knew it would have to be explained eventually, and there was no use putting the complicated conversation off. It wasn't likely to get any easier with time. She finished her tea and set the empty cup and saucer on the coffee table.

"I do. If you don't mind telling me."

"It's not something I share for what I assume are obvious reasons, but I have a feeling your role in this will be a large one. Besides, out of anyone, you may understand the most."

"I have some ideas of how I could help," he smirked.

"Well, then you should know who and what you are dealing with." Onnie sighed, "In the last few months, the rogue guardian has sent dozens of his recruits to suss out who I am. Everything from skill level tests to weaknesses around my relationships with people and routines. He's been relentless in his attacks, and one after another, people have tried to burn down my shop and harm my friends, to name a few." She stopped and rubbed her temples, "At first, we captured and tried to gain any information we could and then disposed of them. We tried to save them, but it was always too late."

"But then they kept coming back," Dany finished.

"What do you mean?" Elaric asked, his expression darkening.

The women looked at each other warily before Onnie nodded, and Dany continued. "The same people we had already…killed came back to try their task again."

Elaric's lips curled in disgust, "Unforgivable."

"Yes," Onnie agreed. "We found that even if we killed his minions, he could return them to a sort of half-life where he would twist their souls into abominations. My only choice was to sever their souls before he could aquire them again."

Dany continued, "The four of us agreed. We would get the information we could from them, and then Onnie would sever their souls so they would be free to enter the afterlife."

"With the added bonus that he would no longer reanimate and torture their bodies."

"It would be wasted effort at that point without a soul," Elaric said.

"That's what we are hoping," Dany confirmed. "So far, none who have had their souls sent to the afterlife have returned."

"That's good." Elaric sighed and rubbed the back of his head. "Wow. Well, things are certainly worse off than I was expecting and probably worse than Abbot was expecting, or his letter would have been more urgent."

The three of them looked up, and Onnie smiled softly when they heard the back door open, and the fire flickered and cracked from the draft. It closed again, and Gabe entered the room, drenched in rain and sweat but wearing a more relaxed face than he'd left with.

He stopped short when he noticed everyone looking at him. "I'll get cleaned up, and we can talk."

"Actually," Elaric interrupted by getting to his feet, "I think you've all told me enough for one night. I have a plan forming in my head, or at least my part, but I think I need some sleep."

"Of course," Onnie said with a smile.

"Thank you again for dinner, Dany," he said with a charming and genuine smile.

She blushed and got to her feet. "Anytime. I'll walk you out."

Gabe walked over and offered his hand. "Accept my apologies, please. I spoke out of line, and if Abbot trusted you and Onnie does, then that's enough for me."

Elaric shook Gabe's hand and nodded. "There is nothing to forgive. Trust is earned, and I have not yet given you a chance to trust or not."

"In time," Gabe agreed.

Elaric inclined his head to Onnie. "Keeper. Tell Mal I said goodbye."

"I will," she grinned. "Be safe. We will be in touch soon."

"Yes, I will find you in a few days."

He followed Dany out the front door, closing it softly behind them.

Gabe crossed the room and dropped to his knees before Onnie. "I was way out of line, and I should not have spoken out as I did."

Onnie rolled her eyes with a smile. "That's all true, but stand up, Gabe, you buffoon," she teased.

He smiled up at her, "I guess I deserved that."

"Seriously," she pulled at him to stand, "you know I hate all that formal crap. It's even worse coming from you. You're forgiven."

Gabe kissed her lightly before she pushed him away and swatted him playfully on the arm. "No, go shower. You smell, and you'll catch a chill."

"Yes, oh great and powerful Keeper!" Gabe roared just as Dany opened the front door. He winked at his sister as he walked down the hall and out of sight.

"Uh, did I interrupt something?" she asked.

"Only your brother being a goof. Come on. I could use some cookies, and tea biscuits aren't doing it for me. I need chocolate."

Onnie said, picking up the tea tray and heading into the kitchen, Dany giggling behind her.

Chapter 5: Rejoining of Bonds

March 2022 - Alku | Elaric Rickson

Elaric pulled his hood up to cover his shaved head in a fruitless attempt to stay dry from the rain that had begun to fall during his visit with the Keeper and her friends. It was only eight o'clock, and he'd only gotten to town that afternoon and had yet to see any of his friends. He quickly texted Marco to find out if he was at the Day Night Cafe and promised to bring him coffee from A Shot in the Dark if he was.

I'll have the Irish for that coffee ready, Marco responded less than sixty seconds later, prompting Elaric to grin and shake his head.

"Sometimes, it's perfect when things stay the same."

He lowered his head, pushed faster through the downpour, and went back through the cobblestone streets to the center of town. From Abbot's—no, Onnie's house, he had to pass the Day Night Cafe to get to the coffee shop, but it was worth the backtracking. Even Stephan, the owner of the Day Night Cafe, agreed that the espresso from A Shot in the Dark was the best.

Elaric shook off what rain he could before he pushed open the glass doors and grinned ear to ear at the nostalgic smell of coffee beans and sweets. A young woman was behind the counter, and after learning her name was Monique and placing his order, she quickly pulled his shots and bagged them up for him to take with him. With a friendly wave and a smile from her, he ducked back into the night and made his way over to his destination.

The warm glow from the cafe's interior beckoned him closer, and before he could grasp the door handle, it swung open, and a man in an *excellent* black suit pulled him inside and into his arms.

"Dude! I'm soaked. You're gonna—" Elaric said with a warm laugh.

Marco pulled back and held him by his biceps at arm's length. "I'll deal with the water. How long has it been, E?"

"Too long for me, but a blink of an eye for you." Elaric was teasing, but his smile quickly faded when he saw hurt flash through Marco's features. His bright white teeth hid from view as his smile dwindled. Elaric promptly scanned the interior, saw only a few tables occupied, and watched the wait staff quickly and efficiently flit between tables.

"Can you get a cover?" Elaric asked, his voice solemn and low.

Marco had an excellent poker face, and if he'd let it slip, especially in public, something was seriously wrong.

Marco released him and quickly turned on his heels. "Yes," he said over his shoulder, and Elaric followed him into the quiet space.

They quickly passed through the dining room filled with tables clad in crisp white tablecloths with crimson roses and a candle in their center. As usual for the dark hours, the red wall curtains were down and covering the cafe walls from the day. The way they transformed this cafe every day, twice a day, never got old, and he didn't think it ever would.

They approached an older gentleman standing beside the door to the kitchen. His shoes glistened, his suit was tailored, and he had a brilliant ginger beard. Before Marco could say anything, the man smiled and rested his palm gently on Marco's shoulder.

"Slow night. See you tomorrow."

"Thank you," Marco said, and the man nodded in response before walking back the way the two of them had come and taking the position at the front where Marco typically was.

"Sure this is okay?" Elaric asked, yet still followed Marco as he led them both into the back kitchens and to an obscured door in one of the corners, the smells of garlic and butter following them.

"He's right. With the storm, its been a slow night and nearly all locals. It's fine." Marco led them up a flight of stairs, down a small hall of doors, and into one near the end. "Come in."

Elaric smiled at the spotlessness that was Marco's apartment. Glass glistened, floors shined, and though modern, the furniture beckoned you to sink into it.

"Shit," Elaric looked down, "I left a trail of rain behind me."

"They've probably already cleaned it up downstairs." Marco took the bag of coffee from him and made his way into the kitchen. "Hang up your coat, and I'll find you something dry to change into."

"It's fine, you don't—" he tried to say before Marco cut him off.

"I already know you haven't checked into the B&B yet. Just do it." Marco called over his shoulder as he disappeared into a dark room down a short hallway.

"I never could win with you," Elaric chuckled but did as he was told, peeling off his soggy coat and unlacing his boots.

Marco reappeared a few minutes later with a stack of clothes in his hands. "I did not realize we were playing a game." His eyes glittered, and his signature grin was back. "Here, you know where the bathroom is. Feel free to shower if you need to warm up. I'll make drinks."

"Make mine strong. I just met the Keeper," Elaric called out as he made his way to the bathroom. Marco didn't respond, but he'd bet money his friend paused for a second or two with his declaration.

Marco's apartment only had one bedroom, and the bathroom was attached. Elaric flipped on the light switch and felt a warm comfort in the unchanged space he'd spent countless time in. Everything was the same. The furniture hadn't moved, and the bedding was the same, making the room smell like Marco. A few books and some pictures were moved around or new, but that was pretty much it.

When he turned to enter the bathroom, he glanced at a dresser and stopped. Atop it was a carved wooden box that Elaric had sent Marco from one of his many wanderings. Behind it was a framed black and white photo of the two of them from the many decades earlier.

Elaric's chest constricted, and he looked back out the bedroom door and frowned. He'd been gone too long this time. He entered the bathroom and saw it was the same, too, and after stripping off the remainder of his clothing, ranging from soggy to slightly damp, he hung everything up to dry and slipped into the buttery t-shirt and lounge pants Marco had given him.

When he looked in the mirror, Elaric entirely shifted back into his base form, and he watched as his skin lightened and his eyebrow piercing and industrial in one ear reappeared. Lastly, his dark hair and blue eyes reemerged. He'd have to apologize to the Keeper at some point for his white lie. He had been in his base form, but the slight shifts to it were enough to make him look different and keep himself safe. There were very few places he was fully and wholly himself, and with Marco was one of them, and that trust went both ways.

Marco was a sanguiste, or what humans would associate with vampires or incubi in their fantasy worlds. The man had lived a long time, and he always had an air of professionalism and polish about him around others. Even that he'd lost his smile in the cafe for those few seconds was worrisome. Elaric rarely, if ever, saw his persona slip like that in public.

Elaric turned the lights off behind him as he wandered back into the kitchen to find Marco slumped over a steaming Irish Coffee at the kitchen bar. He'd discarded his jacket, and his tie was pulled loose. He'd unmistakably run his fingers through his dark hair as it was tousled and entirely transformed him from 'Matra de' perfection' into 'exhausted office worker after a night of overtime.'

Elaric slid into the stool next to him and pulled his drink over. "Alright, now you've really got me worried. What's going on?"

"You hit a nerve earlier, that's all," Marco said without meeting his eyes.

Elaric sipped his drink and gently leaned into Marco's shoulder. Not enough to put weight on him, just enough to ground Marco and remind him he was there. Elaric sat quietly and waited for him to continue, knowing how difficult it was for this man to show anyone his vulnerability.

After a few minutes of sipping and silence, Marco cleared his throat. "I'm sorry. It's just...losing Abbot and Rebecca was hard. You're right. Human lives are but a blip for me, and though yours is longer, it's not by much. Even so, it doesn't make it easier when someone passes just because it goes by faster. Relatively."

Elaric kicked himself. He was an idiot.

"Shit, I'm sorry. I didn't even think about what I said before—"

Marco leaned into his shoulder, now putting his weight on him. Elaric put his arm behind his back and held on to his waist.

"I know you didn't mean anything by it. It's fine. I'm just being over-sensitive about it. There are just times when I am reminded of what I am, and I hate it even more. I meet humans, forge connections with them, and watch them grow. They play with Sam as a kid and you as a young adult, then I enjoy them in their mid-years, and eventually...they leave us. How many times have we done this cycle?"

Elaric let out a breath. "Too many times."

Marco nodded. "Now I see Gabriel, Dany, and Xayn all growing up and getting to that age...."

Silence filled the room, but Marco eventually returned to sipping his drink.

Marco was right, though. Thanks to Marco's eternal life, Sam's curse, and his extended life from the foster princess.... The three of them were destined to watch the people they love come and go. Over and over again. Forever.

The two of them finished their drinks, and Marco made them each a second one to take to the living room's soft, plush, black couch. They each sat at opposite ends of the couch, their feet up and running parallel to each other.

"It's nice to see the full you," Marco said with a soft smile.

"Only with you," Elaric said without a hint of sarcasm, "and ditto. You're sure you don't need to go back down?" Elaric asked.

Marco shook his head, "It's fine. Byron wouldn't have agreed if he needed me. Besides, he'll call if he does."

"If you're sure."

"You're staying, right?" Marco asked and finally met his gaze.

"If you're comfortable with it, it beats the B&B."

"Of course, you're always welcome here. Whether we're together or not." Marco smiled, and some of the tension he'd been holding left his body.

Elaric was thankful that even after dating in the past, they'd parted as friends and had grown even stronger than before. He knew they would do anything for each other, and having that person to return to after, no matter how long, always made Elaric feel like he was returning home. Except, he hadn't been back to Alku for nearly two dozen years, except for an extremely quick day trip a few years ago.

"You've been to Onnie's then," Marco stated, bringing Elaric's comment from earlier back around.

"Yeah, I stopped at the shop earlier today to feel her out and then dropped by Abbot's this evening. I met Dany and Gabriel too, the ones you mentioned earlier, I take it."

Marco smiled with a distant look in his eyes. "Yes. Brother and sister. Their father was Abbot's Guardian." His face darkened, "You know how that ended."

"Yeah.… I can't imagine what they're going through with all this."

Marco tsked at him. "Don't underestimate those three. None of them give a damn about the blood relation, and they will stop at nothing to rid the world of him."

Elaric nodded, "That's good to hear. I assume Abbot wrote you a letter as well?" he asked, switching topics.

"Mmm…." Marco answered while sipping.

Elaric sighed, "I doubted her from just the letter, thinking Abbot was just an overly proud grandfather. Except, she did something, and whatever it was completely incapacitated me on her doorstep. He undoubtedly *under-described* her capabilities."

Marco chuffed, "I'm sure he did indeed. Though, to be frank, I don't think even he understood her power."

After a few moments, Elaric cleared his throat, "Well, I'm glad I returned. It already promises to be entertaining."

He looked over and saw Marco had his head tipped back, resting on the sofa arm. His skin was as pale as ever, and the more Elaric looked, the more it looked paler than usual.

"Marco?"

"Hm?" he responded without opening his eyes or looking up.

"How many nights has it been slow in the cafe?"

Marco smiled and lifted his head. "You could always tell when I was hungry. Other than Stephan, you're the only one who can."

Elaric warmed at the thought, feeling honored to be grouped with a man like Stephan. Marco wasn't a blood-drinking sanguiste and preferred to consume emotions for sustenance. The cafe downstairs was just as much an eatery for its patrons as for its waitstaff. The lively atmosphere, the happy couples, and even Marco's love for his job provided him with enough of a meal to survive—most of the time.

Elaric untangled his legs from Marco's and got to his feet. He took their empty glasses to the kitchen and then returned to him, hand extended.

"Come on. Up you get."

Marco allowed Elaric to pull him to his feet but playfully smirked at him, "And just what are you thinking, E?"

Elaric snorted and draped his arm over Marco's shoulder. "Honestly, if that was what you needed, for you, anything." Marco tipped his head to rest on Elaric's shoulder as he led him down the hallway to the bedroom. "But right now, I think conversation will be enough."

Marco purred like a contented cat and allowed himself to be escorted to his bedroom, where Elaric dug through his closet and drawers, pulled out clean clothes, and handed them over.

"Get changed. I can't see that being comfortable," he gestured to Marco's half-removed suit.

To his relief, Marco accepted the clothes and slipped into the bathroom. Elaric retrieved his cell phone and turned it to silent. The only people who would contact him were in the other room or…dead. He frowned at the sudden loss of his friend again but quickly pushed it aside when Marco stepped out of the bathroom and coughed a few times.

"Sorry," Elaric frowned and pulled down the bed covers.

Marco shook his head and smiled, the small contemplative one he got when he wanted to be polite rather than say what he was thinking.

"Abbot?"

"Yeah," Elaric confirmed. "I set my phone to silent, thinking the only people I care about are you and…." He trailed off and took a deep breath to, once again, push those more raw emotions down for the time being.

"E?" Marco asked, placing his palm on his shoulder. "You need to feel all those feelings. Process. Grieve. Don't repress them on my behalf."

"I will, and I'm not. Now's just not the time. I'd rather you get your fill of happy emotions than sad."

He genuinely meant that. Marco being so sensitive towards the feelings of others meant he'd learned to guard against the more troublesome ones. Elaric knew how much effort that took him and never wanted to be the reason Marco needed to keep his guard up in his own home.

"Now, into bed with you. I'm exhausted, and though it's the middle of the day for you, you look like you could use a lazy afternoon for once."

Marco laughed, a genuine laugh that warmed Elaric's body much more than the coffee. That was the man he missed so much.

"Alright, you don't need to tell me twice," Marco slid into bed and draped the covers over his knees. "Now, if you're not seducing me, what are we doing?"

Elaric chuckled and mimicked Marco's position on the other side of the bed. "I've been gone a long time. I've stories to share."

When Marco's eyes glittered in anticipation of the mental enjoyment and emotions he would receive, Elaric knew that Alku was where he needed to be right now, regardless of the Keeper and her troubles. His relationship with Marco ran deep, and when his chosen family needed him, Elaric would always come running.

Always.

Chapter 6: Growing Unease

March 2022 - Alku | Gabriel Vansand

Gabe stripped out of his soggy clothes and chucked them into the bathtub to deal with after his shower. He turned on the shower taps, let the water heat up, and stepped under the spray. When it hit his body, he hissed, the warm water biting his cold flesh.

Mal, Gabe asked along their Bond, *what do you think of Elaric?*

He's a friend, dude.

Okay, but what do you think of him?

Mal was quiet for a minute, and when Gabe thought he'd been ignored, Mal replied, *I believe Abbot sent him that letter for a reason.*

Gabe sighed, the water running down his face, spattering in front of him. *Alright.*

He put the mysterious shifter from his mind and focused on what he was doing, and ten minutes later, he stepped from the shower and wrapped a towel around his waist.

He quickly dried and dressed in baggy sweats and a thermal shirt before grabbing his soaked clothes and heading to the small laundry room at the end of the hall. He chucked everything in the washer, started it, and then went to find Onnie. His steps seemed to boom in the near-silent house, and he wasn't surprised to find his Cat curled up with her cat, asleep on the sofa in front of the fire.

He leaned on the wall and crossed his arms as he watched her for a few minutes. The slight flush in her cheeks and the rise and fall of her chest as she breathed. She was beautiful, and he had a hard time taking his eyes off her in most situations, but right then, when she was vulnerable and raw, he could fall for her all over again.

Smiling, he quietly retrieved his cell phone from a nearby side table and texted Dany goodnight. After she replied, he set his phone back down and went over to the fireplace and turned it off. Mal opened one eye as Gabe walked by and he put his finger to his lips.

She's asleep. I'll go put her to bed, Gabe said to the feline, who relocated off to somewhere in an instant. *Night man.*

I'll be back, Mal laughed. *Don't steal my spot,* he teased.

Gabe chuckled and carefully lifted his sleeping girlfriend into his arms, carrying her into their shared bedroom. He tucked her into the covers and saw that her clothes had been changed, probably while he was in the shower, and she looked ready for bed. She reflexively pulled the blankets into herself, and Gabe brushed her hair back from her face.

"I love you, Onnie." He kissed her forehead and left the room, clicking the light off and closing the door.

You can join her if you want, Gabe told Mal, who surprised him and appeared at his own feet instead.

Not staying with her?

Kitchen, was all Gabe said and led the way, Mal now on his shoulder. When they arrived, Mal jumped down to the counter, and Gabe dug through the cabinets for a glass and the open bottle of whisky.

"What's up? Still worried about Elaric?" Mal asked, eyeing the alcohol.

Gabe shook his head. "A bit, but not really. You're right. Abbot trusted him, and you guys seem willing to, so I need to catch up."

"Okay…" Mal drawled, "So, then, what is the problem?"

Gabe poured a few fingers of whiskey into the glass and ignored etiquette, instead knocking back the amber liquid in one go.

"I'm not sure."

"For not being sure, that sure was one hell of a nightcap, dude."
Mal stuck his nose in Gabe's glass and quickly recoiled before sneezing
three times.

"My gut says something is coming."

"Well, no shit," Mal sneezed again, "Sherlock. We've been swatting
roaches for weeks now."

Gabe shook his head. "No, not that. Something different. Bigger."

Mal finished sneezing and met his gaze. "Bigger than Jakob?"

Gabe swallowed and nodded, "Yeah."

"Well, okay...." Mal said and stuck his head under Gabe's free
hands for pets. "What do you want to do about this 'bigger'?"

"What can we do besides wait and stay vigilant?" Gabe scratched
the feline's chin a few times before rinsing his glass and putting away
the bottle.

Mal stared at him from the counter, his yellow eyes unblinking.

"Don't look at me like that, Mal. Do you have a better idea?"
Gabe walked to the light switch and looked back to the feline whose
eyes still had yet to blink or look away.

"Sleep well, Gabe," Mal said before disappearing and leaving Gabe
alone in the kitchen.

Gabe sighed, turned off the light, checked the locks, and returned
to the bedroom. When he pulled back the covers and slid in next to
Onnie, she shifted and snuggled closer into his side, and he was more
than happy to wrap his arms around her.

"Gabe?" she mumbled.

"Better be," Gabe chuckled and kissed the top of her head before
holding her tighter and squeezing his eyes closed.

Onnie shifted and slowly opened her bleary eyes. "What's wrong?"
she asked with a frown and a crinkled brow.

"Nothing, Cat. Go back to sleep."

She blinked wearily at him and then stretched up to kiss him.
When she pulled back, her frown deepened, and she licked her lips.
"Alcohol?"

Gabe closed his eyes and smiled. "Can't get anything past you."

"Are you going to tell me nothing's wrong again?"

Onnie's voice was slurring less, and Gabe knew she wouldn't let this go now. His hope for her going back to sleep was gone.

"It's nothing. I just needed a drink after all the commotion earlier." He didn't open his eyes, and he knew she'd be staring at him, his lie thin and so unbelievable he wasn't sure why he bothered.

After a minute of uncomfortable silence, he felt her lips on his once more as she leaned into him. When he tried to deepen their kiss, he hissed as she bit him, and he touched the corner of his mouth with his tongue and tasted copper.

"Liar," she said and then rolled over.

Gabe's eyes were open and wide now, his dark vision returning, and he touched his bleeding lip. He deserved that. He was lying, and if there was one thing Onnie hated, it was secrets. His stomach knotted, and he pressed his palms into his eyes.

He stayed that way for a while, waiting for Onnie's breaths to even, telling him she was sleeping once more, but it didn't happen, and after five minutes, he pulled her back into his embrace.

"Fine. You're right."

When he looked down at her, her green eyes glittered in the dark room, moonlight the only thing keeping them from pitch black.

Her eyes darted to his lip and the wound she'd caused, and he felt her guilt along their Bond.

"I've just got a feeling something is coming, and I hate being blind."

Onnie sighed, "Gabe, something bad is always coming."

Gabe felt a sense of deja vu and couldn't help but laugh. "He really is your cat." When Onnie looked confused, he shook his head. "Not important, but you're right. It's just this time it feels…."

"Worse?" she completed for him.

"Bigger."

"Ah…" she nodded and snuggled back into his side, apparently forgiven, at least for the moment.

"Let's not worry about it now, alright?" He kissed the top of her head and rested his cheek on it, breathing in her scent.

"Gabe?" Onnie said softly, her breath tickling the arm she had pulled against her.

"Hm?"

"Will you tell me about Abbot?"

"Oh," that wasn't what he'd expected. "Sure, what do you want to know?"

"Anything."

Her voice seemed sad, and he shifted, pressing his front to her back. "Hm...let me think." His breath caressed her cheek, and he felt her shiver. "How about when Dany and I were little and got called to the school office on the same day."

He felt her cheeks lift against his arm as she smiled. "*Both* of you?"

Gabe laughed quietly. "Yeah. Dany was caught reading in class when she wasn't supposed to be, and when the teacher saw that the book looked hundreds of years old, she sent her to the office to call Abbot."

"Sounds like Dany. To be honest, can't say I'm surprised."

"She knew who she was the minute she could hold a book." Gabe smiled, his sister's cute kid face beaming at him from his memories.

"And why were you there?" Onnie's soft voice teased.

"Ah..." Gabe stalled a bit. "I got in trouble for fighting."

"You don't say?"

"Hey!" Gabe said with only partial mock outrage, "What's that supposed to mean?"

Onnie snorted. "I didn't have to know you as a kid to know you were a handful."

Gabe pouted, but she was right. He'd caused Abbot a lot of grief over the years, but the old man never cared. He'd treated him and Dany the same, no matter who it was or what trouble they got into.

"You're not wrong," he said, Onnie's hair shifting with his exhale.

"Were you fighting a bully or something?"

This time, Gabe had to try not to laugh. "Nope. I was the bully."

"Wait," Onnie turned her head to try to look at him, "really?"

Gabe nodded, "Yeah, that was the first and last time I did the hazing."

"What happened?"

"Abbot picked Dany and me up from school and took us home. He didn't say a word during the walk. I remember holding Dany's hand and walking behind Abbot, who never turned around. He just kept walking, his hands clasped behind his back. Dany was clinging to her book, and I was nursing a bruised cheek."

He missed Abbot. Gabe loved it when Onnie asked about her grandfather because telling her stories made him feel like Abbot was still here, but he was alone again when the story was over.

"We got home, and he asked to see Dany's book. It turns out it was one of the ones from his rare collection about an old city in Estonia, and she'd been too curious and took it without asking."

"Oy, so she really was always like this?" Onnie giggled. "How old were you?"

"Hadn't even hit double digits."

"Wait, what!?" Onnie hissed in the darkness. "She was reading that at less than ten years old?"

"Are you that surprised?"

Onnie was quiet for a moment, and then she relaxed again and shook her head. "Actually, nope. I'm not. Continue."

Gabe squeezed Onnie once and smiled at her through the darkness. "For me, I just got a lecture. I guess Dany did, too, but she got her book back."

Onnie snorted, "Figures. He didn't punish you two at all?"

"Oh, I didn't say that. We had to sit and feed the ducks after school with him for a week, and trust me, for a kid that age, it was torture."

Onnie giggled, and Gabe snuggled his nose into her hair. The sound of her laughter made him smile uncontrollably, and he was glad it was so dark in the room because he felt his face start to burn. He'd do anything for the woman in his arms, and he felt proud and honored that Abbot trusted him with her life and her heart.

"You two are ridiculous. All three of you, actually."

"Pretty much," Gabe murmured against the back of her neck.

They lay there for a long time, both quiet and, he'd bet, thinking of Abbot. Eventually, Mal appeared, wormed his way into Onnie's arms, and quickly shifted from purring to snoring.

I love you, Cat, Gabe said so they didn't wake Mal.

I love you, too.

He felt Onnie's love along their Bond, and he pulled it into himself, and when he finally felt the sinking feeling in his gut calm, he drifted to sleep.

Onnie Moore

Onnie woke in the morning to birds chirping, the sunlight streaming through the window on her face, and one large male's arm crushing her torso while one feline's tail repeatedly slapped her in the face. She held back both her sigh and her giggle. She never thought her life would end up where it had, but she'd take as many mornings of being crushed and thwacked as she could get.

The other two were still asleep, so she shifted carefully until she could slip out of bed without waking them. She looked down at the handsome man she'd fallen madly in love with and nearly choked when she watched him realize she was missing, but still asleep, he grabbed Mal into a bear hug instead. To his credit, Mal didn't wake either, and Onnie tip-toed out of the room to leave them to their snuggling.

Onnie wandered into the kitchen, put a kettle on to boil, and prepped the coffee maker for Gabe for when he woke up. She pulled a thermos out of a cabinet and filled the tea strainer with Keeper's Tea.

Setting it aside while the water brewed, she went to the entryway, grabbed her heavy coat from the hook by the door, and pulled on her thick, fur-lined boots. When she returned to the kitchen, the water was near a boil, and she didn't have long to wait before she had to snatch it off the base before it began beeping and woke the rest of the house.

Onnie quickly filled her thermos and pulled on her coat. She stuck a banana into one coat pocket and grabbed a muffin before she slipped out the back door and shivered in the cold. The morning air was crisp, and when she took a deep breath, it felt cold in her lungs and stung a bit. She grinned ear to ear and made her way to one of the chairs on the deck and dusted it off before plopping into it, pulling up her hood, and putting up her feet on the railing.

She rarely woke up before the other two, and she probably had the whisky Gabe had drank the night before to thank for the unexpected alone time. She frowned, remembering how she'd bit him, and instantly felt guilty again. The cool breeze blew past her, and she tipped her head back and smiled up at the sky. She hated that Gabe was keeping things from her, and while she realized that she was keeping things hidden from him and the others, what Gabe had lied to hide was silly and small. If he didn't feel like he could share something like that with her, they had some things to work out.

Her mind drifted from topic to topic as she sipped her tea and nibbled on her breakfast. She closed her eyes and listened to the birds who chittered up in their nests and the lapping sounds of the lake, only broken by the occasional small engined boat going by and creating the water's movement. After a time, the clouds cleared up, and the sky shone blue and clear above her. The sun warmed her face, and she smiled like a child.

Onnie felt Mal appear on her lap and immediately take a bite of her muffin. She gently tugged on one of his ears but didn't open her eyes. When he finished his nibbling, he rubbed his chin on her fingers, and she provided him with the scritches he requested.

"Morning, Onnie," Mal said through his purring.

"Mmhmm…" Onnie said and took a few more deep breaths before calling over her shoulder, "You should grab a chair and give me some of that coffee, too."

She heard Gabe's soft laugh from where he stood in the doorway nearly one hundred feet behind her. Much to her joy, he did as he was told, and within a few minutes, he was smiling down at her before he handed her a steaming cup of coffee and kissed her good morning. The taste of his black coffee on her tongue mixed with her tea, and she suddenly regretted getting out of bed.

Gabe broke their kiss and sat in a chair next to her, and she rested her head on his shoulder.

"Morning, Cat."

She held her coffee cup between her palms, the chill in the air and her skin quickly turning it into a drinkable temperature, and Mal wasted no time before he stuck his furry nose in her cup.

"You really have no boundaries, do you?" Gabe said with a smirk, and Mal lifted his head to stick his tongue out before taking another slurp of Onnie's coffee. "You're lucky she's so tolerant, furball."

Onnie laughed and shooed Mal from her cup before taking a sip herself.

"I still don't know why you put up with him."

"Same question," Mal said, and the two males glared at each other.

Onnie sniggered, her calm, quiet morning successfully shattered by these two. "It's not like he's your standard cat. No diseases, no fleas, all that. It is no different to sharing food with you or Dany. Besides, he's so spoiled his paws barely touch the ground."

"See," Mal said with a catty swat of his front paw in Gabe's direction.

Gabe rolled his eyes, and Onnie shook her head. "Behave you two. It's too early for your bickering."

"He started it!" they both said in unison and pointed to one another.

Onnie threw back her head and laughed until her eyes watered, and by the time she'd regained her composure, her two temporary companions had left, and she was alone once more to enjoy the quiet morning.

Chapter 7: Young Love, Old Companionship

March 2022 - Alku | Elaric Rickson

Elaric stood in line at A Shot in the Dark, spacing out, while he waited to order a mid-morning pick-me-up. His mind was all over the place. It flitted from his conversation with the Keeper and her friends a few days earlier to seeing Marco again and how wrecked he was, even if he kept it hidden from everyone else. Then, it wandered into sad territory when the loss of Abbot pushed to the top of his thoughts.

Elaric crossed his arms and inwardly scolded himself. He needed to focus if he would be of any help to the others. He could grieve later.

"What can I get for you?" the young woman behind the counter asked Elaric, pulling him from his mind. He looked around and realized he'd made it to the front of the line and hadn't noticed.

He cleared his throat, "Ah, sorry."

The woman chuckled and shook her head. "No big, we get that a lot."

Elaric smiled back, "Can I have a medium Americano, please?"

"Sure thing! Anything else?" she said while tapping the computer's screen.

Elaric heard a familiar voice float above the din of the shop's patrons behind him, and when he saw Dany walk through the shop door, he smiled and turned back to the barista.

"Yeah, pay for whatever Dany orders, please," he pulled cash from his wallet and handed it to the cashier. "The rest is for you."

She smiled and nodded, "You got it, and thank you. I'll get yours made and call you up in a minute."

"Thanks." Elaric stepped to the side and found an empty, small square table along one of the sidewalls and slid into a sturdy wooden chair.

He groaned when he realized he'd forgotten to tell the barista not to reveal who'd paid for Dany's drink. She wouldn't recognize him in his current form, and he didn't want to make her uncomfortable when some random man bought her coffee.

Elaric's phone vibrated in his pocket, and he frowned when he saw a text from Marco.

You left?

It's way too late. Why are you up?

I woke up and noticed you were gone.

I'm at the coffee shop. I'm not bringing you anything. Go back to bed.

You'll be back later…right?

Elaric rubbed his eyes but couldn't keep the smile from creeping up to his lips.

Yes. Of course. I'll be back before you need to head downstairs. Go back to bed.

Night, E.

As Elaric moved to put his phone back into his pocket, he paused and remembered Dany had given him her number when they'd met the other night. He quickly texted her with his name and current form's description and told her to enjoy her coffee. When she got to the counter and ordered, the cashier told her it was paid for, and then her phone rang. Elaric smiled when she read the text and immediately scanned the room for the person he'd described.

When their eyes met, he lifted his hand in a small wave, and she grinned from ear to ear. His heart beat wildly at her authentic joy, and he swallowed hard. Before he let himself drift too far, he shook his head and cleared his mind. He wasn't in Alku to have a relationship, that would be a bad idea. At least nothing past getting to know the new Keeper and her companions. Even if Dany fit into that group, he needed to ensure the line was kept. None of them could afford to get distracted.

"Hey, can I join you?" Dany's voice pulled him back to the present. She held two steaming cups and handed him one of them. "Monique said this one was yours."

He kicked himself mentally when he instinctively smiled. "Sure, have a seat." He took his cup from her, popped open the lid, and took a deep breath, inhaling the rich aroma. "Thanks for grabbing this."

Dany took the chair opposite him, hanging her long black trench coat over the back of it before sitting down. "No thanks needed, but thank you for the nice surprise." She smiled and sipped her drink as her eyes narrowed, and she seemed to scan him.

Since he was in a form that was new to her, he didn't blame her for the increased scrutiny, so he let her do as she pleased, but then the turnabout was fair play, and he used the time to do the same.

Her shoulder-length hair was a deep purple today, a streak of neon pink framing one side of her face. She was in dark jeans, knee-height boots made of soft-looking leather, and a silky-looking top under a purple blazer that matched her hair flawlessly. Her eyes were lined in black and looked brighter in the shop's natural light. She was stunning, and he was pretty sure she knew it, and that was fine by him.

He saw a blush creep up her cheeks, and he smirked. "You're welcome. I figured I'd try to make up a bit for the commotion I caused the other night."

Dany chuckled and shook her head, "No need. That's pretty much a normal day for us."

Elaric's stomach dropped. "A Keeper fighting with her Guardian is normal?"

Dany's eyes widened briefly, and she emphatically shook her head. "Sorry, not that part. That's rather rare, but Onnie and Gabe tend to… disagree about things still." Dany looked a bit uncomfortable, like she'd revealed something she shouldn't have, and she quickly clarified.

"They haven't known each other for very long. Let alone the um… special situation we're in right now."

Elaric nodded. "Understood. That's enough stress to strain any relationship, especially a new one, and when you add the Keeper, Guardian, aspect…."

"Exactly," Dany's shoulders relaxed, and she sipped her drink.

"I understand, don't worry. I didn't think anything of it."

That wasn't entirely true. He was initially troubled by the out-of-sync interactions he'd seen, but after thinking about it more and now with Dany's explanation, he wasn't as concerned. Mostly. He'd reserve judgment for a while longer.

"How are you liking Alku?" Dany asked.

"Never fails to keep me entertained," he said with a chuckle, "but I think that's part of its charm."

Dany laughed, and Elaric's heart did that flip-flop thing again.

"I know what you mean. Where were you before you came into town," she paused, "and feel free to tell me to bug off if I overstep."

He shook his head, "Nope, I don't mind." He settled his cup between his fingers and fiddled with the heat sleeve on it with one fingernail. "I've been all over the place. I tend to roam more than settle. I think it's part of my, uh, nature…." he said cryptically but saw Dany nodding in agreement.

"I could see that."

"Just before I came here, though, I was in Northern California and, before that, Europe."

Dany suddenly looked past him, and her face lit up.

"Miss Dany!" a little boy said, a little louder than room volume.

In what Elaric could only describe as a practiced maneuver, Dany set down her cup, swiveled in her chair, bent over, and caught the child's body that suddenly dashed past Elaric and launched into her arms.

Dany squeezed the little boy tightly and laughed, "Hey, William!"

"Sorry about that, Dany," a man's voice said from behind Elaric, and he turned to look up at a middle-aged man in jeans and a coat. He wore a baseball cap and stuck his hands in his pockets as he watched the kid who had run from him.

Dany set the boy back on the ground and ruffled his hair. "No problem. William knows I'm always happy to see him, right buddy?"

"Yeah!" the little boy leaned in and hugged her again. "Miss Dany is the best!"

Elaric smiled, and Dany looked between Elaric and the man standing behind him. "Oh, this is William's father, Doug. Doug, this is...." Dany trailed off, and Elaric reached up and offered his hand.

"Andrew. Nice to meet you." He smiled, and the chill of the man's hand surprised Elaric.

"Nice to meet you, Andrew. This here's my son, William. Energetic as always." He beamed, and the light in his eyes was blinding when he looked at his son.

Elaric turned and bent forward a little bit. "Hello William, I'm Andrew. It's nice to meet you, too."

In a typical kid way, William glared at him and held tighter to Dany, his claim staked and his distrust written all over his face.

"Hi," was all he mumbled, and Doug chuffed.

"A bit protective of Dany," Doug said, shaking his head but still smiling.

"It's alright, and I don't mind." Dany pulled the boy away from her and tapped the tip of his nose with the tip of her finger. "Getting something to drink with Dad today?"

William's smile returned as if it had never left, and he nodded. "Yup! We're getting melted chocolate."

Dany's eyes widened, and she gasped. "That sounds delicious!"

"It's my favorite." The boy puffed out his chest, his little body standing an inch taller.

"Well then," Dany ruffled his hair again, "you better get to it. Have fun with Dad, and I'll see you at school this week, right?"

William stuck out his bottom lip, and Doug took one of his tiny hands. "We better get that hot chocolate, William. Let's let Miss Dany go back to her friend, alright?"

William turned to look at Elaric, and his eyes looked him up and down before he looked back at Dany, and his grin returned.

"Finnnneeee…" he bemoaned. "Bye, Miss Dany!" he said with a big wave, letting his dad drag him away and into the line in front of the register.

Dany chuckled, shifted back in her chair, and took a big gulp of her coffee.

"You seem pretty popular," Elaric teased her, and she erupted in a loud enough laugh that a nearby table turned to look at her before returning to their conversation again.

"William is one of my students."

"Obviously," Elaric said, "but I think he's more of a not-so-secret admirer than a normal student. The kid had ice in his eyes when he gave me a once over."

Dany glanced at the boy in line over her shoulder, and he was still watching her and waved when he saw her staring. She smiled, shook her head with a grin, and looked back at Elaric.

"He's a good kid. He'll break many hearts when he's older, but I have a feeling he'll be one to fight for when the time comes."

Elaric enjoyed watching Dany talk about her students, and he pressed her for more stories as they sat and enjoyed their drinks. At one point, Dany got up and ordered them each a second cup, and they continued talking for another few hours. When Dany's stomach growled, she blushed, and Elaric looked at his watch.

"Oh shit," he looked up at Dany with a wince, "I hope you didn't have anywhere to be today.…"

Dany cocked her head to the side, and when she checked her phone, her eyes snapped open. "Oh shit! The meeting!" she quickly cleared her trash, and he jumped up to help.

"I'm so sorry, Dany. I should have watched the clock better."

Dany stopped and covered his hand with hers. "Don't worry about it. I enjoyed myself and can still make it to the library in time."

Elaric nodded and helped her into her coat before pulling on his own. "Can I walk you?"

Dany buttoned up her coat and tucked her hands into her pockets. "If you'd like to, I won't say no."

He gestured for her to head out first and held the door open. Once they were out on the slippery streets, they walked side by side.

"Can I ask what I almost made you late to?"

Dany snorted, "PTA meeting."

Elaric's step hitched. He hadn't realized Dany was a moth—

"Oh, please don't think that way. I am only hosting it." She laughed, and he felt his pulse race.

"Don't get me wrong. I have nothing against kids," he said quickly.

"No big," Dany said reassuringly. "I didn't take it that way. I just saw you go pale. I'm not ready for kids. Maybe someday, but I've got too much other…chaos around me right now. Not to mention the whole, it takes two thing."

Elaric laughed, "Yeah, probably not the most stable time for that."

"I assume by your reaction that you also don't have any." She looked sideways at him, and he felt his ears warm.

He shook his head, "Nope. Same answer as you, mostly. Plus, the um…genetic differences add some factors to consider." She was an intelligent woman, and when he subtly alluded to not being human, she didn't ask him to clarify, making him happy she understood.

"I can imagine." Dany stopped in front of the library steps and turned to face him. "Well, this is my stop.…"

"Thanks for the coffee, Dany. It was nice to talk to someone other than Marco."

"Oh, are you friends with Marco?"

Elaric hesitated. His sexuality was not something he usually talked about, let alone with someone who was essentially a stranger. Additionally, he was interested in her, even though he really shouldn't be. He wasn't quite sure what to say, so he stuck with, "Yup." It wasn't technically a lie, just not the full truth.

She lit up when she heard his answer, and he was instantly confused and wondered if she was interested in Marco. Marco hadn't spoken about her in that way though, quite the opposite actually. Not to mention that he was gay, and there was no way Dany didn't know that.

"I'm glad. Marco's been alone too long." She looked at him sideways and added, "Though something tells me you already knew that."

He shifted his weight from one foot to the other and was saved from commenting when a brunette woman with large round glasses popped her head out the library's front doors and shouted at Dany.

"Dany, you're gonna be late!"

"Shit!" Dany hissed and ran up a few steps before turning around and looking back at him. "Would you like to have dinner? With me...."

Elaric smiled and nodded once, "Sure. I'd love to."

Dany's grin went ear to ear, and her cheeks flushed. "This meeting is only an hour, but I have a bit of work to do afterward."

"Does six work? I can come pick you up."

She nodded, ran up the last few steps to the door, which she took from the other woman, and looked back at him. "See you later!" Then she slipped inside, and the door closed behind her.

Elaric stood there, staring up at the library for another five minutes before it started to rain. He blinked, and his brain resumed functioning again. His phone said it was only three, so he had a few hours to kill, so he turned away from the library and walked back toward the center of town.

With his hands in his pockets and hood up, he walked, staring down at his feet. The cobblestones were slick with the rain, and the familiarity of it made him smile until his heart twisted, and he was again reminded of Abbot.

They had been friends for nearly all of the former Keeper's life. Elaric had been there when Abbot had married Lonnie and the day she and Tory had left Alku. He, Marco, and Sam had spent a few days trading off, staying beside Abbot while he grieved in silence for the loss of his family. Elaric left Alku shortly after that but kept in touch with him between letters, phone calls, and eventually emails and text messages. When Elaric was out exploring the world, he would send things he found back to Alku for Abbot, Sam, and Marco. Like the box still on Marco's dresser full of all the letters Elaric had written him over the years.

Dany was right. He'd been away from Alku for too long this time, and because of it, Marco was suffering, and Abbot was gone.

The smell of lilies made Elaric stop walking, and he turned to look at the building beside him. The local florist was more of a structure of flowers holding up some bricks than a building holding in some flowers. The beautiful scents and eye candy colors made him smile but quickly reminded him of his mother. A familiar voice called out to him before he could walk too far down that path of memories and spiral.

"Hey!"

He turned and saw Onnie standing outside the front of the bookshop, her hand raised in greeting. For a second, he was going to ignore her, considering she didn't know who he was in this form, but when he thought back to her comment about the flickering during their last conversation, he turned back to her and quickly crossed the road.

"Sorry, that was rude, but I, um…don't know your name…right now." She shrugged and then held the shop door open for him. "Come in. You're going to catch a cold in this rain, and you're nearly soaked."

Elaric smirked but followed the Keeper inside anyway. Apparently, it was a day for women to surprise him. When he stepped inside, and she closed the door behind them, Mal appeared on a shelf nearby.

"Yo! What's up, man?"

Once again, Elaric paused but quickly recovered and couldn't hold back his laugh. "This town, I swear."

"Yeah, sorry about that." Onnie turned and scolded the cat. "Mal, you can't just appear when people aren't used to it. You're going to give someone a heart attack one of these days."

"Oh, he's fine," Elaric assured her. "It was just the combination of him and you knowing who I was even while shifted. Just threw me for a sec."

Onnie blushed and fidgeted with the end of her raven-haired

braid. "Shoot...I didn't think about that. I figured I shouldn't shout your real name since I imagine that could end up being messy, but that was as far as my brain got before I called out to you."

He chuffed, drug off his coat, and hung it on the coat stand by the door. "Bingo. I appreciate the forethought." Elaric walked over to Mal and high-fived the tiny, furry paw. "Sup, dude."

"Well, come on in. Want anything? Tea, coffee, water?" Onnie said over her shoulder as she led the way up the center aisle toward the main counter.

Elaric didn't want to put Dany in any awkward positions, so he kept his morning activities to himself and just asked for water since he was pretty sure Marco would have been able to hear the coffee in his stomach sloshing at that point.

Mal jumped down and padded along next to him as he followed Onnie, then he jumped onto the counter without a sound.

"So, I know we just met, but because of Abbot and Rebecca, it doesn't feel like that. Sorry if it's odd."

Elaric shook his head and slipped his hands into his back pockets. "Naw, I know what you mean. Though I'll admit, I don't get it either."

Onnie's soft laughter floated in from the back room, and she reemerged with a water bottle under her arm for him, a small bowl of milk for Mal, and a steaming tea cup for herself. The smell reminded him of Abbot and he recognized it as the same tea she'd been drinking the night he met her, the tea only Keepers could drink.

"There are things I've learned to just accept in my new life. I suggest doing the same since it's connected to this shop. It's just easier." She put the bowl down in front of Mal and passed the water bottle to him.

"Thanks," he took it with a smile.

They each took a sip of their drinks, or in Mal's case, a lap or two, before Onnie's soft smile returned. She set down her cup and pulled a large box of books onto the counter from the floor. "I hope you don't mind if I multi-task."

"Not at all. Do you need help?" He asked, peeking into the box and seeing freshly printed hardback novels.

She shook her head, "I'm good, but I appreciate the offer." She dug into the box, pulled out a few books, and wandered to a nearby shelf. "So, what brings you to my neighborhood?"

"It wasn't intentional. I was wandering, stuck in my head, and ended up here." He put his water on the counter, wandered to the opposite side of the aisle as Onnie, and looked at a beautiful Torha inside a glass case. "I guess it makes sense, though. I used to talk to Abbot when I needed advice."

"Your feet probably thought for you then." Onnie returned to the box and grabbed a few more books.

"Yeah, guess so." Elaric scanned a shelf at eye height and carefully pulled an old leather-bound book out.

"I know I'm not Abbot, but if you'd like to talk, I'd be happy to listen." She paused, and when he turned and looked at her, she was smiling, her eyes soft and gentle. "If you want. No pressure." She turned her back to him and continued shelving books.

Elaric watched her for a moment longer before looking at the book in his hand. It was a book that outlined the various races of the magical world. The real ones. Not vampires and werewolves, but sanguiste and paranams. He let the book fall open where it chose to, and the chapter about the Angel of Death species was where it landed.

He snorted and looked at the sketch that accompanied the list of physical characteristics. Angels. What a joke. He'd met a few in his life and never liked any of them. They were either narcissists or sociopaths. It made sense considering the purpose of their kind and their place in the world, but still. He could do without them.

The sketch was beautiful, though. A delicately scrawled ink sketch of an exceptionally tall and very thin man. Sharp features, with endless black or blue eyes, depending on whether they ferried souls to an afterlife of bliss or repentance. Over one shoulder, they'd drawn a wing that extended from a few inches above the man's head and stopped barely above the floor. They were covered in onyx-colored feathers or cream, depending on their sub-species.

A woman's figure was also illustrated over the man's shoulder, where the wing hadn't been drawn. Except instead of being lanky and imposing, she had soft, child-like features, and her wings came not from her back but from higher up, nearly at her shoulders.

"Find something good?" Mal asked from the counter and startled Elaric from his examination.

"Yeah…not really." He quickly closed the book and replaced it on the shelf.

"I have a question for you, Elaric," Onnie asked from behind the counter, where she was sipping her tea and watching him. He hadn't even noticed when she'd emptied the box or returned to the counter.

"Sure, shoot." He squatted down and glanced over the book spines on a lower shelf.

"What did Abbot tell you about me?"

Mal groaned, and Elaric looked up as the cat rolled his eyes. "Onnie, I thought I told you what he said."

Onnie glared at him, "No, you told me how you and Rebecca aren't the same, and you have no idea." She bent and nearly put her nose against his, "Or were you lying?"

Mal booped her nose with his paw, no claws in sight. "Fine, fine. Ask him."

Elaric rubbed the back of his neck. "Um, probably not what you're expecting to be honest."

Onnie cocked her head, and Elaric realized he'd made her more curious, not less.

"Most of the letter was unrelated," he looked back at the shelf before him. "He was saying goodbye. With you here, he knew he was on borrowed time." Elaric closed his eyes and took a deep breath before clearing the grief in his throat. "He mentioned that he was very proud of you but that you were new to our world and would need trustworthy people around you. Teachers, mentors, confidants, etcetera." He opened his eyes and blinked through the moisture that had begun to pool. "He asked me to come back to Alku and help you if I could."

Elaric stared at the books ahead of him, and he could almost hear Abbot's voice over his shoulder when Onnie said, "I'm proud of you."

Elaric turned his head and saw that Onnie's eyes were also full of unshed tears, but she smiled and held onto Mal.

"I'm sure that was also in the letter," she said.

Mal and Elaric met eyes, and the feline nodded ever so slightly.

"It was."

"Elaric," Onnie said as she walked around the counter and came to squat beside him. Her eyes turned crystal blue momentarily, and Mal purred in her arms. "He meant it. I can't tell you how I know, but…I just do."

Elaric nodded, the only thing he was capable of at that moment.

"And he wanted you to be you. The real one. With people you trust."

Elaric's eyes widened, and he looked down at Mal, whose whiskers twitched as he smiled a goofy cat grin.

"'She's right, Elaric, and you know it, runt.' That's what he'd say, right?"

It felt like the air had been sucked out of the room, and Elaric slipped from his squatting position to sitting on his ass roughly, with the room entirely obscured now by his tears. He rested his arms on his knees and buried his face in them. His emotions flowed freely and all of the grief he'd been unable to process or had been forcing down for Marco's sake began to overwhelm him.

He felt Mal's body press against his side and Onnie's arm around him, and she gently rubbed circles on his back and whispered calming words.

After a few minutes, Onnie spoke softly, "Did you know he was sick? Before the letter, I mean."

Elaric shook his head.

Onnie sighed and hugged him harder. "Seems I wasn't the only one he kept secrets from. I'm so sorry, Elaric. He must have meant a lot to you."

"He did," Elaric said, his voice cracking. "He does."

"And he always will," Onnie said.

He heard the shop's door lock click into place and then felt Onnie hug him tighter as he openly grieved for his friend.

Chapter 8: Awakening Things Lost

March 2022 - Alku | Onnie Moore

It had been a week since Onnie had severed Maurice's soul, and they hadn't seen a roach since. All of them had taken the reprieve to recuperate, which had been desperately needed after so many attempted attacks. Dany joked that she could wear clothes without fear of ruining them, and Gabe spent more time at the school than he had in months.

Onnie had puttered around the bookshop, looked over her shoulder when she wasn't in it, and called her brothers to the point of annoying them. Jace knew something was up when she called twice in one day, but she passed it off as loneliness. She wasn't sure he believed her, but he hadn't pressed the issue.

Today was just like the previous seven and it was starting to feel too quiet around Alku.

Onnie was leaning on the front counter in Abbot's, flipping through a magazine. Her chin rested on her hand, and she sighed loud enough that Mal, who was curled up on the end of the counter napping against the antique register, popped his head up, and squinted at her.

"What's up, girl?"

She sighed again and closed the magazine before wandering over to a nearby shelf in the modern section of the shop and putting it back.

"Nothing."

Mal made a sound that was the cat version of a snort. "Yeah. Convincing." He stood and stretched, his feline body arching while his claws splayed. When he finished, he sat down and stared at her pointedly. "Wanna try again?"

Onnie shrugged, wandered into the small back room behind the counter, and began brewing tea for them. "Honestly? I'm bored. And it worries me." She turned away from the hotplate and kettle and watched Mal saunter into the room and jump onto the small couch against one of the walls. "It's been too quiet. Don't you think?"

"Don't look a gift cat in the mouth, Onnie." He yawned, and his jaw snapping closed in the silent room added an extra touch of irony to their conversation.

"I'm not trying to. I'm glad it's been quiet, and we haven't had many roaches to deal with, but the more quiet it is, the more I fear we are just missing his scheming. I'm training with Gabe, researching with Dany, and taking care of the shop, but I feel like I should be doing more, but I can't prep for what I don't know is coming."

Mal's little cat lips pulled into a smile. "You're most definitely not the standard Keeper. You do realize that nearly all other Keepers in the past had countless days like this, and that was all they knew, right?"

"I know," she said and sat down next to him. "That wouldn't be so bad if I didn't know there was another shoe or seventy about to drop at any minute. Those Keepers probably lived leisurely lives since there wasn't some asshole threatening them every five minutes."

"Also true," Mal said, laying down with his head on her thigh, begging for pets with his body language.

She tipped her head back, closed her eyes, accepted his unspoken request, and repeatedly ran her palm down his spine. "We've come so far, and I've gotten stronger and more controlled with my abilities, but what do I have to show for it? False security."

Onnie heard Mal's low, guttural growl and looked down to see him glaring at her.

"Self-pity is not a good look on you."

Onnie narrowed her eyes at the sassy feline and stopped petting him. "Do you want pets or not?"

Mal growled again but put his chin back down. "Don't shoot the messenger."

She chuckled at him and resumed her tactile tribute to her Link. A few minutes later, the kettle started to whistle, and she carefully nudged Mal off her lap so she could make the tea.

"Want some, too?" she asked over her shoulder.

"No," Mal said so flatly she looked back at him.

"What?"

"You're drinking enough for both of us."

Onnie groaned and rolled her eyes. "Ug, I'm so over the nagging."

Mal hissed behind her, and then she heard his four paws hit the floor as he left the small room without another word.

"Fine, more for me," she mumbled before pouring the boiling water over the tea strainer.

The delicate aroma of hibiscus floated up with the steam, and when it hit her nostrils, she inhaled with a deep breath and closed her eyes. It was relaxing, comforting, and somehow energizing all in one. Truly magical.

It was a specific blend made for Keepers, Guardians, and Links to help increase their receptivity to the Bond and connection to each other and the shop. Rebecca used to blend it for Abbot and Onnie, but the task fell to Mal when she rejoined the shop. Who clearly didn't have thumbs. Thankfully, Mal had taught Mrs. Radcliff what was needed and what to do, and she'd graciously accepted the responsibility in place of the feline.

Onnie carefully lifted the delicate teacup to her lips. Her hand shook just a touch as she took a small sip, instantly smiling as her shoulders relaxed. She hummed her satisfaction, carefully took her tea, and headed for the shop's back corner to Abbot's study.

Even now, after he'd been gone for a few months, it still felt like it was *his* space, not hers. She didn't mind and found it just as comforting as the tea. However, if she were being honest, a part of her was jealous. So far, the shop hadn't created any spaces for just her. It had created the children's area, unlocked Abbot's study, and the small back room and tea area had been there since Rebecca was Link. At this point, Onnie was starting to think maybe this was as large as the shop would get for a long while and she was selfishly disappointed. It was shocking and exciting to find the new areas when they popped up, but the shop was probably preserving energy for the coming battle, and Onnie couldn't fault her for that.

Onnie turned the corner and entered Abbot's study, passing through the archway and running her fingers along the material as she went. Her chest warmed as she approached Abbot's large wooden desk, and she placed her teacup on a leather coaster after another quick sip. The glossy red floor seemed to waver and shiver with the candles and fire on. She shifted to sit on the leather desk chair when something caught her eye behind her, and she froze.

"You're kidding me," she said flatly before calling Mal. *Come here, you're gonna wanna see this.*

Mal appeared in the archway and blinked at her. "I'm still annoyed at you. What is it?"

Onnie stood back up and crossed her arms across her chest from behind the desk. "Fine, be mad, but then I won't let you come with me to explore behind the door that just showed up." She jerked her head toward the room's back corner, smirking until it morphed into a grin as she followed Mal's eyes to the door.

"Oh shit," Mal said and strolled over to the door, walking by her side as they neared it. "What is it?"

"No idea," Onnie said, reaching down and picking him up. "Wanna find out?"

Mal squinted at the door, going silent for a minute before sighing. "Sure. If it's in the shop, it's safe."

"Well, duh," she said before crossing the last few feet between them and the deep chocolate-brown wooden door. "You really don't know what it is, though?"

"Your guess is as good as mine. She won't tell me anything. Suddenly mute. Or deaf." Mal glared at the ceiling.

Onnie giggled, relieved that she wasn't the only one to have pissed off the feline that afternoon.

She placed the hand that wasn't holding Mal on the wood lightly. She didn't expect it to shock her or do anything at all, but she'd learned to be cautious in the last few months. After getting lost in the quilted clearing for two hours the first time it appeared, she wouldn't be caught by the shop's tricks again. Even if Mal had assured her that the shop was only trying to teach her the consequences others would face if they didn't follow the rules.

Heavy iron bolts and fasteners held the door in place, and the handle was one large loop of cold metal. It looked more like the entrance to a medieval dungeon than a door that should be inside a modern-day bookshop. She passed her palm over the door's seam and adjacent wall and cocked her head in surprise.

"There's a cold draft."

"Okay, I can't take it, Onnie," Mal said, squirming in her arms, excitement filling his voice. "I wanna see. Hurry and open it."

Onnie laughed at his sudden impatience and nodded. "Alright, alright. Not mad at me anymore?"

"Still mad, open the dooooor...." he whined.

She chuckled and gently tugged on one of his ears. "Fine, you win." She grasped the heavy iron loop with her free hand and pulled the door...which didn't move.

"What's wrong?" Mal asked, straining his neck forward in an attempt to get closer to the door but not fall out of her grasp.

"Damn, it's heavy. Hold on."

Onnie gently tipped him out of her arms and onto the floor before grasping the handle with both hands.

"Step back in case it gives too quick for me to react."

Mal followed her instruction and stepped to the side. She took a deep breath and pulled with all her weight behind her. After a few seconds of straining, she felt the hinges shift, and a dust cloud billowed out from around the edges. She braced herself and pulled a little more, swinging it open and revealing a dark, *freezing* room beyond the threshold.

"Okay…." Mal said, poking his head around the door frame.

Onnie stooped down to retrieve Mal, and then they took two steps into the darkness. "Can you see? You've got cat vision, right?"

Mal hesitated, "Yes, but no. I can't."

"At all?" she asked, genuinely shocked.

"Zero. It's black. For all I know, it could be empty. Can't see any shadows, outlines, nothing."

A grin crept across Onnie's face in the darkness that Mal couldn't see. "You're brilliant."

"Well, yeah? But why this time?" he sassed.

Onnie closed her eyes, changing absolutely nothing regarding her eyesight.

Mal, the Bond, she said mentally to her Link as she pulled the Bonds for the objects and the room around her into view. Suddenly, outlines and glowing threads pulsed around them, a world illuminated in colors.

What do you see?

Onnie momentarily forgot that others couldn't see the Bond outside the void, and even then, they could only see their connections to others, nothing more. Even Mal couldn't.

The whole room. It's not empty.

For the second time today. Oh shit, Mal said.

Onnie looked behind her, to the wall next to the door they'd passed through. *Ah, here.* She carefully pulled a torch off the wall and returned to the study to plunge it into the fireplace. It sputtered and sparked but quickly lit in a small blaze.

"Watch the whiskers," Mal said, shrinking away from the fire as far as he could while still in her arms.

"You're fine. I promise," she smiled at the fierce warrior. Then she held her arm with the torch further out from her body and away from him. She took them back into the new mystery room, but the torch's light seemed to dim, and she barely got a foot of light around them from the flame. She reached for the room's Bonds again, and it was again aglow with rainbow threads. She traced along them to find something to help them further.

"Is the torch helping you at all?" she asked Mal.

"How about that?" Mal said, and she followed the direction his voice told her he was looking.

"What do you—" When she turned, she saw a sizeable bowl-shaped object that looked like it held a powder or pile of something in it. "Brazier?"

"Worth a look."

"Why not?" She carefully wound her way around the various objects now visible because of the Bond and approached their target. "Sorry," she bent down and set Mal on the floor, "I need a second arm."

Yup. The floor is stone, in case you care.

"Cold paws?" she teased, reaching forward to run her finger along the bowl's edge.

"Extremely. Unnaturally."

That gave her pause, and she decided to be doubly careful in her exploration.

"I think it's…copper? It feels like a hammered copper bowl or something similar." She held the torch as far behind her as possible, leaned closer, and sniffed the air above the bowl, the dry smell of charcoal filling her nose. "Perfect. I think this is what we needed. Step back. I have no idea how potent this will be."

She heard a few fast paws padding behind her, and then she stepped back a bit further. With one last mental request to the shop that she hoped it wouldn't kill both cats due to curiosity, she tipped the torch into the bowl.

For a few seconds, nothing happened, and she was worried that the fuel in the bowl wouldn't catch. Then, a slight draft blew past her from the open door and into the brazier before it flared to life with a deafening roar and a flash of blue flame.

"Yipes!" she shouted involuntarily and jumped back. It was only after her body had reacted that she realized she could have stepped on Mal and, thankfully, hadn't.

They had indeed found an old brazier. It was nearly two feet in diameter, the flame was almost as high as the bowl was wide, and it glowed a brilliant blue.

She took a small step closer to examine it when a second flare-up launched flames eight feet in the air and pulled another squeak of surprise from her at the abruptness of it. There must have been another fuel source along the ceiling that ignited. A small line of fire raced along the stones in two directions before splitting off multiple times in different directions until it formed a sigil on the ceiling that she'd never seen before. The flames didn't stop there and made their way back into four lines, one running down each wall between shelves and other furniture. The fire flowed like water down the stone walls and into three different bowls around the room that she hadn't noticed previously.

The room was fully lit now, and Onnie's mouth was agape. The room was filled with the oldest bookshelves and books she'd ever seen. They stood against the walls in short bookcases, and an old ladder on a rail was in front of one taller bookcases. Trunks were scattered throughout the center of the room, and a few solid-looking tables were dotted around with unlit oil lamps and ink pots with quills atop them.

Mal had also been right about the floor. It looked similar to the cobble streets outside in Alku. Still, it was significantly smoother, probably due to foot traffic over time, considering a few well-worn paths were winding around the sturdy tables.

Onnie turned in a small circle, absolutely in awe of the dark stone contrasting with the blue flames, brown leather covers, and parchment. Dust sparkled in the air and threatened to make her sneeze. It was absolutely brilliant, and she was nearly shocked silent.

"Holy. Shit," she whispered. "Mal, what is this?" When Mal didn't respond, she looked to the floor beside her and saw he was gone. *Mal?*

"Sorry, over here," he said from the floor in the center of the room, staring at the ceiling.

She spun to face him and slowly approached, giving him space since she could see him thinking.

"Have you told Gabe?" he asked after a few minutes of contemplation.

"Oh, no, I haven't." She reached along her Bond to her Guardian and gasped. It felt sort of slippery and seemed to dance just out of her grasp. "I...I can't?"

"That's what I thought." Mal blinked and finally made eye contact with her. "Neither can I. It's because of this." He raised his nose to the ceiling again and the center of the unknown sigil.

"What is it?" Onnie tried not to panic yet and listen to Mal's answer, but she continued to push on her Bond with Gabe.

"That is the sigil of the First Keeper, and I think we need to talk," he said flatly. "Outside."

Then he left the room and returned to the study through the still-open door. Onnie hadn't processed what he'd said right away, and he left her there with wide eyes and frozen in shock.

For the second time that afternoon.

Chapter 9: Something Old, New, Borrowed, and Blue

March 2022 - Alku | Onnie Moore

The instant Onnie's foot met the hardwood floor in Abbot's study, she gasped and clutched her chest from the bombardment of Gabe's emotions along their Bond. Simultaneously, her cell phone scared the crap out of her with its shrill ring from her back pocket. She quickly slammed down her mental walls, blocked out Gabe, and answered her phone, already knowing it was him.

"Are you trying to knock me on my ass—"

"WHERE THE HELL ARE YOU!" Gabe roared, and Onnie yanked the phone away from her face in shock and quickly became annoyed as her ears began ringing along with everything else.

"You want me to answer you, try not screaming at me," she snapped back at him. She assumed Gabe had likely not been able to feel her along the Bond just like she wasn't able to reach him but yelling at her would only piss her off more.

"Cat, don't even—" he started to argue, thankfully not yelling in her ear anymore, but she cut him off anyway.

"I'm fine. At the shop. You should come here, and I'll show you why yelling at me won't get you any answers and will only make me angry."

"I'm nearly there," Gabe said, clearly struggling to hold back the frustration in his voice.

"Then I'll see you soon."

When he grunted in agreement, Onnie hung up and looked at Mal, who was perched on the desk. "Well, that was…intense," she remarked as she flopped onto the couch in the middle of the room.

"Think about it from his perspective. He probably freaked." Mal relocated to her tummy and booped her nose with his small, cold, wet one.

"I'm sure he did. I can't say I didn't either once we realized, but yelling at me won't make it better." Onnie sighed and draped her arm over her face to cover her eyes, a searing headache spreading rapidly outward from behind them.

"Onnie," Mal said, wiggling his nose under her arm, "close the door."

"Can we leave the flames?" she peered out from under her arm with one eye.

Mal nodded, "Yes. It was probably only extinguished because of the stasis it was in."

Onnie pushed on the door's Bond, which closed with a heavy thud from the other side of the room. "We should call Dany, too."

"Put down your walls. You weren't the only one Gabe pissed off." Mal snorted and settled into a more comfortable position on Onnie's lap.

"Oh, crap." When she lowered her mental walls just a fraction, she was relieved to feel Gabe had calmed down a bit.

Dany, are you okay?

What the HELL was that?! Dany shouted with an audible tremble in her mental voice.

I'm sorry. Mal and I found something at the shop that apparently disconnects or dampens the Bond. Honestly, I'm not sure yet, but we didn't figure out that it did for a while. That said, you're going to lose your mind when you see what we found.

Well, I'm heading to the shop, so you can explain then. Dany groaned. *I'm gonna need ibuprofen. Damn, that man can shout.*

Onnie giggled. *You and me both.* Unsurprisingly, Gabe's on his way *here, too, but I think he's ahead of you, so try to hurry. I don't want to explain twice, and I'm unsure how long I can stall him.*

Noted. See you soon.

Dany retreated from their Bond, and Onnie shifted to focus on Gabe's. She gently pushed her sleepy and 'I'm fine, so stop worrying' feelings to him.

I'm SO angry at you, Cat, he replied after a minute.

I know, but once you hear what happened, you'll understand. Probably still be mad, but hopefully not at me.

Dany's on her way, too.

I know. I just spoke with her. I warn you. I'm not explaining anything until she gets here, so don't come in here all on fire and wild muppet arm-y.

Muppet arms, Cat?

I'd pay to see that, Mal chimed in.

Can it furball. You're just as much on my shit list as she is.

Onnie smiled down at Mal, and the feline rolled his eyes.

Breathe, Gabe, she reassured. *Be safe, and see you soon. We're in the study.*

Gabe pulled back from their Bond, and Onnie sighed. "That was so much worse than I was expecting."

"What did you expect? You went dark on your Guardian without notice, along with your Link. He's probably driving here from the school in the shortest route possible, and I mean as the crow flies. Anything in his way be damned."

Onnie snorted and scritched under Mal's chin. "I know. I didn't realize, or I would have told him, you know that. Or waited, but what's done is done, and getting shouty at me won't rewind time."

Mal chuffed and began purring in response to her lazy, mindless petting.

She'd put her arm back over her eyes, and at some point, she dozed off because what felt like ten seconds later, she heard Gabe's voice along their Bond again.

Come on, Cat. Wake up now. Gabe said gently, and she realized he was kneeling next to the couch and softly rubbing the back of her hand that wasn't gripping Mal.

"Sorry," she moved her arm and blinked at the sharp pain caused by the light piercing her retinas.

"It's fine, but if you're up to it, I think you owe us some explanations," Gabe said, kissing her forehead and getting to his feet. When he moved away, she saw Dany smiling but nodding behind him from where she sat on the hearth warming up.

"Yup! I'm a mix of pissed and excited. Not every day you tell me I'm gonna lose my mind over something."

Mal yawned from where he was still curled up on her lap, and she shifted him to the couch as she sat up and straightened her hair and long-sleeved shirt. "I'm honestly surprised you guys waited for me. Why didn't you just go in?"

Dany and Gabe looked at each other and then back to her. "In where?" they both said in unison.

Onnie yawned and tipped her head toward the door behind her, "New door."

She watched, and both her best friend and boyfriend shifted their gaze to the corner of the study and then squinted. Dany's eyebrows eased slightly faster than Gabe's, and she suddenly whooped and jumped in the air, her sudden and extreme movement making the fire flicker.

"Holy shit!" Dany exclaimed and ran over without a second thought.

"Dany!" Gabe shouted, and his tone halted his sister in her tracks instantly.

"What!?" She shouted and spun on her heel to complain to him. "Don't tell me you're not excited."

"Of course I am," Gabe said, slowly walking to the door. Onnie giggled when she saw how hard he was trying to cover up his barely restrained interest with his serious, brooding Guardian attitude. "Did you already forget that Cat went dark in there," he turned to look at her to back him up, "You were in there, I assume?"

"Can't deny it," Onnie shrugged.

Dany groaned, a smile still plastered to her face. "You suck. Fine." She crossed her arms and feigned a pout, "So, we can't go in?"

"I didn't say that…." Gabe said, and this time, his face and tone betrayed his excitement.

Onnie laughed and made her way past them and over to the door. "I understand your hesitation, Gabe, but now that we know this room has some shielding or dampening property, I think we'll be fine. Mal can correct me if he thinks otherwise. He was with me the whole time."

Mal appeared, perched on Gabe's shoulder. "Naw, it's safe. You'll see, but I can tell you with zero doubt this may be the safest room in the entirety of the shop. Current, past, and future."

Even Onnie paused at that. Mal evidently hadn't told her everything, and she felt her excitement re-building.

"See! Let's go!" She said before spinning around and pulling on the cold iron handle again, except this time it pulled far easier, and the room was already awash in blue flames, its glow mimicking her, Mal, and Gabe's eyes for a split second.

"Woah," was all Dany and Gabe managed to say as they stood outside the room for a minute or two. Once their brains engaged and Dany realized what she was looking at, she quickly rushed past Onnie and went to the nearest trunk. On the other hand, Gabe had his eyes glued to the ceiling and the symbol that now blazed blue above them.

Onnie took a few steps into the room and turned to face Gabe as she walked, "You gonna stand there all afternoon?" She had intended to tease him but paused when she saw Gabe's expression hadn't shifted to playful as she'd expected. "What is it?"

Gabe narrowed his eyes, still looking at the ceiling. "I'm not sure. I just get the feeling that there's something important we're missing."

"Of course we are!" Dany scolded, her upper body popping out of one of the trunks she had been spelunking in. "This room has only been open for like an hour, and considering the sigil on the ceiling is the First Keeper's, I'd say it's been closed a long while."

"Wait, it's what?" Gabe asked.

"She's right," Mal added, pushing his paw against Gabe's cheek. "You really can go in, though. I think I can explain a little. Won't fully chill you out, but should take the edge off."

Onnie snorted, made her way to one of the larger tables in the center of the space, pulled out a spindly wooden chair, and sat down. She crossed her arms, partly to reinforce her point and also because it was still freezing in the room.

"You heard the cat. Get your ass in here. I wanna know."

Dany glanced between her brother and Onnie before carefully closing the trunk she'd been rummaging through, pulled out a chair beside Onnie, and mirrored her impatient posture.

"What she said."

Finally, Gabe's skeptical side cracked, and he sighed, but Onnie could see the slight smile on his lips. "Fine. You win." He crossed the threshold and shivered but walked over to Onnie's other side and carefully sat in another chair. "Can't say I trust the furniture."

"Dude, people were not built like you way, *way* back when." Mal teased and jumped off his shoulder and went to sit in the middle of the table to face all three of them.

"What does that mean?" Gabe replied in mock offense.

"He means you're a behemoth," Dany interjected, and Onnie quickly erupted into a giggle fit.

"Oy!" Gabe griped, playfully leaned over, and poked Onnie in the side. "Quiet you."

Onnie inhaled a deep breath and nodded. "Okay, okay. Sorry." She turned to look at Mal and tried her best not to start laughing again. "Mal, please explain."

The three of them could now listen to the feline attentively once the tense atmosphere had finally been broken.

"Obviously, the shop didn't always look like it does now, nor was it in Washington originally. Hell, it wasn't even a shop, to begin with."

"It grew as the knowledge of the world did," Onnie said rhetorically, and Mal nodded.

"Okay," Dany added, "Judging by the First Keeper's mark on the ceiling, this must have been one of the very first rooms the shop ever created."

"Bingo," Mal nodded. "In fact, this *is* the first room."

Onnie coughed, choking on nothing as the impact of what her Link was saying fully hit her. "This is the first room? Like the first... first...?"

"Yup," Mal said.

Onnie's eyes were wide as she stared at Mal. "I mean, like from before, this was a shop."

Mal nodded again, "Uh huh."

"As in, the shop's original location—" Onnie started.

"Yes!" Mal shouted with a chuckle. "The very first, initial, wasn't even in this country, but somehow is, or seems to be, a room where the first person became what we call a Keeper, resided."

Onnie snapped her jaw shut and crossed her arms on the table in front of her so she could put her head down on them. "Even for me, this is insane."

"Careful, Cat, don't drool on the thousands-year-old furniture." Gabe teased.

"Oh, like you have room to talk, behemoth man," Onnie shot back without raising her head. "You break it, you buy it."

Dany giggled softly, and Onnie reached to check Mal's amusement via their Bond, and she found it exactly as it should have been. Her head shot up, and she slowly scanned the room.

"What's up, Onnie?" Dany asked, trying to follow Onnie's sight path.

"I just instinctively reached for our Bond again and then remembered earlier. Mal, why is this room affecting that?"

"Ah, to be honest, I'm not quite sure on that point. Dany might actually know more than I would," he looked at Dany, and Onnie and Gabe did the same.

Dany pursed her lips, and her brow wrinkled in concentration for a minute or two while they all sat still and stared at her. She shifted in her seat a few times, stood up, paced a bit, and then sat back down.

"Okay, so I have a few theories."

"After all that, I'd hope so," Gabe quipped, earning himself a sisterly glare.

"Okay, first is, maybe the sigil that we now associate with the First Keeper is actually a ward of some kind. Think of the ones Xayn has all over our houses."

"Alright, not bad," Gabe nodded. "Next?"

"Or, there may be something in here that's so old it has an effect we don't know about."

"So," Onnie said, working through Dany's theory out loud, "maybe there's a book or object in here causing it? So it's not the *room* per se, but a thing in it?"

Dany shrugged, "Could be. No clue."

"I have one more theory," Mal said, raising a front paw to get their attention like a child would in school. "As Onnie pointed out, this room shouldn't even be in this location…so what if it isn't?"

The three sat quietly with confused expressions as they stared at Mal.

"That's it?" Gabe asked, skepticism heavy in his voice.

Onnie could feel herself frowning. She felt like something was pushing on her intuition, but it kept dancing just out of reach.

The door appeared. It was stuck, probably because of disuse, age, environmental changes shifting the wood, or something else. It was dark inside. Unnaturally dark. So dark that Mal couldn't see. Then there was the cold. It was too cold. Not to mention the blue flames, which sure as hell were not natural, at least not in their current context. Onnie looked over to one of the four braziers and into the flames. The color was also the same as her eyes when she pulled a lot of power from the shop or when she was overly emotional.

So what did that give her? Dark, cold, Keeper blue colored flames,

Bonds that became deaf to those outside the room, and where telepathy was isolated to only those within the room.

"Oh, my god," she blurted without thinking.

"What?" Gabe asked as he leaned forward to look closer at her, her random outburst probably confusing him.

Onnie looked at her brilliant Link. "You're right, Mal. This room isn't *in* Alku. We're in the void."

Gabriel Vansand

When Onnie said they were in the void, Gabe's skin chilled, and his teeth clattered together. It had been cold before, but now it was as if his body realized it hadn't responded to the degree it should have been.

"What!" Dany shouted shrilly and got to her feet.

Both he and Mal winced at her outburst, and Onnie just looked up at her and sniggered.

"Damn, Dany," Gabe said, rubbing his ear closest to her.

"What?" she said, stomping her foot and crossing her arms. "Do you not realize what this means?"

"Not fully, but it does mean I'm extremely glad when we are in the void normally that we can't feel the cold."

Onnie giggled, "Yeah, you and me both."

"Are you really worried about the temperature right now?" Dany glared at him, and he figured he'd teased his sister enough.

"Alright, I get it. Wait," realization struck Gabe, "you've never seen the void before, have you?"

When his sister turned away and pouted, he knew he'd hit the nail on the head. Their entire life, Abbot had talked and taught them both about the Bond and mentioned the void a few times. From what Gabe could piece together, the void that the older man had seen was not quite the same as what Cat could, but it sounded close enough. Abbot hadn't had the power to bring anyone to the void with him as Onnie could, so he and Dany had never experienced it. Except now Gabe had. And Dany hadn't.

"Why didn't you ever ask me?" Onnie said and walked over to pinch Dany's side playfully. "I mean, it's literally black, but I'd have shown you."

I had no idea, Onnie said to him and Mal. *I bet she feels left out.*

"It's...not a big deal," Dany said, her tone of voice betraying her true feelings.

"It is to me," Onnie stated and crossed her arms. "I'm an idiot. You're brilliant, no doubt there, but everyone on the team should have first-hand experience with the void and the Bond, not just theoretical. I'll take you. First chance I get."

Gabe saw Dany's cheeks tint, and he couldn't deny Onnie's observation, but more than that, she'd acknowledged Dany's feelings of isolation, knowledge gap, and wounded pride with a single sentence. Then she'd fixed it.

Damn, she's good, Mal said to him, verbalizing his exact thoughts.

I was just thinking that myself.

Even though he'd only spoken to Mal, Onnie glanced at him, and with the look she gave him, he'd swear she'd heard him too.

"Alright, you two," Gabe said and got to his feet, "I'm cold, and that's saying something. Cat, you'll need to bring a sweatshirt in here with you."

Onnie was always cold, so if he felt it, she was most likely frozen solid and was just ignoring it in favor of her excitement.

Dany snorted, "Come on, let's go. We can talk more in front of the fire while eating Mrs. Radcliff's cookies and drinking the tea you ordered for me."

"I'm glad you like it," Onnie said from behind Gabe.

He heard Mal jump off the table, and they met eyes as the feline walked past him to lead the precession out the door. When Gabe glanced over his shoulder, the two women weren't following. Instead, Onnie hugged Dany, and both had their eyes closed and smiles on their faces.

"Mal, let's go make that tea. My teeth are chattering, and my jaw's already sore." Gabe said, giving them privacy and following Mal.

"At least you've got shoes on. This floor is *frigid,*" Mal complained as they exited the room and returned to the study.

Thanks, Gabe. Onnie said along the Bond right before he stepped into the other room.

He answered quickly, *Just don't stay in here too long. Mal's right, it's frigid.* Gabe didn't wait for Cat to respond. Instead, he left the stone room, and followed the feline, complaining of frostbite.

Chapter 10: The Calm Before the Storm

March 2022 - Alku | Onnie Moore

Onnie bent over to pull a stack of books from a box at her feet that had arrived the day prior. She read their titles as she placed each of them on their respective shelves. Apparently, the box she was unloading was all fiction, as they seemed to be one fairy tale after the other. A romance here, a mystery there. All the magic and ghouls and knights a person could want.

Except for Onnie.

Less than a year ago, she was bored, lost, and looking for where she belonged. Well, be careful what you wish for. Now, she only wanted to run away from the massive responsibility that had been placed on her shoulders. Too bad running wasn't an option. Not that she'd do it anyway, even if she had the chance. There was too much in Alku that Onnie loved to give up out of fear, but that didn't mean that some days it didn't weigh on her more than others.

Her Bond with Gabe pulsed, and she felt his worry over her shift in mood as her mind drifted down a darker path. She closed her eyes and smiled, reassuring him that she was okay and he shouldn't worry. After a minute, he backed off again, and she could feel him retreat into his own mind.

They had both gotten better at their wordless communication over the past few months, and Gabe had begun asking, not assuming, when her mood shifted too quickly or drastically. She appreciated his calmer approach and tried to remember that even though he'd grown up with a sister, he was clearly not a woman, nor did he understand how deeply hormones could affect mood and mental thought.

Onnie smiled when she remembered the first time Gabe and Mal came home, and she and Dany had been lying on the couch, both victims of biology simultaneously. There had been a plate of chocolate chip cookies on the table, multiple empty ice cream containers, and a huge pot of their favorite tea, and both of them had heating pads on their laps while they sat in the darkened living room. She and Dany had looked up at the two males who had been smart enough not to open their mouths, and instead, Gabe refilled their tea while Mal curled up to replace the hot pad Dany had been using with his warm, furry body.

There was only one book left in the box Onnie had been unpacking, and it had only taken her roughly twenty minutes to plow through most of the backlogged stock she had. She shelved the final book and was about to close up for the day when the front door burst open, clattering against the wall and startling her half to death.

"Oh shit!" Dany cursed from under her fancy purple raincoat as she struggled to pull the door closed. "What the hell kind of mutant storm is this!" she shouted over the downpour and roaring winds.

Step back, and I'll close it!

Dany quickly shuffled back, and a second later, the shop door swung shut with a bang and then locked with a loud click.

Onnie rushed over to the stained glass window that had thankfully been closed, but she looked through the clear panes of glass and frowned. "What the hell is going on out there?" The downpour was clearly audible when she was closer to the door, even inside, and the sky was an ominous swirl of greys and black.

"I have no idea. It was drizzling when I left the library, and by the time I got here, it morphed into a hurricane or something."

Onnie narrowed her gaze out the window even more. "Magic?"

Dany shook her head, "Didn't feel like it, but you're the expert."

"Hmm...." she nodded and projected herself onto the sidewalk in front of the shop's door. Her non-corporeal form stood unphased by the water and wind as she looked to the sky for any oddities. Everything looked normal, and nothing felt nefarious, so she shrugged before returning to her body.

"Everything looks fine, and I don't feel any strange magical mojo or anything."

"Magical mojo?" Dany said with a snort. "Is that a technical term?"

Onnie rolled her eyes and helped Dany peel off her wet coat that had only partially protected her from the amount of water she'd endured. Though in Onnie's opinion, no raincoat would have saved Dany from the hell outside her door.

"Gabe still at the school?"

"Yeah, and if this storm stays this bad, he will probably volunteer. Alku uses the gym as a rescue center during disasters. Everybody pitches in from around the community."

"Oh," Onnie said, surprised. "I didn't realize Alku had so many disasters. They should probably have included that on the brochure."

Dany scoffed at her, "Smart ass. So many magical beings in one place, sometimes there are...accidents."

"Do I even want to know?"

"Probably not," Dany said, smiling, but then she smirked. "Well, there was that one time we got so much snow that people had to be dug out of their houses, and then Elsi and a few others went around defrosting infrastructure. Most people hung out in the gym, the cafe, and A Shot in the Dark for the night."

"I guess having an elemental witch with an affinity for fire comes in handy. What about the day walkers?"

Dany giggled, "They all made it home. A mix of Gabe, Xayn, Stephan, and a few others made sure they were safe. I'm pretty sure Sam reverted to actually being seventeen for the day, considering he and Vanessa basically sled the entire way home. Pulled by local dogs and everything."

"Ah huh," Onnie said, smiling as she walked deeper into the shop. "Come on back, and I'll make you some tea to warm up." She led the w ay to Abbot's study and over to a trunk in the corner next to the new door they'd found the week prior. She placed her palm on the wooden door briefly before opening the chest.

"Here, I have extra clothes, and they'll be dry." She pulled out a pai r of baggy sweatpants and a soft long-sleeve thermal before passing them to Dany. "Well, the shirt will fit. Sorry about the pant length."

"It's fine, thanks," Dany said, stripping off her wet clothes and dropping them to the wood floor in a soggy heap.

Onnie grabbed them and laid them on the hearth in front of the fireplace to dry. "Why'd you brave the storm and come all the way over here anyway?"

"It's not that far, Onnie, and it really was only misting when I left," Dany said, rolling her eyes. "Besides, I was going to take you to The Day Night Cafe for a girls' night. Now, I guess we're eating in."

Onnie crossed her arms before her chest, "And what if I had other plans?"

Dany put her hands on her hips and raised one eyebrow. "Ha! Yeah…right."

"Oy!" Onnie threw her hands up, "Why can't I have other plans?"

"Fine," Dany said, reaching out for her soaked clothes. "I'll go."

Onnie groaned, "Shut up and put the sweats on. You know I don't have any other plans."

"I know!" Dany cheered and resumed getting dressed. "Hey," she looked around, "where's Mal? Exploring the First Keeper's room?"

"Chasing the quilted mice in the clearing reading room."

Dany snorted, "Really?"

"Yup. I think the shop is enjoying its time as a more...physical being this incarnation."

Dany laughed. "I bet. Rebecca was a force to be reckoned with, but somehow, I think she saw things differently than the shop did and definitely way different than Mal does."

Onnie nodded and left the study to make tea in the back room, Dany following her.

"I know. It's odd. Their personality sometimes feels like two completely different beings instead of one manifestation and one spirit of the same essence. Especially after finding a new room. Mal not knowing much about the First Keeper's Library was a bit…unsettling."

"I bet, but If I've learned anything in your short time as Keeper, your powers are far more advanced than in the past. Perhaps it's you that's helping them be their own people?" Dany squinted in confusion, "Felines? Building?" She sighed and then flopped onto the couch. "Oh, whatever. You know what I mean."

Onnie laughed, "Yeah, I do." She focused on making tea and pulled out the serving set since she'd not used it since she'd cleaned and put it away the night before.

"So," Dany said after a minute or two of silence, "what do you think of Elaric?"

"If he is who he says he is, I think we've found a good ally."

"I think he is. I trust him."

"You barely know him, Dany. What's to trust?" Onnie smirked at her best friend but did a double take when she saw Dany suddenly very interested in her fingernails. "Dany…."

"What?" she said, still not looking up.

"Uh oh, I know that look." Onnie ran over and squished beside her on the couch, "Spill it."

Dany blushed, "Ug, fine!" She smiled and crossed her legs on the couch. "We've gone out a few times."

"What!" Onnie screeched. "When?"

"Last week."

"Alright," Onnie said, getting up from the couch and opening a cupboard. "Forget the tea. This calls for wine."

"Well, that wasn't the reaction I was expecting," Dany admitted while getting up and pulling the kettle off the hotplate.

Onnie stopped, "What reaction did you expect?"

"I half expected a lecture, really."

"Why would I do that? You can date whoever you want. Besides, he seems like a nice guy."

"He is," Dany smiled.

"Good. Now you open the wine," Onnie handed her the bottle, "and I'll find something for us to eat."

"Deal!" Dany grinned and began peeling the foil from around the cork.

Onnie shook her head at her friend before heading back into Abbot's study and her stash of snacks to find something for them to split with the alcohol.

Elaric Rickson

Elaric shook the water from his dark black hair and then shivered, but not from the cold. The storm that had rolled in from out of nowhere that afternoon was brutal, and he'd put money into it being magical. He ducked under the overhang outside of the Alku school gymnasium and pulled out his phone to text Marco and Dany and make sure they were somewhere safe. He hoped Dany was with the Keeper as he knew her Guardian was not. He sent a quick message to both and looked up as an older woman obscured behind a large golf umbrella came up the walk. She visibly struggled as the wind tried desperately to rip everything in her arms from her grasp.

He quickly reached out and steadied the umbrella in her hand, and opened the gym door for her.

"Here, let me get that for you." He smiled, and she thanked him before they slipped inside the brightly lit shelter.

While he fought the wind as he attempted to close the door behind them, he heard the umbrella snap closed, and then she scurried off deeper into the room. When it was shut, he ran his fingers through his hair in an attempt to wring some of the water from it. Eventually, he gave up and focused on his clothes, which weren't much better. His combat boots and baggy jeans were drenched, and thankfully, he'd grabbed a leather jacket instead of a fabric one, so at least his torso was dry. Mostly. He didn't remember Alku being this…wet in the past, but he was glad that his normal clothing was a fit for it either way.

The gym was filled with the people of Alku of all ages milling about happily. There were tents inside the space and electric extension cords running throughout the room that snaked off and connected to people's electric burners and space heaters. Little ones wore pajamas and ran around in one corner of the gym playing tag, while the older ones sat in groups playing cards and gossiping. All of them looked utterly unphased by the storm raging on outside and he was glad they felt safe enough to let the adults do the worrying while they could just be kids.

Across the room, he spotted Gabriel helping set up a tent for a young mom who rocked her toddler in her arms. Elaric made his way over and raised a hand in greeting. "Can I help?"

Gabriel looked up from the tent poles in his arms and narrowed his eyes at who he assumed was a stranger to both himself and Alku. After a second of hesitation, he nodded to a second pile of poles.

"Sure, man. Can you help put this tent up?"

"No problem." Elaric smiled at the mom and looked down at the sleeping girl in her arms. "Man, she must be tired to sleep through this."

"She's a trooper, that's for sure," the woman smiled sweetly at the child.

Elaric nodded, walked over, and stooped down to pick up the poles at Gabriel's feet before whispering, "Elaric," so only the other man would hear.

Gabriel stopped for only a fraction of a second before the corner of his mouth raised in a small smile. "Thanks for your help."

"Anytime."

The two of them worked silently for a few moments, finishing the tent quickly and leaving the mother and daughter to their privacy. Gabriel led Elaric to a small office off of the gym and handed him a dry towel.

"You look drenched."

"Thanks, it's gnarly out there." Elaric ruffled his hair with the towel and tried to keep from flinging water all over the small room.

"Crazy storm," Gabriel said, sitting in his chair and putting his feet on his desk. "No way it's natural. It came on too quickly for that."

"Agreed," Elaric said, slumping into one of the smaller chairs. "You talked to the Keeper yet?"

"Mmhm…" Gabriel nodded. "She and Dany are at the shop. Cat says the storm's not magical."

Elaric narrowed his gaze, "We both know she's wrong."

Gabriel sighed, ran his hand through his damp brown hair, and tugged lightly on the ends of it. "Yeah, and that's what scares me. What magic is it if she doesn't know, even by instinct, what it is."

"The rogue guardian," Elaric said plainly. "I've been watching him. Well, his minions more specifically, while they have been watching you guys."

"You what?" Gabriel said, dropping his feet to the floor and sitting upright in his chair.

Elaric raised his hand, "Don't worry. He can't trace me back to you guys, and none of them have ever seen me in any form at all. I've been very careful, but before we can plan, we need to know what we're dealing with."

"I agree, but that was stupid. There's no reason for you to be acting alone with this."

"I don't intend to. I need all four of you for my idea to work," he smiled.

"You have a plan?" Gabriel asked with curiosity.

"A start to one, but now's not the time to talk about it." Elaric shivered. "We need to keep an eye out. Something's not right."

Gabriel ran his hand through his hair again and then nodded. "You're right," he got to his feet, "Come on. Let's go check on the residents."

Elaric stood and followed him to the door when Gabriel stopped. "By the way, what's your name this time?" he asked, causing Elaric to laugh.

"Let's stick with Andrew."

"Andrew?" Gabriel asked with skepticism.

"Yeah, I recently started using it, and so far, it seems to be working out."

Gabriel chuckled and shook his head, "What a life you have, Elaric and Gabe, by the way, please."

Elaric smiled and followed the Guardian back out to the townspeople, and as they walked, his cell phone vibrated in his pocket. He smiled when he saw Marco's reply.

Still downstairs. Had some patrons, and now we won't let them leave due to the storm.

Good, he replied. *How are people feeling?*

A few seconds later, Marco replied, and Elaric smirked at the response.

I'm fine, don't worry. Since you've been back, things have been easier. Be safe. This is no mere storm.

He worried about Marco in a room full of people whose emotions were likely less than favorable, but there was little he could do for him at that moment. *I will be, and yeah, I don't think it is either, neither does Gabe.*

Elaric finished his conversation with Marco and slipped his phone back into his pocket just as the older woman whom Elaric had held the door for scurried up to Gabe with a worried frown.

"Gabe, where is Onnie? She is alright, isn't she?"

Elaric hadn't noticed much about the woman earlier as she'd been hidden behind her gigantic umbrella. Without it, he recognized Elanor Radcliff, the town's local florist and one of Abbot's friends. Mud clung to her rubber boots and was smeared on her canvas apron, but when he looked over her shoulder, the direction she'd come from had no mud tracks, as he'd expected.

"Of course, she's fine, Mrs. Radcliff. She's at the shop with Dany right now." Gabe bent down and kissed the older woman's cheek.

"Oh, good heavens, I'm so glad," she said, clutching her chest. "Was she the one who conjured this storm?"

"No, but she's trying to figure out who did. Don't you worry." He shot Elaric a look that clearly said, 'keep your mouth shut,' before taking her arm and leading her to a small tent off to one side. "I pulled out my spare tent for you. It's all set up and ready."

"Oh, my boy! Thank you." She poked her head inside the tent to look around.

"Of course. Now, if you need anything, just ask, alright?"

"Yes, yes," she said with a wave before disappearing inside the tent, only to reappear a second later. "Have you talked to Xayn?"

Gabe smiled, but Elaric noticed it didn't quite reach his eyes like his earlier one. "Yes, he and Grandma Yvonne are at Green Cottage. They'll be fine."

"Oh good, I couldn't reach her," she said before ducking back inside the tent.

Elaric jerked his head to one side, and Gabe followed him a few paces further from the tent. "The Keeper thinks it's not a magical storm."

"I know, but the townspeople don't need anything more to frighten them. Cat will figure it out, or she's right, and it's a natural storm, and we really do have nothing to fear."

"You're sure?" Elaric wasn't convinced, but he knew very little about the balance of information in Alku since he'd returned, and he would just have to trust Gabe.

"I'm sure. I trust Cat with my life."

"Alright." Elaric looked at the tent where the older woman's bottom was sticking out the door as she rummaged through the tent's contents.

Gabe followed his gaze and smiled. "Mrs. Radcliff. She's a nymph. Most of the town has their own outdoor supplies, but that's not something she would need, so I lend her my spare set."

They looked over as she fought the tent's zipper, which had caught her apron's tie.

"Uh-huh," Elaric said. "Cute lady. It's been a long time since I've seen her, and not in this form."

"Interesting, but yeah, she is," Gabe said warmly. "Come on. I could use your help making sure everyone is settled in and fed for the night. Hopefully, we won't lose power, but if we do, I'd like everyone asleep before that."

Elaric nodded, and with one last look at the florist, he followed the Guardian into the fray.

Onnie Moore

Onnie was very aware that she had drunk far too much. Likewise, so had Dany. They were draped over large pillows piled on the floor before the study fireplace. Their cheeks were rosy from the heat and the alcohol, and Dany had a minor case of the hiccups. Mal pretended to nap on the couch but had one eye open, staring at them from across the room.

Onnie took a big gulp of her wine and wrinkled her nose, "I wonder if Elaric has ever been a woman before?"

Dany giggled, "Oh! Now, there's a question I'd like to know the answer to, but even better, would that make him a lesbian?"

"Oh god, you can't ask him that!"

"Why not?" Dany said, sitting up. "That could be fun!"

Mal groaned from the couch, and both women looked at him in surprised silence.

"Do you have something to add, Mal?" Onnie asked with a chuckle.

Mal rolled over on his back and pretended to hurl up a hairball.

"Oh, you stop that!" Dany said and flung a pillow at him.

Right before it hit him, he disappeared and reappeared on her stomach, where he leaned forward and licked the tip of her nose before smiling and returning to the couch.

"You little furball!"

Onnie was rolling on the ground with laughter, wine precariously sloshing out of her cup onto the wooden floor.

"You two are lucky I haven't called Gabe yet. You're a mess." Mal chided and blinked slowly at them with his best disappointed adult expression.

"We are not!" they slurred together.

He cocked his head to the side, and they erupted into more giggles.

"We're just having a bit of fun, Mal. Don't worry. Everything's fine," Onnie said, stumbling to her feet and flopping on the couch beside him.

"Famous last words, Onnie." He said as she picked him up and snuggled him to her, peppering him with loud kisses.

"Blegh, get a room, you two," Dany teased, throwing back her head to finish her wine.

Mal growled and squirmed out of Onnie's grasp. "You two stay here and gossip. I'm going to find your Guardian. Maybe he's rightly concerned about this storm." He glared at both of them one more time and then relocated.

Onnie frowned, "Uh oh. I think I pissed him off."

Dany shrugged, "Don't worry about it. You're allowed to live a little sometimes."

Onnie nodded and then felt Gabe pushing along their Bond. *Cat, stop drinking. It's becoming quite challenging to stay sober over here.*

Onnie winced, "Shit."

"What?"

"We forgot that when I get drunk, Gabe gets the side effects, too."

Dany's eyes widened, and a slow smile spread across her lips before she cracked up. Slowly, Onnie joined her in laughter.

Sorry, Gabe. I'll make some coffee.

Dany is a horrible influence.

Onnie could tell he was smiling, though she wasn't sure if that was because of his amusement or the alcohol. Either way, she felt better.

"Come on, you. Let's make coffee."

Dany stuck her bottom lip out and pouted, "Spoilsport."

"I know, I know." Onnie lumbered to her feet and offered the other woman a hand, pulling her to her feet. "I have whipped cream...." Onnie tempted.

Dany immediately perked up and headed for the backroom. "Don't have to tell me twice!"

Onnie shook her head with a wide grin and followed behind her best friend.

Elaric Rickson

Mal, Gabe, and Elaric sat in the small gymnasium office with smiles all around. The office door was closed, and most of the people beyond it were sleeping soundly after an eventful evening of fussing on Gabe's part.

"I swear, that woman will be the end of me," Gabe laughed.

"The Keeper?" Elaric asked.

"No. Dany," Mal and Gabe answered together.

Elaric chuckled, "I could see that. She seems like the type to lead with her heart."

Gabe smirked at him but didn't comment further. "By the way, you can call the Keeper, Onnie. I'm surprised she hasn't given you a lecture yet, actually. She hates being called Keeper."

Elaric's brows came together in confusion, "But she is the Keeper. It's a great honor and responsibility, and she is worthy of the title."

"She feels like it makes her more important than everyone else, and that's not how she sees herself," Mal commented. "Besides, Onnie is not one for doing what she's been told."

"I noticed," Elaric chuffed.

"You can keep calling her Keeper…." Gabe added, "But be aware, she has an entire speech about the topic."

"Got it. Don't piss off the Keeper," Elaric snorted. "Onnie."

"Exactly," Gabe said, crossing his arms. "She can be frightening when she's mad. Not in a bad way. I trust her with everything, but evil and the immoral should be wary of her. She has a lot of power and doesn't hesitate to use it once someone is proven guilty."

Elaric nodded, "The town seems to trust her."

"Not trust," Mal said, shaking his furry head. "Love. Onnie is a kind soul and the people of this town flock to kindness. Even more than that, though, she's genuine. They'd do anything to protect her."

"And she them," added Gabe.

"She sounds a lot like her grandfather," Elaric said.

Mal nodded.

"Can I ask how you knew Abbot?" Gabe said carefully, and Elaric appreciated the man's concern.

Elaric smirked, "Ten-year-old runt chased after Sam and me."

Gabe snickered, "That makes so many things make sense now."

"Yeah. He was just an energetic boy living in Alku, and Sam and I honestly felt bad for the kid. He was obviously lonely, and while not an Outsider, he seemed to stay on the periphery of things."

"People probably sensed he was the Keeper, even if no one knew it yet," Mal added.

"Very possible." Elaric agreed.

He smiled fondly at the memories of a young Abbot chasing Sam in the park on sunny days. Or when they used to have sleepovers at Stephan and Vanessa's once Abbot had grown a bit older. Marco watched out for the young Abbot, too. Everyone did. Mal was probably right, but Keeper or not, they all loved Abbot for being Abbot.

"Sorry if I brought up stuff better left buried," Gabe said apologetically.

"Don't be. I was just remembering."

After a few minutes, where each of them was lost in their heads, Elaric stood and stretched. "Well, I think it's best if I head off to get some shut-eye myself."

"Do you need gear?" Gabe offered.

"Naw, I'm good. But thanks."

"Of course, dude. Sleep well."

"Night!" Mal said, waving a paw.

Elaric quietly left the small office and closed the door behind him, trying not to wake anyone. He went to the corner of the gym the kids had been using as a play area and lay on one of the gymnastic mats. He pulled off his jacket, rolled it under his head as a pillow, and closed his eyes.

It only took a few minutes for him to drift off to sleep and even less time for him to sit bolt upright and wide awake.

Chapter 11: Dark Deceptions and Decisions

March 2022 - Alku | Elaric Rickson

Something was wrong.

Elaric quietly got to his feet from his makeshift pallet and blinked to adjust his eyes to the darkness. He checked his phone and saw he'd been sleeping for a few hours, reinforced by the gym still fully dark and full of sleeping people. He squinted across the space when a sliver of light came from the direction of the gym's door. A slight silhouette slipped outside, and his gut told him whoever it was and whatever they were doing, it wasn't good.

He grabbed his jacket and then crept past the tents and people sleeping on the floor in sleeping bags, doing his best not to wake anyone before he understood the situation. When he reached the door, he quietly eased it open and slipped outside into the pouring rain. The sky was black and moonless, and the howling wind created an eerie atmosphere that made the hairs on Elaric's neck stand on end.

The little figure he'd followed was nowhere to be found, and he continued to squint through the darkness for any indication of them. A minute later, he saw a figure step into the street, but it was clearly an adult, not the child he'd been searching for.

"Hello. Do you need a place to wait out the storm?" Elaric shouted above the winds. "You can come inside." The figure didn't respond, and Elaric took a few more paces toward them, now wary of the stranger. "Did you see a child come out here?"

At his last question, the figure raised their arm in front of them and splayed their fingers. A young girl walked out from the shadows, her movements robotic, and her eyes were glazed-over and unblinking. She approached the stranger, stopped before him, and turned to face Elaric.

"What do you want with her?" Elaric said as his body reflexively prepped for a fight.

"Summon the Keeper," the figure bellowed with ease over the din of the rain and wind.

"What do you need of the Keeper?" Elaric asked with more bravado than he felt.

"Do not question, or I will kill the child!" He twisted his hand, and the little girl turned her face to the sky and opened her mouth. "Do you wish to see her drown?"

Elaric recoiled in terror. "Return her to me, and I will summon the Keeper."

The figure cackled and turned the child's head back to normal, where she then spit up the water in her throat and mouth. "Summon quickly, human, or I may decide I don't need hostages."

"One sec, big man," Elaric said, holding up a finger and pulling his phone from his pocket, his eyes never leaving the child. He dialed Gabe quickly, and Mal appeared at Elaric's feet as the Guardian picked up.

"Outside. Now." Elaric nodded to Mal, who disappeared as quickly as he'd appeared. Elaric looked back toward the stranger and put his phone away. "Alright, you've got what you wanted. The Keeper is on her way. Now, give me the girl."

The man hissed, the sound unnatural and pulling on Elaric's memories just out of reach. The man was laughing.

"Fine, you may have the girl." He flicked his fingers toward her, and then she blinked a few times and shook her head. She walked towards Elaric, still in a daze, but the figure interrupted when she was only halfway to him.

"Oh, but I forgot. One parting gift."

He swirled his finger in the air, creating a black thread of smoke before blowing it towards her back too quickly for Elaric to reach. The little one looked confused momentarily, but it was short-lived, and she began screaming.

The girl dropped to the knees of her soaked pajamas, clutching her head, as she screamed a raw and powerful scream unlike anything Elaric had ever heard.

He was already running towards her before his brain registered that his feet were moving. She continued to wail, now in his ear, as he cradled the young child in his arms, trying to calm her but not succeeding against whatever magic she'd been hit with.

The gym doors slammed against the wall as Gabe threw them open and stormed into the rain to confront the dark stranger. He stepped in front of Elaric and the girl, shielding them with his imposing form and a long carved staff in his hands.

"Leave this place!" Gabe shouted into the wind and rain.

The dark stranger's laugh was different this time, and it was a deep-rumbling cackle that Elaric almost mistook for thunder. The man beckoned Gabe with an upturned palm and unblinking eyes.

"Guardian, you would make a fine addition to my army. Join me."

It wasn't just the man's laugh that had changed. His voice had shifted as well. Elaric watched Gabe take two steps forward before hesitating on the third step. He shook his head and roared with anger.

"STOP!" he shook off whatever compulsion he was nearly under and brandished his weapon higher. "You cannot have me, and you will not harm another person in this town!"

When the stranger looked down at Elaric and the girl still in his arms, he knew what was coming before it even began. He closed his eyes and braced for the same agony that the young girl was still screaming from and he shifted to put himself between her and the man.

Before the pain came, he heard Gabe growl. Elaric looked over his shoulder and saw the Guardian standing even closer to the stranger, and his staff was raised as the stranger staggered back.

"I said," Gabe panted, "You. Will. Not. Hurt. Another."

The stranger sneered, "How noble you think you are, Guardian. How wise." The stranger shifted and stood taller than before, and Elaric assumed his weak facade was a ruse. "Thank you."

The pit in Elaric's stomach grew as he watched the stranger pull his arm back, and then he hurled a ball of black billowing smoke toward the gym. Its trajectory was too far over their heads to reach and went straight for the building where it would envelop them all.

Time seemed to slow as Elaric's brain registered their error. The rogue guardian didn't want to hurt Gabe. He wanted to cripple him. How better to destroy a kindhearted man than to rip his friends and family away from him as he watched, powerless to stop it.

The smoke flew towards the crowd of people who had come running outside a few minutes earlier when the young girl's screams woke them. Their faces were filled with terror as they watched the unknown evil stream toward them.

A flash of light lit up the night sky, blinding Elaric and burning away his dark vision and everyone else's. When he could finally pry his eyes open again, the glowing light emanated from between him and the stranger. The darkness that had been thrown was pulled back in their direction and consumed by the light's origin as a black hole does to space. When it was entirely absorbed, Onnie stood at the point where it had been extinguished.

"This is how you seek my attention!" she bellowed. Like the stranger's, her voice was magnified to be heard over the rain. "You do not know me as well as you think, rogue!"

Even from a fair distance behind the Keeper, he could see the blue glow of her eyes shining in the dark—a blue beacon of knowledge and protection. Elaric glanced to his side, where Gabe had moved to, and the Guardian's were also glowing.

"You will not harm another, and you should have listened to my

Guardian when he warned you. Now I have lost my patience and my mercy." Onnie said, her voice low with barely contained fury.

The look on her face gave Elaric both fear and hope. This Keeper was raw, feral, and unstoppable, and she'd shredded any last doubt he had of her being the one they'd been waiting for.

"Oh, I did not come here for your mercy, *child,*" the man mocked. "I simply wanted to introduce myself properly."

Fire flickered in the stranger's eyes, and Elaric couldn't suppress the shiver it pulled from him. Something wasn't right, and they had to be missing something. If the storm wasn't magical as the Keeper thought, then Jakob had other motives, and there was no way this altercation would end well.

"We are the residents of Alku. See how we band together and protect what we love even as you try to break us. Even Alku itself weeps for your incompetence."

The man tsked, his slightest sounds and whispers still reverberating loud and clear over the storm's wrath. "My my, how you've protected the young one."

Elaric watched as the man made a grabbing gesture with one hand and then yanked at the air, not even bothering to look at his young victim. The girl in Elaric's arms abruptly ceased wailing, only to return her face to the sky, where the falling rainwater began to drown her for a second time.

"No!" Onnie bellowed and then disappeared before reappearing inches from the stranger and roughly grabbing his forehead with one hand. Her fingers glowed, and light chased the darkness from his eyes as she purged the evil from his body and soul. As the last traces of it left the puppet's eyes, the young girl regained control over her body and began retching up water for the second time that night. Elaric kept his eyes on Onnie but softly whispered to the little one and gently patted her back to assist with her retching.

The rain continued to pour down around them, now silent as Alku itself seemed to focus on the Keeper's manipulation of nature just as the townspeople did.

"Rogue guardian, hear me now!" Onnie bellowed with her eyes closed. "If you want a fight, I will happily rip you apart, but if you come after the citizens of Alku instead of me directly, *EVER*," the ground shook from the force of her words, "again, then I will not strip you of your soul when we meet, and you will have wished that I had. I will be keeping your pet. I thank you for the gift."

A wave of energy burst from the Keeper and radiated outward from her. Elaric listened as windows shattered in the distance from the sonic boom, and car alarms began wailing on the more distant streets. Lightning struck trees, and wolves howled in the nearby forest as hundreds of winged beasts flew from the trees. Then, the rain, which had been silent, stopped.

Finally, the stranger slumped to the floor and landed in a heap, unmoving at Onnie's feet.

She turned around slowly to face those behind her. Elaric watched as the color began to drain from Onnie's face rapidly, and he'd wager she wouldn't be upright much longer. Everyone stood stunned, but Onnie broke it.

"I'm sorry, everyone. You're safe now. Go back inside and get out of the wet."

The little girl Elaric was holding had stopped coughing, and her mother ran over to take her from him. He released her to the crying woman, got to his feet, and looked at Onnie. Gabe casually walked to her side and offered her an arm for support. The strength the woman showed in front of the people she served was astounding. Elaric was sure he could only see her struggling because he was so close to her.

"Cat," Gabe said quietly.

"I can hold on for a few minutes. Get everyone back inside," she squeezed his arm gently, and he nodded.

"Andrew," he called to Elaric, "Can you stay with Onnie?"

"Of course," he answered and swapped places with Gabe. Then he leaned down to whisper in her ear, "It's Elaric, though you already knew that."

She smiled with what looked like a lot of effort but took his arm either way. "Dany is with Mal. They are inside. I...relocated us here and dropped them off in case things went poorly."

"You can do that?" he questioned reflexively.

She nodded, and he must have visibly relaxed, for her smile grew even more prominent. "Only the second time, but yes. I'm glad you care so much about her. Be careful, though. You wouldn't want me as your enemy, Elaric." She winked at him, and he involuntarily gulped.

She returned her focus to the people being rushed inside by Gabe, and Elaric looked down at the man at their feet.

"What are we going to do with him?" he toed the man with his boot.

"Hmm?" Onnie said distractedly before looking down. "Oh, I'll have Gabe bring him to the shop and deal with him tomorrow."

"What are you going to do?"

"Honestly," Onnie sighed, "I don't know. There's not much to be done with him. I'll probably have to strip his soul and have Dillon take care of the body. From the quick look I got, it was already in tatters. The rogue guardian doesn't leave much when he's done with his pawns and without Xayn's tonic, I was more rough with it than normal."

"But you said..." Elaric began.

Onnie shrugged, "I lied."

He could feel her starting to shake now, and he indicated to the gym with his free hand. "Come on. I'm surprised you're still on your feet."

She nodded weakly and took one single step before Elaric caught her unconscious body just above the ground.

Once the Keeper's strength gave out, the gym was filled with a flurry of activity and remained that way for a few hours before everyone had calmed down enough to return to bed.

Dany and Elanor rushed from inside the gym when Onnie collapsed, and they asked him to carry her inside, where they had made a soft pallet for her in the center of the tent cluster. He laid her down to sleep off whatever she needed to while Elanor sat at her side and brushed Onnie's wet hair from her face in a motherly gesture.

He and Gabe split up to watch the two exits of the gym while Dany and Mal roamed among the frightened and tearful as they tried to calm them.

No one spoke of the power that the Keeper had shown, even though it was something she was not supposed to have. She had saved them all, and he could see reverence and respect in the expressions of those who passed her sleeping form. A few even stopped and bowed their heads, and he could see their lips as they whispered to themselves or their gods.

Elaric's mind kept returning to the moment Onnie appeared in a flash of light. Keepers of the past were mental creatures. Capable of telepathy and short-range astral projections. Their power lay in their connection to the knowledge they guarded and the being it had become over the millennia. Never had he heard of a Keeper with the skills of this young woman.

He checked on her often during the night. Her breathing was never more than shallow, and her skin was never as rosy and pink as before. He was concerned, and when he asked Gabe, he got the same brave face answer he was telling everyone else. Gabe had to play the role of Guardian and portray that sense of strength and control, so Elaric searched for Dany, knowing she would tell him the truth.

The woman and her head of emerald green hair was sitting with the mother and little girl who had been attacked. They were only a few feet from Onnie, and Elaric watched as Dany's eyes searched her friend's face very carefully. When he got nearer to the woman, Dany smiled, and he returned it.

"Hi," she said timidly.

"Hey," he said, sitting beside her and scratching the feline in her lap on the head. Mal purred in response. "I just came to check on you." He looked over to the mother and child and nodded once, "How's she doing?"

The woman looked at the sleeping child in her lap and brushed her delicate curls off her forehead. "She'll be alright. Onnie will help her when she wakes up."

"She can do that?"

"Yes," Dany said. "This little girl's name is Miranda. She's one of Gabe's students." Dany hesitated briefly before adding, "And she doesn't speak."

"Oh, I'm...sorry?" Elaric added but cocked his head when he saw Dany's expression.

"Except with Onnie," the mother said, beaming. "I don't know what it is about that woman, but she brings my daughter back to me each and every time I hear them talking."

"Does she ever talk to you afterward?" Elaric asked a bit nosily.

The woman sighed, "A bit and only for a few hours, but I will take every minute I can."

"I'm sure."

"Thank you, by the way. For protecting my daughter," the mother said gently.

"No thanks needed. Besides, she did most of the work." He looked again at the pale Keeper sleeping a few feet away, and his resolve to enact his plan grew even stronger. "Dany?"

"Hm?"

"What's really happening with the Keep—" he stopped, "Onnie, right now? Gabe won't tell me anything."

Mal stretched on Dany's lap and looked up at Elaric. "She's fine. She just needs sleep."

Dany nodded, "She over-extended herself. She does that." Dany shook her head and groaned. "I can't wait to see the shop in the morning."

"What's wrong with the shop?" Elaric asked. At the same time, he pulled his phone from his pocket and texted Marco to check-in.

Mal answered instead of Dany. "She pulled a lot of power from it tonight to save the townsfolk, and it has taken a beating in return. We will have a mess to clean up when the sun rises."

Dany sighed, "Onnie is a very powerful Keeper, but that power has limits, and one of them is that she can only use so much of the shop's magic before she...makes a mess."

"She's good at mess-making," Gabe said, entering the circle and sitting beside Onnie. He brushed her dark hair back from her forehead just as Elanor had and checked it for a fever. "I just wish she'd make less of them."

Dany snorted, "She says the same about you, dude."

"I know," Gabe said with a small laugh, "But my messes drive her crazy. Her's nearly kill her."

"She'll be alright, Gabe," the mother said, shifting her daughter on her lap. "Have faith. She knows what she's doing."

"I hope so," he mumbled before leaning down and kissing her cheek.

"I may not have known her long," Elaric added, "but I know she'll be fine." Gabe didn't say anything, and Elaric could see the worry over his lover etched into his face.

Elaric's phone vibrated, and he relayed the message to the others. "Oh, by the way, Marco had a group of stranded tourists at the cafe. Everyone's fine, and the staff is escorting people back home and to the bed and breakfast now that the rain let up."

"Good, makes it easier that they weren't here. Less work for the wards." Gabe said, and the tension in his shoulders visibly eased.

Dany smiled, "I'm glad he's fine."

He and Dany had talked about his past and current relationship with Marco, so Dany's genuine relief gave him a minor case of the butterflies. While she knew the two of them were friends, had she not approved of or been comfortable with their relationship, he would have kept his distance from her. He and Marco were a packaged deal of sorts, and whoever he dated had to accept that.

"We should all get some rest," Gabe said. "I have a feeling our Keeper will need our help in the morning."

Dany nodded, resting her head on Elaric's shoulder with a small smile. He wrapped his arm around her and closed his eyes.

Thank you, Elaric, Onnie said in his head just as he slipped off to sleep for the second time that night.

Chapter 12: Assistance Asked, Assistance Given

March 2022 - Alku | Onnie Moore

Onnie woke the morning after the storm with the worst headache she'd ever had in her life. She groaned softly and rolled over, bumping into Miranda, who was snuggled up beside her. The little girl had worry lining her brow and cooed uncomfortably in her sleep. Onnie placed one finger on the child's forehead and closed her eyes to enter the void.

Miranda, can you hear me?

Onnie? Where are we?

It's okay, Miranda, you're sleeping, and you're safe with me and your mama. I'm going to make you feel better. You have a headache, don't you?

Uh-huh, and there are monsters in my dreams.

I know, don't worry, I'll make them go away.

Onnie slipped further into the little girl's mind, leaving a link between the young girl's consciousness and her own. She didn't think Miranda would notice as the darkness left inside her was purged, but just to be safe, Onnie scrutinized her Bond. The corruption hovered over a few threads and wasn't difficult to locate. She wrapped a small portion of her remaining energy around the mist and tugged it off Miranda's Bond and into herself. Then she rolled away from the little girl before opening her eyes and coughing out the darkness. Onnie's throat burned and felt raw, but she ignored it. Instead, she focused on the black mist as it rose and dissipated. Just like when she relaxed her hold over the corruption within herself, Onnie felt slightly nauseous.

"Cat?" Gabe whispered from beside her, his eyes open, watching the last bits of mist vanish.

"Don't worry. It's harmless now."

He kissed her forehead, "Explain later. How are you feeling?"

"Killer headache. I'm never drinking again." She waited until just a touch of concern shone in his eyes before smiling. "I'm kidding. Yes, I remember what happened last night. Don't be so concerned."

Gabe exhaled and glared at her with his eyes, but his lips smiled, and his Bond gave away his amusement. "Cat, not funny."

"I'm sorry, I know."

Onnie looked around the dimly lit gym and smiled when most occupants were still sleeping soundly. Dany was snuggled up in Elaric's arms, and Miranda's mother was sleeping on her and Miranda's pallet nearby.

Mal? Onnie asked along the Bond.

At the shop, Onnie. We have some work to do today.

Ug, be right there.

Onnie whispered to Gabe, "Be right back." Before he could argue, she closed her eyes and projected herself into the shop.

She stepped back in shock when she saw the utter destruction she'd been the cause of. Scorch marks lined the walls and ceiling. Most of the bookcases lay atop one another, tipped over, and their contents spilled out into a puddle of words on the floor. Glass cases lay shattered, their contents topsy-turvy. Dust twinkled in the air and made a glittering mess over everything. Even the register had shifted on the front counter.

Onnie walked hesitantly down the center aisle and stopped at the counter. The logbook and her favorite of the antique teacups lay ripped and shattered on the floor with Mal sitting beside them.

"I'm sorry, Onnie."

Onnie sniffled and held back her tears. *It's my fault. I knew the consequences when I pulled the power I did.* She pressed the heels of her hands into her eyes and apologized to the shop. *I'm so sorry I hurt you.*

"You saved the town, Keeper. You did what you had to do," Mal said sternly. "We forgive you."

Onnie nodded and knelt at Mal's level. *Let me wake the others, and we'll head over to start sorting this out.*

Mal shook his head, "Don't rush them. This will all be here when you return."

But—

"Take care of the others first. The shop can wait."

Alright. Onnie stood and turned to look at the destruction she had caused once more. *It's hard to believe I did this.*

"You didn't," Mal said with finality. "The rogue guardian did when he attacked Alku."

Onnie nodded and opened her eyes, blinking through tears.

"Cat?" Gabe said quietly.

"She's fine, but I have a lot of cleaning up to do."

Dany yawned, and Onnie looked over to see her stretch carefully in Elaric's arms so she didn't whack him. "We, Onnie, not you."

"Dany's right. This isn't just your fight. It never has been." Mrs. Radcliff said, walking over to them, her face bright but somehow already covered in dirt smudges.

"Exactly," another person added from the small crowd that had gathered while she'd been at the shop.

"You have our loyalty and our help, Onnie," said Miranda's mom, Erika.

"Thanks, everyone," Onnie said, sitting up and smiling at the still-growing crowd. "I hate to ask…." she trailed off.

Dany stood up. "Onnie, I'm pretty sure everyone here agrees with me when I say this, whatever you need. Just ask."

More people had gathered around now, and everyone nodded and murmured their agreement. Onnie stood and went to stand by Dany's side and took her hand.

"The shop is in ruins." A gasp came from the crowd, and she shook her head. "It's alright. I did it. The power I pulled last night to dispel the darkness was immense, and the shop suffered the backlash, but it's nothing we can't rebuild, but I need your help."

Elaric stood and stretched. "Keeper, leave the repairs to us." He smiled, "But...after breakfast and coffee?" He winked at her, and she nodded with a laugh.

"Of course, Andrew." Onnie looked around at her town and nodded, "Alright, you heard the man, breakfast, and coffee. Then we rebuild."

The crowd cheered and dissipated as everyone cleaned up their gear and prepared for the day.

Elaric quietly cleared his throat, getting her attention. "Mind if I have a word with you three?" he said, looking between her, Dany, and Gabe.

"We can use my office," Gabe said, leading the way to the door into the small closet-esk office.

The four of them sat and stood around Gabe's desk, and Onnie called Mal.

Can you join us? I think you may want to be here for this.

He appeared on the desk in front of her, purring like crazy and nuzzling her face. "I'm fine, Mal," she laughed and scratched his head. "What's up, Elaric?"

Elaric nervously shifted from one foot to the other a few times before taking an empty seat and a deep breath. "I think I have a plan for how you can get one step ahead of the rogue guardian."

"We're listening," Gabe said, crossing his arms and standing behind Onnie in one of the student's chairs since Dany had stolen his behind the desk.

"I—" Elaric hesitated, "I am going in as a roach."

Dany sat forward in her chair and shook her head, "Ah, no. No way."

"Hear me out," Elaric started.

"Why? This is crazy!" Dany got to her feet. "The man's insane.

162

Deranged. We've seen what he does to his pawns, and there's no telling what he'd do to a spy."

"I'll be fine, Dany."

"No. I won't let you, and neither will Onnie." She turned to her with pleading eyes. "Right?"

Onnie rubbed her face, "First off, are you telling us you're going to do this or asking for our help, Elaric? Because if you want to do this *with* us, you should ask, not tell."

Elaric started to defend himself, and Onnie realized she was scolding him.

"Look," she stopped him, "I'm not saying you can't go. It's your life, and you can do what you want with it, but if you want our help and blessing, we need to talk about this more."

"Understood."

"What?" Dany asked, confused. "You're okay with this?"

"No," Onnie said sternly. "But I am not a dictator. Elaric can do what he wants to. All we can do is try to help and not be judgmental when doing it. Right now, I am listening to his plan and thinking of how I can keep him safe. It's better he does this with our help than without, right?"

Dany opened her mouth as if to say something and then shut it before sitting back in Gabe's chair. She crossed her arms and then her legs, her eyes narrowed at Elaric. "Fine, what's your plan?"

"Alright, I admit, I don't have much of a plan. I was thinking I would take the form of someone, posing as one of his pawns, and get as close to him as possible. Take on some of the more critical missions for him, and we could all pull our punches. Maybe I could learn something to help stop him."

Dany rolled her eyes, and Onnie thought about his offer a minute longer before she spoke. "Well, I think you may be on to something, but there's no way he won't see you for who you are with powers like his. Hell, he may have noticed last night, though I doubt it. He's too brazen not to have flaunted it and exposed you."

"You think he'll be able to see through my forms?" Elaric asked, stunned.

"Yes. Absolutely."

"Then you're not doing it," Dany snapped. "It would be suicide."

"Or a benefit for him," Gabe added, earning himself a glare from his sister.

Onnie shook her head, "No, he would see it as a weakness. Something he would be unable to control. You could be anyone, do anything, tell his plans to whoever you want."

"Precisely," Elaric said with pride.

"He can't know that," Onnie said with a shake of her head. "But…."

"I know that, but," Gabe said with a smirk down at her. "What are you thinking?"

"If I bind his powers and lock him in one form, the rogue won't be able to tell what he really is."

Elaric paled, "Bi—bind my powers? Unable to change?"

"I know it sounds frightening. You've been able to change on a whim all your life, but this is the only way I can think of to keep you safe. It's not permanent. Not to mention, you've got the foster princess' blood. He'd never believe a transmogromorph would be on his side."

"I…I will have to think about it," Elaric said, visibly shaken.

"You're the one who asked us to bless this mission of yours," Gabe interjected.

"Gabe, stop," she said, resting her hand on his arm. "That's fine, Elaric. I understand. We can talk again in a few days once everyone has settled down."

Elaric nodded but stared at the floor in front of him as he processed.

"Well, I need coffee," Dany said, standing and stretching like a cat. "Onnie, come with me?"

"Sure." Onnie looked up at Gabe, "Can you stay here and assist everyone home? The storm's passed, and I want to head into the shop as soon as possible."

"Of course," he bent down to kiss her forehead. "I'll meet you over there as soon as I can."

"Mal, would you stay with Miranda for a bit? Maybe until she wakes up?" Onnie gave him a few scratches under his chin, and he made an agreeing sound.

"Okay, then, coffee it is."

Onnie smiled at Elaric as she passed him and placed her hand on his shoulder. He smiled weakly and patted the back of her hand with a nod.

She squeezed him gently and looked at Dany, "Lead on, captain."

Elaric Rickson

"She really wants to bind my powers?" Elaric asked once the women had left the office.

"Yup. What did you expect?" Gabe said with a smile. "She'd be sending you into the lion's den draped in raw meat otherwise. You'd do well to listen to her."

"I do, and I will, but I don't know how to be *me* without my shifting," Elaric put his head in his hands. "Ironic, isn't it?" he chuckled.

"You'll still be you, just temporarily unable to play practical jokes on your friends."

Gabe squeezed Elaric's shoulder where Onnie's hand had just been, and the difference between the two hands was immense, though they both provided the same feeling of warmth and support.

"Come on, man. I'll make you a cup of terrible teacher's lounge coffee, and we can start getting these people back to their homes."

"You drive a hard bargain," Elaric smirked, but his face fell quickly, and he sighed. "Fine, but I'm not promising anything more than thinking about it."

"Dude, you don't have to do anything. But you proposed it, and if you want the Keeper's backing, you will have to deal with her demanding your safety as a non-negotiable."

"Yeah, I guess."

Elaric followed Gabe as he led them across the yard into the main building of Alku's only school. The main structure looked relatively undamaged except for tree debris everywhere, but he didn't immediately see any shattered windows. When they entered the building, Elaric shivered.

"I'd bet the main power went off at some point. It's freezing in here."

"Most likely. The gym is on a separate circuit since the town uses it as the emergency area." Gabe opened a door, and they walked into a tiny kitchen, yellowed and faded. It looked like an ad for an eighties hospital.

"Man, this place could use an upgrade."

Gabe laughed, "Yeah, we upgraded the classrooms and the gym first, the teacher's space we haven't gotten to yet."

"Makes sense. What about the library? Dany was telling me about how important that is to the town."

Gabe looked sidelong at him and smirked. "She did? Huh, you two seem to have gotten close quickly."

Elaric stopped, "Look, I know she's your sister, but I swear—"

Gabe held his hand up to stop him. "Dany is a smart woman. I trust her judgment. If she chooses to spend her time with you, that's her business."

"Thanks, man."

"Besides," Gabe smiled, "You've nothing to worry about with impressing me. You proved yourself last night."

"Thanks, I was only doing my part. I wasn't deceiving Onnie when I said I wanted to move here." Elaric looked over to a corkboard on the wall beside him filled with yellowed notices and inspirational posters. Marco's paler-than-normal face from the other night flashed in his mind, then Abbot's, then Sam's. "It's overdue, actually."

"That's good to hear. Alku would be lucky to have you, and I think you need a place like this. One where you can belong and make a difference."

Gabe passed him a paper cup filled with the darkest coffee Elaric had ever seen before the large man knocked back his own in just a few gulps.

"It's best if you just down it. This isn't coffee you drink for taste. We can pick that up on our way over to the shop later. I'm sure Dany and Onnie will need a second cup by then."

Elaric swirled the pungent brew in the cup a few times before tipping his head back and swallowing it quickly, the bitter taste making him pull a face and wince.

"Damn, that's horrible."

"Yup," Gabe laughed, taking Elaric's cup and tossing it into the bin with his own. "You'll get used to it."

"Blegh," Elaric said with a slight cough, "not sure I want to."

Chapter 13: A Piece Ripped Out

March 2022 - Alku | Onnie Moore

Even though Onnie already knew what awaited her in the shop, when she opened the front door, her breath caught, and Dany had to grab her shoulders and steady her.

"Woah, you good?" Dany questioned, concern in her voice as she searched Onnie's face for information.

Onnie nodded and swallowed, "Yeah. Just a lot."

Dany nodded with a slight frown, "I know."

"Even knowing how bad it was, being here in person feels different. Worse."

"I can't even imagine, but either way, let's get inside, and we can catch our breath. It's still stupidly cold out here, even without the rain."

"Yeah," Onnie said, stepping out of Dany's grasp and standing on her own again. She could feel Gabe checking their Bond, and he must have felt her momentary shock. She took a deep breath, regained control over her emotions, and sensed him recede.

"I'm fine now," she entered the shop and tried not to flinch when her boots crunched on glass beneath her feet.

"Should we see how bad it is before we start? Or do you want to just jump into something?" Dany asked, following behind her and gently closing the door behind them and latching it.

"We should look around first, I think. I didn't go further than this room when I came over. I have no idea how the other rooms—" Onnie's voice faltered as her chest began to pound, "Oh shit."

She'd forgotten about the First Keeper's Library. Panic rose in her throat, and she dashed between debris, splintered wood, and torn pages to get across the room. As she ran, she pulled on the Bonds for the objects in her path to move the more significant things out of her way so she didn't damage them further. It left an easy route for Dany, who was right on her heels.

"Onnie, what's wrong?" Dany said from right behind her. Only before Onnie could answer, Dany had figured it out. "Crap, the First Keeper's room!"

"Exactly!" Onnie gasped as the soles of her shoes slid on the hardwood in Abbot's study. The room hadn't been spared, but thankfully, it did look less shattered than the main room. When she looked for the wooden door in the corner, she found it closed but still there.

"Please, please, please," Onnie begged whoever was listening as she finished her wild sprint across the room and collided with the door. She yanked, using her whole strength and body weight on the icy handle. What little panic she'd repressed flared and rippled along her Bond when it refused to budge. "No, you can't do this. Open up, damn it!"

A second later, Dany appeared at her side, grabbed onto the handle, and helped pull, but after a few attempts, she stepped back and sighed. "Onnie, it's no use."

Cat, what's going on? Mal, are you with her?

Am now, Mal replied before relocating next to Dany.

"Onnie, you need to stop. It's not going to open."

Dany was calm and rational, and Onnie knew she was right, but her emotions were taking over, and she barely even heard the woman beside her.

What the hell is going on? Gabe asked, his voice frantic with worry and unease.

The First Keeper's room won't open, Dany replied.

"It can't. It has to open. I'm not," Onnie tugged on the handle, punctuating each word, "ready, to, let it go too!"

After months of trying to assimilate to life in Alku, Onnie finally had a space where she could be Onnie, not the Keeper. No Bond. No need to control her emotions. No one in her head except herself. It was just her and the books. She couldn't, *wouldn't,* lose that.

Onnie, you need to stop. You're going to tire yourself out. The shop will open it again when it— Onnie cut off Mal's mental attempt to calm her.

No! I refuse! Onnie shouted down their Bond and then sunk to her knees, her hands still clinging to the iron handle above her.

"Onnie, it'll be okay," Dany said, squatting beside her and gently rubbing her back.

At some point, Onnie started crying, and when she looked up at her best friend, she saw a blurry face but still heard Dany's breath hitch.

"Oh, Onnie," Dany said before wrapping her arms around her and pulling her over to cry on her shoulder.

What's going on? Onnie heard Gabe ask the group.

I think we'll be fine, Gabe, Mal assured.

Then everyone went silent, and Onnie would bet they were all having a side conversation without her.

I'm sure it'll reopen, Onnie, Mal said, trying to comfort her, but she didn't need his guessing.

She closed her eyes, and even though she knew it wouldn't work, she went to the void and tried to project herself into the room beyond the door. As expected, she was unable to, and nothing happened. Undeterred, she tried again and again, repeatedly, but not once did it work. She thought she'd slipped between a crack and made it inside at some point but quickly saw she'd failed again.

At the furthest edge of her mind, her attention was drawn to a pressure that had been steadily increasing, but she'd been too frantic to notice it until then. Onnie switched her focus to it, and a bit overzealously, she shoved herself at it mentally, and then she felt it release, popping like a bubble.

Peace, Onnie. You'll see it again.

Who are you? Rebecca?

Rest, young one, the voice whispered, and then Onnie was back in her body, sprawled on the floor in front of the First Keeper's door, her head in Dany's lap. Onnie looked up at her and saw Dany's tears running down her cheeks.

When a small motion out of the corner of her eye drew her attention, Onnie looked over at the archway into the study, and she saw Gabe and Elaric rushing into the room. Gabe's expression told Onnie everything she needed to know.

Then, her world went black.

Elaric Rickson

Gabe cursed beside him, and Elaric looked over and saw one very, *very* pale man.

"What's up?"

Gabe clutched his chest and quickly made eye contact before he dashed off at a full sprint to the gym door.

"Woah, dude," Elaric said, running behind his new ally.

Judging by the reaction to whatever had happened, the Keeper must be the cause, and Elaric hoped Dany was alright, too. He followed behind Gabe, the two of them sprinting down the slick cobble streets and vaulting over shrubs and low fences to shorten their route to, probably, the shop as much as possible.

Gabe cursed under his breath a few times, but after checking and seeing that Elaric was behind him once, he never looked back. The pair ran through the rain-soaked, debree-covered streets of Alku and drew more than a few concerned stares and shouts as they passed. Neither stopped focusing on getting to the Keeper as fast as their legs would allow. Thankfully, the school wasn't unreasonably far from Abbot's shop, and few people were back on the streets yet.

They skid around the final street corner, and Gabe yanked on the front door only to find it locked. After a second, he tried again, and it opened without issue, and they both quickly slipped inside.

Elaric had seen some shit in his life, but nothing could have prepared him for the carnage that was the bookshop.

"You're fucking kidding me. She did *this?*" He asked no one in particular, especially since he already knew the answer. The amount of broken glass was overwhelming, and looking at the bookcase corpses, he knew there was no saving most of them. Onnie hadn't been exaggerating. They did have a lot of work cut out for them.

Elaric refocused and saw that Gabe hadn't stopped running. Instead, he bolted down a path with less shrapnel and continued deeper into the building.

"Cat!" Gabe's shouts didn't carry very far, the sounds being swallowed by the fractured pieces of the shop. "Cat!"

When they approached a brick archway in one of the back corners, Gabe ran faster and rushed inside. Elaric could hear sobbing, and when he made it into the room, his mind went blank. Dany was on the floor in one corner of the room, her body heaving with sobs, tears streaming down her face with Onnie's head in her lap. But that wasn't the part that froze Elaric in place. The Keeper's eyes were glassy, staring straight above her at nothing, and they were ice blue. She turned only her eyes and looked over at him and Gabe. She seemed to register their arrival for a split second, but then her eyes closed, and she went limp.

Elaric stayed out of the way as Gabe slid to his knees beside his sister and leaned over his partner.

Mal disappeared from beside Onnie so Gabe didn't collide with him, and he reappeared by Elaric's feet. When he looked down, Mal disappeared again, reappeared on Elaric's shoulder, and whispered in his ear.

"Hey."

Dany sniffled loudly, and he and Mal refocused on her.

"Gabe, she suddenly remembered the First Keeper's room and panicked that something had happened to it when she pulled all that power last night. When we got here, she and I tried pulling the door open, but it wouldn't budge. I thought she had finally accepted it, but then she collapsed and became catatonic. I think she was trying to force her way inside mentally. Then you came in."

Elaric was impressed at how quickly Gabe had regained his calm as he began to check Onnie's breathing, pulse, and then placed the back of his hand on her forehead.

"She's got a fever." He looked at his sister, "When did they change to blue?"

"When she touched the door, I think." Dany sniffled again but seemed to be regaining her composure as well.

Elaric glanced around and saw the fireplace on the other side of the room, and the that couch was nearly upside-down in front of it.

"Give me a sec, Mal," he whispered before walking over to the couch, and by the time he'd bent over to correct it, Mal had moved to perch on the mantle over the hearth.

Elaric called over to Gabe, "Bring her over here. I'll get a fire going. Dany, can you shake out these blankets?" He pointed to the tipped-over basket in the middle of the room but he didn't wait for anyone to respond or even start moving. He just went over to the fireplace and set about lighting it. Mal was right above him, and Elaric saw his slight nod before the feline whispered, "Thanks."

"Course," Elaric paused. "Can you do me a favor?"

"Anything."

"Can you go check on Marco for me? I planned on going before —" Elaric stopped when Mal held up a paw.

"Be right back," then he was gone.

Elaric smiled, refocused on the stack of wood and kindling, but kept his ear out for what was happening behind him. Gabe had shifted Onnie over to the couch, and Dany was snapping blankets as she shook the dust and debris from them. When he'd gotten the fire roaring, Elaric turned around and saw Gabe was tucking the blankets around Onnie and brushing her sweaty hair from her forehead. Dany walked past the pair and over to him, wrapping her arms around his waist, her nose buried in the sweatshirt beneath his jacket.

"Thank you," she whispered, and he hugged her tighter.

"No thanks necessary. What else can I do?" He asked quietly enough so as not to disturb the other two.

Dany shrugged and shook her head. After a few minutes, she sniffled and stepped back. "I think she probably just over-exerted herself last night more than we realized, and her body is telling us that. She'll be fine."

She looked over to her best friend, Dany's expression filled with worry and then she crossed her arms in front of herself in a comforting and protective self-hug.

"I'm sure she will be. For now, why don't we leave these two here for a few minutes and get some food and supplies? None of us are in top shape, and we can't afford anyone else getting sick."

When Dany turned to look at him, he suddenly struggled to breathe, and in that instant, he knew something had changed. He remembered Abbot's letter and how he'd described Dany and Onnie's friendship. Elaric's understanding of the Keeper's Prophecy finally clicked, but before he could think anymore about it, Dany smiled and nodded.

"Yeah, you're right." She returned to Gabe's side and gently placed her hand on his back. "Gabe, we're going to go get supplies and stuff for Onnie. Okay?"

Gabe looked up at his sister, and Elaric warmed at the affection in their exchange. "Yeah, watch her for a second," he got to his feet.

"Course," Dany said, taking his place beside the sleeping woman.

Gabe walked toward Elaric and stopped in front of him. The Guardian looked like shit. His skin was pale, his hands were still shaking, and his Keeper blue eyes glistened with unshed tears for the woman he loved.

"We'll get some food, fresh clothes, and medicine for Onnie. That okay?"

Gabe didn't say anything for a few seconds, and just as Elaric thought maybe he'd made a mistake, Gabe held out his hand to him.

"Thank you...for last night and this morning. That's twice you've stepped up to help complete strangers. I don't care what it is, as long as it doesn't interfere with me protecting those two women over there, you have my support, trust, and anything else I can provide. You need only ask."

Elaric smiled as he took the man's hand and was pulled into a hug. "You don't need to thank me. She's Abbot's flesh and blood, and I'd do anything for him and, by extension, her."

When they broke apart, Gabe smiled again. "One day, you'll have to tell me more about the old man and why Dany and I have never met you."

Elaric chuckled, "That you know of."

Gabe laughed, and Elaric saw Dany jump from the sudden sound. "Fair enough. Can't argue with that."

The two of them walked over to the couch, and Gabe looked around the small, chaotic mess of a room. "Where'd Mal go?"

"Ah," Elaric said hesitantly, "He's doing me a favor. I asked him to check on Marco since I hadn't gotten over there."

"Got it," Gabe said and dropped the subject. Elaric wasn't sure if it was due to discomfort or an intention not to pry, but it didn't matter for now.

"Ready to go?" Elaric asked Dany and held out his hand to help her up.

"Sure," she said with one last glance at her friend before accepting his help and getting to her feet.

"Oh, quick question," Elaric asked, causing them both to look at him. "Ah...what door?

Chapter 14: Meeting in the Middle

March 2022 - Alku | Elaric Rickson

For a moment, Elaric wondered if he'd slipped into speaking a different language because neither Dany nor Gabe said anything. He didn't know if it was the lingering shock or something else, but they stared at him in disbelief as if he'd just confessed to being an alien.

"Ah...should I not have asked that?"

Dany broke from her stupor first. "Ah, no, it's fine. Answer me something," she said as she crossed the room to where she and Onnie had been when they'd arrived. She never broke eye contact with him, and when she stopped in the corner of the room between a large trunk and an empty section of wall, she finally spoke again. "What's behind me?"

There was nothing sarcastic in her tone, and Elaric hesitated but answered honestly. "A...wall?"

"Just a wall?" Gabe asked from beside him.

"Yeah? Is that...bad?" Elaric paused, "Wait, are you telling me there's a door there?"

Both siblings nodded in unison.

"And I assume it's not one of those hidden trick doors judging by your expressions."

They both shook their heads in unison again.

Elaric sighed and nodded once. "Sure. Okay.... Let's get going, Dany."

He'd deal with the mysterious invisible door another day. With that, he turned and wandered back towards the front of the shop.

As he meandered through the wreckage, he began to truly understand the scale of the damage, and he was more impressed that such a tiny human could cause so much of it. He wasn't sure you could have made more of a mess if you'd intentionally tried to.

As he walked, he occasionally stopped and picked something off the ground. An old book that looked unharmed, a framed photo with missing glass, the knob off of a drawer, and even a metal tea kettle. He carried all of them to the front counter and placed them down gently. There was no sense in breaking them if they'd already managed to survive. Mostly.

His phone began to vibrate in his pocket, and he glanced at the time. It was ten in the morning and far past the time Marco should be sleeping, but his name and face still flashed across his screen.

"Hey," he said in a hushed voice.

"How is she?" Marco asked, his voice relaxed and personal, meaning he was home, alone, and had removed his persona for the night.

"Honestly, not sure. She's got a fever and passed out, but beforehand, she was in some sort of trance or something."

"Hmm...."

"Yeah, from the sounds of it, she was terrified that something she cared about might have been broken when she used all that power last night, and judging by her reaction, it wasn't spared the devastation."

"What about the others?" Elaric could hear a faucet running in the background and was surprised that Marco hadn't called him from bed, considering the hour.

"Wrung out, but fine, I think. I assume Mal stopped by for me?"

Marco chuckled softly. "Yes, he did. You didn't need to worry about me."

"Nice try. You know that doesn't work."

"I know. You'll worry whether it's needed or not." Marco paused and cleared his throat, "Thank you."

"Always. Now, what are you still doing awake? It's way too late for you."

"I was just warming something to drink, and now I'm back in bed. Besides, the number of emotions and adrenaline people were running on last night was intense, and I had trouble blocking it all out."

"Are you alright? Do you need anything?"

Marco laughed again sleepily. "No, I'm fine. I've settled now, and I think I can sleep." When he yawned, Elaric grinned.

"Alright, that's my cue. Go to sleep. I'll be back later tonight. Probably early, didn't get much sleep last night either, as expected."

"Sounds good…." Marco's voice slurred, and Elaric shook his head and rubbed his eyes with his free hand.

"Sleep well, Marco."

When he didn't respond, Elaric hung up and put his phone back in his pocket.

"You really care about him," Dany said from behind him where she was leaning on the wall. She smiled and chuckled when she realized she'd made him jump.

"You scared the crap out of me."

"Sorry, I didn't mean to eavesdrop." She walked over, and he could see her cheeks were pink, and she wouldn't meet his eyes.

"Does it bother you?"

That got her attention, and her eyes snapped up to meet his. "What? Your relationship with Marco?"

Elaric shrugged, "That and the whole bisexual thing."

She shook her head emphatically. "Not at all. Xayn, one of Gabe's best friends, is gay, for the record, and I consider him a brother. I accept him, so no, I have zero issues with you being bi. As for Marco, also no issue there. I adore him, and frankly…" she trailed off.

"What is it?" Elaric asked, his curiosity peaked since Dany usually seemed to say whatever was on her mind.

She sighed and looked back at him. "I think he's been struggling. For a while."

The woman could have punched him in the stomach, and it would have hurt less. Elaric sighed and closed his eyes. "Yeah. I know."

"He just always has this…" she struggled to find the word, "mask on."

Elaric couldn't help his reaction, and he laughed, which probably made him look extremely creepy.

"I'm sorry, I wasn't laughing at you. You're right. He does." Elaric gestured for Dany to lead them to the shop door. "Let's walk and talk. Obviously, you know Marco is a sanguiste, I assume."

Dany nodded in front of him as she carefully picked her way through the splintered bookcase shards.

"Do you know what his preferred diet is?"

Elaric wasn't going to reveal anything that was Marco's private business, but if Dany already knew, he might be able to fill in some gaps.

"Emotions."

"Correct."

Dany led them outside and closed the door behind them with a soft click. They tucked their hands into their pockets and bundled up tighter to the cold. He started walking toward the city's center and the Day Night Cafe to begin by ordering some food for the group. Dany fell in step beside him, and he smiled.

"Marco is extremely old." Elaric grinned, and Dany snorted. "Sam, Marco, and I have been friends for a long, long time."

"Wait, really? I mean, I knew Sam and him. Obviously. They are practically family despite their…backgrounds."

"Yup. I'm also significantly older than I look. Good genes," he winked at her, and when she doubled over laughing, his chest warmed at the sound.

When she stopped laughing, she tilted her head and looked at him. "So, did you live in Alku? I mean, I guess you must have."

"Kind of. Never officially. I've been coming to Alku and staying for a few years or months since I was a kid. The only time I guess you could say I lived here was when I was with Marco." Dany hesitated for a second, and he could tell she wanted to ask him something. "You can ask anything. I promise I'll try to answer if I can."

"When was that? How long ago?"

Elaric grinned, "Ah. That. Well…" he looked at the sky and mentally calculated the years. "I think it was the eighties."

"Wait, so did you know our dad?"

It was his turn to laugh. "Not those eighties."

Dany stopped dead in her tracks and turned to look at him. "The eighteen eighties!?" she said with a screech.

Elaric could only nod. "I told you it was over a long time ago."

"For fucks sake," Dany said before resuming their walk, "that's an understatement." She was quiet for a few minutes, and he saw her thinking through something in great detail.

"Penny for your thoughts?" he teased.

"Oh," she jumped a little. "Sorry, I was trying to figure out how to phrase this in the least offensive or narcissistic way possible."

Elaric stopped walking and put his hand on her forearm to pull her to a stop. "Dany, I told you, you can ask or say whatever. I'm pretty hard to offend, besides," he looked around and realized they'd wandered into City Center Park and were effectively alone. "I know it's only been a short time, but I really do care for you, and I'd like to see where this can go between us."

To his surprise, the stoic woman before him turned a radiant shade of pink, and he had to hold himself back from doing or saying anything that might embarrass her further.

"Ah…" she squirmed a little, "me too." She took a deep breath and looked him straight in the eye. "Okay. I wanted to say that I'm glad you and Marco have each other, and I trust you that it's over, so… don't change anything on my account. Behaviors or whatever."

To his surprise, she blushed even deeper, and it snapped his final bit of restraint, and he swept her into his arms and kissed her deeply.

When he'd regained his sense of place and released her, it was his turn to be crimson.

"Ah…sorry about that…."

She laughed, the sweet sound crisp like wind chimes on the breeze. "Don't be."

He cleared his throat. "Thank you. Marco means a lot to me. I will always love him and be there for him, but he's more family than ex at this point in our lives."

Dany smiled and quickly kissed his lips before taking his hand and restarting their walk. "Good," she smirked sideways at him.

"You're truly amazing, Dany."

"Nope," she said, "I was just raised well. Abbot and Gabe saw to that. To each their own as long as they don't hurt others."

"If only there were more Danys in the world."

She shivered, "Nope, one's good. Can you imagine two of me?" Dany looked over at him, and when she saw his face, she paused and then giggled like a kid. "Oh, shit, wrong person to say that to, I guess."

He joined her in laughter. "Honestly, I'm not sure the world would survive two Danys. We should most definitely stick to just the one."

They continued talking and laughing for the next hour while they ran their errands and then returned to the shop.

Onnie Moore

Onnie didn't have the energy or will to move. Granted, she was in her mind and didn't have a physical form *to* move, but still. She felt empty. For a few short days, she had had a haven. A safe space she could hide in where no one could find her or needed to worry. But now it was gone.

I should have been more careful last night. I shouldn't have used so much power.

If she had held back a bit more, then maybe the shop wouldn't have closed off the First Keeper's room. She was probably being punished for acting so recklessly.

You are aware that you've been reckless then.

Onnie reflexively tried to put up her mental guards, but when she could not, she realized she was too tired to be concerned.

Who are you?

The voice was silent momentarily, and Onnie thought maybe they had left, or she'd dreamed it.

I'm most definitely real. I'm sorry it took me so long to reach you, Onnie. Thank you for taking such good care of me so far.

Wait…you're the shop.

That I am. I am the First Keeper. I am so glad you enjoy my library.

Onnie was stunned. *Are…you real…? Please say you're real, and I'm not passed out in a ditch somewhere with a head wound.*

The First Keeper laughed, and it was such an incredible sound. Onnie wanted to bottle the feeling it gave her.

I am real. So are you, though right now you're a bit over-extended.

Eek…. Somehow, Onnie knew she was about to be lectured or scolded.

Both.

Crap. Well, I suppose I deserve it.

You most certainly do. However, I think Gabriel and Dany will have both of those covered. I'd prefer to just converse with you while I have the chance.

Oh…I'd like that. Um, should I call you First Keeper? Quite a mouthful, but I also don't want to be rude or disrespectful.

You may call me, Kushima.

That's beautiful and, somehow, perfect.

Thank you. It's been with me for countless years at this point, though it's been an age since I've heard it. Now, back to the scolding. While I won't do that, I want to discuss what happened.

Onnie suddenly felt like a petulant child. *You saw me, didn't you? Trying to open the door.*

I did.

Why did you lock me out? Are you angry with me? For last night?

I am angry with you, but not for last night. I would not have provided you with the power you desired had I not trusted you with it.

But...look at what happened to the shop. That's all my fault. I was careless. Impatient. Arrogant.

Yes, what happened to the shop was a result of your actions. However, given time and training, you will be able to channel our power efficiently and effectively without backlash. Similar to the Transference when it was triggered, things that were negligible for other Keepers will be magnified for you, and the impossible will be possible.

I'll be able to control it? Everything we've found says this is just what happens when a Keeper uses that much power.

That's because they were not you.

Onnie didn't know what to say to that. She wasn't sure if that made her scared or confident. She was nothing special, but the shop, Kushima, was unmistakably more knowledgeable, so...maybe she was right.

Wait, so then why are you angry with me?

I'm angry because you're acting recklessly and alone.

Onnie couldn't argue with that.

I'd like to discuss your reliance on the Keeper's tea, not to mention the souls you are currently hiding within your Bond. However—

The darkness around Onnie felt like it expanded and then constricted. Kushima's voice droned on, but Onnie couldn't focus on it. She was pretty sure she would have fainted if she had been in her body. Unaware of whether Kushima was still talking or not, Onnie blurted out, *How do you know about the souls?*

When it comes to the space within the shop's walls or you and your Bond, there is nothing I cannot hear unless you prevent it. We are a part of each other.

Is that why you shut me out?

Oh my, Onnie. I did not shut you out. May we start from the beginning?

Yes. Please.

Would you do something for me first?

What?

Please focus on your body. Feel your Bond flowing through you. Picture yourself. Your fingers. Your palms, up to your arms, and down to your toes. Can you see yourself?

Onnie did as she was told, and after a few minutes of focusing, she mentally opened her eyes, and when she looked down, her body was within the void. *I assume this is another form of astral projection?*

Correct. Similar to the Transference. Usually, when you are in the void, you're...conscious and aware of what's around your body. Think of it like looking through a window versus entering the dwelling. Currently, you're more in the void than normal.

I see.

Onnie turned over her hands and inspected the back of them. Other than the missing tactile sense, it was her body all right.

Why did you want me to do this? Not that I mind.

I find it easier to speak with you when I can see your body language. Then, I can focus on what you're saying and showing while remaining outside your unspoken thoughts. I may not be able to grant you complete privacy, but I shall endeavor to do my best.

Onnie chuckled and began pacing the void as she spoke. *I appreciate that.*

As promised, I shall start from the beginning. You are not shut out from my library permanently. However, as you've so brilliantly figured out, that space exists within the void, and as such, its rules are not the same as those in the physical world. I wasn't trying to harm you. I was trying to preserve it for you. We are both unstable after last night, and I wanted to ensure I didn't need to remove it permanently.

Oh, Onnie stopped pacing and looked at what was functionally the floor. *I'm sorry. I overreacted.*

Nonsense. How were you to know? In fact, had you not reacted and tried so hard to reach it, we wouldn't be speaking now.

The pressure feeling....

Precisely. Returning to the Keeper's tea, due to the vast quantities of tea you've been consuming, your determination to reach me, and my own understanding of what rules we could…bend, we met in the middle.

Then I guess I'm thankful, but…am I really drinking too much tea? I mean, it's just tea, right….

Young one, you know better than that.

Ug, Onnie groaned and flopped onto the floor to sit cross-legged. *I guess, but how will I be able to beat the rogue guardian without more… oompf?*

Kushima laughed again, and Onnie couldn't help but smile in response.

Actually, I do agree with your need for it. However, I'd like to come to an agreement with you.

Oh?

Promise me you will tell me everything that happens pertaining to our power when you're outside the shop. Communicate with me. Don't think you are alone.

I thought you could read my mind anyway.

Would you prefer that I do? If you're honest with me, I will do my best to provide you with as much privacy as possible.

Really?

Of course. Onnie, we are going to be together for a long time. I need you to trust me, and I, you.

Alright. I promise. Onnie paused. *Do I genuinely think I'm alone?*

Young one, you know that answer as well.

I don't. I have Dany, Gabe, and Mal. I just…also….

There are things you would rather keep private. That's understandable, and while it'll be more challenging to keep things from me, we will try our best. Everyone should be allowed to have things known only to their heart, and even Keepers should have some secrets.

Thank you.

None needed. Shall we now discuss those souls you're carrying?

Ug, yeah…. How badly have I screwed up?

I told you I would not scold you—quite the contrary. I think you've made a wise, well-thought-out decision considering the circumstances.

Wait, really?

Is that so surprising?

Actually, yeah. Gabe and Dany would be fuming with me right now and probably put me under constant mental and physical surveillance, not to mention stopping me from saving any more people.

I do believe they would indeed react in that way.

Onnie couldn't hold back her giggle as, evidently, Kushima hadn't just been watching her the past few months. *So, if you're not angry, what would you like to know?*

Well, firstly, I'd like to compliment you. Being a Keeper of mere months and rationalizing how to utilize the Bond the way you have and manipulate it to do your will is no small feat. Power we have, but that wasn't power. That was your cunning.

Onnie was one hundred percent blushing, either in the void, in her physical body, or both.

I would like to offer a suggestion, not because your solution wasn't adequate, but because—

Kushima, you don't need to justify your advice. As you said, we need to trust one another, and if we are going to be able to, I'd like it if you could never hesitate to tell me what is on your mind, even if I might not like it. Though not applicable in this instance. I'm not so arrogant as to not utilize your knowledge and experience.

That makes me very happy to hear, young one. Now that you can access my library, you have access to a void space that isn't transient. I'd suggest that you shift the souls from without your own Bond, and instead, we store them within my library.

I think I understand. Onnie stood to resume her pacing as she thought, *because it's shielded or whatever it is, no one can use their Bond to see within that space. Wait, but couldn't Mal see the Bond, and I was able to speak with Gabe once he was inside the room.*

Correct, but that's because Mal is a part of me. Only the three of us are...suited to manipulating the Bond within my library. When inside, the others are blind, deaf, and mute unless you or I are to assist them.

I see... If that's the case, wouldn't I have to explain to Mal? He'd for sure tell Gabe.

I agree, but I can assist with that. He may be a part of me, but we are not the same, and I still have some Keeper secrets of my own.

Oh, that would piss him off if he knew.

Onnie returned to the floor and laid on her back with her head pillowed on her arms.

It would indeed. Spitfire of a feline, he is.

Onnie closed her eyes, one void replacing another. She suddenly felt exhausted, and her eyelids were heavy. She should say goodbye to Kushima.

You'll never need to say goodbye, young one. I'll always be with you. Sleep now, and remember, you're not alone.

Onnie smiled as she felt herself gently nudged out of the void, and her mind returned to her body, the last words she heard being nearly a whisper.

Thank you for fighting to reach me, daughter mine. The millennia have been seemingly endless and lonely.

Chapter 15: Healing Wounds

March 2022 - Alku | Elaric Rickson

Elaric stretched his arms above his head and bent backward, his 'Andrew' form's spine cracking with a satisfying pop. He looked around the front room of Abbot's and watched as dozens of people milled about, picking up splintered wood, carefully boxing books and loose pages, and sweeping glass shards into bins.

It felt like the entire town of Alku had turned out to help clean up the bookshop. Elaric had met a ton of new people as Dany brought them over to make introductions, her charm and warmth putting everyone at ease as they worked. The day prior a group had come to check on the shop's windows and Dany introduced him to what was apparently, Alku's local construction crew led by a human named Michael. They had finally finished replacing the windows around town that had been damaged and the bookshop was their last stop but luckily hadn't had that issue. Which was a blessing, a small one, but considering everything else that could have been a problem, was, he'd take what he could get.

"Andrew," Dany said from across the room, and when he looked up, she waved him over.

He carefully stepped over neat piles of debris and slipped between a few people carrying heavy boxes of books from place to place.

"What's up?" he said as he approached where Dany was leaning on the front counter. A muscular, tanned-skinned, dark-haired man stood beside her, and his lime-green eyes sparkled.

"I wanted you to meet Xayn," Dany said, indicating to the man. "Gabe, Sam, and Xayn grew up together. I mentioned him the other day."

Xayn cocked his head and smirked at Dany. "Well, two of us grew up at least." He held out his hand, and Elaric took it gladly.

"Ah, Marco's mentioned you a few times, too."

"Friends with Marco?" Xayn asked with a raised brow.

"Actually," Elaric liked the guy already. "I also grew up with Marco and Sam, just not the same time you did."

Dany snorted, and Xayn laughed with her. "Small world, then."

"Incredibly," Elaric added. "What brings you in? Here to help out?"

"In a way. I'd like to replace some of the smaller wooden objects that were destroyed." Xayn frowned, "I think I might be able to help. A little."

Dany smiled and grabbed Xayn's arm. "Stop it. You'll be a help, and I'm sure Onnie will appreciate it."

"I agree," Elaric added.

He knew by Xayn's lime-colored eyes he was a hedge witch, and if he were planning on making anything for the shop, it would probably be warded.

"To be honest, I've found a few things that might be in your wheelhouse to replace."

Dany mouthed, "Thank you," from behind Xayn's back before, shooing the man to follow Elaric. "You heard him. Off you get."

Xayn laughed and followed behind Elaric, his eyes taking in the damage as they walked.

"Incredible, isn't it?" Elaric asked over his shoulder as he led Xayn to the front of the shop.

"Yeah…."

"What about this?" Elaric stopped and picked up two of the many pieces that the coat rack was in.

Xayn's eyes lit up, and he grinned, "That's perfect!" He took a few fragments and stuck them into the backpack he carried. Then he reached over and picked up a small incense holder. It looked unscathed, but he turned it over in his hands as if he were looking for something.

"Should I worry?" Elaric asked tentatively.

Xayn looked up and raised one eyebrow, "Hm?" Elaric looked at the incense holder, and Xayn's face brightened when he understood. "Oh! No, it's fine. I just have an idea."

"If you've got an idea, take it. I'm sure Onnie won't mind. Chances are it'll be a bit before she returns to the shop anyway." Elaric said, glancing around the room for other tempting possibilities for a hedge witch.

"Yeah, I think I will. Won't take me too long to modify it either."

"Oh," Elaric swiveled to look deeper into the store, "By small chance, can you do anything with candles?"

"Yeah, why?"

Elaric gestured to Xayn, "Sorry, back we go. There are some in the study area, and they weren't damaged," he led the way back through the shop and smiled at Dany as they passed, her expression amused, "but you may find something to add."

"Sure, I can take a look."

When Elaric stepped through the archway and into the study room, he noticed Xayn's eyes widen, and then his brows creased together. "Never seen this room?" Elaric asked.

Xayn shook his head. "No, I mean, yes. I have. It was months ago, and I didn't know it had opened back up."

"Ah, got it." Elaric pointed to a few wall sconces with candles set within them. "What do you think?"

Xayn blew out one of the flames and carefully pulled the candle from the holder. When he dripped a few bits of wax, Xayn stuck his free hand underneath the drops and caught them.

"Crap."

"You okay?" Elaric glanced around the room, looking for something cold enough to stop the burn and harden the wax.

When Xayn laughed, Elaric looked back at him. "Sorry, I'm fine. Common trade injury. I didn't even feel it." Xayn held his palm up, and Elaric noticed the skin was covered in calluses. "Thick skin."

Elaric sniggered but relaxed, "If you say so."

"I was more concerned for the floor." Xayn carefully looked at the candle and then more at the sconce. "Yeah, I think I can make these a bit...more." He chuckled and then returned the candle to its rightful place.

"Mind if I ask? Curiosity, not suspicion or anything." Elaric leaned back on the desk and watched Xayn's demeanor shift completely as his confidence in his craft changed everything from his expression to his posture.

"Sure. Abbot used to spend a lot of time here reading, and I remember Gabe talking about how it used to give him headaches. I'm thinking of something to reduce anxiety and soothe. Not enough to put Onnie to sleep as she researches, but enough to increase focus on whatever she wants instead of eye strain and muscle fatigue."

"You can do that?" Elaric was genuinely impressed. Most green witches he'd known stuck with plants and focused on tonics, poultices, and healing applications. It already surprised him when Xayn actually agreed to modify the candles to begin with.

Xayn nodded emphatically, "I can."

"Huh. Cool."

"My grandmother is your traditional green witch. She specializes in plants and their healing uses. I learned to branch out." Elaric snorted, and Xayn chuckled, "No pun intended."

"Just wanted to try something different?"

Elaric hoped he wasn't prying, but after Dany's comment about Xayn, Elaric had asked Marco about him. Marco, being Marco, didn't say much. Xayn's business was his own, but Elaric got the feeling that Xayn may have struggled a bit in Alku. Being gay in a big city was difficult enough. Alku was anything from big, even if it was highly tolerant.

Xayn shrugged, "My grandmother is a master at what she does, and I am constantly learning from her, but...."

When Xayn trailed off, Elaric felt like crap, "I didn't mean to pry."

"You didn't. You said you grew up with Sam?"

"I did, in a way. I've never lived in Alku, but we've been friends for years. Why?"

"Ever slept at his home?"

"Sure, long time ago, though. Why?"

Xayn inhaled deeply, "I started because of him. When Abbot told Gabe and me what a day walker was and what they endured...."

"Ah, yeah. I get it."

Light from the candle Xayn had recently been holding flickered behind him, and Elaric frowned at the man's tortured profile.

"Hey, Xayn?"

The lime-green stare returned to meet Elaric's. "Yeah?"

"Look, I know you've known Dany your whole life, and from what she's told me, you're basically her second brother." Xayn smiled, and Elaric realized it was the most genuine one he'd seen on the man's face so far. "I just wanted you to know that she and I are dating."

Xayn cocked his head to the side in confusion, and Elaric continued.

"But, many, many years ago, I dated Marco." Elaric hoped Xayn would feel like he had a friendly ear if he needed one, even if Elaric didn't come right out and say it. "In case you heard any rumors or anything," Elaric added before smiling. "I don't need her brothers on my back. Either of them. Gabe already knows, too."

While Xayn was still processing Elaric's comments, with her impeccable timing, Dany popped her head around the study's archway.

"Hey, you two. All good?" she grinned, but it faltered when she saw Xayn's blank expression.

"Yeah, I think so," Elaric said and walked over to kiss her cheek. "I need to head back up. Xayn?"

The man quickly looked over. "Yeah?"

"Nice to meet you, man. Get my number from Dany. It's always nice to have more people to share a coffee with in Alku. Maybe you could catch me up on what's changed since the last time I was in town."

"Ah, su-sure. Thanks."

Elaric nodded and squeezed Dany's forearm gently as he returned to the shop's front room. Dany would know best what to say to Xayn to ease the man's discomfort. It hadn't been Elaric's intention, but he'd learned over the many years that conversations dealing with vulnerabilities were rarely comfortable, but that only meant they were even more important to tackle.

The shop still had quite a few people buzzing around and thankfully, most of the damage had been contained in the main room. With everyone's help, they'd made significant progress in a short time. He was confident that once Onnie woke up, they would have completed most of the work.

No one had started picking up the sitting area where Onnie served tea, and Elaric made his way over to see what attention the space needed.

Most of the area was undisturbed, or at least it looked like it had endured an earthquake, not a typhoon. Elaric hefted the weighty antique chairs back to their feet and set their side tables in their rightful places. There were a few dozen books on the floor after having fallen off of nearby shelves, but nothing looked damaged, and he was able to get them put back pretty quickly.

"Hey," Dany said from over his shoulder.

He smiled, put the last few books where they belonged, and got to his feet.

"Hey," he gestured to the recently corrected chairs, and they each sunk into one of them. "Oh wow," Elaric closed his eyes and tipped his head back.

Dany chuffed, "You alright?"

"Yeah, just sore and tired. More than I expected." Elaric took a deep breath and looked at Dany. "He alright? I hope I didn't offend him or anything."

Dany shook her head, "No, just shocked him, I think. He'll be fine."

"Okay, good. You've got impeccable timing, by the way," Elaric grinned.

"I was passing by and heard the last bit." She snorted, "I know Xayn well enough. I could tell by his response what he was thinking."

Elaric smirked, "Well, I appreciate the assist. Marco told me Xayn had gone through the typical...inner turmoil with his identity."

"Yeah, he did," Dany frowned. "Thankfully, he was here. I'd imagine we're way more accepting than other places."

Elaric scoffed, "That's one hell of an understatement."

"Thank you," Dany said in an uncharacteristically small voice.

Elaric held out his hand, and to his relief, she took it, and he pulled her into his lap. When she snuggled into his arms, he closed his eyes and enjoyed the feeling of warmth she gave him.

Gabriel Vansand

Gabe heard a soft knock on the front door, and he got up from the couch and opened it to see Xayn on the porch, looking a bit shell-shocked.

"Xayn? What's up?"

His best friend blinked and looked around, apparently having walked without thinking, and was now slightly disorientated.

"Never mind, it doesn't matter. Come in." Gabe stepped to the side, and thankfully, Xayn entered the house. "You eaten?"

"Ah, no...."

"Great," Gabe led the way into the kitchen. "I haven't since yesterday."

Xayn groaned behind him, and Gabe couldn't entirely suppress his smile at Xayn's caring nature.

"How is she?" Xayn asked before taking his bag off and settling into a bar stool.

"The same." Gabe sighed, "Not sure if that's a good thing or not at this point."

"She'll be fine, Gabe. Just let her rest."

"I know," he pulled open the fridge and dug around for ingredients to make sandwiches.

"You need rest, too, though. When was the last time you slept?"

Gabe paused and thought of lying for a split second so he didn't worry Xayn or get himself a lecture. Ultimately, he sighed and was honest.

"Night before the storm."

Xayn groaned, retrieved his bag, and dug through it. "Dude. You're just as important as she is. Here," he held out a small green jar filled with liquid. "Don't argue. Drink it."

Gabe snorted. He knew better than to argue with Xayn when he was in herbalist mode. He held out his hand, quickly uncorked the bottle, and downed its contents in one go.

"Never understood how you could get it to taste like vanilla without putting any into it." Gabe rinsed the bottle in the sink, dried it off, and returned it to Xayn for cleansing and reuse.

"Neither do I. Ask Grandma. Even when I read her recipe, I have no idea how she manages that taste with those combinations." Xayn grinned from ear to ear, and Gabe mirrored his smile.

"Grandma Yvonne is one hell of a green witch, that's for sure."

Gabe carried their sandwich fixings and two plates to the bar in front of Xayn. Without hesitation, he reached for the plates and began building their food while Gabe pulled out drinks.

"So...I met Dany's boyfriend at the bookshop...."

Gabe smirked, "Thoughts?"

"Well...."

"Wait," Gabe turned around and looked at Xayn, who'd frozen mid-mayo slather. "What was his name?"

"Andrew...why?" Xayn said, his head cocked to the side.

"Were you alone when you met him?" Gabe shook his head. "Sorry, never mind. I guess it doesn't matter. Andrew's name is Elaric."

Now, Xayn looked extraordinarily confused.

"He's a transmogromorph," Gabe stated and watched as Xayn's face processed through what he'd said until finally grasping it.

"Ah. No, we were surrounded by people fixing the shop," Xayn said, answering Gabe's earlier question.

"Yeah, that's what I figured. Don't take it personally."

Xayn looked down and slowly returned to making their sandwiches, but Gabe narrowed his eyes at him.

"Xayn, talk to me."

"Hm?" Xayn looked up, but his eyes were far away.

Gabe sighed and swapped their drinks for cider, and took the stool beside his friend.

"I know that look. What's on your mind? Did you not like him?"

"Oh, no. That's not it. Seemed like a nice guy." The corners of Xayn's lips turned up slightly, "Dany and he seem to get along well."

"It's still new, but yeah, from what I gather. So, why are you so in your head then?"

Xayn put down the cheese he'd been holding and looked away. "He mentioned he used to date Marco."

"Yeah, and? From what I hear, that wasn't even this century. Literally."

Xayn chuckled, and Gabe couldn't hide his smile.

"It just caught me off guard, I guess," Xayn said, returning his gaze to his hands.

Gabe sighed and put everything he'd been holding on the counter before pulling his chosen brother in for a hug.

"Xayn, you're not alone. You never have been and never will be."

Xayn hugged him back and nodded into his shoulder. A minute later he sat back and returned to making their lunches.

"I'm sorry," Xayn said softly.

"Nothing to be sorry for. I know it's been a rough few weeks, but her wrist healed, you've talked it out, and it's all good now."

"I just feel like—"

"I swear, Xayn, if you say it's your fault, I'm taking your sandwich back," Gabe teased but still could only frown. "She slipped. You weren't even home. It had nothing to do with you."

"I should have been home."

"Why?" Gabe asked, crossing his arms.

"Because that's where I belong. In that forest. With my Grandmother. Not in town."

Gabe growled, and he felt Mal press on their Bond with concern.
I'm fine. Trying to talk sense into Xayn. Sorry.

Let me know if you need backup, Mal said, and Gabe sent him feelings of gratitude.

"Xayn, let me ask you something."

"What?"

"We both know Grandma Yvonne is...nearing that point." Gabe swallowed roughly. That woman was family to him, too, and he knew his words hurt Xayn, but he needed to get through to him.

"Do you want things to end up with her like me and Abbot? Don't do what I did." Gabe looked down and felt when Xayn looked over at him. "Don't regret anything. Spend time with her and make happy memories. Help her in the garden. Sit with her while she crochets."

When Gabe's voice wavered, he squeezed his eyes closed momentarily.

"She'll be gone eventually. We all will. Don't waste what you have left feeling guilty over something. Whether you actually should own that guilt or not."

A minute later, Xayn pushed a plate toward him, Gabe's favorite sandwich atop it.

"I promise," Xayn said after a few minutes. "Now eat. You need sleep. I'll stay while you nap."

Gabe's heart hurt for Xayn and himself, and he missed Cat, but he stuck his lunch in his mouth, comforted in knowing he wasn't eating alone.

Chapter 16: Recovery and Regrets

March 2022 - Alku | Onnie Moore

Onnie could hear voices nearby, and when she tried to focus on what they were saying, their words slipped through her grasp like the finest sand. She switched to scanning her body and could feel when she was able to wiggle her toes. She moved up and took a deep breath, her chest rising and falling. The tips of her fingers tingled, but after further inspection, she had probably not moved them in quite a while. Lastly, her head. Surprisingly, she didn't have a headache but felt like she'd woken up from a lovely nap. Once her senses returned, she tried to focus on the voices again.

"She'll be fine, Gabe, as I told you yesterday. Just keep giving her a green bottle twice a day to help her body keep its strength up." Onnie recognized Xayn's voice and was glad he'd come by to help. Not just for her sake but Gabe and Dany's, too.

"Thanks, Xayn," Gabe's voice said, not far from her. It was slower than usual, and Onnie could guess he was sleep-deprived.

"I'll walk you out," Dany's voice said from farther away.

Onnie refocused on her body and recognized the softness beneath her. She was home in bed, and when she moved one finger back and forth slowly, she felt the tell-tale texture of her quilt.

Gabe sighed, and she felt him rest his head on the bed beside her. "Cat, you need to come back now. I need you."

I'm here, Gabe. It's just taking me a few minutes to get my body to behave.

She felt Gabe shift beside her, and he lifted her hand and pressed the back of it to his cheek. "I've missed you."

How long?

"Three days."

Damn. How's the shop? What about the town? Has the storm fully passed? Oh, no, how's Dany? I'm sure I scared—

"Cat, breathe. Slow down, and we'll go one at a time," Gabe said calmly as he brushed her hair back with a delicate finger.

Alright. Can you get me some water, please?

"Sure, I'll be right back."

When she was confident that Gabe had left the room, Onnie opened her eyes and winced. Even though the lights were off, the room was blinding compared to three days of sleeping and being in the void. It wasn't long before Gabe was back with a glass of water, and when he saw her eyes open and her attempting to sit up, he rushed over and supported her back with his free arm.

"Why didn't you ask me?"

"Because I knew you'd worry, and I'm fine. It's just really bright." She accepted the glass of water and drank it all in one go, handed the empty glass back and then flexed her fingers in front of her. "Stiff."

"I'd imagine so," Gabe said, setting aside the glass and sitting beside her. *Mal, she's awake.* Onnie heard Gabe say along their Bond. Two seconds later, Mal was sitting on the bed on Onnie's other side.

"About time you quit lazing about," he teased with a goofy grin.

Onnie laughed and scratched under his chin. "Sorry about that. I was practicing for my Sleeping Beauty audition."

"I'd cast you," Mal said as he leaned into her hand and purred. "Good to see you, Onnie."

"Are you hungry?" Gabe asked, shifting to the foot of the bed and pulling her feet into his lap to rub the tingles out of them.

"Nope, but I assume that's Xayn's doing."

"It was. How'd you know?" Gabe smirked.

"I was awake a few minutes more than you realized. I heard him leaving."

"He's good people," Mal said as he settled into her side and got comfy.

"He is," Gabe said, his eyes sparkling.

The three of them heard the front door slam, and they all jumped. Gabe was on his feet and heading to see what happened, but before he made it through the bedroom door, Dany dashed through it and dove into Onnie's lap. Onnie's head whacked the headboard behind her with a loud crack, and for a second, she saw stars.

"Dany!" Gabe shouted, but Onnie held up her hand to stop him and then wrapped her arms around the woman who was acting more like an anaconda than a human.

"I'm sorry, Dany," Onnie apologized and squeezed her friend back.

"You should be!" Dany shouted into Onnie's stomach. "Do you have any idea how much you scared me!"

"Gabe, would you mind picking up some soup from the Day Night Cafe?" Onnie asked, adding, *Need a few minutes with her,* along the Bond.

"Of course. Elaric is in the living room if you need anything." He nodded once, frowned at his sister, and left the room, closing the door behind him.

"I'll go with him. I want a slice of tiramisu," Mal said before disappearing from the bed beside her and leaving the two women alone.

Onnie held onto Dany for a few more minutes until she shifted her body to laying more beside Onnie rather than atop her like a human blanket.

"Will you tell me what happened while I was asleep?"

"Honestly, not much. Gabe rarely left your side, so Mal spent most of his time at the shop with Elaric and me. I slept in Gabe's room at night, and it was pretty much rinse and repeat."

"I'm sorry I caused so much trouble."

She was genuinely sorry and hated seeing her friends worry over her. That said, she'd do it all over again just for the chance to meet Kushima. Realizing she'd forgotten, Onnie searched along her Bonds, and her heart returned to normal when she heard the now familiar voice.

I'm still here. Do not worry.

"No one's mad or anything. We were just worried. You've never been out for this long before. Was it just because of the storm?"

"Ah…." Onnie trailed off. She wasn't ready to tell the others about Kushima yet. "Mostly. That and shock, I think. Seeing the shop like that…."

"I get it," Dany said quietly, and Onnie felt a bit guilty for lying to her friend, but she'd explain it all when she was ready.

"You said you, Elaric, and Mal were at the shop. How much do I owe you, and how much work do I have left?"

Dany snorted. "Oh, you don't owe us anything, but Mrs. Radcliff, Xayn, Marco, Sam—"

Onnie groaned, interrupting her laundry list of debts. "Why? How much did they all do?"

Dany pinched her side. "Stupid, because they care. About you, the shop, Abbot, whatever it is. That's why they helped. As for how much, well…seeing as you can go back to work whenever you'd like, I'd say homemade cookies for the next six years at least."

"You fixed it all!" Onnie shouted and sat up in bed, turning to look down at Dany's grin of pride.

"I mean, it's not back to how it was before, but it's mostly the same. We saved what we could, but not everything made it."

Onnie's chest started to feel like someone was stepping on her, and she must have looked like something was wrong because Dany was sitting up beside her in a second.

Cat?

Sorry, I'm fine. Onnie took a deep breath and focused on controlling her emotions better.

"You good?" Dany asked, creases wrinkling her brow.

"Yeah, I just realized how much everyone had done and how much they care, and it got a bit overwhelming for a second."

You are not alone, young one. Kushima's soothing voice made Onnie nod with a smile.

"Of course, we care! I know you just hit your head. Sorry about that, by the way," Dany said with a chuckle and carefully began feeling for a lump on the back of Onnie's skull from the headboard, "but did you really not think that after everything you've done and all of the relationships you've formed that people wouldn't help? Actually, I'd have been impressed if you'd kept them away."

"What happened to the roach?"

"I called Dillon and he took care of it. That one was in pretty bad shape."

"Okay, thank you," Onnie sniffled and then laid back down. "I know I just woke up, but I think I will close my eyes a bit more. Will you stay?"

"Of course," Dany snuggled up beside her.

Onnie closed her eyes and checked on her friend's Bonds individually. Everyone seemed worn out but relieved, and she hated that she was presumably the cause of the exhaustion. Mal felt her checking on him, and he pressed back on their Bond in a way that scolded her and said she should stop worrying over much.

Not wanting to cause more grief, she pulled back from the Bond and tried to rest. She quickly drifted off into sleep, but she did manage, *Thank you,* in Dany's mind before she did.

"Cat," Onnie heard Gabe say from beside her. "You should wake up and eat something."

She opened her eyes and saw that the room was dark, and Gabe was kneeling beside the bed. When she tried to sit up, she felt a weight on her right side, and when she looked down, Dany was curled up on the blanket beside her, breathing softly.

She didn't leave? Onnie asked Gabe.

Nope. You've both been sleeping for about ten hours.

Onnie looked at Gabe in shock. *Why did she sleep—wait. She's not been sleeping either, has she? Did any of you?*

Gabe smiled and softly held her cheek. *Cat, you already know my answer.*

An involuntary groan escaped, just enough to rouse Dany, who yawned and stretched.

"Hey, feeling better, Onnie?"

"Yes, just hungry."

Gabe got to his feet, and Mal relocated himself to the foot of the bed from wherever he'd been. "Did someone mention food?"

She looked at Dany, and they both erupted into giggles.

"Yes, Mal," Gabe said and poked the feline's tummy. "Let's go. You just volunteered to help me."

Mal groaned, "How would I help? Did you forget the lack of thumbs?"

"I'll find something. Let's go." Gabe nudged the cat off the bed and smiled at Onnie and Dany before leaving the room.

Onnie sniggered, "Those two. Really."

"The bromance is real," Dany said, flopping back on the bed.

"You feeling better?" Onnie asked, laying back down beside her.

"I do. I didn't mean to fall asleep, though," Dany said through a yawn.

It still takes me by surprise sometimes how much they all care, Onnie said to Kushima.

While I understand, it should not. They scream it loudly at you in their every action and word.

Onnie groaned, and Dany glanced over with one eyebrow raised.

Young one, why not take this opportunity to show your Sister the Bond?

Oh, that's an excellent idea. Thank you.

My pleasure.

Onnie reached for her Bond with Gabe, Mal, and Dany. *Hey, Gabe, while you cook, mind if I keep Dany?*

Sure, but what's up?

Onnie grinned at Dany beside her. *I wanna show her the void.*

Really!? Dany exclaimed and tensed up her body.

Shesh, Mal said with a laugh. *It's not that great.*

Shut it, you! Dany retorted.

Have fun, you two, Gabe said.

Onnie pulled her focus back to Dany. "Ready?"

Dany's head nodded like a bobblehead doll. "Yes, yes! What do I do?"

"Well, first, you'll need to calm down," Onnie chuckled.

"Got it," Dany shut her eyes immediately and began to slow her breathing.

This is making her far happier than I expected, Onnie said privately to Kushima.

I believe your observation in my library was correct. Likely, this means quite a bit to Dany.

Better make it good, then. Onnie sniggered and slowed her breathing to match Dany's.

I will remain quiet but will be here should you need me.

Thank you, Kushima.

Onnie closed her eyes and reached for the darkness at the edge of her sight with little effort.

Dany, focus on the darkness at the edge of your eyelids. Try to reach for it.

Onnie pulled up her and Dany's Bond to monitor her friend's progress. The purple strand leading into the void and eventually to her friend pulsed in time with Dany's breath.

Good. Now, I want you to try to reach for me. See if you can find my Bond.

Dany found it quickly, and Onnie shivered, understanding the feeling she often inflicted on others to prove a point.

You're there. Now, look down. Do you see—

Dany gasped, and Onnie materialized herself in the void.

Alright, I'd like to try something further. Think of yourself. Picture yourself within the void. Stand beside me.

Half a heartbeat later, Dany shimmered into being beside Onnie.

There were tears in her eyes, but her smile was blindingly bright. So was their Bond, and Onnie brought it into the void for Dany to see. The green strand of Onnie's Bond originated at her heart and drifted out to Dany's purple Bond. They met at the center, a tangle of colored threads gripping each other like tentacles.

Hey, Onnie said.

Oh, my gods, Onnie! This is...just wow. Dany looked down at their Bond and squinted.

Onnie couldn't hold back her giggle. *Yeah, not all Bonds are that bright.*

Really? Dany leaned forward to inspect it.

Something occurred to Onnie, and she switched to talking to Kushima. *Does she see it the way I do?*

No. Young one, not even I see it the way you do.

Onnie blanched, both in the void and where she lay resting on her bed beside her best friend.

It's...brighter...right here. Why? Dany asked and indicated to where Onnie saw their threads entwining.

That's the point where our Bonds are connected. Do you see yours as purple and mine as green?

Dany nodded. *Does everyone have a different color?*

Yes. Mal's is yellow. Gabe's is...actually. Onnie closed her eyes in the void and brought her Bonds with Gabe, Mal, and the shop to where Dany could see them.

Oh! There's more!

Dany was at least seeing the Bonds in general, even if it wasn't precisely as Onnie did.

So, this is Mal's? Dany pointed to the yellow strand that started at Onnie and headed into the void. A yellow strand also connected to Dany's purple one, but the glow was significantly lower.

This one? Dany pointed to the red thread that was Gabe's. The brilliant woman's eyebrows wrinkled, and she looked between it, herself, and where it vanished into the void.

Gabe's?

It is. Red. His is also connected to you, but because your relationship with Gabe is so much stronger and built up than your one with Mal, it's noticeably brighter.

Oh, that makes sense. Wait, so could I talk to Gabe without going through you?

Onnie shook her head. *No, you may be connected to him, but your Bond isn't how you're talking to him telepathically. You're still going through mine for that. Similarly to you only being able to enter the void by piggybacking off me.*

Dany frowned, and Onnie saw her look at the last Bond Onnie had made visible—Kushima's.

That one's...different. It has to be the shop, right? Onnie nodded, and Dany began to inspect it closer. *I can't tell what color it is....*

It's not a color. It's opalescent.

Oh, that makes sense. So many Keepers over the years blended into her with their own colors.

Onnie heard Kushima laugh softly.

Dany stopped her investigation of the glowing Bonds and looked back at Onnie. *Is this what you see all the time?*

Yeah, no. Well, this is what I saw before the Transference.

And now?

Onnie closed her eyes once more. *I'll only leave it up for a moment, or it'll be overwhelming. Ready?*

Uhh, no? Dany said honestly.

Onnie pulled up the Bonds within the bedroom and filled the void with light. She heard Dany's gasp, and when she checked on her friend, the woman spun in circles, trying to take it all in.

It's, it's everything. It's like we're in the room, only it's made of.... You can see everything.

I can. Onnie reached for the Bond of the pillow in the window seat and gently pulled it to her.

Okay, that's unbelievable. Seriously, have I died? This can't be possible.

Onnie snorted. *Yeah. I know.* She slowly dimmed all the Bonds, including their own, so they were alone in the void again.

Onnie, Dany said, her eyes sparkling, *Thank you. Truly.*

I'm sorry it took me so long.

Dany shook her head emphatically. *No, it was worth it.*

Have any questions?

Like a million, Dany declared, and Onnie rolled her eyes.

Yeah, I guess that was a stupid question. Anything you want to ask here, specifically?

Her friend's face fell, and she looked toward the floor. Dany's sudden shift in demeanor made Onnie worry.

What's wrong?

Onnie, you shouldn't be able to do any of this. Dany looked up, and her eyes were sad. *Are you...does it....* Dany sighed. *When you pull too much power, or whatever it is exactly that happens, does it hurt or...whatever the Bond equivalent is?*

Well, that was the last thing I thought you'd ask, Onnie said with a smile. *Not really. It's not physical pain, not when I am doing whatever it is. Afterward, I'm mostly exhausted and have a headache.*

Dany nodded and looked away again.

Come on. Let's go back, and we can talk more, but I think we will miss dinner at this rate. Onnie smiled and tried to reassure Dany that everything was fine.

How do I do it?

As strange as it sounds, close your eyes again and walk back.

Dany giggled. *Somehow,* Onnie watched Dany close her eyes as instructed. *I can't see it being that....*

Onnie returned to her body and grinned at Dany, still beside her. *...easy.*

Dany looked down at the pillow Onnie had moved with the Bond, which was still in her hands.

"I need wine," Dany said matter-of-factly.

Onnie laughed loudly, and she and Dany were a mess of giggles when Gabe came in to get them for dinner a few minutes later.

Chapter 17: Plans and Promises

March 2022 - Alku | Onnie Moore

"So, here's what we know so far," Dany said, sitting on the floor beside Onnie, curled up in front of the fire. "It's not much."

Gabe and Elaric sat on opposite sides of the couch in Abbot's study at the bookshop while she and Dany snuggled in blankets, sipping hot cocoa, the scent of chocolate filling the space. Mal lay in Onnie's lap, his paw or nose occasionally slipping into her drink to lick up the cool whipped cream.

Everyone was tired, with dark circles under their eyes from the long week of repairing Abbot's or fretting over Onnie. Still, the shop sparkled with renewed vigor thanks to the devotion and hard work that the entire town of Alku showered her with while Onnie recovered. Onnie was touched by the number of people who came out to help her and the shop, and she smiled every time she saw the new carpeting and glossy wooden bookcases or smelled the lemon-scented wood polish Mrs. Radcliff had made especially for her.

Elaric looked different again today, this time wearing the face of a fraternity boy with short blonde hair and a baby face. He wore fraying jeans and a UW sweatshirt, and a backpack lay at his feet. Onnie wasn't sure he'd ever been to college, but if he hadn't, she was sure he'd fit right in if he wanted to. He smiled when he caught her staring.

"This one doesn't flicker much, right?"

She shook her head, "Nope. How do you keep them all straight? I mean, do you even know who you are right now?"

Elaric smirked, "I'm always me, just the face changes, but I think you're asking more about the personality part. Acting, and years of practice. From frat-kid," he gestured to his current form, "to pissed-off corporate office worker, I've become most of them."

"Yuck, frat boys. I think," Onnie said, smiling over her mug, "I feel better knowing you can act like a jerk. It will make this easier and more believable." Instantly, the room became more solemn.

"Let's get this over with then," Dany said, setting her mug on the hearth behind her.

Onnie frowned, put her arm around her friend, and rested her head on Dany's shoulder before she looked back at Elaric. "You're sure about this? I won't restrict you to one form unless you're one hundred percent sure."

Elaric locked eyes with Dany, who looked away. "I've thought it through, and I'm sure. It's the right thing to do."

When no one objected, she continued. "Okay, so here's what I think step one is. I found a ritual in my grandfather's books that theorizes a way to manipulate a Bond that isn't tied to the shop."

"The same one we used for Dany?" Gabe asked.

"Not exactly. My Bond with Dany was…easier for a few reasons. Mostly because you're blood-related and because of her role. Occasionally, a more advanced Keeper could link up with the Head Sister for short periods." Onnie shook her head. "But for Elaric, from what I've found, strengthening a Bond with a complete wildcard is frowned upon, if someone could even accomplish it. It's basically permanent, and if the new Bond were made with someone with ill intent…." Onnie trailed off.

"They could cripple the Keeper," Elaric stated flatly.

"Exactly," Onnie confirmed.

Dany quickly turned to look at Onnie and frowned. "So, both of you are at risk? What happens if Jakob tries to take him over like the other roaches?"

"Actually," Onnie said, looking down at her lap, "it's possible that he could manipulate me, Gabe, Mal, and the shop." She paused, "This has to be a group decision. None of us are unaffected. Elaric and I have talked about this already, and both agree that this still should be done, but we can't do it—"

"Won't," Elaric interjected, his eyes not leaving Dany's.

"Won't," Onnie corrected herself, "Do it without the four of you consenting."

"What is the ritual?" Gabe asked, rubbing his chin.

"It's pretty simple, actually. It's a bastardized version of the ritual I underwent to become the Keeper, just kind of…reversed?" Then she shook her head. "Kind of. I'll meet Elaric in the void, strengthen our existing Bond connection, and make a few modifications."

"He'd be able to feel your emotions?" Gabe asked out loud before adding through their Bond, *I don't know if I like that, Cat.*

"To an extent," Onnie said with a shrug. "I'll be able to put up walls and close him out if I need to, but the last bit of the binding will pretty much make it a moot issue."

"How so?" Gabe asked.

"To bind his powers, I will hide them behind a wall in *my* mind, not his."

"Why yours?" Dany asked.

Elaric leaned forward to speak. "We don't know how powerful the rogue guardian is. It's just too risky to keep my powers with me in case he breaks my defenses."

"Won't you not having your powers be even riskier? What if something happens and you need them?" Dany said.

"Don't worry," Onnie said with a smile, "I wouldn't strip him of his powers and leave him defenseless. Our Bond will be faint and nearly undetectable but still there."

"Yeah, I'll be able to reach out to Onnie mentally if things go south."

"And then I'll unbind his powers."

"So, there's a backup plan," Gabe nodded.

"An 'oh shit button,'" Elaric smirked.

"And you're okay with this?" Dany asked Elaric directly.

"I am," he nodded. "You trust Onnie, so I will too. She won't send me to my death."

"He will kill you if he finds out," Dany said coldly.

Onnie swirled her hot chocolate around in her cup, and Gabe rubbed his temples.

"I know," Elaric said flatly, "But it's a risk worth taking."

"I'll do everything in my power to keep him safe, Dany," Onnie said, gently squeezing her friend's hand. "All of us will. I promise."

"That may not be enough." Dany untangled herself from the blankets, got to her feet, and took her hot chocolate with her. "I'm going home. See you tomorrow."

When she was out of earshot, Gabe cleared his throat. "My sister."

"It's understandable," Onnie said, staring into her cup. "She cares."

Elaric stood. "Thanks for everything, Onnie. I'll meet you tomorrow to start the setup."

"Yeah."

"I'm going to walk her home." He nodded to Gabe and left, too.

The three of them sat silently for a few minutes until Gabe came over and sat where Dany had been. He put his arm around Onnie and kissed her temple.

"You're sure this is the right thing to do, Cat?"

"I am."

"What about you, furball?"

Mal paused his paw, which was nearly inside Onnie's cup, and nodded. "Yup. I think it's our best option. Besides, what Onnie's going to do shouldn't even be possible, so I don't think that Jakob would even know to look for this type of deception."

Gabe sighed, ran his fingers through his hair, and tugged on the ends. "Alright. Then I think we do it."

Onnie nodded and snuggled closer to Gabe's side, sipping her cocoa while she scratched the top of Mal's head.

This will work. It has to, she said to Kushima along the Bond.

Elaric Rickson

"E, you're positive this is the right thing to do?" Marco asked from across the coffee table.

They were sharing a meal before Marco had to go downstairs for work, or at least Elaric was having dinner, and Marco was having a pre-breakfast snack.

"Honestly, no. I'm scared shitless." Elaric sighed before putting a bite of ravioli in his mouth. The handmade pasta filled with gooey cheese and mushrooms slathered in the creamy sauce was one of his favorites from downstairs, and living with Marco undoubtedly had its perks.

Marco crossed his arms, tipped his head back against the couch, and closed his eyes. It was difficult for Elaric not to stare at him considering he was still in his pajamas since it wasn't quite time for his shift. Every time Elaric saw the man without his mask on, he felt relieved.

"And Onnie hasn't found any other way?"

"Way for what?" Elaric asked before sipping the most delicious wine he'd ever tasted. "Not having to bind my powers?"

"Yes."

"Not really, but we stopped looking. Once we realized we would do that, we focused more on how to do it safely than finding other options."

Marco's head snapped forward, and his eyes narrowed. "You. Stopped. Looking."

Elaric froze, recognizing that tone, even if Marco rarely used it. "Shit."

While Marco was relaxed and genuine around him, every so often, Elaric forgot the man was a sanguiste and an extremely old one.

Currently, it wasn't entirely his friend and former lover across the table from him, nor was he the friendly Day Night Cafe employee. This was the 'I've seen some shit, and it changed me' Marco. This was the man who had been broken, beaten, and had everything taken from him. Here Elaric was, telling him that there was a chance that he could be taken from him, too, if something went wrong.

Elaric felt the slight pressure of Marco's intimidation begin to build. Intimidation was similar to mild hypnotism and was what sanguiste used to frighten their targets in place so they could feed. Even if Marco didn't consume blood, he rarely let his control over his instincts slip, not even a small amount. Now, Elaric watched as his pupils dilated, his breathing became nearly imperceptible, and if you didn't know him, his intimidation would have you praying for a quick death. Marco was deeper into his instincts than Elaric had seen in decades, and it was all directed at him.

He slowly lowered his fork to his plate and carefully slid the bowl and wine glass away from him and into the center of the table.

"Marco, I understand why you're pissed—"

"You think I'm angry?" Marco's voice said in a low growl from over Elaric's shoulder, making him shiver.

He'd blinked, and Marco had moved. Human fiction about vampires did stem from reality, but Outsiders weren't aware that the myths they perpetuated were based in fact. A sanguiste was ordinarily dangerous, but if they succumbed to their base instincts, they were nearly unbeatable—the world's first bipedal predators, and to Marco, Elaric was currently that prey.

He weighed his options and decided it was best to stay silent and submissive and just let Marco talk for now.

"I'm not angry, E. I'm *fucking terrified,* and you seem to have decided that the first option was the best option. When is the first idea *ever* the best idea?"

Elaric could see Marco out of the corner of his eye, and he was surprised to find him shaking ever so slightly. Marco's flesh-piercing teeth were visible even though he usually kept them concealed near constantly, and while this sanguiste preferred emotions, it did not mean he *couldn't* feed on blood or rip out a man's jugular.

Granted, Elaric knew he was realistically in little to no danger. Marco would never allow himself to lose control that far, and considering Stephan was downstairs in the cafe, he'd intervene if Marco truly lost it. That didn't mean Elaric had to make it harder on the man who was clearly suffering, though.

Elaric spoke softly and calmly, "What would you like me to do, Marco?"

There was no answer for quite a few minutes, and just when Elaric thought he would have to shift in his chair, Marco's forehead dropped onto his shoulder.

"I can't lose you too, E," his voice shook, and his words cracked.

Elaric took a deep breath now that he was confident Marco was back in control. He reached up and wrapped his arm around Marco's shoulder and was surprised when he fell to his knees and gripped Elaric around the waist.

Elaric's heart broke for the man who never showed weakness to anyone, even himself. Yet, here he was, crumpled in his lap, fractured by his recent losses and terrified of the future.

"I can't lose you either, and I promise you, I'll come back." Elaric gently ran his fingers through Marco's silky hair. "You're the only family I have left, Marco, but if I don't do this…" he sighed and swallowed hard, "If I don't do this, there might not be anything left for me to return to. That man isn't going to stop, and after seeing what he's capable of the night of the storm, he's not just looking to destroy the Keeper. He wants to burn it all down. Everything. This has something to do with the Prophecy, too. I can feel it."

Marco was still quiet, but Elaric felt the slightest nod of his head, and he was thankful he was at least listening.

"I have people I want to protect. You. Dany, Onnie, and Gabe. Sam, Vanessa, and Stephan. Hell, even Abbot."

"Has Dany been involved too?" Marco mumbled into Elaric's torso.

"Yes."

Marco's shoulders heaved as he took a deep breath and untangled himself from Elaric's lap. He sat back on his heels, and it took every atom in Elaric's body for him to stay in his chair. The torment on Marco's face was heart-piercing, and Elaric hated that he was the cause of any pain for him.

"Alright. I know she cares for you and how dedicated to Onnie she is. She wouldn't allow either of you two to do anything that wasn't as safe as possible." He looked away from Elaric and off into the empty space of the apartment. "Just…promise me. Promise me I won't have to bury you, too."

The last word of Marco's sentence was barely audible, and Elaric's control had reached its limit.

Elaric slipped to the floor, mirrored Marco's position, knee to knee, and turned Marco's face to look at him. He held the back of his neck and stared directly into his eyes.

"I swear it."

Marco nodded, and Elaric pulled him into a hug. "There's one thing you could do for me in return, though."

"Anything," Marco responded without hesitation, his arms still around Elaric's neck, holding on to him and unwilling to let go.

Chapter 18: Trustwalk

April 2022 - Alku | Elaric Rickson

It had been a week since their plan had been decided, and Elaric had spent most of it running errands for Onnie or spending time with Dany and Marco. The former, he now truly understood why all of Alku was willing to stand with her. She was a strong, fierce woman who didn't hesitate to put herself in harm's way for what she believed in and was highly empathetic and compassionate to those around her. He'd seen how Gabe looked at the woman sometimes, and it was easy to tell that the Guardian was grumbling on the inside. His job was a difficult balance between lover, friend, and protector, but the pair seemed to be doing alright.

And then there was Dany. After her initial shock at the danger he'd be walking into, she pulled away from their group for a few days. Eventually, she gave her blessing but said she would not be a part of it. She wouldn't be able to live with herself with his blood on her hands. Onnie talked to her, and from then on, Dany had her fingers in everything. She wanted to know every detail, check on all aspects of the ritual, and review every contingency plan. It didn't take long for her to drive herself to exhaustion.

Elaric could guess what Onnie told her friend without asking. The best way for Dany to feel confident that he would be okay was to know that everything would be handled perfectly, and what better way than to oversee it yourself? So, instead of his blood on her hands, she'd know that they'd done everything possible to keep him safe.

Dany's devotion to their plan and his safety was also what finally convinced Marco that Elaric wasn't going on a suicide mission. He was sure that if Dany hadn't changed her mind, Marco would have teamed up with her to lock him up somewhere.

So the day they'd all been planning for arrived. Dany would facilitate the ritual that would bind his powers, and he would start on his path to infiltrate the rogue guardian's organization.

One of the tasks Elaric had to complete for the ritual was to find the form he would take when undercover. He, Marco, and Dany had spent a tiring evening as Elaric had changed into two dozen forms before the pair had finally approved and said he looked like the kind of scum Jakob would use to do his bidding. The form they'd settled on was a greasy-haired man with a big beer belly. He looked down on his luck and on his last leg. He was the sort of person with a wife who left him and a kid who wrote him off. A perfect specimen for the rogue guardian to recruit to his cause. A man who wanted to hurt someone just to see them bleed.

Now, Elaric stood outside of the Keeper Mausoleum, a place he never thought he'd visit. Before Abbot, he hadn't known any of the previous Keepers well enough or cared to see their final resting place. Now that he was outside the great stone building, he was overcome with the sense of presence around him. He felt the power and the knowledge seeping from within and trying to comfort him. Considering Onnie and the others were already inside, it was likely that the spirits of past Keepers knew what they were about to do.

A warm gust of air rushed past his back, and he smiled reflexively. He'd know Abbot anywhere. With his friend by his side, Elaric knew they'd be alright. Onnie had promised, and he trusted her word.

He took a deep breath, inhaling the smell of pine, green grass, and fresh flowers, settling his nerves even more. He was about to do something extraordinary and good. The aspect of impossibility aside, a

Keeper was about to alter his Bond, connecting them together, and he would protect her with his life. Elaric was more than honored.

Waiting out there all day? Onnie's voice questioned in his mind.

He smiled and shoved his hands into his jacket pockets, his Converse making little noise on the worn stones as he walked. It felt like even his shoes knew to be silent and respectful. The earthy smell of moss tickled his nose yet was quickly replaced by incense and spiced herbs. He followed the short hallway into the antechamber and squinted as the darkness gave way to the candle-lit room. The walls were lined with sleeping forms in alcoves. Tiny plaques beneath each of them listed their names, race, and along with their time of life. A quick scan showed that the sleeping figures extended far back into the chamber and that many more Keepers were memorialized in Alku than Elaric had realized. He shook his head in awe before continuing to a small room in the back.

Voices echoed softly but ceased once he entered the room. Gabe stood in one corner wearing a guarded expression and a sword on his back, while Onnie smiled at Elaric as he entered, before closing her eyes and placing her hands on Abbot's effigy. Dany bustled around the room with bowls of fragrant water, white cloths, and blankets, only sparing him a small smile and a nod before returning to her preparations.

Elaric stood and watched them for a while. They existed comfortably with one another and moved around each other like actors in a silent film. He wondered if they were communicating telepathically or were just that familiar with one another's presence.

Both, Onnie said intrusively. *We warded the mausoleum from the inside and have increased the receptivity of others within to telepathy. It should make our task a bit easier for you.*

Elaric smirked and shook his head before standing next to Onnie. One of her hands was on Abbot's forehead, and the other was gripping his hand, which was made of stone. She opened her eyes, took one of Elaric's hands, and placed it on Abbot's shoulder.

He misses you, Onnie said, and Abbot's voice responded before Elaric could ask who missed who.

Oh, I bet he does. He misses all the trouble we used to get into.

Abbot? Elaric asked, though fully aware of the answer already.

You used to be so quick. What happened, Elaric? Pick an old man as your form this time around.

Elaric gasped, removed his hand from Abbot's shoulder, and stepped back. Onnie smiled softly.

"Don't worry. He can't hurt you."

"But he's dead," Elaric stammered. "How?"

"Keepers never truly die, Elaric. Their bodies fail, and their souls meld with the shop's life force. With the increase in telepathy, you're able to speak with him."

"That's crazy."

"I know. I will give you some privacy if you'd like to talk more. I spoke with him all night."

He hadn't noticed it before, but her eyes glistened with unshed tears as she left him to talk to the ghost.

He looked at Gabe, who still had his arms crossed, but now Elaric understood the man's mood. Abbot was like a father to him and Dany, and this must not be easy on him.

"Gabe," Elaric asked, "did you...did you get to speak with Abbot?"

Gabe blinked a few times and eventually focused on Abbot's stone form. "Yes, sorry. We've spoken."

"I can let you—"

"No," Gabe said, pushing off the wall with his boot. "I'm going to patrol," he said to no one in particular and walked out of the room.

Don't mind him, Onnie said. *Talking to Abbot was difficult for him. We never got to say goodbye.*

Elaric nodded, stepped up to the dais, and smiled down at the older man's form before he held on gently to his hand.

How you doing, pipsqueak?

Not such a pipsqueak anymore, runt. Abbot's voice chuckled as they teased one another. *How are you, my friend?*

I'm— Elaric stopped and looked over at Dany, *scared.*

Of the ritual.

And what it would mean to fail.

Abbot made a tutting sound. *Think as if you'll fail, and you already have. You know that. You've already overcome more significant obstacles in your life so far than many others will face in their entire lifetime. Don't get distracted, and you'll do fine. My Onnie was right to trust this task to you, and you were right to trust her. She will keep you safe.*

She's an amazing woman, Abbot. You should be proud.

I am. And of Dany and Gabriel, too. All three of them have grown into strong young folks to be proud of.

Dany....

Be careful with her, Elaric.

Elaric's brow knit into a frown. *Of course, but why do you say it?*

Dany...has a part to play in the prophecy that has yet to be made clear. She's essential, Elaric. Just as you, Gabriel, and Onnie are. The prophecy needs all four of you. You must protect her.

I will.

Promise me, Elaric. Promise me you'll watch out for her. Gabriel won't always be able to.

Always. I promise. Elaric glanced over at Dany and smiled. She wore a frown as she precisely measured herbs and poured them into a large wooden bowl filled with water. *You did a good job, Abbot, with all three of them.*

Four. You're a good man, Elaric, not just because your DNA tells you so. You were dealt a bad hand, but you made the best of it, and I'm proud of you for it. I will never be able to express how much our friendship meant to me, both as an outcast child and as an adult.

Thank you, Abbot.

Have you told them of your past?

No.

You can trust them.

Elaric did not respond. He had tried trust before, and it wasn't something he easily granted. *I'm not sure they need to know.*

They may not need to, but I think it would be good for you to have others who understand you besides Marco and Sam.

Elaric was quiet as he mulled over Abbot's words in his head. *About Marco....*

Abbot sighed. *I can only imagine.*

Yeah, I've never seen it this bad before, Abbot. It's like he's...been hollowed out. He's fragile and scared.

He was a good friend to me even when I got too old to keep up with him.

I've seen him grow attached to humans before, but you were different.

Did you ever ask him why? Abbot questioned.

Ah...no...I didn't realize there was a real reason. Elaric chuckled. *I already knew you were special, Abbot. Was there more?*

Yes. Much.

Elaric hesitated, *Can you tell me, or should I not ask?*

I reminded him of Niamh.

Elaric felt the blood drain from his face.

Before she was killed, of course, Abbot added quickly.

I...I had no idea. Elaric squeezed his eyes shut, his heart hurting for Marco once again. *So, he didn't just lose you.*

He probably feels like he lost her a second time.

Oh, Abbot... Elaric groaned.

I know I ask a lot, Elaric, but please, help him heal from this. He needs you. Of that, I don't have any doubt.

Yeah, but now I'm doing this. No wonder he nearly lost control when I told him.

He knew I would pass someday, but I don't think the abruptness of it was something he was expecting.

Not at all. None of us were. Someone had been keeping secrets... Elaric scolded gently.

It was not something any of you could change. Why would I burden my family with that knowledge?

Elaric rolled his eyes and pressed one palm to his forehead. *Because I would have come back sooner.*

You're home now. That's all that matters, runt.

Pipsqueak, you just wait. When I get there....

Abbot laughed, the sound making Elaric smile to himself.

They were quiet for a few minutes, and Elaric became increasingly lost in his thoughts, but eventually, Abbot pulled him back to the present.

I think Onnie is ready to begin, Elaric. You must get started.

Thank you, Abbot. Rest well, my friend.

Take care of them—all of them.

Elaric nodded and released the cold stone hand.

"Are we ready to start?" he asked Onnie.

"We are."

Elaric took a deep breath and looked down at Abbot's form once more, and then he nodded.

"Then let's get this over with."

Onnie Moore

Be careful, my dear. This is no small ritual. Abbot's voice spoke along Onnie's Bond with her Grandfather.

Since they had increased her receptivity to the Bonds within the mausoleum, her web of colors pulsed stronger than it had ever before. Most Bonds that connected the little things in the world were often so insignificant that they were effectively invisible to everyone but her. Yet even now, dozens of strands glowed that she had never noticed before, their light too faint to do anything with. For a brief moment, she was fearful for the souls she'd hidden within her own Bond, but even she could still not see them without significant effort.

Abbot's pulsed brighter than when her Grandfather had been alive, and his voice rang in her head as if he was standing next to her.

I know Grandfather. I've read the books. I know what is at stake.

Onnie.

Yes?

That boy is very special to me, don't get over-confident. No matter how much of that tea you've been drinking. You and I both know that what you're about to do shouldn't be possible and while I have no doubt you'll succeed, you need to treat this like you could fail.

Onnie heard him but said nothing. She knew what was at stake and refused to believe she couldn't do it. She saved the town a week and a half ago. She'd protect Elaric and save them all this time.

"Okay, so here's what we need to do," she said aloud before adding, *Gabe, we're ready,* along their Bond. "Elaric, you and I will lay along the two hollowed grooves here," she pointed to the floor beside the epitaph of Abbot. "We will be head to feet with Gabe sitting behind my head and Dany at yours."

"Alright," Elaric said with a nod.

"The two of them will guard our bodies while our minds converge, and I connect our Bonds and weave them together."

"Do I need to do anything to help facilitate that?" Elaric asked.

"You must focus on keeping your mind open to mine no matter what. If you close off your mind before I am finished, there's a chance something will go awry."

"What does that mean?" Elaric questioned as Gabe reentered the stone room. "What could go wrong?"

"I could cut your powers off from you permanently, or the backlash could burn us both out, or any other consequences from a long list I don't have time to cover now."

"You didn't tell me that, Cat," Gabe said with a frown.

"I told you there were consequences if it were to be interrupted. This is just one example of that. You two need to guard our bodies well." She looked at the three frightened faces before her and shook her head. "I'm sorry, but we knew there would be risks. We will be fine as long as everyone does their part."

"You should have told us," Dany said, crossing her arms and looking away.

"Are we doing this?" Elaric spoke up, his tone sharp, exposing he was more nervous than he was letting on.

"Yes, lay here," Onnie indicated to the hollow furthest from

Abbot.

Dany stood beside him as he sat atop the blankets laid out on the floor. She squeezed his shoulder before he laid down and then she went to sit cross-legged behind his head.

"Gabe, you do the same as Dany," Onnie asked, then laid down on the blankets in her hollow. "Dany has a bowl of purified water and cleansing herbs. Each of you dips a white cloth into it and wrings it out. Dany will guide you through the rest after Elaric, and I close our eyes. When we do, you cleanse our brows and then cover our eyes with the warm towel. Then you two will hear nothing more from us."

"But you'll still be speaking, right?" Dany asked. "Will we hear any of it?"

"Perhaps you'll hear bits, but mostly, I'll be weaving the Bonds together, and Elaric will be assisting in small increments. That will be the only time we are communicating."

"Alright," Dany said.

"Be safe, Cat," Gabe added.

"We will be," Onnie said, laying her head down. "Ready, Elaric?"

"As I'll ever be."

Onnie closed her eyes and listened to Gabe and Dany dip their cloths into the bowl between her and Elaric. The water splashed back into the vessel, and Onnie focused on the sound drips made. She listened to the random splashes and drops and made patterns out of them in her mind. She focused her breathing and slowed it down.

One, two, three, she counted as she breathed in. *One, two, three,* she breathed out.

This time, when she inhaled, she smelled the cleansing herbs: sage, rosemary, mint, and cinnamon.

Her ears picked up the faint flickering of the candle flames around them, and she pictured them fluttering in her mind. Their heat traveled into her body and warmed her flesh. Their light revealed hidden pathways in her mind. She was walking, twisting and turning, with no end in sight.

Elaric? she called out into the void but got no response. The Bonds she had with her shop, her Guardian, Link, and the past Keepers pulsed around her, each one leaving her body from a different point and spinning off like a spider's web in a different direction. The yellow strand from her right hand was Mal's, who was watching the shop, but when she thought of him, his tiny furry body appeared and fell in step beside her.

Hey Onnie.

Mal, are you really here?

You know the answer to that, Keeper. I'm never truly anywhere, but yup, it's me. I figured you might want some company, and I'd also be here to help if something goes south. Besides, the shop is slow, and Elanor said she'd keep an eye out since she was working out front today.

Alright, thank you.

I am here as well, Onnie, a feminine voice said clearly, and Mal smiled and looked up.

That's new, Mal replied.

I know that voice, Onnie said. *You spoke to me after Abbot's funeral. You're the shop.*

Before entering the mausoleum, Onnie and Kushima had decided to act as if they'd never spoken. Less to explain later and remove a potential distraction if the others found out.

Yes, though then it was merely chance that you heard me. You've boosted your mental powers significantly of late, and I am able to communicate with you thanks to this ritual.

Mal purred, *Are you okay with what Onnie is doing?*

Yes, it's the right choice, but she knew that.

I did, Onnie smiled. *Thank you for saying it, though. I have so many questions, but I suppose now really isn't the time.*

Correct again, my dear. You better get going. Elaric can't last long in this trance. His mind isn't accustomed to the void like ours is.

Right.

Onnie's heartbeat increased, and she sped up her mental walk through the silky Bonds around her. Pulsing off in the distance was a pearlescent strand, the colors spinning and wrapping around themselves. It was similar to the shop's Bond, but instead of one bundle of shimmering threads, it was a multitude of colored threads forming a shimmering bundle. Instinctively, she knew it was Elaric and as she approached the brightest spot, it rippled and wavered, its glow dimming slightly. It reminded her of the flicker she saw when he was in any form he was less accustomed to. She used the bright spot to follow the Bond to where it joined her own, but the wavering hadn't lessened.

Elaric, you have to unblock your mind. Let me in, don't be afraid.

Mal skipped ahead of her and jumped over to the root of the strand. Elaric's form shimmered into existence, but just as Mal's feet would have hit the void's floor, a chasm appeared beneath him, and he relocated to beside Onnie again.

We have a problem. He's still closed off, and as the chasm gets wider, we will have a harder and harder time reaching him, Onnie.

He's frightened young one, I think he needs the help of your Sister. He trusts her.

Onnie turned and rested her hand on the pulsing purple Bond that ran from her to Dany. *I need your help. He's afraid and not letting me in. Try talking to him?* Onnie felt Dany's agreement and removed her hand, giving them as much privacy as possible.

Elaric's form pulsed and strengthened a few minutes later, and he stood across the chasm.

Hello, Keeper. My apologies. I was somewhere dark and…unpleasant. Thank you for sending Dany.

Elaric bowed his head, and then his forehead scrunched in concentration. Slowly, the chasm's width closed, and he stood before Onnie, smiling.

I did it?

You did, Onnie nodded. *Now, let's get this done so we can go home. I need a cup of tea. Palms up, please.*

Elaric held his palms out, and she rested his Bond within them. Almost immediately, his hands started to glow in matching colors with his Bond. Onnie examined the cord, finding the individual threads, and searching out the correct one that would lead her back to Elaric's chosen form for their plan. When she saw a grey thread, she tugged gently, and his current form shivered, and then he was standing before her as the greasy, downtrodden man he would be using.

Okay, I am going to separate this thread from the rest. Then, once it's isolated, I will tie off the remainder and pull them to me. I will intertwine them with my own Bond, and you will no longer be able to access them. Are you ready?

As I'll ever be, Elaric gulped. *Do it.*

Onnie began unwinding the grey thread from the main bunch that was his base form's Bond and the individual threads that were his acquired forms. As she touched each thread, Elaric's form shifted. A teenage girl, a pregnant mother with fiery red hair, and a sizable lumbering man with a shaved head. Even a young boy.

She wondered what it would be like to be able to change oneself at a whim, and Elaric chuckled.

I will tell you when you're not holding my many lives in your hands.

Fair enough, Onnie smirked and continued to unwind the grey thread. *I think we are almost done, just this one more thread....* As she reached for the last thread, Elaric changed shape into a young version of Abbot. Far younger than the one she'd known, and Onnie froze.

It's not what it looks like, Onnie. I swear.

Explain, now. Before I rip your Bond from your body, she growled, startling herself with her reaction.

Calm yourself, Keeper, Mal said, brushing against her ankles even though she couldn't feel him. *Elaric is on our side. Hear him out.*

It was a prank. I knew Abbot when he was a kid, and we used to play together. Every few years, I'd come to visit. I would take his form, and scare the crap out of him. It was all in good fun. I never used it to impersonate him or hurt him. I would never. He was my best friend for a long time. He's family.

How old are you? Onnie whispered.

Many years older than Abbot was. My kind doesn't age like humans do. Think of it like reverse dog years, but I'm the equivalent of a thirty-year-old human. Roughly.

How can I trust you?

Trust us, Kushima said.

Abbot added, *He speaks the truth, Onnie.*

Fine, she pursed her lips. *It's not like I have much choice anyway, do I?*

Not really? Elaric said with the grin Abbot often had around Sam, the young day walker who looked after him when he'd gotten older.

Onnie pulled the last form's thread from around the grey one, and then she released the one she'd singled out. Elaric shifted back into his undercover form and winced.

Ew, I hate this one. I'm such a sleaze.

Onnie nodded but focused on her task, braiding the strand with Elaric's remaining forms that she would be keeping safe. She wrapped her own around them in a slip knot then she tugged gently on her Bond, watched as the braid slipped free, and started to weave its way back to Elaric. She grabbed it mid-flight and re-knotted it once more.

Okay. I have the forms, other than the one you're in. Your main Bond and the one you've chosen, are still with you. I think we are all set.

Good. This is way too much time in my own head if you ask me.

I'm used to it, I guess, Onnie shrugged.

Question for you.

Go ahead, she replied.

What if I need my powers? You release them, and then what?

I'm not sure. The spell says you will regain them. I assume it takes a few minutes for them to weave back into your Bond fully, but a piece will always stay with me, like when the yarn of a sweater sheds.

What if I need you to unbind them early? Do we have to do this whole ritual again to rebind them?

I'm...not sure. Do you know? Onnie asked Kushima and the others.

You do not, Keeper. You will be able to rebind them with deep meditation at first and with increased ease as you continue to do it. I'd suggest you both spend a bit of time practicing.

Well, that's good, Mal purred. *Can we go home now? My tail is stiff.*

Oy, Onnie fluffed the cat's fur before picking him up. *Come on you.* *She held out her hand to Elaric, and he smiled when he took it.*

Thank you, Keeper.

You're welcome. Will you tell me stories of Abbot?

It would be my honor, he beamed. *Let's go home.*

Protect each other, Abbot said just before they left the void.

Chapter 19: Two Can Keep a Secret

April 2022 - Alku | Onnie Moore

"What's up, Cat?" Gabe's voice said through the now unnecessary phone pressed to her ear out of habit.

"This is your warning. I'm going to go into the First Keeper's Library for a while."

Onnie promised to give everyone a heads-up when she needed to go into the room that muted their Bonds. In return, unless they had an *excellent* reason, they were not allowed to keep her from it or, more importantly, intrude.

"I don't like it. No one is with you. What about the shop?" Gabe was being careful not to step over their agreed-upon line, and she enjoyed watching him struggle as he tried to phrase his concerns in a way that would not break her rules.

"I closed for the day. Besides, I can always come out if I need to."

"And how do you think you'll know if you *need* to step out?" Gabe said with smug satisfaction, and Onnie was positive he was smirking in his office at the school.

Onnie tucked a notepad under her arm, stuck a pen into her braided hair, and picked up her thermos of tea.

"How about a compromise? I'll ask Mal to watch the shop, and he can come get me if needed."

"Accepted."

Onnie added quickly, "With the agreement that he does not interrupt me."

"That's between you two. Thank you, Cat."

Onnie sighed but smiled. "You're welcome. Talk to you later."

"Yeah," he said and then hung up.

Mal, can you hang out at the shop and play gopher for me this afternoon?

Sure, why?

I want to go into the First Keeper's Library, and I promised Gabe that you'd watch the shop and come get me if anything comes up.

Mal appeared on the edge of the cold marble counter in the shop's front room. "Got it."

"Thanks, Mal," Onnie gave him some scratches and snuggles. "Can you please, please, promise you'll stay outside the room, though?"

Mal rolled his eyes, "So, how am I supposed to tell you to come out?"

"Ah," Onnie said with glee, "come on. I solved that." She led the way to the back of the shop and into Abbot's study, where she grabbed a blanket on her way past the sofa and then walked to the door in the corner of the room. On the wall next to the door, at about waist height, was a bell with a long string that hung to an inch above the floor.

"I needed a way for Elaric to come to get me too since he can't see the door...."

"I can't tell if I should be offended by your blatant lie or honored you even bothered to try." Mal stretched his back and jumped onto the desk. "I know Elaric can see the door now that you've woven in his Bond, but I appreciate you thinking of me."

Onnie felt her cheeks flush at being caught red-handed. She had lied a bit. Before they'd bound Elaric's powers, she had planned on installing the bell for him and Mal, but she didn't get to it until it no longer mattered.

"Fine, caught me."

"It's fine. Now, get." Mal said before jumping down and heading back to the front of the shop. "I'll come check on you every hour, deal?"

"Thanks, Mal! Love you!" Onnie called over her shoulder as she pulled the door open with no small amount of effort and slipped inside.

When the door fully latched closed, the blue flames within the room slowed their dancing, and the room went nearly silent. Onnie headed for one of the most extensive tables in the room, draped her blanket over a chair, and set her notebook and thermos down, carefully avoiding any of the ancient papers, books, or notes.

She took a deep breath in through her nose and out through her mouth. Once with her eyes open and then again with them closed. When she opened them again, a newly familiar face stood before her.

It is good to see you again, Onnie, Kushima said with a warm smile.

"I will never get tired of seeing you standing in front of me," Onnie said as she approached the slender and porcelain-skinned woman.

Kushima wore a deep blue cloak, the hood up, obscuring most of her dark hair beneath it. Her cheeks were slightly rosy, and her eyes sparkled crystal blue, their subtle glow mixing with the flames in the room around them.

"Actually, are my eyes blue right now too?"

Indeed. Though it's been made more manageable and less exhausting, we're using quite a bit of power presently.

Onnie raised her hand, palm out, and Kushima mirrored the motion. They pressed their palms together, Onnie's corporeal and Kushima's projection passing through it. It had become their sort of greeting, and even though they could not feel one another, it still made Onnie feel like she was being hugged.

Kushima smiled, and they each took a chair at the table.

What would you like to discuss today, young one?

Onnie carefully unscrewed the cup cap of her thermos and poured herself some tea. The First Keeper's Library was always colder than she preferred, and even if she hadn't needed the Keeper's tea, she'd have brought something with her to take the edge off.

"Would you help me remove and store the souls in here safely? I'd also like to learn more about souls in general if you'd be willing."

My knowledge is your knowledge, Onnie. Kushima smiled, her perfect white teeth matching her pale skin as if she were more doll than human. *I also think it's time to remove the souls you carry. They will be safer here, and you will also feel better without them weighing you down.*

Onnie nodded in agreement. "You're right. The more of them I protect, the more difficult it is to hide them, and I worry the others will find out. On top of that, I don't want to harm the souls I do have."

Agreed.

"So, do you already have a way for us to store them in mind, or are we starting from zero?"

I have thoughts on the matter, but ultimately, how we proceed is your decision.

Onnie set her cup down and scowled. "Alright. I guess it's your turn for the lecture."

Kushima's eyes went slightly wide, and the corners of her lips curled up in the slightest smile.

"At least you don't call me Keeper, but please don't treat me like one either. I'm just Onnie. Your partner, not someone to be treated differently just because of some title."

Kushima sat with a stunned look on her face for a few heartbeats and then started laughing and clutching her side. Even though she was not a physical being, her projection responded like it would have when she was alive.

Alright, I understand and respect your wishes. It's amusing. I've heard you give that speech to others many times. Never did I expect to be on the receiving end of it one day.

"Eh, I hope that wasn't rude of me," Onnie flushed. "I may have forgotten for a second that you're the First Keeper. You probably deserve the pomp and circumstance more than I do."

Kushima stopped laughing and gave Onnie her own scolding glare.

Perhaps from others, but never from you. Let's agree that we are, indeed, partners. We speak our true thoughts without fear and always stay honest.

Onnie held her palm up in front of her a second time, and Kushima did the same, their greeting becoming a version of a pinky promise.

"I promise."

Kushima smiled again, her eyes glittering in the matching firelight. *Shall we get to work?*

"Let's," Onnie said, pulling her blanket around her shoulders and tucking herself in. "So, what were you thinking?"

Ah, Kushima said, pacing the empty area nearest their table. *I have never done this before, and neither has another Keeper in history, but I have no doubt you'll be fine. We'll be fine.*

"I'm sure we will be. We can do it. Together." Onnie smiled and sipped her tea.

Precisely. I think we follow your already perfected process and bury them in a Bond. However, instead of placing them in your Bond, we bind them to something in here. I'd suggest a few in each brazier.

Onnie sat forward, tapping her pointer finger on her chin. "I see where you're going. The fire burns so bright that even if someone looked closer at it, they'd pass right over them, assuming they were a flicker within the flame."

And if we split them up, checking in on them will be less exhausting— one smaller bundle at a time versus all at once.

"I like it. Will they be safe woven into something inanimate, though? I'm actively holding them within my Bond. Granted, it takes minimal effort, but still."

That's where I think I can assist. Look closer at that flame and tell me what you see.

Onnie cocked her head to the side. "Oh, alright."

She got to her feet and went to stand in front of the nearest brazier bowl. "Nothing with my eyes." She saw Kushima nod beside her, so Onnie closed her eyes and pulled at the Bonds around her. The blue flame's Bond flashed blindingly bright, the matching blue color filling her field of vision. She looked closer and just focused on watching the strands. After a few beats, she realized what she was supposed to see, pulled back out, and opened her eyes.

"Clever. It has a pulse."

It does. Fire is one of the elements that build the universe. It does not bleed but breathes, dies, and actively adapts to its surroundings. I believe if we set the correct conditions, the flames would aid us.

"I'm in. Let's do it," Onnie returned to her chair and sunk into her blanket.

I believe it would be wise for you to check in with Mal prior to retrieving them. You once told me you seem to lose time exploring that deep.

Onnie groaned, "You're right. I just don't want to get back up." She chuckled but dragged herself to her feet again and walked to the room's entry. Before she grasped the handle, she looked over her shoulder at Kushima. "Would you mind tucking yourself out of sight for a moment? Then we don't have to project you a second time."

Of course.

Kushima nodded, made her way to the same side of the room as the door hinge, and took a chair in the corner that situated her behind a few other pieces of furniture.

"Perfect," Onnie opened the door and stepped one foot to the other side of the door frame. She looked around for Mal and found the room empty.

Mal, I came out to warn you I'm going to meditate a bit, so this is my hour check-in.

Thanks, girl. I got you covered. I'll tell Gabe not to freak.

You rock.

I know. You owe me a sugar cookie.

It's yours. See you soon.

Onnie slipped back into the First Keeper's Library and firmly re-shut the door.

"Alright, I think we're settled. Ready?"

Kushima returned to her side and nodded with a smile.

Onnie was shaking and sweating, but thirteen souls sat on the table between her and the First Keeper.

"Wow, that never gets easier."

I'm sorry, Kushima frowned. *It's not something I can assist with.*

"No big. Knowing you were watching my body for me allowed me to focus more and worry less about being caught. It was a huge help." Onnie sat back in her chair and slumped over, her exhaustion pulling on her shoulders.

If you're sure.

"One hundred percent. Thank you," Onnie smiled wearily. "Give me one more minute, and we can start transferring them."

Take your time. You haven't been gone an hour yet, though perhaps you should check in before we begin again.

"Yup, not wrong." Onnie leaned back and closed her eyes for a minute. "I hate that I have to do this, Kushima. I don't want to hurt people."

I know, young one. We all do. Yet, nonetheless, you continue—a testament to your strength.

"Strength or stubbornness?" Onnie said with a grin to the ceiling.

Kushima chuckled. *Correct.*

After a minute, Onnie sat up straight and rubbed her eyes. "At the end of the day, it's better I do it than he does. If this is what needs to be done to protect them, I will continue to do it. I just wish, once, someone would choose the other path we offer."

Perhaps, one day, someone will.

"I hope so. It would be wonderful to help someone continue their life, not end it." With one last deep breath, Onnie stood and stretched her back. "Alright, let me check in with Mal, and we can get this wrapped up. Next time," she turned and looked at Kushima, "I'd like to talk more and play with souls less."

Kushima smiled, the corners of her eyes crinkling, *Agreed.*

"Okay, be right back," Onnie felt a sense of deja vu when she had nearly the identical conversation with Mal as she had the hour prior. She promised it would only take her one more hour, so now she had to hustle, but she wasn't sure she could keep Gabe out much longer. At some point, his concern and curiosity would win out, and he'd poke his head in to check on her.

As she approached Kushima, who stood with her arms in front of her, fingers delicately laced together, Onnie paused for a second. She tilted her head to the side, and squinted, making Kushima squirm.

"Um, Kushima…."

…*Yes?* She responded with hesitance and a slight pause in her voice.

"I didn't notice it until now, but…um, why do we look so alike?"

Onnie stepped closer and inspected the woman more intentionally. To her surprise, Kushima's eyes widened, and Onnie was confused about why she looked frightened.

"What are you hiding?" Kushima looked genuinely uncomfortable, and it made Onnie's stomach sink.

Kushima looked away. *Would you be angry if I said I'd like to have this discussion another time?*

Onnie hadn't expected that. She figured Kushima would tell her it was a coincidence, but her response nullified that. There was definitely a reason.

"…No, not angry. Will you promise to explain eventually, though?"

Kushima nodded but still hadn't looked back at Onnie.

"Alright." Onnie forced the concern from her mind and a smile to her face. "Shall we get these to their new homes?"

Yes, let's, Kushima replied and stood beside Onnie, in front of a copper bowl. *I don't think you'll need to do anything wildly different than you did when you held them. You must ensure they are exceptionally secure, as you won't feel it if they slip.*

"Understood," Onnie took a deep breath and squared her shoulders. "Ready?"

Yes.

"Got my back?" Onnie said with a genuine smile this time.

Always.

With a single nod, Onnie closed her eyes and began their task.

Chapter 20: A Way In

April 2022 - Alku | Onnie Moore

Onnie was sitting on the couch in her living room with her feet in Gabe's lap. She was exhausted from her day with Kushima, but she was also strangely energized. Without the thirteen souls tucked into her Bond, she felt less weighed down and more optimistic about their situation. She'd underestimated how much their darkness and corruption had affected her.

"Mal, any idea how many letters Grandfather sent out or who he sent them to?" she asked.

"I'm not exactly sure. I wasn't told any specifics," Mal said with a stretch as he lounged in front of the fireplace, "but I would guess about a dozen."

"The letters were all good things, Cat," Gabe added.

"You knew he sent them too?" she said, wiggling her toes until he rubbed them with his thumbs.

"Only after Elaric mentioned it. I asked Stephan if he got one. He did." Gabe sat forward and poured her a cup of tea from the china set on the ottoman. "Abbot just wanted to ensure his allegiances were passed to you and to his granddaughter."

"Oh," Onnie examined her fingernails.

She'd had so little time with her grandfather, and after the way her family had treated him in the past, it still slightly surprised her when she found instances of him caring for her as if their troubled past hadn't existed. Onnie wished she'd had more time with him, selfishly for her own reasons and to try to make up for her family's lost time.

Cat, where'd you go?

"Sorry, I was thinking about how lonely Abbot must have been, knowing he had an entire family only a few states away." She sighed, "and that they wanted nothing to do with him. Or knew nothing about him."

"It wasn't like that, Cat. He knew about you and your brothers. He and your grandmother talked a lot and were still close. When she passed, he did lose contact because your Mom rarely called, but he kept tabs on you as much as he could."

"I'm glad he and my grandmother kept in touch. She always felt a little lonely, too. Mom, my brothers, and I tried to help, but there's never a substitute for your first love."

"Sadly, no," Mal said between licking his paws.

"Cat," Gabe said, leaning towards her, "thank you for caring about Abbot even though you only knew him briefly."

He softly kissed her lips, and she leaned into him.

"Blegh, I'm outta here," Mal said before disappearing. *Call me when you're done with the lovey-dovey stuff.*

Onnie laughed, "Gabe?"

"Hmm?"

"We are going to be late for our date," she murmured against his lips.

"Shit. Call Dany and cancel," he smirked.

"Gabe!" Onnie chided and started to get up. Gabe pulled her back down to him and peppered her face with kisses. "We are not canceling on Elaric's last night with us," she gently pushed him away. "Come on, you fiend."

She got up from the couch and giggled the entire way to her bedroom.

"Get dressed, lover boy."

When she heard his grumbles about a man's needs, she shook her head as she walked further away.

Elaric Rickson

He, Dany, Onnie, and Gabe were walking through City Center Park after dinner. Dany held his right hand, and her other arm was woven around Onnie's left arm.

"We have to make sure your powers are rebound sufficiently," Dany whispered to Elaric.

"Of course, Dany, I trust Onnie. I'll be fine." Elaric beamed at the Keeper he'd grown rather fond of.

"You have my word, Dany," Onnie smiled. "Now, let's hit the shop for some tea and dessert."

"More tea, Cat?" Elaric heard Gabe whisper to Onnie, who merely shrugged him off.

He's only worried about you.

I know, Elaric, but he doesn't need to be. I have it under control. I simply like the flavor of Elanor's teas. That's all.

If you're sure, he nodded before smiling down at Dany. "Tea and dessert sound good to you?"

"Onnie made sugar cookies, so yeah, I am so in!" Dany skipped in her leather boots, and Elaric suddenly needed a cold shower more than caffeine and sugar.

"Then it's settled. Lead the way, you two," he said to Onnie and Gabe.

Gabe nodded and pulled Onnie from Dany's grasp, and they walked a few steps in front of him and Dany now that the road was too narrow for the four of them to stay shoulder to shoulder.

When they were far enough away, Elaric glanced at Dany. "What do you think of Onnie's tea habit? She seems to be drinking a lot of it recently, and if I'm not mistaken, she's drinking Rebecca's blend, isn't she?"

"Yeah, it's the Keeper's tea," Dany frowned. "I've told her a few times that I think she's drinking too much of it, but she either gets defensive or waves me off. Everyone sees it but her. You've seen her powers and what she's capable of. She's way beyond what Abbot could do."

"Does that have more to do with her being the One than the tea?"

Dany shrugged, "I have no idea."

"Has she asked the shop?"

"What do you mean...ask the shop? You mean Mal?"

"No, Dany, I mean the actual shop. When we were splitting my forms, the shop was talking with us. As in the First Keeper."

Dany stopped walking and crossed her arms before she frowned down at the floor. "That can't be possible, that shouldn't be possible." She shivered, and Elaric pulled his coat off and draped it over her shoulders.

"Why not?" Elaric gently pulled Dany back to walking as they were now much further behind Onnie and Gabe, who had continued to walk and talk. "Onnie is the First Keeper's descendant. If anyone could speak with her, it would be Onnie."

"I know, but," Dany shivered a second time. "Gods, why is it so freaking cold!"

We have company, Onnie said to their group plus Mal. *Act like you know nothing. Gabe and I will walk us to the forest behind the school.*

"Hey, Dany," Gabe shouted over his shoulder. "I forgot something in my office. Can we take a detour there before the shop?"

"It's the opposite direction, Gabe."

Gabe glared at her over his shoulder. "So? It's not far, or does that mean I need to up your training?"

Dany groaned. "Fine, fine."

Elaric smiled and pulled Dany to him. She stiffened before relaxing into his side. "You okay?"

"Yeah, nothing to do with you," she smiled weakly.

"Ah, okay then."

The four of them walked through the park, with only the sound of the light snow on the ground crunching beneath their shoes. A few people milled about in the dusk with them, but nothing like a big city would have. Alku was a quiet town in a small valley, and every time Elaric came to visit, he would eventually go stir-crazy and hit the road again. As more time passed, he became acutely aware of how he'd made the wrong choice. He pulled Dany closer and pressed a kiss to her temple. This time, he could see himself sticking around. Marco needed him, and he needed Dany.

"Onnie mentioned you were looking at real estate in Alku," Dany said, breaking the silence.

"I am. Abbot always wanted me to stay closer, and I always came up with an excuse for why I couldn't. I was thinking about that, actually," he smiled at her. "Alku used to stifle me. I knew every person, every shop, and all the trails. There was nothing new to explore. It was...quiet."

Dany snorted, "You must have been around in the good times then. Lately...well, you've seen it. It seems like we never catch a break."

Elaric snagged a flower from a cherry tree as they passed under it and tucked it into the clip in her hair. "I'm sorry if I sounded insensitive. That wasn't my intention."

"No, I know," Dany said with a soft smile. "You're right. When Alku is calm, it's...a bit suffocating."

Elaric snorted. "Abbot used to say that was what he liked about Alku. It would smother him in its calm, and he could just be. I used to think the man was crazy, but then I went back out and saw more of the world. Now, I think he may have been on to something."

"I've never lived outside of Alku."

"You're not missing much. The world is a wonderful place to visit, but it seems you have a great life here."

Dany nodded. "It's better now that Onnie is here. She thinks this town saved her, but she has no idea what it was like before she got here."

"Tell me about it?" he asked with unmasked curiosity.

"It was like Alku was a husk. Abbot was so sick, and everyone knew it, yet we could do nothing about it. We couldn't help him, and we couldn't survive without him. I remember meeting Onnie on the first day she came to Alku. I walked to the coffee shop before my shift and could feel the difference in the air. People smiled at one another on the street, waved when you passed their storefront and stopped to chat with neighbors. No one had done that for years. Everyone had walked through the days with their heads down, waiting for someone to come in while Abbot was weak and cause trouble for us. A weak Keeper is a vulnerability, and Abbot pushed Alku *extremely* close to destruction by waiting to call Onnie."

"I had no idea."

"No one outside of Alku did. You'd have to live and breathe this place every day to notice. No one said anything or did anything that would upset Abbot. He was our only protection, the shop's only protection, and, more importantly, our friend. We didn't want to hurt him by showing him how much he was hurting us."

"That's honorable, Dany, but I can't help but think there was some lasting damage done by not speaking up. Isn't that how Onnie has found herself in this situation in the first place?"

"You're right," Dany said as they crossed into the school grounds. "We should have spoken up. *I* should have."

"Now, you know that's not what I meant. It's not your burden to tell the wise old Keeper he was being thick."

"I know, but he was a father to Gabe and me. We should have said something. Then maybe Onnie would be safe. Maybe Alku would be safe."

Elaric stopped and held onto both of Dany's upper arms. He bent his knees and looked into her eyes.

"Stop that." He kissed her lips softly, and when he pulled back, he saw her passion simmering under the surface. "Come on. We've fallen pretty far behind now."

Dany looked up to where Onnie and Gabe were and giggled. "Oops, you're right. We'd better catch up."

Onnie Moore

Another one of his men? Onnie asked Gabe. "Dinner was great, thank you," she said out loud.

From what I can tell, yes. He's following along with us on the sidewalk outside the park and not being very stealthy about it. "You're welcome, Cat. I'm glad you enjoyed it." *Looks like Jakob is getting lax in his choice of minion.*

"I did, though I require a sugar cookie." Onnie smiled up at him. *Well, the man in black was one hell of an act to follow. He survived how many years?*

A dozen? Maybe more, but however he was made into a Link must have been too much effort to repeat. "Well then, let's get you to the shop. I need to swing past my office and grab my phone charger first."

"No problem," Onnie smiled. "I'm sure Dany and Elaric won't mind." *Should we lead him to the clearing or the shop?*

Less clean up in the clearing. "Very true," Gabe nodded.

We have company. Onnie said to both Mal and the group. *Act like you know nothing. Gabe and I will lead us to the forest behind the school.*

"Hey, Dany," Gabe shouted over his shoulder. "I forgot something in my office. Can we take a detour there before the shop?"

"It's the opposite direction, Gabe."

Gabe glared at her. "So? It's not far, or does that mean I need to up your training?"

Dany groaned, "Fine, fine."

Okay, let's lure him to the school, and we can use the yard if we have to. No one should be around this time of day. Gabe suggested to Onnie. "What color did you frost the cookies, Cat?"

I'd rather not play with souls around the townspeople, Gabe, she scolded. *We need to get him to the forest.* "A bunch of colors, nothing special."

"Sounds good," Gabe said with a nod. *Understood.* "What would you like to do tonight?"

"I don't know, cookies and a movie?" she said with a shrug.

"What did you have in mind?"

Gabe caressed her hand in his as they exited the park. The snow was heavier out of the trees, and the cobble streets were slick with ice.

"Watch your step, Cat."

"The snow is beautiful," she smiled with genuine joy. A light dusting of big flakes rested on every surface and glistened in the lamplight. "I'm still not used to the snow, but I do like it."

"I know you do. When this is all finished, we should spend some time in the mountains," Gabe said with a wistful look in his eye.

"Am I allowed to do that?"

"What do you mean?"

"Am I allowed to go on vacation? I know Abbot came to see me once, but other than that, he never left Alku, did he?"

Gabe turned somber, his frown visible even in the low light and from her lower perspective.

"No, he didn't. That was his choice, though. I think he stayed because he felt a sense of duty to Dany and me. He became our family after ours left. I don't think he wanted to chance it and leave us vulnerable in case Jakob came back and tried to turn us on Abbot."

"Can't imagine that would actually happen," she stated.

Gabe shook his head, "Of course not!"

Onnie slowed their walk as they approached the school grounds, allowing Elaric and Dany to catch up.

Are you ready? she said to everyone. *Mal, meet you in the clearing?*

Course, though, I want snuggles. It's cold.

We're ready, Elaric responded. *We'll follow your lead.*

Let's get this damn cockroach. I want my promised sugar cookies! Dany added.

"I have to run in and get my charger. Dany, come grab your planner. You left it on my desk the other day." Gabe said to his sister and offered her his arm.

Dany laughed as she passed Elaric his coat back and then took Gabe's arm. "Damn, I've been looking everywhere. Why didn't you tell me earlier, jerk."

"We'll wait here, Gabe," Onnie said, shaking her head at the pair. "Hurry up, I want cookies, too."

She and Elaric stood waiting for the siblings to slip around the corner of the gym and out of sight.

Once they were gone, she spoke again. *Go out the back and split up to cover the tree line. Elaric and I will feign boredom and take a trail.*

"Elaric, wanna walk? I'd like to learn more about you since you're interested in my best friend and all."

Onnie smirked at the transmogromorph who had settled into Alku and now used his real name and a single form. People were getting to know him as Elaric and old friends were happy he'd returned. Onnie, personally, liked him very much and was only teasing with her comment. As far as she was concerned, Dany had her blessing. Not that she needed it.

She gestured for him to follow her along a thin trail that headed directly from the back of the school into the forest that bordered it.

I knew I should have worn flats! Dany grumbled in frustration.

Onnie snorted and covered it with a cough into her elbow. As she and Elaric reached the edge of the forest, Onnie looked for Gabe's Bond and found him a few dozen yards down the tree line. She looked for Dany and found her the same distance in the other direction.

When she and Elaric entered the forest, a chill spread over her body, raising goosebumps under her coat and making her shiver.

He's close, she warned.

She looped her arm through Elaric's and used him for balance, closing her eyes and searching the nearby area for life. A few squirrels and some rabbits in their dens were the largest creatures she found until she saw the blood-red Bond pulsing off of a man hunched behind a tree further down the path from them.

She opened her eyes and spoke to the group. *Middle-aged man, one hundred paces down the path. I'd guess he's just another roach.*

"I haven't been in this forest yet," Elaric commented to keep their charade up. "It's beautiful, and the snow makes it feel even more magical."

"I love it. One of my favorite things in Alku is jogging in this forest. Gabe does, too." Onnie added with distraction in her voice.

We are nearly there. Elaric, let him attack me. He won't hurt me.

He stiffened beside her, but only a heartbeat later, he nodded with a subtle tilt of his head.

Elaric, you know about Wayward Clearing, right?

I do.

Good.

When they finally passed the tree the roach was using for cover, Onnie felt him following close behind them as they walked. She quickened her pace just a bit and led them to Wayward Clearing. When she and Elaric emerged into the ring of trees, she went and sat upon the large rock in the center and Elaric followed her. Both of their backs were to their assailant.

Onnie closed her eyes and smirked as she watched the man's Bond approach from the corner of her vision. He stepped hesitantly closer and closer. When she heard him raise his hands to grab the back of her coat, she grabbed his Bond and froze him in place while she chuckled.

"You've got to be kidding me," she stood and turned around to see the face of her would-be attacker. "You're going to have to try harder than that if you expect to catch me unaware."

What she could only describe as an evil man was caught in her hold. Not only were his eyes filled with hate, but he had the look of a cunning salesman who would scam a cancer patient from their medications.

She waved her hand dismissively. "Whatever. Now, it's my turn." Onnie circled the man slowly until she once again stood facing him. "Let's start with the obvious one. Who sent you?"

She didn't feel like playing games, so she unfroze the man's head.

Elaric came to stand beside her, his hands in his coat pockets, a calm nonchalance about him.

We are just outside, Cat. Gabe vouched for him and Dany.

I'm here too, just up, Mal said from atop one of the clearing's trees.

"You know who I work for, Keeper," the man sneered. A scar on his lip ran up to his eye and pulled when he spoke, giving him a distorted and haunted look, and it only added to her earlier judgment of him.

"The rogue guardian," she stated.

"He is rather fond of that title but prefers to go by Jakob. He knows how much your Guardian loves hearing that name." The man's head tried to turn to search the clearing for Gabe. "Where is the dear son of my Master?"

"Never far," she said, narrowing her gaze. "Next question. What do you want?"

"My my, you're rather boring, aren't you? Fine," the roach rolled his eyes. "I was to bring you back to my Master so he can rip your powers from you and keep them for himself."

"Finally! We are getting somewhere!" Dany said, entering the clearing. "Sorry, Onnie, I didn't want to miss the fun." Dany approached Elaric's flank and stood defensively at Onnie's back.

"What does he want with my powers?"

"Oh, I don't know, but I can hypothesize," he rolled his eyes again, and Onnie restrained her annoyance at his flippancy. "To rid the world of Keepers and their self righteous arrogance."

Onnie flipped her ring into her palm and, with her other hand, found the vial in her pocket.

"And you said we were boring?" Gabe said, entering the clearing and stopping behind the roach with a brooding expression.

"Oh, is that sonny boy? Hello Gabe, it's a shame your bed mate caught me. Daddy said hello and was looking forward to the reunion."

Gabe's anger and revulsion rolled off him in waves, and Onnie had to slam a wall down between their Bond, glaring at him once before refocusing her attention on the filth in front of her.

"Last question. Where is the rogue guardian?"

"To quote, 'never far,'" the roach said, and something flashed behind his eyes that Onnie couldn't quite place, but she'd seen it before. In the pawn from the night of the storm.

"Fine, you had your chance."

Onnie pulled the vial out and popped off the cap before downing it. Then she took two steps forward and gripped the man's neck, her fingers wrapping around to the top of his spine where his skull met with it, and then she ripped the soul from the man's body, his mumbling figure hitting the snow on his knees with a soft thud.

"I need a cookie," Onnie stated as she, with disgustingly practiced movements, hid the soul within her Bond while her friends were preoccupied.

We've got another to protect, she said to only Kushima.

I'm sorry.

They never choose the other path, Onnie said with a sigh.

Then she exited the clearing in the direction of the shop, not looking back.

The five friends sat in Abbot's study at the shop, with hot drinks and a plate of sugar cookies between them. Mal was switching between lapping cream from a small bowl on the hardwood beside Onnie and licking the frosting off a cookie she held for him.

"I'm so full, but you are too good to pass up," Dany said to the cookie in her hand with a laugh.

Gabe scoffed but took another bite of the one in his hand.

"What?!"

"It's just a cookie," Onnie smirked.

"Nope, pretty sure it's some rare Keeper power we never knew about," Dany grinned.

"Sounds like we may need more research materials," Mal said with a matching grin.

"Oy," Onnie rolled her eyes at the pair. "I really don't need some new super-Keeper power, thank you. I've got enough going on with all the other ones."

"I'm sorry you had to do that tonight, Keeper," Elaric murmured.

Onnie was about to scold him for calling her Keeper, but she saw him staring at the floor, his brow creased in discomfort.

"Now that I have seen it, I'm even more sure I need to do this. I will find a way in tomorrow, and we'll start this."

Mal burped, breaking the tension.

"Maldwyn, how rude!" Onnie said, pulling the furball into her lap and tickling his tummy.

"Hey!" he purred and squirmed. "I can't help it if your cookies are so tasty."

Dany laughed and got to her feet. "It's not the cookies, Mal. It's the cream." She stretched and yawned. "I'm out, guys. I need some sleep. I'll text you in the morning, Onnie."

Elaric stood too and collected his and Dany's cups. "I'll walk you home."

"Thanks," Dany smiled, and then she and Elaric headed out, leaving Onnie, Gabe, and Mal alone in the shop.

"Come here, Cat," Gabe said from the couch.

Onnie downed the rest of her lukewarm tea, stood, and stretched before snuggling up in her boyfriend's lap.

"Night, you two. See you at home," Mal said and disappeared.

"Smart cat," Gabe said with a chuckle. He tipped Onnie's chin up with his fingers and kissed her softly. "I think we should pick up where we left off. What about you?"

"It's like you can read my mind, Guardian," Onnie paused, "But ah…maybe we should do this at home."

Onnie thought of Kushima and heard a soft chuckle along their Bond, and then it warmed slightly.

Chapter 21: Letting Go

April 2022 - Alku | Elaric Rickson

Elaric stood in the front room of the bookshop in the downtrodden man's form he and the others had chosen for him. He was nervous and scared, but he had resolved to play his part, and he would.

"You have everything you need?" Onnie asked him. "You look perfect, by the way."

He laughed, his current form's voice as greasy as his hair. "I'm fine, Keeper. Thank you."

Onnie stepped up to him and rested her hand on his cheek. "Elaric, be safe. Don't do anything stupid, alright? Stay in contact and..." she grinned, "kick his ass, but save some for us."

He nodded once to her before looking at Gabe and Dany, who stood a few paces closer to the shop's door.

"I'll be fine, you two, don't worry."

"That's what they all say," Dany added before hugging him so tightly he was tempted not to let her go. After a minute, though, she sniffled and stepped back, and swapped with Gabe.

Gabe shook his hand and patted his back. "Keep in touch, man."

"Will do." He looked over his shoulder at Onnie. "Ready?"

"Yup, go for it."

Elaric pulled open the bookshop door and stepped out onto the sidewalk.

"Fine bitch, keep your fucking money." He tucked a ripped paper bag full of worn books further under his arm. "Someday, you'll pay for this!" He shouted and slammed the door as hard as he could, to the point where he legitimately lost his balance. He fell to his hands and knees in the sludge and cursed Onnie more.

"Wench and her high and mighty bodyguard. How dare they laugh at me."

He saw Elanor across the street giving him the stink eye, and he really hated acting like an ass to those he was friends with.

The man whose name was Harry, scowled, "What're you looking at, old woman?"

"You shouldn't speak to people that way, especially not Onnie."

The woman had always been vibrant and good to her core, and it seemed as if nothing had changed over the last few dozen years.

"What would you know about it? Mind your own business, and I'll mind mine."

He dragged himself from the floor and started the long hobble down the street toward the outskirts of town where he could call a taxi. It was good that his mind was in shape because this body was not. By the time he reached the road leading out of Alku and to the tunnel that led through the mountain, he was huffing and puffing like a lifelong smoker. Maybe he had been. He had no idea.

"Going somewhere?" a rough, feminine voice asked from the shadows of the tunnel behind him.

Elaric grinned while his back was still to her but quickly put his scowl back on his face.

"Who's there?" he asked into the dark as he spun around.

"Just a friend."

A young woman stepped from the shadows, no older than twenty. Her hair was stringy, her nails dirty, and from what he could tell, she hadn't had a bath in days. She looked gaunt and strung out, and it was difficult for him not to offer her help instead of asking for it himself.

"Or at least, I hope to be. The name's Gemini and I have a proposition for you, Mr...." she trailed off.

"Mr. Benson, but you can call me Harry." Elaric sidled up to the girl and gave her his best creeper look. "Tell me, Gemini, why do you want to be my friend?"

"Because I have a colleague who may be of use to you. I saw what happened outside that bitch's bookstore." The girl circled him, openly evaluating him. "She had no right to throw you out like that."

"Hell no she didn't, but what can you do about it?"

"Me? Nothing," she said dismissively.

"Then we're through here," he turned to walk away, and she jumped in front of his path.

"But my boss can help you get revenge on that Keeper bitch."

Bingo, we're in, Elaric said to Onnie.

"What's a Keeper?" he asked naively.

"Oh, you'll learn all about them and their guard dogs. Why don't you come with me and meet my boss? He can explain more."

"And if I say yes," he looked sideways at her.

"Then I take you straight to him, and you hear him out," she smirked, "and if you don't like what he has to say..." she shrugged, "then you can leave."

That was a bald-faced lie, he thought to himself, but he nodded to the roach. "Fine. Lead the way, Gemini."

She walked towards him and looked deeply into his eyes, and when something flickered behind them, he gulped, not acting for the first time since leaving the shop. A fire burned within them, and a darkness looked back at him that momentarily had him doubting their plan.

Jakob was pure evil, and Elaric finally realized what it meant to be walking into the lion's den, and Gabe had been right. Elaric was one prized hunk of meat.

Onnie Moore

Elaric hadn't been gone long, but the minute Dany couldn't hear his voice on the street through the window, she'd begun pacing in anxious circles.

"We shouldn't have let him go," Dany said, chewing on her thumbnail.

"Dany, it wasn't your choice. He chose to do this," Gabe said, walking over to pull Onnie into his side as he spoke.

"Stop it. I don't care if it was his choice. We shouldn't have let him talk us into this."

Dany sagged against the counter, her head into her hands, causing Onnie's heart to ache for her friend. She honestly didn't know what she'd do if she and Gabe were in that situation instead. If she were being honest, she'd probably have been just as distraught.

"Hey, Dany..." Onnie said delicately.

"What?" Dany groaned without lifting her head.

Onnie looked up at Gabe before squeezing his forearm, stepping away from him, and walking over to her friend.

"How about we get some coffee, something delicious from the Day Night Cafe, and then come back here and hit the books a bit? There are a few in the First Keeper's Library I want your opinion on."

Dany looked up and narrowed her eyes. "Are you trying to distract me with coffee and delicious pastries?"

Onnie laughed. "Partly, but the opinion part is also legit. The best thing we can do for Elaric now is to find something we *can* do and bring him home faster."

Dany rolled her eyes and looked at Gabe, who had crossed his arms and merely shrugged.

Mal yawned and stretched. "They're right, Dany."

"Ug," she groaned before rubbing her face three times and pushing away from the counter. "Alright, alright. You're not wrong. What about Elaric though, can't you not communicate along the Bond while you're in there?"

"We tested it. I can still feel him metaphorically poking me. I assume it's because I'm holding the rest of his Bond or something."

Dany nodded with a small frown, "Okay. Fine."

Gabe smiled at his sister as Onnie went to get her bag. "Gabe, could I ask you and Mal to watch the shop for a bit?"

"What's in it for me?" Mal said, appearing on Gabe's shoulder.

Gabe tipped to the side, unbalancing the feline, and Mal disappeared only to reappear on the front counter. "Brat."

Mal swiped the air with his claws in mock anger, "Jerk."

Onnie and Dany giggled at the two 'men' having a cat fight as they grabbed coats and bags.

"Behave, you two," Dany said.

"And, of course, we'll bring you something." Onnie stepped up on her tip-toes and kissed Gabe's cheek before following Dany down the center aisle and to the shop's front door. "We'll be back soon."

When Dany opened the door for them, a young couple, followed by two giggling teenage girls, entered the shop and passed by them. Onnie grinned at Dany.

Just keep going. They'll manage.

Consider your slippers forfeit, Mal retorted.

I'll pull them off the shelf for you when we get home, Gabe added.

Both women chuckled and quickly slipped outside and closed the door. Mrs. Radcliff waved to them from across the street, and Onnie smiled before she and Dany headed into the center of town and to A Shot in the Dark to grab a coffee first.

Onnie slipped her arm around Dany's and pulled her closer. "You know I'll do anything in my power to protect him, right? Hell, even if it's not in my power, I'll probably still do it."

Dany snorted and nodded, a small, sad smile playing on her lips as she gazed at the cobblestone street they walked on. "I know you will."

"That doesn't mean you can't still worry. It's allowed."

Dany's smile grew slightly wider. "He owes me a date, so he'd better come back."

Onnie raised an eyebrow at that. "Do tell...."

"It's nothing, really, and it's not even important," Dany said lightly.

"It is if you think it is, and you've obviously got it on your mind."

Dany didn't respond for a few minutes, and they quickly crossed the street and made their way to cut through City Center Park.

"I asked him to go see a movie with me. One of the ones the theater plays that are historical. Ya' know, black and white and all that."

"That sounds fun! Is he into movies?"

Even only knowing Elaric briefly, Onnie figured even if he weren't interested, he'd have taken Dany anyway, if that's what she wanted.

Dany giggled, "Well, they're showing a few films during the summer festival that are from the twenties."

"Yesh, really old. You weren't kidding." Onnie wasn't a film person, but she could appreciate the history and film making behind it all.

"Ah...yeah...Elaric saw them when they first released." Dany grinned, and Onnie's jaw dropped.

Sure, she knew Elaric was older than they were. It was literally in his genes, but she didn't often think about *how much* older he was since he often chose forms that were late twenties to mid-thirties.

"Oh snap. It's easy to forget, huh?"

"Yes and no," Dany said with a sly grin. "Sometimes he acts exactly as he looks, but occasionally, something will slip through, and I can't help but notice it."

"It sounds like you two are hitting it off, then. I'm glad."

Onnie smiled, pulled open the glass door into A Shot in the Dark, and held it open for Dany. They stepped into the medium-length line to order their drinks, and their conversation shifted to light and fluffy topics. After they'd ordered and waited for their coffee, they returned to the streets of Alku and made their way to the Day Night Cafe, a short distance away.

As they approached the cafe, a young man began waving his arms over his head at them with excessive amounts of vigor.

"Onnie! Dany!" Sam said with a low shout.

"Hey, Sam!" Dany said and waved in return.

When they reached the cafe's front, Sam hurried over and crushed them in one giant group hug.

"How you doing, Sam?" Onnie asked as he stepped back and held the door open for them.

"Nothing one way or the other, to be honest," the teenager replied, following them to the counter.

Lucky, Onnie thought to Dany, who hid her giggle behind her coffee.

"Picking up lunch?" Sam asked and stepped behind the counter to join the young woman also on shift.

"Yeah, that's the plan," Dany said, looking up at the menu.

"Why are you looking at the menu?" Onnie teased, "It's not like we don't know everything on it."

"Hey, you never know," Dany said, hip-bumping her, "one day, it could change."

"Actually…" the young woman behind the counter said softly. She was looking at her feet, and her ears were slightly red. "There is something new." Onnie saw the woman's eyes quickly flick to Sam, and then the color on her ears spread to her cheeks, too.

"She's right," Sam grinned. "Vanessa added a new sandwich. Tomatoes, mozzarella, basil, and balsamic. The best part is the bread she developed for it, though."

"Sounds delicious. What do you think?" Onnie asked the girl, startling her into a wide-eyed stare.

"M-me?"

"Course." she smiled, and Dany nodded along beside her. "Have you had it before?"

The young woman nodded shyly.

"Any good?" Dany asked.

"Mmhmm," the girl responded, but she grinned and nodded emphatically this time. "The bread is amazing."

She must have realized how excited she'd gotten, and her eyes quickly looked at Sam before she blushed again and went quiet.

Oh, take pity on her, Dany said to Onnie.

"One of those for me, then. Dany?" Onnie prompted.

With her order complete, Onnie left Dany to finish for the others and gestured for Sam to step aside with her.

"Yo, what's up?" he asked when they were out of earshot with the rest of the cafe's patrons and staff.

"You know about Elaric, right?"

Sam sighed and rolled his eyes. "Yeah. Marco filled me in. Stupid shifter. Was there no other way?"

Onnie frowned at Sam's use of the derogatory term for transmogromorphs. "Possibly, but this is what he chose to do, and after he promised to follow some of my conditions. I felt it was better that we were with him than for him to go alone."

"Suppose. He better come back, though. I don't want to have to clean up his mess."

Sam looked angry, and Onnie wasn't quite sure what had set him off.

"What's up?" she said as she sipped her coffee. "You seem...pissed off."

"I am. Elaric always does this. He runs off somewhere, leaves Marco and me here, and then I have to deal with the fallout. I swear if he—"

Onnie cut him off quickly, "Stop that."

"Stop what?"

"Please. I need you to stay positive. Sounds like Marco does, too." Onnie glanced at Dany. "Not to mention...."

Sam said nothing more after that, and when Dany joined them once she'd finished their order, he groaned. Then he mumbled, "Fine," under his breath, and went to assist the young woman with their order.

"What was that?" Dany asked Onnie in a whisper.

"Honestly?" Onnie rubbed her eyes, "I think he's acting like a teenager."

Dany snorted, "Like a real one?"

Onnie nodded, "Yeah, I think he's mad that Elaric left, and I'd guess he never talked to Sam about it."

Dany got quiet, and when Onnie looked over, Dany was staring at Sam, a slight frown on her lips and a crinkle in her brow.

"Yeah, I think you're right, but I can't blame him if that's the case. I mean...he's known Sam for a really long time, too."

"I wonder why he didn't mention it then," Onnie said. "It's Elaric, so he wasn't trying to be hurtful, there must have been a good reason."

"Yeah...." Dany agreed, her frown deepening.

Gabriel Vansand

Gabe watched as Onnie took the first bite of her sandwich, and her eyes widened.

"Oh, my god," she said through a mouthful as she inspected the bread.

"That good?" Dany asked, reaching over to pull a small piece off and shove it into her mouth before her face mimicked Onnie's.

Gabe couldn't help but laugh at the two of them and they both glared at him. When he opened his mouth to tease them, Onnie shoved her sandwich into it before he had the chance. He rolled his eyes and took a bite of the sandwich, and it took every ounce of his self-control not to make the same face they had. Instead, he kept a poker face and shrugged.

"It's fine."

He lied.

Onnie glared at him again and narrowed her eyes. *Can't fool me, jerk,* and she pushed along their Bond, proving she knew what he was genuinely thinking, or at least feeling.

He chuckled, "Fine, you're right."

He leaned over and tried to snag a second bite, but she quickly pulled her arm to the side and out of his reach. Mal chose that moment to appear, and his tiny cat mouth chomped down on it instead, and he ripped off a bite, dragging a slice of mozzarella out along with it as she reflexively pulled away.

"Hey!" Onnie whined, "My sandwich!" She bonked Mal on the head with the tip of her finger, but Mal kept chewing.

Gabe sighed, and when he looked up, Onnie was watching him, her head slightly cocked to the side. He forced a smile and took another bite, keeping his emotions calm and in check. Their eye contact was again broken when Mal tried swiping a piece of tomato from Onnie's sandwich.

"Oy!" Onnie scolded. "You have your own!" she pointed to the tuna sandwich that lay open on a paper plate on the ottoman.

"Yeah, but yours is better," he grinned and tried again to catch his quarry.

By now, Dany had finished her food and was leaning back in her chair, sipping her coffee and occasionally egging on either Mal or Onnie, depending on the situation.

"Instigator," Gabe said gently, poking her side.

"Hey!" Dany squirmed away with a giggle.

Gabe returned to his food, content in watching his family enjoy themselves.

"You good?" Dany said softly.

He glanced over to see his sister eyeing him warily. "Yeah. Why?"

Dany shrugged, "You don't seem okay."

"Just ready to be done with all of this crap."

Gabe saw Onnie's eyes flick over to meet his, and then she lowered them quickly. When she got to her feet and picked Mal up, he knew she and Dany had been talking about him along the Bond.

"Come on, Mal. I hate waiting for water to boil alone. Sit with me while I make tea." Onnie said, exiting the room, the cat in her arms.

Once she was out of earshot, Dany shifted in her chair to face him. "I don't like it either, Gabe, but it's reality."

"I know, but I want it over. Our family has done nothing but cause her grief for—"

"Ah, I misunderstood," Dany said, cutting him off.

When Gabe looked at her, he was both surprised and proud to see his sister's stone-faced expression. The one she wore when she was fighting.

"What?"

She shook her head, "You're still thinking of him as if he were our father, aren't you?"

Gabe flinched, "What?"

"When you think about what's happening with all this, how do you refer to him?"

"Ah," he looked into his lap, "you're...right."

"He's not our father, Gabe. If anyone was, it was Abbot. As far as I'm concerned, Jakob isn't even our blood. He's just a stranger. Horrid one, but a stranger."

Gabe sighed and rested his head back on the chair his father...no, Jakob, had given Abbot.

"You're right." He smirked at her, "Because, of course, you are."

She chuckled and shook her head. "I'm lucky. I have fewer memories. It's...easier for me."

Gabe reached over and took his sister's hand. "Thanks, Dany."

"No problem."

Hey, you two, I'm going to go across the street and see Elanor. Taking Mal with me, and we'll be right back.

We'll be here, Gabe replied.

"You doing okay?" he asked Dany.

"No," she answered quickly, and he nodded.

"Anything I can do?"

Dany was quiet for a second but eventually shook her head. "No, but thank you."

"You got it, sis. Tell me if that changes." Gabe said and ruffled her hair, earning him a throw pillow to the face.

It didn't matter. He'd take a thousand pillows to the face if it kept his sister smiling.

Chapter 22: Meeting the Rogue

April 2022 - Alku | Elaric Rickson

Elaric shivered as he entered a dank, heavy-feeling room. Lichen lined the walls, and moisture rolled down the ceiling to form puddles along the ground. There was an incessant dripping sound that, even after only a few minutes, made his skin crawl. The stone room looked to have been carved from the mountainside and not recently. He made a mental note to tell Onnie and the others about the rogue's base as soon as possible.

Harry followed behind Gemini, who continued to prattle on about something or other. He'd stopped listening, or at least Harry had. Elaric wasn't sure what helpful tidbit she'd let slip, so he kept one ear out for her and yet acted disinterested as Harry would. So far, she was a typical teenager, but hopefully, all her drivel would pay off.

"Wait here," she said, leaving him in a large stone room like the others they'd passed through.

Except this one had floor-to-ceiling windows on one side and an empty, large wooden table in the center. The room gave off a sense of dread, and Elaric would bet money the rusty brown puddles weren't from any metal objects.

Gemini left the room, going back the way they'd entered, and he was left alone to wander. He crossed the room to look out of the large windows and gasped as the mountains and valley around Alku came into view. He must be inside one of the tallest mountain range peaks that ringed the town. Now, he understood how the rogue knew all of their actions. He had been watching them for who knows how long.

"Do you like the view?" a deep voice said from behind him.

Elaric spun and came face to face with Dany and Gabe's father, Jakob—the rogue guardian. Elaric had met him a few times while he was still Abbot's Guardian, but that man and this one were nothing alike. The man wore long black robes, head hooded and arms tucked into his sleeves. Elaric couldn't see his face, but his intuition told him he didn't want to. With the newcomer in the room, the air now smelled slightly foul and rotten, and it had an unnaturalness that Elaric couldn't place.

"It's alright," he answered with as much boredom as he could muster. Harry wouldn't give a damn about a pretty view and would only be interested in the revenge part or the exchange of assistance.

"Not an outdoors man, I take it."

"Only if I have to be," Harry said with feigned disinterest.

"Pity."

The man turned his back on Harry and walked over to the wooden table, which now had a complete feast atop it. He had only been in the room a few minutes, and Elaric was positive he'd not heard anyone bring food in during the short time he'd had his back to the table.

"Can I interest you in something to eat?"

Elaric circled the table, keeping his eyes still on the robed man before him.

"Why?"

"Because we're friends, or we will be." The robed man inclined his head. "You must be hungry, you eat, and I'll talk. I'd like to explain why I want revenge on that entitled shop owner you met today."

Harry raised his hand, "I don't need to know your issue with the girl, just what you're going to do to help me get back at the bitch."

"You will need to understand my reasoning. It is imperative for the operation to succeed."

Elaric rolled Harry's eyes. "Whatever you say, boss. I'm here in your," he gestured around the room, "lair. You can tell me whatever you want."

"Gemini, would you join us?" the robbed man called slightly louder that his speaking volume.

The young girl came bouncing into the room, smiling. "Sure thing, what's up?"

"Please inform our guest of the history of Alku. I have other business to attend to."

With that, Jakob left the room as quickly as he'd entered.

"What was that all about?" Harry asked. "One minute, he was going to tell me his grand master plan. The next he's gone?"

"Oh, something came up with the Keeper, I bet. I'll tell you all a bout her. I am the Master's favorite and know the whole story."

Elaric quickly brushed his Bond with Onnie and sent her a warning. He had no idea what was happening, but it couldn't be good. He had a feeling the rogue wanted to vet his new minion, and if he was leaving in the middle of the process, Onnie was in for something.

"So, her magic is evil, and the Master wants to steal it so she can't hurt Alku anymore," Gemini prattled on.

"Wait, what?" Elaric asked, realizing the girl had been talking to him.

"Yeah, there's real magic." Gemini looked smug and proud that she knew something he didn't.

"But you said this Keeper was evil?"

"Oh yeah," she drawled, reached for a strawberry on the table, and popped it into her mouth to chew loudly. "Super evil. She hoards all these books about magic, keeps them for herself, and doesn't let other people learn stuff."

Elaric snorted, "Sounds like a real tyrant."

"She is. You've met her." Gemini grabbed a finger sandwich and took a large bite out of it.

Elaric forced himself not to laugh at the absurdity of the entire situation. The Keeper was hoarding magic, a Guardian truly turned rogue, and somehow that guardian had powers that shouldn't be possible. He was going to 'free' said magic, and none of this seemed odd or out of place to the Outsider sitting across the magic feast from him. They knew their foe was powerful, but the level they expected was nowhere near reality. He needed to find something they could use and get out. Fast.

Elaric refocused on the food before him and watched the young woman skeptically. She ate with gusto, and considering how thin she was, the food she was consuming was either not as it seemed or simply a rarity for her to be granted.

"Did you bring this food here?"

Gemini shook her head, still chewing on a dinner roll. "Nope. Master did."

Harry narrowed his eyes at her and then the plate of fresh fruit and vegetables in front of him. He reached out and poked a grape. It felt real, and Elaric wasn't sure what he'd expected the grape to do, but it didn't matter.

"Have some," Gemini said with a mouthful and pointed to a plate of cheese and tomatoes.

Harry nodded slowly but reached for the plate of food. "So, how can I fit in with all of this?" He shoved a grape tomato between his teeth, its juice spattering down his greasy chin.

Gemini shifted to reach across the table to grab another piece of food, and Elaric caught sight of multiple minor puncture marks behind her neck, no doubt where her regular fix was administered. He wondered if she was even aware of the drugs or injections at all. Perhaps she didn't suspect the rogue was drugging her. After hearing her devotion to Jakob, be it magically enhanced or authentic, it was unlikely that she would have protested whatever he wanted.

"Master can't go into town. Too many people know him. He used to live there or something." Gemini rolled her eyes. "I have no idea why anyone would want to live in a dump like that place, but whatever."

"So, I'm his gopher?"

Gemini shrugged, "Doubt it. We're not really allowed to go into town that often."

"Allowed?"

She nodded, "Yeah, we don't want anyone to know we are here, duh. What if they followed us back or something?"

Elaric wanted to bash his head against the table in front of him. This girl was impossible to talk to, and he was getting nowhere.

"What about the others. You said you were his favorite. Are there more people helping him?"

She nodded, "A few, but all of them are out of Alku right now."

"Why would they be outside of Alku if his goal is the woman at the bookshop?"

She shrugged and took another bite.

"When will your master return?"

Gemini laughed at him. "He's your master too now, silly," she grinned and then looked over his shoulder.

Elaric didn't need to turn around to know that Jakob was once again behind him. The foul smell on the air had returned, and the hairs on the back of Harry's neck stood on end. Carefully, Harry rotated on his stool, looked up at the dark hooded figure, and smiled.

"That he is. Welcome back…Master."

Elaric choked down the bile and single tomato he'd eaten and plastered the sleaziest smirk he could manage on his face while simultaneously thanking whoever was listening that he was as old and practiced with acting as he was.

"Gemini has told you of our goal, then?" the rogue asked.

Elaric saw that the hood of his cloak had not rippled with his exhale. When he looked closer, none of the fabric had moved.

"She has," Harry looked over at the girl for a moment before back at the man he now served. "How can I help?"

The rogue was silent momentarily before he strode to the window overlooking Alku and shifted to tuck his hands into his sleeves behind his back.

"Are you afraid to die?"

Harry mulled over the question, then answered. "No, but I would like to do a few things before I kick the bucket. Would be a shame not to get to. There are a few people I'd like to...."

"Kill," the rogue stated.

"Make bleed. Death would be lenient."

Elaric watched the posture of the two others in the room, and while Gemini was highly focused on the rare feast still, the rogue had resumed his statuesque stillness.

"Understood," Jakob said after a moment. "I need spies. I want to know where she is, what she's doing, and who is with her at all times."

"Want me to tail the broad? I can do that. But what's in it for me? After we take care of the bitch bookseller, I'd like to pay my ex-wife a visit."

While Jakob was silent, Elaric took the moment of quiet and let his eyes map the room. The door where the rogue had disappeared through earlier was now open just a crack, and when Elaric looked at it, he couldn't suppress a shiver. He had no idea what was behind that door, but he knew one thing. If he went into that room, he'd likely never walk out of it again.

Harry looked back at the rogue's cloaked figure, and Elaric was sure the man was watching him in the glass's reflection.

Eventually, the rogue's hooded head nodded once. "Good. Let's begin."

Onnie Moore

"Hi, Elanor," Onnie said, entering the small florist across the street from the bookshop. "I just stopped by for some more tea if you have it."

The older woman smiled as she looked up from the large vase in which she was arranging flowers.

"Hello, Keeper," she responded warmly. "I have a bit left, but until some of mine and Yvonne's herbs re-grow, I'm afraid I won't be able to make more." The nymph stuck one last rose into the center bunch of flowers and dusted off her hands. "Let me get it from the back. Give me one second, dear."

While she hurried off, Onnie perused the shop and stopped to smell various plants as she passed them. There was lavender growing by the front door in a large pot, and a few long, low, rectangular pots were terraced up with some wooden supports, each with a different color pansy, mum, daisy, or other smaller flower within them.

"I love coming in here," Onnie said to Mal, who was sniffing a pot of hydrangeas.

"Me too. I come sit with her a lot."

"Good," Onnie smiled down at him. "I'm sure she likes that."

Mal nodded and returned to his sniffing and Onnie to her wandering.

A few decorative pots with ivy, pothos, and other house plants were tucked between larger brethren. Elanor's shop always smelled heavenly. A cross between the forest bordering Alku and a field of the most fragrant flowers. Even though a large portion of the flowers she grew to sell were in her fields at home and Onnie had never seen them, Elanor's magic was a particular type of wonder, and Onnie adored learning more about it and the older woman who had grown into such a friend.

"Alright, young lady," Elanor said, returning to the front of the shop with two mason jars filled with tea. "You've run me dry, and I know you won't want a lecture, but..." she passed the jars to Onnie with a frown. "Do be careful. You're drinking it awfully fast."

Onnie slipped the jars into her shoulder bag and clasped the old woman's gnarled hands in her own.

"Elanor, thank you. Both for caring enough to make the tea and for warning me of the dangers. I promise I will only use as much as needed to overcome the threat we're facing, and then I will reduce my intake. Is that a fair agreement?"

"Fair has nothing to do with it, Onnie, but it'll do." The old woman stood on her tip-toes and kissed Onnie's cheek. "Take care, my dear."

"I will. Thank you." Onnie smiled and made her exit, Mal waving his paw at Elanor before following behind Onnie.

Once back on the street, she carefully checked on Gabe and Dany, both of them safe at the shop. She was about to check on Elaric when she felt him brush against their Bond first, and a sense of warning came over her.

She pulled away from him, shut her eyes, and opened her mind to the Bonds around her and was instantly overwhelmed by the amount of them. She flinched and dimmed them again before opening her eyes.

Prior to the Transference, she had only been strong enough to see Bonds with intense focus and even then, there weren't very many. After the Transference with her increased power and control, she was starting to see more with less effort, and viewing every Bond in Alku on a busy Saturday was not a smart move on her part.

"Do you have a headache, Keeper?" a voice said beside her.

Onnie relocated her bag to the shop before she spun, a roundhouse kick flying up to assault the man who'd invaded her space. A split second before she struck him, she saw the stranger was robed, and she slammed her mental walls up, stopping her kick and landing in a defensive stance. Gabe instantly pushed at her mental defenses, and Mal appeared at her feet.

"Jakob, I take it," Mal said to no one in particular.

"In a past life," the robed man responded. His arms were tucked into his sleeves, and his hood entirely obscured his face.

Onnie quickly shifted only her eyes to scan the street around them, and she was thankful that there were no townsfolk around. She needed to focus solely on what was before her, not the well-being and safety of innocent bystanders. The fraction of a second before Onnie looked back at the rogue guardian, she noticed Elanor had her face pressed against the glass window of her shop, staring out, but frozen in place.

Mal, Onnie projected along their Bond. *He's frozen everyone. What power is this?*

Keeper, he's done nothing.

Onnie's stomach sank, and she felt genuine fear for a fraction of a second, but it was not of the rogue.

"You are more powerful than I ever imagined for one so young and so naive. Yet, for one with so much power to have so little control over it. To not even know that you are using said powers..." he tsked. "Such a disgrace, and why I must take them from you. It's for your own good and for the good of humanity that no one being shall ever have that much power again."

"Sure, you can try and take my power. I'll even say that I'd be intrigued to see what you did with it, but either way, it will never happen." Onnie smirked, "But do feel free to tell me the rest of your plans before you leave. I love an evil monologue."

"My, my," he said as he stood, still motionless, as he mocked her. "You are your grandfather's blood."

"Then you should know I won't relinquish my powers without a fight."

The rogue seemed to chuckle, but the sound made her skin crawl.

"I would have expected nothing less from the *One.*"

Onnie felt him capitalize the last word as he said it, and a deep sense of foreboding washed over her.

What is he talking about? Onnie asked Mal.

When she didn't react, the robed man began to pace in a small circle around her and Mal. His clothing made no sound, and his hood never slipped.

"Oh, she doesn't know?" he said to Mal, "but Link, you would surely not keep something of this importance from your Keeper. And her Guardian, he must know as well, along with that worthless sibling of his."

"What is he talking about, Mal?" Onnie said through clenched teeth.

We will talk about it later, Onnie. Now's not the time.

"Oh yes, enlighten her," the man mocked more. "Tell your little Keeper how she's the most powerful Keeper since the first."

"Jakob, stop this," Mal said, spitting.

"Tell her how she's a direct descendant of the first Keeper." He had completed his circle around her and Mal now, his mocking working its way under her skin.

"STOP THIS!" Mal shouted.

"How she will bring about the fall of the magic!"

"BE GONE!"

Mal jumped at the former Guardian, and Onnie, though confused, attacked in tandem, trusting her friend's actions. Before either of them could make contact with the robed figure, he disappeared, his laughter still ringing in her ears.

Chapter 23: Fallout

April 2022 - Alku | Onnie Moore

Gabe and Mal were seated on the living room couch, looking extremely nervous as their eyes flicked toward the front door and pretty much anywhere but at Onnie. At least they knew they were in trouble.

"Explain," Onnie said with her fists on her hips. "And I expect it to be the *full* explanation."

After the rogue guardian disappeared, Onnie barely warned Mal and Gabe before she ripped them from where they stood and relocated them and herself to the house. She wasn't sure what she was about to hear, but whatever it was, she knew it wouldn't be good.

Onnie, try—

I will talk to you later, Kushima. I have a feeling we will want privacy and a longer amount of time. However, don't think I'm not angry at you, too.

Understood.

"What do you want to know, Cat?" Gabe asked in the overly calm voice he used on his students when they were on the edge of a breakdown.

"How about all of it?" Onnie threw up her hands. "What the hell was he talking about? What did he mean by the 'One' and the fall of the magic? On top of that, what do I have to do with it?"

Mal shifted his weight between his front paws on the couch cushion. "Onnie, you have to understand—"

"Understand!?" Onnie cut him off, her voice a shrill shriek. "How can I understand what I *don't know about?*"

Gabe and Mal's eyes went wide as Gabe paled and Mal's tail fluffed in response to her wild anger.

"Cat, please sit down, and we'll explain."

"If I sit down, you'll tell me everything," Onnie informed them before plopping in a wing back chair opposite their couch. "Fine. Start." She crossed her arms in front of her chest and shut her mouth.

Gabe cleared his throat. "There's a prophecy. It's ancient."

"What does it say?"

Mal nodded. "With the coming of the final Keeper, the First shall be reborn. Of power unnatural and Bonds unbreakable, endless shall be their vigilance."

"For fucks sake," Onnie groaned and rubbed her eyes. "That can't be it. What's the rest of it?"

"When surrounded by devoted and carrying the willing, the magic of all shall be stolen. Under heavens of blood or heavens of ice, the strength of the One shall unleash it." Gabe finished for Mal.

"Right," Onnie leaned forward with her elbows on her knees. "Let me repeat that. A descendant of the First Keeper will be extremely powerful and either decide if the world is fucked or if all is hunky-dory and still breathing when everything is all over?"

Gabe smirked, and Mal nodded in agreement before speaking. "Pretty much, though the prophets may have phrased it a bit less terrifyingly."

Onnie glared at the feline, and she heard him gulp.

"At least that's my opinion," he said, becoming suddenly very interested in one of his paws.

"My apologies, I'm not in a Shakespearean mood right now." Onnie stood up and paced in front of her chair once, twice, and then sat back down. "Where did this prophecy come from?"

"Dany would know the specifics better than I—" Gabe started to explain, but Onnie held up her hand to stop him.

"Of course, she knew about this too. Am I the *only* person who had no idea?"

She felt her emotional control slip and ripple through her Bond and wasn't surprised to see Gabe and Mal wince. A part of her felt bad, and she hated hurting them, but right then, she was struggling to have any sympathy. She took a deep breath and calmed down her emotions, and instead of inflicting them on the pair, she locked them out completely. When she felt Gabe metaphorically tap on one of the walls she'd raised, she strengthened it until she couldn't feel his presence in the slightest.

"Cat, don't do that." Gabe's frown was pitiful, but she didn't care.

"Don't what? Keep things from you?" She rolled her eyes. "Hypocrite."

Gabe's eyes flashed blue, and he got to his feet. "Alright, enough!" He towered over her, his face a mix of pain and anger. "Yes, we kept this from you. What were we supposed to do?"

Onnie stood and mimicked his position, their bodies leaning over the tea set on the ottoman, faces a foot apart.

"How about trust me! We're supposed to be a team! *ALL OF US!*"

The last sentence she said aloud and mentally directed at Kushima, who'd been listening.

"Onnie," Mal said calmly, almost monotone from his place on the couch. "Partners trust each other, and sometimes that trust means trusting them when they do something you don't like. Like protecting you."

She locked eyes with the feline, and for a few seconds, they just stared at each other, but then she stepped back, her heart racing and hands shaking from all the adrenaline running through her body.

"Fine," she took another deep breath and returned to her chair.

After another minute, Gabe sat back down and crossed his arms before looking away from her. The three of them sat silently and calmed down. When she felt more in control, Onnie stood up and went to the kitchen. She pulled out her favorite tea cup and began making a pot of Keeper's tea, tempted to make it strong enough to peel paint just to spite everyone.

What do you have to say? Onnie asked Kushima now that they could focus on each other more.

Nothing that hasn't already been said.

So, you also think I'm too weak to know the truth.

Absolutely not!

Onnie could sense Kushima's frustration down their Bond as Onnie had only blocked out Gabe and Mal. Kushima sighed, and Onnie could picture her pained expression.

It has nothing to do with your strength. You can even use the Prophecy as proof if you don't believe me. You're the most powerful Keeper ever to exist. Or, you will be. You're still growing and learning.

Magic power has nothing to do with the power of understanding. You honestly don't think I could have mentally taken being told the truth?

Kushima was silent, and Onnie had her answer, which ripped through her like a thousand pieces of shrapnel.

She focused on brewing her tea, closed her eyes, and took in the wonder of the Bonds around her in the kitchen. No other Keeper had ever seen the Bond in the way she could. They'd never teleported people or things. They'd never ripped souls from human bodies, and they never had to grow themselves at the pace she had and still needed to do. They were all passive. Even the few Warrior Keepers that had existed. None of them did more than settle a few disputes or use their powers to defend the people they were charged with. Not one of them had to go on the offensive like she needed to.

Am I still not good enough... will I ever be?

You were good enough the day you began your Transference, Onnie. You still are. You're the Keeper of Prophecy. You're my flesh and blood. Nothing you could do would make you incapable or unworthy.

But that's a lie. She pulled on a few Bonds within the kitchen, objects shifting and moving in response. *You cannot believe only half of a prophecy. You're ignoring the part where I'm unnatural and the skies of blood.*

Kushima was quiet for a second, but her voice was firm and direct when she finally spoke again.

You will not. One interpretation of the Prophecy, the one I believe in, is that depending on the outcome, either good or evil will reign. You need only look around to see which future you will usher in. Having seen your interactions with the people you care about, even those who wish you harm, I am confident you will help positively shape the future. Just think, if you could ask the fourteen souls you have provided sanctuary, I'd wager they would say the same. Even when they were initially your enemy.

This is why you wouldn't answer my question of why we look alike.

Yes.

You had the perfect opportunity to tell me everything, why didn't you?

It wasn't something I felt I could tell you on my own. Mal, Gabe, Dany, and Abbot all chose to keep it from you. I couldn't go against their wishes.

You promised. We promised.

I know.

Kushima's voice was filled with genuine agony, and Onnie didn't feel like being angry at her any longer. She was already angry at too many people.

Onnie saw Gabe enter the kitchen with Mal on his shoulder. Their Bonds pulsed as Gabe tried, once more, to reach her. She opened her eyes but didn't look at him, instead choosing to watch the steam rise from the kettle's spout.

"Cat?" He said softly, more timid and careful than she'd ever heard him before.

"I can't even stand to look at you right now," she said in a calm and measured tone. "Just go out for a while. Both of you."

"Cat, don't be like that—" Gabe said, taking a step forward.

"No," Onnie said sharply. "I might want to talk to you later, but right now, go to Dany's or something and just leave me alone."

Onnie poured her tea with her back turned on two of her best friends. Her Guardian and her Link.

After a few minutes, she heard the front door close and sighed. She walked to the freezer, pulled out a frozen pasta dish, and stuck it in the oven while she drank some of her tea. She quickly checked her Bond with Elaric and found him safe, so she pulled out her cell phone and called her mom. After the first ring, Tory picked up.

"He called you," Onnie stated.

"Nope, but he did text. Tell me, what has you so upset you're not talking to Gabe and Mal."

"I found out they'd been hiding a huge secret about me. What's worse is I found out from the big bad evil dude we are supposed to be stopping." She sighed, slumped into the bar stool, and put her head on the counter.

"Okay, start at the beginning. You told me there was some guy after you, so I couldn't come in for the funeral. What aren't you telling me?"

Onnie winced at the worry in her mother's voice. "This is why I didn't want to tell you. I didn't want you to worry."

"Connie Moore, I am your mother. It is my job to worry about you, *especially* if some freak is trying to hurt you!" her mom scolded loudly.

"I know. I'm sorry. Can I start over, and I'll tell you the whole story?"

"Yes. You better. Lewis," her mom shouted away from the phone, "get in here. You're going to need to hear this."

Onnie rolled her eyes and sighed. "Tell me when you're ready, and I will start from the beginning."

Two hours later, Mal reappeared on the kitchen counter, his head down, his paw holding a white bit of fabric.

"Maldwyn, I am still so mad with you I could—"

"Keeper," he cut her off. "I am here as your Link. You still need protection. I will go lay in the library and leave you alone, but stop acting like a child." With that, he disappeared again.

"Was that little Mal?" her mom asked over the phone as Onnie swirled her fork in her now cold pasta.

"Mom, he's an omnipotent representation of an entity that's existed for thousands of years. He's not a 'little' being," Onnie scoffed.

"Stop that sass, missy. He's a cute and fluffy cat to me," her mom teased. "Just because you're some hot-shot Keeper who will save the world, doesn't mean I can't come there and kick your butt."

"Sorry, Mom, today just sucked," Onnie said, chewing and setting her fork down into her now-finished oven pan. "I think I am going to nap for a bit. I'm tired of being the Keeper of Prophecy everyone is counting on. I want to be nobody for an hour."

"Oh honey, they aren't counting on you because you're the Keeper. They're doing it because you're you. Take a nap, and you'll feel better. I love you."

"I love you too, Mom, and you too, Lewis."

"Love you, kiddo," her stepdad answered.

"Call me later," Tory said in parting. "Bye."

"Bye."

Onnie left her dinner mess where it was and refilled her teacup, taking it and the pot with her into the living room. She put both on the coffee table and lit the fireplace. Then, she grabbed her quilt and snuggled up on the couch, tea in hand, shivering from the cold and dread seeping into her bones.

"Mal, I am so mad at you and Gabe," she whispered into the empty room.

Mal appeared on the couch by her feet and bowed his head.

"I know, Onnie, but you have to know we have your back. We didn't want to overwhelm you all at once." Mal slowly walked closer to her from the other end of the couch. "With Abbot's death and then the shop being trashed, and then the roaches and Jakob, it's not like we've had a ton of time to tell you or to add any more stress onto you."

"But you should have told me either way. I had a right to know.

Gabe knew how angry I was when I found out everyone knew I was the Keeper before I did."

"Do you think maybe that's why he didn't want to tell you?"

Mal nudged her teacup with his paw. She tipped it down so he could take a sip, and he hissed.

"Onnie, what did you do?"

"What do you mean?" Onnie said before sipping the tea. "It tastes fine."

"Onnie, how much are you brewing? That tea is way too strong."

Mal jumped to the ottoman and poked his nose into the teapot, his whiskers disappearing into the depths. When he pulled his head out, his whiskers popped out and splattered the deep crimson liquid across the room. A few droplets hit the fire, roaring to life with brilliant blue flames.

"Keeper," Mal said formally, "you are brewing this way too strong."

Onnie drained her glass defiantly and then refilled it, all while she glared at him.

"I think it tastes good this way. I like it stronger."

"You're not just increasing the taste. You're increasing the magic. You need to be careful. I'll get Dany to come over. I think she can help."

"I'm not a child, Mal," Onnie said, standing and shrugging off her blanket. "Stop treating me like one and start treating me like your Keeper."

Mal hissed, "Start acting like one, then!"

Onnie picked up the feline and tossed him to the floor.

"Go sleep somewhere else. I'm taking a nap."

With that, she sat back down, rolled herself up in her blanket facing the back of the couch, and closed her eyes.

Gabriel Vansand

"The flames turned blue?" Elanor said to Mal. "Oh, that's very not good. She's brewing it way too strong."

"I know, Elanor, but what can I do? She's shut me out." Mal gestured to Dany and Gabe, too. "She's shut all of us out."

Gabe stood with his back leaning against the florist's door frame, arms crossed and a scowl on his face. "Elanor, she's out of control. You said it yourself. She practically stopped time this morning and had no idea. She shouldn't be able to do that."

"Especially without meaning to," Dany added. Her hair was bright purple today, with silver streaks running through it, and it suited her entirely black outfit with combat boots. "If she's already this powerful and can't control it...."

"Cat needs an intervention. She has no idea how reliant we can become on that tea if it's used irresponsibly."

"Gabe, man, you didn't see her. The shade of blue her eyes flashed when I confronted her," Mal shivered. "Pure ice man."

"She can't be acting alone," Dany added, "and at the worst possible time. Has she even mentioned Elaric?"

"Is that all you care about?" Gabe hissed, "Your boyfriend?"

"How dare you!" Dany shouted at him. "Of course not. I love Onnie, but she's not just my friend. She's also my Keeper, and one of *her* friends is putting himself in danger for her, and I want to know how he's doing."

"Doesn't feel like you care."

"Dude," Mal scolded, "you know that's not true, not to mention harsh."

"And unfair," Dany added. "Whatever, I'm done here."

Dany picked up her purse, kissed Elanor on the cheek, and left the shop, not bothering to look at him on her way out.

"What the hell, man?"

"What?" Gabe shrugged. "I only said what everyone was thinking."

"No, young man," Elanor frowned and shook her head. "You most certainly did not."

With that, one of the women Gabe considered family left the front room of the shop, angry at him, just like his sister.

"I'm going to the shop," Mal said before relocating, leaving Gabe by himself.

"And now I'm the bad guy," Gabe scoffed, "and I can't even go home."

He pushed open the flower shop's door and stepped out into the dewy evening air. He stuck his hands in his pockets and went to City Center Park in the direction of his office at the school. It was too cold to go for a run, but he could get a workout in and maybe blow off some steam.

It had only been a few minutes into his walk that Gabe knew he was being followed by someone within the trees. He pressed along his Bond with Onnie and still found nothing but a solid wall. It wasn't as if he couldn't handle whatever the threat was himself, so he pulled his hands free from his pockets in case he needed to react quickly and let whoever was following him continue to do so as he walked to the school.

When he reached the door, he unlocked the front entrance to the gym and didn't bother locking it once he was inside. Instead, he jumped onto a stack of workout mats and swung up to a girder above the door, where he crouched and waited. Sure enough, the gym doors squeaked open after just a minute, and a man entered the dark interior. Once the door was shut and the man was a few paces in, Gabe dropped from the support beam behind the stranger and put him into a headlock.

"Who are you, and what do you want?"

"Dude, it's me," Elaric said with Harry's voice.

Gabe immediately dropped his hold and stepped back, his hands raised. "I'm sorry, man, I didn't know it was you."

"I told Onnie I was coming to see you," Elaric said with a wrinkled brow.

Gabe sighed. "She's not speaking to me. Come on, I need a drink."

Elaric followed behind as Gabe led the way to his office, unlocked the door, then his filing cabinet, and retrieved a bottle of scotch and two glasses.

"Want one?"

"Sure. Tell me why the Keeper and her Guardian are on the outs?" Elaric said, lowering his life-weary body into one of Gabe's life-weary office chairs.

"It's not just me. She's not speaking to Dany or Mal either."

Elaric whistled. "Damn, what happened? I've only been gone a day."

"Your new boss happened. He made a guest appearance at Elanor's and told the Keeper she's the Keeper of Prophecy."

"She didn't know?" Elaric said with wide eyes.

Gabe downed the shot and a half in his glass and shook his head. "Nope."

"Abbot never told her?" Elaric asked before he took a swig of his drink but quickly swallowed. "Wait, *you* never told her?"

Gabe slumped forward in his chair and rubbed his eyes. "No. I thought I was doing the right thing. She's had so much change so quickly, and I thought she deserved to settle in a little more before we brought it up."

"Gabe, my man, you're her Guardian and her boyfriend, she's not your ward. That wasn't your call to make."

"Yeah, well, then I pissed off Dany and Mal. So, now we are all spread out, and you're here, sneaking up on me, so obviously, something is going on. I can't help but think dear old dad did this on purpose."

"That's what I came to tell you," Elaric downed his drink and poured them both a second glass. "I met Daddy dearest today, and dude, is he a piece of work."

"I can imagine. What happened?"

"Well, Mr. Dark and Moody has a minion, his favorite apparently," Elaric rolled his eyes. "Gemini. She's a twenty-something chick who needs a bath and a stable home, but she's with him instead for some reason. She has this crazy idea that the rogue wants to steal Onnie's powers and share them with the world because the 'tyrant Keeper' is hoarding all of it for herself."

"That's absurd," Gabe scoffed.

"You have no idea. His lair screams evil and broody. There's blood on the floor and water dripping from the ceiling," Elaric took another drink. "Though," he nodded, "he has the best view of Alku I have ever seen. His base of operations is on a mountain peak to the west of Alku. Complete with floor-to-ceiling glass windows overlooking the valley."

"Sounds posh."

"Maybe after a good scrub, but the blood turned me off," Elaric shivered.

"So, he plans to steal Onnie's powers. I could have told you that. What does he want with them, for he sure as shit isn't giving them out to the poor like some magical fucking Robin Hood."

"If I had to guess, he's going to activate the prophecy and turn the sky red."

"Fucking great," Gabe said, knocking back his second double.

Onnie Moore

Onnie woke up to Dany's shouts and a pounding on the house's front door.

"Onnie, open this door right now!"

"Coming, Dany, I'll be right there."

Onnie blinked rapidly and rolled off the couch and to her feet, where she yawned with a stretch. When she checked the grandfather clock and saw she'd been asleep for nearly two hours, she quickly opened the door to a very angry Dany. Her best friend pushed past her and stormed into the kitchen, leaving Onnie to lock up and grab her teapot and cup as she followed after her.

"What's up, Dany?"

"You!" Dany spun and spat out. "What is wrong with you?"

"Me?" Onnie asked, placing her teapot on the counter as calmly as possible. "I'm not the one who kept a huge secret from my best friend."

"We didn't keep a secret, Onnie. We kept you safe. There's a big difference." Dany rolled her eyes as she filled the kettle with fresh water before practically slamming it on the electric base.

"You took away my choice! You're no better than Abbot!" Onnie shouted, and then she saw her eyes flash blue in the kitchen window's reflection. Then her teacup shattered on the counter beside Dany, and they both jumped from the suddenness of it.

"Then I am proud to have kept the secret," Dany said calmly. "Abbot was a wonderful man who loved you, cared about your wellbeing, and could look past all of that and ensure Alku stayed safe as well. You're acting like a child."

"I'm so tired of being called a child. Ever think that if I weren't being coddled and allowed to think for myself that maybe I'd act less like one?"

Onnie sighed and looked at the shards of the teacup scattered throughout her kitchen. She was still angry but couldn't deny that Dany was right. The proof of her lack of control and temper tantrum was visible in every porcelain shard.

"Dany...." Onnie sniffled, tears close to the surface for the first time that day.

Dany turned and embraced Onnie, rubbing her back and squeezing her gently.

"It's fine, Onnie. I'm sorry you think we were trying to hurt you. You know we would never do that. We just wanted to let you be you before you had to be this great savior of magic."

Onnie chuckled, sniffing back tears. "I can't be some great savior, Dany. I can only be me."

"Then we'll all be fine. You just have to be you, Onnie. You've proven that that's enough over and over."

Onnie stepped back and lowered her mental walls, finally composed enough to let the others back in. Elaric was knocking, so to speak, and she directed him to Gabe. She may be well enough to talk to Dany, but right now, Gabe could face all the saving the world mumbo jumbo as punishment.

"Let me clean up this teacup, and we can go sit by the fire, and you can tell me everything."

"How about we take it to go, and someone else can explain it? She'll know better." Dany pulled two thermoses from the kitchen cabinet above the stove and filled both bottles.

"Who?"

"I know you've been talking to the First Keeper, Onnie, Elaric told me. He didn't realize I didn't already know. She will be able to tell you far more than I can. Besides, she was there when it was foretold." Dany dropped a tea bag in each mug and sealed them up. "Here. It's chamomile."

Onnie scowled but didn't protest as she took the thermos. "Thanks. Want me to drive?" she asked as she went to turn off the living room fireplace and get her coat.

"Naw, let's walk. It's barely raining." Dany said with a smirk, and once Onnie was in her coat and boots, she led the way out of the house.

I'll see you soon, daughter mine.

Chapter 24: Introducing the First Keeper

April 2022 - Alku | Onnie Moore

The cool air was doing Onnie's mood some good. As she and Dany walked to the shop, neither spoke other than to point out a pretty tree or flower or to reply to other Alku residents' greetings.

House is free, Onnie said to Gabe. *You can go back now. I'm with Dany. Talk to you later.*

She didn't wait for Gabe's response, just cut off their connection by raising her mental walls once more, though not to the same degree she had earlier. She still wasn't ready to talk to him, but she also knew better than to leave their emotions connected and make things worse.

They weren't far from the shop when Mal appeared beside her and Dany and silently padded along with them. He relocated when they reached the shop entrance and Onnie unlocked the front door. When she entered, she was nearly knocked off her feet by the grief and love that washed over her.

I'm sorry, Onnie.

Onnie grinned up at the ceiling, and when Dany laughed, Onnie saw Dany had reached out to steady her.

"Sorry, I think the First Keeper feels a bit guilty."

"I'm so jealous that you get to talk to her. She's got to be so interesting," Dany said as they made their way to Abbot's study.

"Want to say hi? I might be able to act as a conduit?" Onnie offered while she turned on the fireplace and sat on the hearth to warm up.

"Really!?" Dany squeed. "Yeah, of course!" She skipped over to Onnie and sat cross-legged on the floor in front of her. "What do I have to do?"

Onnie rolled her eyes. "Nothing, goof."

She closed her eyes, slipped into the void, and pulled her, Dany, and the shop's Bonds into view. When she found the spot where she and Dany's Bonds intertwined, Onnie pulled a thread of the shop's to wrap around that connection point loosely.

Dany shivered when Onnie manipulated her Bond. "That feels strange."

Onnie smiled but kept twisting their threads.

Hello Sister, the First Keeper said along their, now joined, Bond.

"OMG!" Dany shouted. "How do I respond?"

Onnie left the void and laughed so hard she nearly choked. "However you want, Dany, she can hear you."

Dany blushed, but it quickly faded as she paled. "Oh gods, has she always been able to hear me?"

Yes, dear, the First Keeper responded, and Dany's blush quickly returned.

"Now, I want to know what that look is for," Onnie teased. "Does it have to do with Elaric?"

Dany laughed. "Oh no, but I did have my first kiss in the shop's science fiction section."

I was embarrassed for her.

"It was so bad!" Dany giggled. "It was like he was trying to see what I had for lunch." She made a face like she'd sucked on a lemon. "Blegh."

"Wow, I so need to hear about this one day," Onnie snorted. "And poor First Keeper for having to witness it."

I was unable to look away, Kushima answered with a chuckle.

"Ewww, I feel so bad. What else have you seen!?" Dany squirmed.

More than I have ever cared to. Some of it would make your stomach turn. While other times, I just have to sit back and watch the horror.

"I've never thought of it that way," Onnie said, sipping her tea. "You can only watch. There's not much you can do if someone is doing something you don't like."

Exactly. Last year, when I was attacked, all I could do was scream out to you.

"That must have been horrible. So, what's changed? Why can you communicate with Onnie now?"

It was Onnie's turn to blush and lower her head, and she tried to prepare herself for a lecture.

"I may be drinking a lot of tea."

That's an understatement, my dear, but one I will let slide.

"Onnie!" Dany scolded. "I knew it! How much are you drinking?"

She's cleaned out Miss Elanor.

"ONNIE!" Dany's voice screeched, this time making Onnie wince. "Call Gabe now and tell him to get his ass over here. And summon that cat of yours. It's time for an intervention."

Onnie looked away, not wanting to see her friend's disappointed expression.

"Dany, I need the tea. If I am going to be strong enough to kick the rogue's ass, then I need as much power as I can get."

I'm afraid I do have to agree with her here, Dany. I've been doing my best to keep Onnie's powers in check, but she needs to be as strong as possible if she's going to survive against Jakob.

"There has to be a safer way, though. She exploded a teacup this afternoon!"

"Dany...." Onnie groaned. "She can't always see outside the shop."

My dear young one, shame on you. You promised to tell me everything concerning this tea and your growing powers.

"Does she know you basically froze time this morning, too?" Dany interjected.

The shop's interior got exceptionally quiet, and Onnie could feel the literal structure warring between holding its breath and lashing out at her. The First Keeper said nothing, and neither did the two women for what seemed like an eternity. Finally, Onnie broke the silence.

"Keeper?"

I am SO mad at you right now, Connie Moore. Call your Guardian and your Link. We will discuss this as a group.

Onnie's shoulders drooped, and she felt herself slipping into her practiced posture of invisibility.

Dany whistled. "She used your full name."

"Yeah, second time I've heard it today."

"You pissed off the most powerful entity on the planet. Good going, girl."

Not wanting to piss off anyone further, Onnie reached out to Gabe and Mal, the latter appearing on the hearth beside her instantly.

"Onnie...what did you do?" he accused, but she ignored him.

Gabe, the First Keeper, requests your presence at the shop.

The first, what? Cat?

Just get here, please.

Are you alright? Gabe sounded genuinely worried about her, and she flinched.

Yes, I'm sorry. Just stressed. I pissed off the shop.

Yes, you did, foolish girl, Kushima said so only Onnie could hear.

On my way...but, Cat?

Yes?

I'm sorry.

I know.

They both pulled away, and Onnie left Gabe to focus on his surroundings as he made his way to them. Then she sighed, "Alright, he's on his way."

Onnie scratched behind Mal's ears, and when he leaned into her palm and purred, she pulled him into her lap for a snuggle.

"Why is the shop so upset, Onnie?" Mal asked.

"Can we wait for Gabe?"

Mal narrowed his eyes at her but eventually gave up and gently nipped at her palm. "Fine."

"Oh, I um…connected Dany's Bond to the shop temporarily. She can hear the First Keeper, too."

"Oh," Mal snuggled down into Onnie's lap. "That makes this so much easier." It only took a few seconds for Mal's eyes to narrow up at her. "Wait, too?"

Onnie nodded shyly. "Yeah, um, I'm sorry I didn't say anything."

Mal growled and pointedly looked away from her, and Onnie felt his upset along their Bond.

Mal?

What?

Are you that angry at me?

No.

Okay…then, what is it?

Why didn't you…tell me? Just makes me feel…not sure….

Onnie pulled Mal closer to her face and rubbed her nose in his belly fur. *I'm sorry, really. It hasn't been very long, and I was still processing, to be honest.*

Mal was quiet for a few minutes, and Onnie glanced at Dany, who was also frowning at the feline. His mental voice was incredibly soft and diminished when he finally spoke again.

Best friends talk to each other. I'm sorry you didn't feel like you coul—
Nope. Stop it, Mal.

Onnie scolded and used her pointer finger to tilt his chin up and look into his blue eyes. Even that they had changed color at all proved he was really hurt, considering Mal's rarely shifted.

First off, hypocrite. That said, I don't want to talk about that right now. Second, you are my best friend, and I know I can tell you anything. I was going to, but I was scared. She looked away before continuing. *I figured you'd be mad at me. Or disappointed.*

Mal sighed, and she felt him shift so he could stand in her lap and bonk his head under her chin. *Guess we're even. I'm sorry, too.*

Onnie gently tugged on both his ears and smiled before brushing her nose against his in a butterfly kiss.

He good? Dany asked Onnie.

Yeah. Was hurt I didn't tell him. Says we're even now.

Dany snorted, and Mal turned to look at her. "So, you've met Master K then."

"Master K?" Dany scoffed. "Really, Mal?"

He's called me that since the day I created him—little shit.

Onnie and Dany burst into laughter, Mal followed soon after, and even Kushima seemed amused.

You're lucky I like you, feline.

"You know you do. I'm not nearly as dull as Rebecca was."

"Mal!" Dany and Onnie scolded together.

"What?" Mal protested. "She was an old woman even when she wasn't."

Onnie poked his belly. "Still, be nice. That said, I always did want to ask about that, actually. Was Rebecca always an older woman, or did she age?"

"Mentally or physically?" Mal asked.

Dany spoke up. "Well, I know she aged physically. She was younger when I was a kid."

She did age. Kind of, the First Keeper began. *Rebecca had to give the appearance of aging while not surpassing Abbot, but she also couldn't be an unruly young woman while he was figuring things out. Rebecca started around her thirties as a mentor for Abbot and a friend. As he grew, and when your grandmother moved away, she slowed her aging until he caught up. Then she aged as he did.*

"Her personality was always old, though," Mal said, licking his paw.

Onnie bopped him on the head with her pointer finger and scolded him again. "Mal."

She was, Kushima agreed. *Tell me honestly, Onnie. I'm old. Very old. Do I seem as old as Rebecca?*

Onnie giggled and shook her head. "Nope. Not in the slightest. Actually, why is that? Shouldn't you have some super old English dialect?"

"Yeah, like Shakespeare or something," Dany interjected as Onnie sipped the tea she'd forgotten.

I can has't one if 't be true i did want to, but i've't hath lived longeth enow to learneth mod'rn speech patt'rns

Onnie snorted chamomile up through her nose, and Mal disappeared and relocated to Dany's lap to avoid the liquid as Onnie coughed it up into her sweatshirt sleeve.

Everyone dissolved into laughter, and the four of them spent the rest of their time waiting for Gabe, mimicking the shop's different era speech patterns and swapping stories about what the shop had witnessed over the years.

Gabriel Vansand

Gabe entered the shop to sounds of giggling and general mischief— nothing like what he'd been expecting. He locked up behind himself and felt a warmth radiate down his Bond with Onnie. It felt different, though. There was something else there he couldn't recognize, though it felt familiar.

Hurry up, Gabe, Onnie teased.

An insuppressible smile spread across his face. It had been so long since Onnie laughed that genuinely, and hearing it rang like music in his ears.

Sap.

Shit, sorry, he winced. He hadn't realized how loud he'd thought that.

Onnie laughed again. *It's fine. I just never knew how lovey-dovey my big, tough Guardian was.*

Who are you, and where is my Keeper? He growled down their Bond.

Cool your jets, turbo. I'm about to be ripped a new one by four of the most important people to me. Least you can do is let me tease you a bit first.

Gabe shrugged off his coat and hung it by the door, running his palm over the front counter as he passed it and tapping the bookshelf full of scrolls as he walked by it. Gods, he loved this place. When he turned the corner and headed into the study that had once been Abbot's, he froze. Dany and Onnie lay on their backs, feet up on the hearth, fire blazing, with Mal on the mantle, looking more than a little disgruntled.

"It's about time you showed up, man," Mal hissed.

"Why?"

"These three have been losing their minds."

"Well, that's—" Gabe paused, "three?"

Onnie pointed to the ceiling and smiled. "She says you're handsome."

Dany snorted, and Onnie dissolved into giggles so hard that she stopped breathing for a few seconds.

"Yeah, we aren't the only ones keeping secrets, dude. Onnie can talk to the First Keeper."

"The First Keeper? Like the shop?" Gabe plopped on the sofa roughly and rubbed his eyes. "Why didn't you tell me this?" he asked Onnie. "For how long?"

"Since Abbot's funeral and the Transference." Mal answered for her.

"WHAT!" Gabe shouted and stood up reflexively, watching Onnie, Dany, and Mal flinch.

"Cool it, Gabe, even I felt that," Dany said, rubbing her forehead. "Is that how it always is?" she asked Onnie and Mal.

Onnie nodded. "When he or I lose control, yes."

"Wait, you felt that?" Gabe asked Dany, who nodded upside down at him. Gabe roughly sat back on the couch and rubbed his temples with his fingertips. "Okay, start from the beginning."

Well, he'd told them to start from the beginning, and twenty minutes later, Gabe felt like his head was caving in. Dany was now linked to the shop through Onnie temporarily. Mal knew Onnie could talk to the First Keeper…sort of, and Onnie had been hiding the extent of her use of the Keeper's tea, and the First Keeper knew about all of it.

"I'm sorry, Cat," Gabe said, pulling her to him and crushing her in his arms.

"For what?" her muffled voice said through his sweater, and he could feel her grin against him.

"I have been so stupidly self-absorbed, and I didn't even know all this was happening. You're supposed to trust me. Talk to me. I'm your Guardian, for fucks sake."

"Mal, let's give them some room, shall we?" Dany said, picking up her friend and carrying him out of the study.

"Gabe," Onnie said, pushing him away. "It's not all your fault, you know. I am responsible for myself. I am choosing to drink the tea." She pointed her finger at him, "And for what it's worth, I would do it again, and I will." When he opened his mouth to retort, she placed her fingers on his lip. "No, even the First Keeper agrees. Isn't that right?"

Onnie sat quietly for a second, looking at the ceiling, before she looked back at him and smiled confidently. "See, she agrees."

"Cat," Gabe chuckled, "I can't hear her."

"Oh," Onnie giggled. "Oops."

Then she closed her eyes, and a few minutes later, Gabe shivered before he then heard a motherly, yet authoritative, female voice in his mind.

Hello Guardian. I'm so glad to finally speak with you.

It's an honor, First Keeper.

The First Keeper laughed softly. *Oh, quit that. I could hear you capitalize that. I'm just a Keeper like your Cat here. Very apt nickname, by the way. Suits her to a T.*

Onnie blushed, and Gabe kissed her cheek. *I know. Did you have to give her a real cat, though? Couldn't her Link have been a human, like Rebecca?*

And what type of human does she lack, Guardian?

Uh...well....

For a girlfriend, she has Dany. A mentor, she has me. A protector, she has you. She needed a companion who would be with her no matter what. Someone who would love her for her and provide her comfort. He would not be suitable for any other role.

Gabe rolled his eyes and sighed. "Yeah, you're right, Mal's perfect."

Onnie cocked her head to the side.

"Were you not listening?"

"No, I try not to eavesdrop. Just because I can doesn't mean I should."

He kissed his Keeper then, pouring his love for her down their Bond, and when the First Keeper cleared her metaphorical throat, he kept going. He kept going until his phone rang, and Dany cursed him out for knocking her on her ass in line for coffee. Then she cursed him out more, then informed him that she and Mal were grabbing dinner and would be back soon and told him not to do anything she wouldn't do while she was gone.

When he told Onnie and the First Keeper, he became even more confused when they both laughed.

"Do you know something I don't?" he asked both women.

"Yup," Onnie barely choked out.

And that's how it will stay, Guardian—some things a brother doesn't want to know about his sister.

Gabe pulled a face, and Onnie kissed his cheek. "Come on, let's talk logistics. You spoke to Elaric, right?"

"I did. He's infiltrated Jakob's organization and is earning his trust. He came to 'attack' me tonight, but he doesn't think it was a real assignment, only one to see how stupid he would be."

"So, the rogue is trying to hunt for better minions now?"

"Sounds like it. He wants smarter but still manipulatable, and this Gemini chick is his recruiter. Elaric said she didn't try to make a pass at him, but she made it clear she was the 'Master's' favorite." Gabe's stomach turned at the whole situation. "She's also the one that said the rogue was upset because we caught another roach."

"At least that's something. I'd hate to make life easy for him," Onnie rolled her eyes. "So, how did you leave things with Elaric?"

"He's going to report back that he didn't confront me but instead followed me into the school and overheard valuable intel that we were on the outs after the new information you learned earlier today. He'll tell of dissension within the ranks and a weak support system around you."

"He'll paint me as alone and vulnerable," Onnie nodded.

"Exactly."

Onnie sighed, "And so it begins."

Chapter 25: Body and Mind

May 2022 - Alku | Onnie Moore

"Okay, Onnie. Close your eyes and try to picture your shield," Dany said from a few feet in front of her.

They were in the school's gym, practicing and experimenting with Onnie's novel control over the Bond and seeing how far they could push her limits while getting creative in how she used it.

"Why am I closing my eyes?" Onnie asked curiously but followed instructions.

"You can project a shield while looking at what you want to protect. I want you to try to create one when you can't see it."

"When would I need to shield something I can't see? How would I even know something needed shielding to do it?"

"No clue, but what's the harm in knowing how? Blindfold, dark room, hell, it might even come in handy when you're in your astral form."

That's actually a pretty good plan, Onnie thought to Kushima.

Of course, it is. She's your Sister and best friend, after all.

When Onnie smiled, Dany whacked her butt with a foam sword. "Hey, focus. Stop gossiping with the First Keeper."

Onnie snorted but did as she was told and tried to visualize the training dummy she knew was across the room from her.

"Should I be using the Bond or fully blind?"

"Hmm…" Dany said, her voice originating from a different place in the room. "What's easier?"

"Using the Bond. I can basically still see that way, though, remember?" Onnie shrugged.

"Yeah, I do. Okay, try using it, and we can step up to fully blind afterward."

"Got it, coach."

Onnie pulled her and Dany's Bonds into view, and their light began to glow around her. Dany was circling her, their Bond pulsing bright, a visual representation of their connection forever. Onnie knew they were the only beings with heartbeats in the gym, so she widened her sight to include the objects closest to her. The training dummy wasn't far, and Onnie was slightly surprised that Dany hadn't moved it to try to throw her off.

"How are you doing?"

"Shoot, sorry," Onnie said, realizing that Dany was oblivious to the mental investigation she had been doing silently. "Everything's fine. I was being too methodical."

"No worries. This is for you, so if that's what you need as a building block, do it."

Onnie smiled before refocusing on the training dummy and slowly pulling power through her connection with the shop and its reserves. She was careful how much and how fast she used, but worked as quickly as she dared, weaving glowing gold Bond fibers into a mesh. She pictured the threads going over and under each other, creating a small pattern before she replicated it, over and over, becoming faster the more she completed. When she had enough, she draped it over the dummy, enveloping it in the shimmering gold mesh. Then, she opened her eyes.

Dany was standing beside the shielded object, and there was a soft glow of golden light in a halo around it. Onnie watched as the inquisitive woman reached forward to poke at it cautiously with her finger. Nothing seemed to happen from her perspective, and Onnie only felt a minor brush against the power she was sustaining before Dany's finger passed through it and touched the leather beneath it.

"Okay, I see it, but I don't think it's working," Dany said, poking it again.

Onnie giggled, "Try being threatening. Your pointer finger isn't scary, so it's not activating."

"Oh, okay then."

Dany stood up straight, and in the next second, she roundhouse kicked the dummy with incredible force for a woman with her build. The shield activated alright, and she was thrown across the room, the suddenness ripping a shout from her. Before Dany hit the floor, Onnie froze her in mid-air, gently lowered her back to her feet, and unfroze her.

"Sorry, reflex." Onnie winced.

Dany's wide eyes closed as she doubled over in laughter and braced her hands on her thighs. When she'd regained a bit of composure, she grinned at Onnie.

"No, I deserved that. Part of me figured it wouldn't work, and I'd pass through and hit the bag. I should have known better than to doubt you."

Onnie snorted. "Well, I'm glad I was right. Seeing as you've got such lofty expectations for me."

"Should we try again?" Dany stretched her back and walked across the gym to the training dummy.

"Yeah, let me see if I can do it this time and make it invisible."

"Ooh, great idea!" Dany crossed her arms and turned to stare at the training dummy.

Onnie closed her eyes again and repeated what she'd done previously. Once she was confident the shield was up, she was ready.

"It's up, and you can see it, right?"

"Correct."

"Okay, I wanted to ensure it went up before I tried. Give me a sec."

"Got it. Want me to tell you if it changes?"

"Yes, please."

Onnie saw the shield pulsing and glowing in the void, a brighter light source than all the other Bonds, with the exception of hers and Dany's.

Kushima, any suggestions on making this invisible?

Hmm…the issue is that it's glowing in the world, correct? Not just the void?

Yup, I'd like to see if I can make it invisible so someone wouldn't know it's there.

After a minute of thinking, Kushima responded, *Could you cover it up?*

With what?

Kushima chuckled, *No idea.*

Onnie snorted. "Sorry, Dany. I'm brainstorming over here. I'm not sure how to do this if I'm honest."

"Could you, I don't know, put something over it?" Dany suggested.

Onnie grinned, her eyes still closed. "That's what the First Keeper said, too."

"Nice!" Dany said, seemingly proud of herself.

"Wait, let me try something…."

Onnie carefully retracted the power she'd been feeding the shield but didn't unweave it.

"Wait! It's working!" Dany's sneakers squeaked against the floor a few times, and Onnie saw the woman's Bond bouncing and knew she was jumping up and down.

Onnie pulled the remaining power from the shield, and when it was empty, she felt it unravel.

"Damn."

"What? It looks invisible to me."

"It is. Because I broke it," Onnie laughed. "Let me put it back up, then I'll explain."

For the third time, Onnie wove the shield using the shop's power, and this time, once it was up, she retracted all of the power except a small portion—a drop compared to an entire lake's worth.

"It came back and then disappeared again. Should I test it?"

"Yeah, but please test it a wee bit less this time," Onnie teased.

"Yeah, yeah," Dany said, a grin in her voice.

A few seconds later, Onnie heard Dany's fist strike the bag and felt her pierce the shield.

"Um, was it supposed to do that?"

"Yeah. Let me catch you up, and I need your opinion," Onnie said opening her eyes again.

She walked to the stack of gymnastics mats on the side of the room, picked up her water bottle, downed half of it, switched to her thermos, and took a few gulps.

"Okeydokey," Dany said, coming to join her. She used her palms to push herself up and sat on a stack of mats.

"So, the first time, I created it the same way as before, but then I removed the power from it, but it wasn't stable, and it dissipated."

"Ah, makes sense. Power is what gives it any form at all. Remove all of it, and it ceases to exist." Dany said, unscrewing her water's cap.

"Exactly. I figured that would be the case, but I would have kicked myself if that was the answer and we hadn't tested it. I was hoping I could leave it up as a sort of shell and reactivate it when I needed it."

"Good thought. So the second time when I punched through it?"

"I didn't remove all of its power and left the barest amount. Just enough to have it hold its form."

"Didn't work."

Onnie shook her head, "Nope. When you punched through it the second time, I felt you easily break past what little power remained."

Dany gulped her water, and her brows creased as her brain worked through the problem. Onnie took the time to drink more of her tea and check her cell phone.

"So, does that mean," Dany wiped her mouth with the back of her hand and re-capped her water, "you have to re-add the power when it's needed?"

"Think so."

"Hmm," Dany said with even more of a wrinkled forehead. "That's going to rely on very fast reflexes, right?"

"One hundred percent and it will become visible again until we learn to hide it. That's where I need your opinion. I have two thoughts. One, we add to my training how quickly I can pour power into it after creating it. Or, two, we scrap the invisible idea and just focus on the speed of creating it. What's more important, creating it quickly but staying visible, or creating it slower while keeping it hidden?"

Dany's eyes narrowed, "Ooo, that's a good question...."

What do you think? Onnie asked Kushima and included Dany in their conversation.

Yeah, good point. What do you think, First Keeper?

I think both options are valid, which doesn't assist you much.

Onnie giggled. *Correct. Not at all a help.*

Instead of telling you which I think is more correct, let me rephrase the options.

By all means, Dany said and flopped onto her back on the mat stack.

Onnie, which scenario will grant you more control and stability over the flow of power? Will you be at risk of pulling too much too fast if you have to create it quickly or if you have to activate it reflexively?

Oh, snap, Dany said, sitting back up. *That's a great point.*

Onnie crossed her arms and paced in a small circle. *It is a good point.*

Dany and the First Keeper continued chatting, but Onnie had basically tuned them out, her pacing and thoughts too loud to hear them. She needed to ensure the safety of the person she was protecting while also ensuring the shop wasn't hurt again. Both options set her up for disaster. The only difference was that one was more of a delayed destruction. She could create the shield slowly and carefully while no one noticed, but then she'd have to power it in a snap scenario. She groaned and rubbed her temples.

Young one, do not worry so much.

Yeah, you're thinking so loud even I can feel your stress.

Dany slipped off the mats and draped her arm around Onnie's

shoulders.

Yeah, sorry. I'm just trying to figure out the safest way to not over-extend the shop again.

We heard. Dany and Kushima said in unison.

Onnie chuffed, *Sorry.*

Even we can hear you, Mal said, joining the conversation.

Ug, really?

Onnie was now not only stressed but angry at herself that she had been so preoccupied that she'd let it drift through her Bonds.

Sorry, all.

Not a big deal, Cat. Can we help? Gabe's Bond fluttered as he sent her his love and support.

Onnie thought for one more second and then answered them all.

I think we should focus on creating it as fast as possible. Once I can make them quickly, I'll switch to creating them fast in stealth mode.

I think that's a good plan, Gabe said.

Yup, Mal added.

As you wish, Keeper, Kushima teased.

"Let's get started then," Dany said.

Onnie felt her best friend's evil grin and glanced up to find she'd been correct. Suddenly, she felt it was going to be a very long afternoon.

Onnie flopped onto her back on the mat behind her.

Gabe, your sister is trying to kill me. Save me.

Mal appeared at her elbow but quickly relocated when a towel flew straight at him and landed on Onnie's face. He reappeared on her other side and sniffed her forehead.

"Damn girl, you smell."

Onnie drug the towel off and swatted him with it, and once again, he was gone. This time, he had relocated to the other side of the mat out of her reach.

"Jerk," she teased.

Dany laughed and plopped herself down next to Onnie. "You're doing great, but I do think it's time for a break. Dinner?"

"I can't move." Onnie groaned. "My everything hurts. Brain, body, and I'm pretty sure if my mental self had feelings, she'd be covered in blisters."

I'll be to you guys in twenty, Gabe said.

"All the more reason you need food." Dany poked Onnie's side with her finger. "Besides, you did great today. We deserve a treat."

"We?" Onnie rolled her eyes but grinned. "Didn't you just say *I* did great?"

"Hey! I helped!" Dany giggled and tickled Onnie, their laughter echoing in the empty gym.

Onnie wiggled away as she pulled in deep breaths and tried to talk through her laughter.

"I give!"

Dany smiled and scootched over to lie down beside her. "Really though, you did good, Onnie."

"Thanks," Onnie said sleepily as her eyes closed. "I hope…it was… enough…."

Sleep, young one. We'll wake you when Gabriel gets there.

Elaric Rickson

Elaric stood, skulking in the shadows of the forest bordering the school. Hours earlier, he had seen Onnie and Dany enter the gym in their training clothes. He assumed that they would be doing an entire training session, in which case he knew he'd have some time to kill. He had waited as Harry for a few minutes to confirm that the two women would be staying in the gym, and once satisfied, he made a quick trip to get coffee and do some eavesdropping.

That had been hours ago.

Elaric shifted, Harry's feet sore from standing for so long, but he ignored it. The pair had to finish their session soon, considering the sun was going down, and he could wait a few minutes longer.

As if summoned by thought, Gabe's car pulled into the school's parking lot and the spot closest to the gym. After locking the car, he entered the gym and disappeared from view. Thankfully, Gabe had been in jeans, not workout clothes, so Elaric assumed he was there to pick up the other two, not join them.

It only took a handful of minutes for him to be proven correct when all three exited the building and made their way to the car. Dany smiled, big and beautiful, and poked Gabe's side playfully, most likely teasing him about something. Gabe merely reached for her and put her in a faux headlock before releasing her and telling her to get her ass in the car.

Onnie looked exhausted. Whatever she and Dany had done must have been intense because she was more motion picture zombie than bright and witty Keeper. Even Mal walked beside her on the asphalt, not in her arms.

Elaric frowned at seeing her so worn out. She stiffened slightly, and neither Gabe nor Dany noticed. Then he felt the softest brush along his Bond, making him grin like a fool. That woman was incredible. Even in the state she was in, she knew he'd been nearby watching them.

He returned the brush against their Bond, and she visibly relaxed. She didn't press him further, and neither did he. Clearly, he was the one following them, and there was nothing to discuss, so they would each carry on.

Onnie was the last to get into the car, and when she did, she stared out the window, lost in thought. Or at least that's how it looked. Gabe didn't drive too near to where Elaric was hiding, but close enough that for a fraction of a second, his and Onnie's eyes connected.

Then they were gone.

Elaric stretched and carefully trudged out from the shadows and down the cobbled streets toward the bed and breakfast where Harry had been staying. He ambled and put an expression of boredom and introspection on his face, but his ears were listening.

Mrs. Radclif hadn't disappointed him, and the local florist had turned out to be more than an innocent older woman. Instead, she was the mastermind behind his entire rumor mill. One of the others would tell her a bit of information, and within hours, Harry would find out and be able to report it back to the rogue. Of course, none of it was factual information, or at least not *fully*, but that was fine. Not only did Mrs. Radcliff pass around the false rumors, but she also had a way of passing along the information so that those spreading the gossip knew what was real and what was staged.

The nymph had missed her calling, and Elaric smiled when he remembered the younger Elanor and how the woman was still the same even after so many decades.

Harry passed the flower shop and took the long way back to his arrangements to settle in for the night. As usual, the fragrance that rippled off the shop was intense and bordered on overwhelming to Elaric but stayed just shy of that line. It smelled amazing, but he frowned at the feeling it gave him nonetheless.

Flowers reminded him of his mother and his childhood, and his mind began taking him down memory lane, which was never a wise choice. He missed Marco and wished he could stop by the cafe, but it was too risky. Elaric would have to deal with his past on his own. Instead, he quickened his pace and left it behind him.

He was already tired of his situation and wanted to go home. It had been less than a week, and he knew it would be many more before he would learn something valuable. The faster he could be of use, the faster he could get out.

Harry would return to the mountain tomorrow and deliver what he'd learned about the Keeper and her companions.

Elaric, on the other hand, would try to remember to take one day at a time and that his days wouldn't be like this forever.

Chapter 26: Further Understanding

April 2022 - Alku | Onnie Moore

Onnie leaned on the bathroom counter with crossed ankles as she watched Gabe, who was currently leaning over the sink, shaving. He had a towel wrapped around his waist as he got ready for work, his hair still dripping every so often.

"What's your plan after classes today? Do you have to stay late again?"

"Yeah, I'm almost done, but not fully. I have to get the last of the stupid state fitness test plans prepped."

As Gabe drug the blades of his razor over the stubble on his cheek, Onnie was drawn to the sound, and when she inhaled, the light perfume of his shaving cream made her think of her brothers when they'd all been growing up and shared a bathroom.

"Alright, well, Dany has a PTA meeting at the library, and I'm pretty sure if we ask Mal to babysit me one more time, he really will pee in your slippers." When she giggled, Mal appeared on the counter next to her.

"I will. That's a promise," Mal's reflective eyes narrowed at them both.

"You know I don't need a babysitter right…."

"Cat," Gabe said, shifting his eyes to her but continuing to draw the blade down his skin, "we've gone over this."

Onnie pushed away from the counter, threw her hands up before facing the mirror, and began to apply some basic makeup for the day.

"I know, I know. We can't have me alone because it might put Elaric in a bad spot if he had the opportunity to act and didn't."

"Exactly," Gabe said with a slight upturn at the corners of his lips.

"How about this," Onnie turned and pointed her eyeliner pencil at him. "I'll go to the Day Night Cafe. I can sit and have dinner and then visit with Marco. I'll be safe there, and there's no way Elaric would be held responsible for avoiding an attack somewhere so public."

Mal and Gabe looked at her and then at each other before Mal nodded. "She's actually got a point."

Gabe rolled his eyes, "I know."

"Ha!" Onnie jumped and cheered.

"But," Gabe said, mimicking her minutes prior and pointing his razor in her direction, "you'll teleport, transfer, warp, whatever you want to call it. You won't walk there alone."

"Deal! I bet Marco would let me use his apartment or the hallway or something."

"Fine," Gabe agreed, even if it was begrudgingly.

"Thank you."

Onnie scratched the top of Mal's head and gave it a quick peck before she went to Gabe's side. She used his shoulder to pull down his clean-shaven cheek and kiss him, too.

"Really, you two. It means a lot. I know you're trying to help, but I'm going crazy."

"I know, Cat," Gabe said, kissing her forehead and then returned to finish his shaving.

Onnie brushed her teeth and finished her makeup, a grin on her face that she couldn't shake off. While Gabe dressed, she went into the library to pack her bag for the day. When she entered the room, Mal relocated to a pile of blankets on the floor and yawned.

"You just woke up. How are you already tired?" Onnie teased as she shoved a notebook, her favorite pen, and the shop's finance log into her bag.

"I'm a cat. We're nocturnal," then Mal closed his eyes.

Onnie shook her head, "You're a physical manifestation of the world's collection of knowledge. Not a cat."

"And being a manifestation is hard work," he said without opening his eyes.

"Fine," Onnie said, bending to scratch under his chin. "You coming into the shop later?"

"Pick up a hot chocolate for me when you get your coffee, and I'll be there." Mal cracked one eye open, and Onnie glared at him.

"You're one spoiled cat."

"I think you'll find I'm a physical manifestation of the world's collection of knowledge. Not a cat."

Onnie stood up and shouted down the hallway, "Gabe! I'm gonna need a new Link," and left the library. Mal's laughter followed her into the front room, where Gabe met her, dressed and ready to go.

"Why?" He smirked, walking her to the entryway and helping her into her coat.

"He's too little Link and too much sass."

You like my sass.

"See!" Onnie said with mock annoyance and locked up the house as Gabe walked to the driver's side of his Audi.

"A Shot in the Dark first?" Gabe asked while he started the engine, and Onnie pulled on her seatbelt.

"In what universe would the answer not be yes?"

Gabe chuckled, "Ever think he's learned his sass from you?"

Onnie fiddled with her heated seat and pretended not to hear his comment, but he laughed, and she knew he wasn't buying her sudden and temporary hearing impairment. She leaned back in the incredibly comfortable seat and watched the streets of Alku as they drove by. The distance from the house to the center of Alku wasn't very far, and most days, they walked, but with both of them having late nights recently, they were driving more.

"Wanna go for a run this weekend?" she blurted abruptly, breaking the silence.

"Sure, but what made you think of that?"

She saw in her window's reflection that Gabe was watching her out of the corner of his eye.

"I just realized we haven't lately, and it's my first winter in Alku, even if it should be spring. I haven't gotten to see much of the area covered in snow. I don't want to miss it."

This time, Gabe turned his head to study her a bit closer, and she was expecting him to call her on her lie, but he returned his focus to the road and didn't comment. It was only a tiny lie. She didn't want to miss the snow...in case it was the only winter she'd have in Alku. With the prophecy weighing on her, Onnie had to admit there was a scenario where she didn't make it to the other side.

"Alright. Want me to call Xayn? Maybe he can show us some pretty forested areas. Hell, even just Green Cottage in the winter is magical to look at. Literally."

Onnie smiled, her reflection returning the expression. "Yeah, I'd like that."

Gabe reached over and clasped her hand while they drove the rest of the way to the coffee shop. From there, he kissed her goodbye and continued to the school, leaving her with Mal, who appeared once his promised payment was purchased and she'd exited the shop.

"I still find it amusing that no one in Alku gives it a second thought that I'm walking down the street with a cat." Onnie pulled her scarf closer around her and hovered her nose over her coffee's steam.

"Why? People walk cats all the time now."

Mal was playing Dante's version of the floor is lava with the snow as they walked, and Onnie was amused as she watched him tip-toe around the deeper sections of powder, flicking the water off his paws if he stepped into it.

"Yeah. With leashes, Mal."

The feline grinned up at her as they continued toward the shop. When they were on Elanor's corner, Onnie made it a point to wave to the friendly nymph sitting at one of her front windows, drinking her morning tea before customers came in.

"Your cocoa's on Abbot's desk. See you inside."

Mal promptly relocated while she opened the shop's front door and pulled out the wooden sandwich board before heading inside.

Brat.

Onnie giggled under her breath, knowing he'd found his cocoa. In its cup. With the lid on.

I'll be right there. Let me get the sidewalk settled so I don't have to put my coat back on.

It didn't take her long to get the sign where it needed to be and to check on the potted plants beside the door, which looked healthy and weedless. Lastly, she pulled a small wooden box from beside the coat rack and sprinkled a few handfuls of the salt on the sidewalk.

Finally finished, Onnie shrugged off her coat and scarf before hanging them on the wooden coat rack near the front door. She stopped, gently ran her hand over the piece of furniture, and smiled.

He was very particular in his choice of wood, Kushima said. *He was telling Dany about it when they were making the repairs. He wanted something he could ward for you.*

Always thinking of others. Xayn's one of those people the world wouldn't be the same without.

Indeed.

Onnie hung up her things and turned on all the lights and oil lamps in the shop with Kushima's assistance. After unpacking her bag and grabbing a shallow bowl from the backroom, she went to Abbot's study and the spoiled 'physical manifestation' that awaited her and demanded cocoa.

Onnie was sorting through a box of old books, her cell phone held to her ear by her shoulder.

"Thank you, Marco. You don't know how much this means to me."

"Onnie, you never have to thank me for spending time with you. Text me when you're ready, and I'll ensure the apartment hallway is private." Marco's reply was filled with a smile Onnie could feel through the phone.

"Perfect. Then I'll see you in…" she looked at her phone before finishing, "Thirty?"

"Lovely, I'll see you soon," Marco said, ending their call.

Talked to Marco. I'll go over in about a half hour. Onnie told Gabe so he'd stop asking her what her plans were every ten minutes.

I'll let you know when I'm heading out then, and maybe I can pick you up.

Warm feelings from her Bond with Gabe pushed against her, and Onnie grinned to no one.

Sounds like a plan. Thanks.

Gabe pushed one last wave of emotions toward her and retreated from her mind again. Then Onnie felt the familiar tingle on the back of her neck that warned her of an incoming customer. She placed the book she was examining back in the box on the front counter and looked up as a young girl dragged a woman behind her by the hand through the door.

"Miranda!"

Onnie darted around the counter and down the aisle, where she squatted to the little girl's height and was rewarded when Miranda launched herself in for a hug.

"Hey, girly! How are you?"

Onnie looked up at Miranda's mom with a quick glance and was relieved to see Erika was smiling. Onnie always felt a little guilty that Miranda only talked to her, but Erika always assured her that she wasn't envious, simply happy to see her daughter speaking.

"I'm—" Miranda's little-used voice squeaked, and Onnie saw the tips of her ears turn red. "I'm good," Miranda stepped back and grinned.

"I'm so glad," Onnie said, holding both her hands. "How about Mom? She doing okay, too?"

Miranda looked at her mom, then grinned even wider and nodded. "Mommy's good. Right, Mommy?"

Onnie looked up, and the woman's eyes glistened with unshed, happy tears. If Onnie could give the two of them a chance to talk whenever she saw them, she would never hesitate to speak to the sweet girl whenever she could.

"I'm good. Thanks for asking, Onnie."

"Of course!" Onnie looked back at Miranda. "So, to what do I deserve this lovely surprise visit?"

"I want a book, and Mommy said you might have it. She says you have *lots* of books. Like more than Miss Dany."

Onnie swallowed her laughter and made a mental note to tell Dany how she was dissed later.

"Well then, let's see what we can do, huh?" She got to her feet and kept one of Miranda's hands. "Now tell me, what are you looking for?"

"I wanna book about a prince."

"Alright, anything else?" Onnie asked, leading them to the start of the quilted clearing. When they found the first few quilted leaves on the ground, she tipped her head back and whispered to Erika, who wasn't missing a moment of her child's speaking and had followed behind them.

"Don't lose sight of us. Wayward," was all Onnie said, and she saw the understanding in the woman's eyes.

"I want the prince to win. I want him to beat the bad guys. He has lots of friends and a cat!" Miranda said, her eyes lighting up suddenly, and Onnie knew she was making this up as she went along.

You listening? Onnie asked Kushima. She would need her help finding an exact match for this girl's desire.

I am.

"Okay, so, a prince, beat the bad guys, lots of friends, and a cat. Anything else?" Onnie asked with genuine interest.

Miranda's forehead scrunched up while she thought, and they continued to walk. When they reached the quilted clearing and the reading space for the kids, she jumped and shouted. "How about one where the prince saves everyone in the world, and his favorite color is blue!"

It felt like the floor dropped out from beneath Onnie, and it took every ounce of her control not to show her fear to the innocent child before her.

"Ah...."

When her voice shook, Onnie looked at Erika, who was wide-eyed, and Onnie assumed she also knew of the prophecy.

Young one....

Gabe's presence touched on Onnie's Bond, and she quickly pacified him and refocused on Miranda.

"Hmm..." she said, feigning her pondering. "Let me think...."

Kushima.

I know.

How?

I genuinely have no idea. However, isn't this the young girl who was taken during the storm?

Yes.

Perhaps there's a connection there.

Onnie closed her eyes and took a deep breath. She quickly slipped into the void and examined Miranda's Bond for anything out of place but, thankfully, found nothing suspicious.

Do we have a kid's version of the prophecy or something?

We do.

When Kushima answered, Onnie followed her instructions and found it on the shelf a minute later. She pulled it off and flipped through it.

You guys couldn't even give me the kid's version? Onnie joked and was relieved when Kushima chuckled.

"Okay," Onnie turned and faced mother and daughter. "How about this one?"

Onnie relocated from Abbot's to the hallway on the second floor of the Day Night Cafe, where a few apartments were located.

"Onnie!" Marco's smooth voice said from his apartment's doorway that she'd just appeared in front of. "It's lovely to see you."

She smiled and walked into his open arms for a hug, his slightly taller but slender body wrapping around hers. "You too, Marco. How've you been?"

"Plenty of time for that," he gestured for her coat and bag, which he hung up and set inside his apartment. Then he grabbed his suit coat from the hook next to the door and pulled it closed behind him. "First, a meal. Stephan would like to see you as well."

"He's here? I feel like I haven't seen him much recently."

Onnie allowed herself to be directed down the stairs and to the door from the residential hallway into the kitchen of the Day Night Cafe.

"I mentioned you were coming, and he changed whatever plans he had." Marco held open the inconspicuous door and ushered her through it.

The kitchen of the Day Night Cafe was a wonder of the world if Onnie had any say about it. She'd only been in it once during the night shift, but Vanessa's calm and relaxed vibe during the day was gone and replaced with organized chaos. The day's kitchen was modern impressionist dancing, and the night's was the Russian Ballet at the height of the winter season. Chefs, bartenders, servers, and various other staff slid past one another in the bright white room. They never collided, spilled, and made little excess noise above their voices and the classic kitchen sounds. They weren't silent or robotic. They each smiled and conversed freely, which was felt soothing and methodical. Onnie found it so relaxing that she was pretty sure she could fall asleep watching them.

The single high-top table along one wall with four stools tucked beneath it was a constant in the kitchen, no matter what time of day. Stephan was sitting at one tonight, his fingers tapping away on a laptop. With little surprise, Stephan closed his computer and turned to smile at her before they'd even made their way fully into the room.

"Evening, Onnie," he said, standing and hugging her in a manner similar to how Marco had done earlier.

"I really hope you didn't change your plans for me. I could have come to see you when it was more convenient."

As she hugged him back, she inhaled the sweet cologne he wore and was reminded of his son, Sam. Their smells being very similar.

He tsked at her and kissed her cheek before returning her to Marco's side. "Not an inconvenience at all. Would you like something to eat?"

"If you're sure. Yes, I'd love something."

Onnie's stomach growled at the thought of the deliciousness it was about to receive, and she rolled her eyes when both sanguistes heard it and smiled.

"Cheaters."

Marco chuckled softly as he buttoned his coat and slipped entirely into his maître d' mode.

"Would you prefer to eat here or in the dining room tonight?"

"Whatever. Both are fine for me."

Stephan nodded and held out his arm for her to take. "Then let's utilize the dining room this evening. We have a wonderful cellist playing tonight."

"Sounds lovely."

She was led out of the kitchen by Stephan and over to a corner table with ample privacy. Behind one chair was a wall, and on the other, a tall potted plant. Additionally, there were no other tables nearby.

These two men never did anything without intention, so she also assumed there was a reason behind that particular choice tonight.

Onnie took her seat when Marco pulled it out for her, and then he stepped away to fetch a menu. To her surprise, Stephan took the other free seat at the table.

"Would you mind if I joined you?" he asked as Marco returned.

"Not at all," she looked up at Marco, who smiled a bit wider than he usually did and she caught a glimpse of his sharp white teeth, which he usually kept concealed, shining in the low light.

"I'll join you after a bit. For now, you two enjoy," with that, he returned to the front of the cafe.

Onnie watched him go, and Stephan picked up on her shift in mood with ease.

"Don't worry, he's alright."

She looked at her dining partner, whose smile was small and sad, his eyes wearier than they had been in the kitchen.

"Is he really, though?" she said under her breath, but Stephan didn't respond.

Their dual introspections were interrupted by their server stopping to take her dinner order and a glass of wine for Stephan. The kid was clearly nervous about serving his boss and his guest, and when she recognized him as the same server from her first date with Gabe, she hid a small smile behind her hand. This time it wasn't a Guardian making the younger sanguiste anxious, it was his boss and she felt a little guilty for inadvertently causing anxiety again for the man a second time.

Once it was just her and Stephan again, Onnie sipped her wine, the crisp tartness of it making her tongue tingle slightly. They talked of light and fluffy topics while waiting for her meal and as she ate, and when she was finished, she set down her fork and sipped more of her wine.

"So, tell me about Elaric."

Stephan looked away from the cellist and at her with a passive expression.

"If Marco and Abbot knew him for so many years, you also had to. Am I wrong?"

Stephan smirked, "You are not. What would you like to know?"

She set her glass down and laced her fingers in her lap patiently. "What do I need to know?"

Stephan's expression shifted to a subtle one of fondness. "Sometimes I forget that you're Abbot's Granddaughter."

The fondness drained from his face, replaced with slight worry, and Stephan settled into his chair a bit more as he sipped his wine and then began watching Marco across the room. After a moment, he looked back at her.

"I presume you know of their relationship in the past?" When his voice showed no hint of judgment or prejudice, Onnie was relieved but would have been extremely surprised to find the man anything but accepting.

"Only that there was one, to which I say, good for them. Especially since they seem to get along extremely well even after it ended."

Stephan nodded, the corners of his lips turning down a fraction. "They do. Though it was a mutual decision to end it, both amicably and long ago, they have never ceased being incredibly important to one another. No one on this earth knows Marco as Elaric does. Not even me."

That surprised Onnie a bit. Marco and Stephan were basically family, so what did that make Elaric?

"Are you aware of how the sanguiste kind came to be, Keeper?" Stephan said, taking another sip of his wine.

With his shift into calling her by her title unmistakably intentional, Onnie sat up a bit straighter. "I am."

"But do you know the history written in the books or the one that truly came to pass, I wonder?"

The rare smirk on Stephan's face was one of intense amusement, and Onnie knew this was going to be an interesting conversation.

"I would hope the latter, but judging by your phrasing, probably the former. Enlighten me?"

Stephan finished his wine and placed the glass on the table between them, the residue of the blood-red wine still clinging to the sides of the glass. A moment later, Onnie's plates were cleared, and once the waiter had left, Stephan continued. Not that it truly mattered, most of the staff were sanguiste and would over hear their conversation anyway.

"Sanguiste have been around since the beginning of man. When man evolved into its bipedal form, it began to grow and evolve quickly, and one of the first things it did was create religion. Not as you and I would think of today, but a religion all the same. With that religion came the crossing of planes of existence."

"Planes of existence?" Onnie repeated, confirming she had heard him correctly and that she had indeed not learned the true history of the sanguiste.

"For ease of conversation, let's refer to it as the Underworld."

Her face must have given away what she'd been thinking because Stephan chuckled when he saw her switch from shock to confusion to interest. Or perhaps he saw or felt it through her emotions.

"With religion came the belief in death and the afterlife and with that, the Underworld and its inhabitants."

"Are you saying that Hell is real?"

"Probably not as you are picturing it, but yes, it is. Along with other planes, but that's a much longer conversation and not one fit for this location."

Kushima, I can't imagine he's lying about this.

He is not. Listen to his story, young one.

"Alright, continue. Please." Onnie took a large gulp of her wine and refocused.

"Man has not changed much over the millennia. Just as he is now, he was curious and thirsty for power then. One human called forth a denizen of the Underworld and made a pact with them. Near immortal life in exchange for their soul upon death."

"You're kidding me?"

Stephan's lowered eyes and slight head shake told her all she needed to know.

"Sanguiste consume either the life-blood of the body or the life-blood of the soul to survive. So, our connection with humans led to the growth of our species and continuation of the agreement, even until this day."

"Blood or emotions," Onnie said, referring to their nutrient source.

Stephan nodded and stared at his wine glass for a while before looking back at Marco, who was chatting up an elderly couple in the opposite corner of the restaurant.

"Immortality is extremely lonely, and while Elaric's kind may not be truly immortal, they have significantly extended lives. Elaric has been at Marco's side and vice versa since they met. They each provide the other with something no one else can."

"Understanding," Onnie stated.

Stephan looked at her and shook his head, "Unwavering loyalty. They would each do for the other whatever is needed for their survival, for one cannot live without the other anymore. They've seen too much together and been through too much. Watching loved ones die, wars be fought, prejudices come and go. They truly love each other in a way I can honestly not say I've ever seen anywhere else in all my many years."

Onnie gazed into her wine glass and saw her reflection frowning back up at her. "But what about Dany...."

She couldn't help but worry for her best friend, who was growing to love Elaric and had been friends with Marco since she was a child.

"My dearest," Onnie glanced up at Stephan, and he smiled, warmth radiating from his eyes. "Not all love is romantic, and while those two may have held that form of love for each other at one point, what they have now has far exceeded that. Dany is safe to love Elaric, and I believe he will return those feelings. However...." When Stephan's voice trailed off, Onnie's stomach sank as realization set in.

"She's a human."

"Indeed."

Onnie squeezed her eyes closed. *I understand now.*

Do not think of it as a negative, daughter mine. Elaric having and loving Marco does not lessen his feelings for Dany. Nor will any finite duration of time they may be given.

When she opened her eyes, Stephan was watching her. "I understand. Thank you for telling me the true history."

"Anything for my Keeper," he said with a nod before looking past her. "Marco, would you be so kind as to take my place?" Stephan got to his feet and straightened his suit coat. "I must return to work, I'm afraid."

"With pleasure," Marco said, appearing at Onnie's side and resting his hand on the back of her chair. "Dessert?" he asked with a smile.

"Why don't you take it upstairs?" Stephan suggested before leaning down to kiss Onnie's cheek. "Thank you for a lovely meal, Onnie."

"Please, let's do this more often," she said with a smile and genuine sincerity.

"You call—I'll be here." With that, Stephan nodded once to Marco and returned to the kitchen.

Marco offered Onnie his hand and gently helped her to her feet. "Shall we then?"

Onnie glanced around the dining floor, and when she saw another man at the restaurant's podium, she nodded. "Let's."

Once again, she was led into the kitchen, except this time Stephan was nowhere to be seen, and she and Marco went upstairs to his apartment.

"Please," he opened the door for her, "Come in. Sit wherever you find comfortable. I'll be right back."

When she nodded, he walked in behind her and headed into a room down a short hallway. Onnie wandered over to a soft-looking couch and sank into it with an outward sigh.

I'm exhausted.

It's been an interesting day, Kushima replied.

I think I understand Elaric a little better now.

"Would you prefer a place to rest?"

Marco's voice startled Onnie out of her head, and she saw he'd removed his suit coat and was walking towards her, a slight frown on his lips.

"I'm sorry, no," Onnie grinned. "I'd prefer to talk. It's just been an….interesting day," she snorted.

"I'll get us something sweet then." Marco's small smile returned, and he went into the kitchen and began plating two slices of cheesecake. "So, what made the day so exhaustingly interesting?"

"Ah...." Onnie pushed herself to her feet and changed to sitting at the kitchen bar. "Unexpected conversations. You know Miranda, correct?"

"The little one who prefers to stay silent?" Marco asked as he passed Onnie a plate and fork.

"Prefers?"

Marco smirked but said nothing more.

"Well," Onnie slid her fork through the end of the cheesecake, and her mouth watered despite having just eaten. "She came in wanting a new book to read and described to me what she wanted."

Marco brought his plate over and sat beside her. "Sounds normal so far."

"She described the Keeper's Prophecy down to the detail of the color blue." Onnie stuck a bite in her mouth and was pleased to see Marco look as shocked as she had been.

"Well, then." Marco took a bite of his cheesecake and chewed thoughtfully. "I'd agree. That would make for an interesting day."

Onnie laughed, and they ate in their contemplative silence until Marco broke it with an uncharacteristic request.

"When can he return, Keeper?"

His voice was low, and Onnie's whole being ached at the longing in it. When she saw that his head was lowered and he'd asked without looking at her, her heart hurt with how much Marco's posture looked practiced at trying to be unobtrusive. Just like hers often was.

"That's really up to him, but I hope quickly."

Marco said nothing more as they finished their desserts. It wasn't until they both had clean plates and were sitting on the couch that Marco finally broke the silence.

"I'm being selfish. I know that."

"Stop that," Onnie snapped without hesitation. "You are not, and I won't let you think that. We all want him to come home, and I can't imagine how you must feel, so please, don't stop wishing for him to come home." Marco smiled, but Onnie saw it didn't reach his eyes. "Marco?"

"Hmm?" he looked up at his name.

"Will you allow me to try something?" she shifted on the couch and scootched closer to him.

Kushima, this alright with you?

Be careful for Elaric's sake, but yes, please do.

"Ah...sure," Marco shifted and sat more upright and facing her. "What are we trying, out of curiosity?"

Onnie held out both hands, palms up. "Please, give me yours." Marco did as he was asked, and she gave them a slight squeeze. "Close your eyes and focus on your breathing. Make it even and calm."

"Alright." Marco did as he was told, no questions asked, and Onnie closed her eyes once he had.

She viewed the Bonds around her and focused on Marco's, which glittered like gold before her. Carefully, she searched for where his connected to Elaric's and felt Marco shiver beside her.

It's alright, that was me, she said along the Bond as she pulled a single of their connected threads and fused it with a single one of her own.

After a few minutes of Marco's patience and her focus, she softly nudged Marco mentally.

Focus on Elaric.

What am I supposed to think abo—

Onnie felt the instant Marco had connected with Elaric's Bond in his subconscious, and she quickly put a wall between them.

Sorry, we need to be extremely careful.

What was that? Marco's mental voice sounded a mix of frantic and hopeful.

I connected a small portion of his, mine, and your Bonds. I wanted you to feel that he was alright, not just take my word for it.

Marco didn't say anything for a few minutes, and when he did, his voice shook.

Please, I'll be careful. Can I feel it one more time?

Yes, but I need you to promise you won't reach out to him. I don't want to spook, distract, or put him in jeopardy.

Understood.

Slowly, Onnie lowered the barrier she'd risen, and she felt Elaric's consciousness move toward Marco's. They brushed against each other with the smallest of contact, and then she nudged Marco's once and began separating them all once again.

When she had finished and re-opened her eyes, she found Marco staring at her, his eyes glassy.

"Thank you."

She pulled him into her arms and squeezed him tightly.

"You're welcome, Marco."

Chapter 27: Foundings and Foundations

April 2022 - Alku | Onnie Moore

Dany's coming for tea, apparently, Onnie said to Kushima while simultaneously waving to a customer as they left the shop. *When I mentioned that I wanted to learn more about the prophecy and Keepers in general, she pretty much informed me she wanted to know, too and was on her way.*

Kushima laughed softly, and Onnie felt her amusement and affection for Dany via their Bond.

That's alright with me, though, your Sister most certainly knows nearly as much as I do.

Onnie snorted. *Probably right.*

It was about fifteen minutes until Dany said she'd be at the shop, so Onnie wandered into the backroom and put on the kettle.

Kushima, is there anything you don't want me to ask her? I don't want to put you in an awkward position.

Appreciated, however, do not fret. I'll let you know if something comes up in our conversation.

Onnie nodded and pulled a tin of cookies from the small cabinet next to the hotplate. When she popped off the lid, shortbread, biscotti, and lemon drop fragrances hit her nose, and she grinned.

"Mrs. Radcliff's cookies are magic," Onnie stilled. "Wait, are they?"

This time, Kushima's amusement made Onnie blush at her blurted-out question, but Kushima merely added, *Quite possible, especially with that woman in particular.*

After replacing the lid on the tin of sweets, Onnie set it on the serving tray and began collecting everything for when Dany arrived, which was nearly fifteen minutes exactly.

"Onnie?" Dany shouted from the front of the shop.

Why are you shouting? Onnie giggled along their Bond. *I'm in the sitting area. I made tea.*

Oops, habit, I guess.

When Dany entered the sitting area, Onnie noticed her friend's cheeks were slightly pink, and chances were she'd felt embarrassed over her shouting.

"Hey," Onnie smiled warmly and began pouring them each a cup of tea. "How's the library?"

Dany groaned, flopped into one of the chairs, and went dramatically limp. "It's fine."

Onnie chuckled and wiggled the fingers of one of her hands in Dany's direction. "That's fine?"

She passed Dany her cup as the woman sat up and added a few cookies to her saucer.

"Yeah, it's nothing. I was working on the plan to restore the library, and it's just a lot."

"I'm sure it is. Let me know if something changes, and I can help."

Dany nodded before sipping her tea with a contented sigh.

Onnie pulled a shortbread cookie from the tin, but Mal had relocated beside her elbow before she'd put it in her mouth. She glanced down at him where he sat on the arm of the chair next to her and looked between her and her cookie repeatedly.

She rolled her eyes and held it out to him. "I swear you only like me for the food."

Mal already had the cookie in his mouth, so when he responded with, "Not true," around the sweet, it lost some of his intended reassurance.

Dany laughed and poked his side. "Honestly. You'll eat anything."

The cat stepped into the chair and continued his nibbling after retorting, "Not anything. Have you ever had one of Elsi's cookies?"

"The Elsi who runs the occult shop and spelled my ring for me?" Onnie asked with a tilt of her head.

"Yeah," Mal said around a chew. "Don't."

Dany giggled, "He's right. She tries, but food is not one of her strengths."

"Noted," Onnie said with a grin before taking a large gulp of her tea and retrieving another cookie for herself to replace the one Mal had absconded with.

After a few minutes of contented sipping and nibbling, Dany cleared her throat. "So, you wanted to know more about the prophecy and Keepers in general?"

"I do. I've learned a lot already, but considering I had no idea about the prophecy, my assumption is you withheld a few key books intentionally."

Dany winced.

Onnie held up her palm. "It's fine. What's done is done, but now I'd like to know. The First Keeper offered to tell me," Onnie grinned. "Though she mentioned you probably know as much as she does."

A second blush crept up Dany's cheeks, and she shook her head emphatically, but the First Keeper cut off her protests.

She is correct, Sister. I'm confident you could teach her all that she needs to know. However, I will be able to provide some first-hand accounts.

"Hello, First Keeper," Dany said with a glance to the ceiling. "Thanks for that."

No thanks needed. It's but the truth.

"Well," Dany looked at Onnie, "what do you want to know first?"

"Don't know what I don't know, for the most part," Onnie shrugged. "That said, I don't know the actual origin story of the Keepers. Gabe told me a few things about some of the early Keepers during the Transference, but nothing before that."

"Sounds like a good place to start, then." Dany looked up again, "Please interrupt whenever."

I will.

Dany settled into her chair more and sighed in contentment once comfortable.

"Well, the first Keeper—" Dany hesitated. "Damn, it feels odd talking about you like you're not here."

Onnie heard Kushima laugh, but Dany carried on.

"The First Keeper was born around 3400 B.C.E., and at least from what records I've seen, you were human, right?"

I was. Not much older than you two when I became the Keeper.

"If you were the first, did you just...make it up?" Onnie smirked.

Mal chuckled, "Nope, she was a classic case of voluen-told."

"Really?" Onnie said, slightly surprised.

While he's not exactly incorrect, it was closer to being nominated. Brat.

Dany smirked, "It was a group of magical beings, right?"

Yes. Much like the Transference, a representative from several races and species decided that at the rate humans were evolving, magic's extinction wasn't wholly unfathomable.

"Wait, they thought humans would destroy magic?" Onnie frowned.

"At the time, humans were one of the younger races. Sanguiste, paranam, even hedge witches are older."

Onnie opened her mouth to ask what a paranam was, but Mal beat her to it.

"Animal shifters."

"Thanks," Onnie said, breaking off a piece of her cookie for him. "Wait, humans are younger?"

Didn't Stephan say sanguiste were created from one of the first humans? Onnie asked only Kushima.

You're partly correct, Kushima said, answering Onnie's question so everyone could hear her. *It's not that those species were older than humans. It's that they evolved faster. For example, a hedge witch is still human. Just one advanced enough that they are receptive to the magic of the soil.*

"Good point," Dany agreed. "Humans may have been the first to exist, but we fell behind on the evolutionary line very early on."

"Okay, so you were nominated to be...the Keeper?" Onnie said, rubbing her forehead as she tried to cram more information into her brain.

Yes. I was, quite literally, to be the vessel for the information. Through magic and ritual, I was changed from a human into something...more. I spent my life learning, and when my time finally ran out....

"All that effort was," Dany paused. "Is rewarded the right word?"

Kushima laughed once more. *Yes, I'd say so now. Perhaps not in the beginning, though.*

Onnie frowned and looked down at the red tea swirling in the cup in her lap. Kushima presumably blocked her emotions, but her voice still told the non-verbal footnotes.

Don't fret, Onnie, Kushima reassured. *I did agree with Dany's use of the word reward. While I was made into the entity I am now, another Keeper was chosen. Over the millennia, I have witnessed and experienced incomparable amounts to what I would have had I remained simply a human.*

Dany glanced at Onnie and then between them said, *She sounds so sad.*

I know. The amount of loneliness....

Onnie took a deep breath. "I get it. Though, I can't help but think of my conversation with Stephan last night."

Indeed. The situations are somewhat similar.

Dany raised one eyebrow, and Onnie shook her head. "Later. Not important right now."

"That's basically it, though. After the First Keeper, subsequent ones were found, they bonded with her and eventually began housing physical records, not just internalized information."

"Where was the first location?" Onnie asked.

"Mediterranean," Mal yawned.

"Oh."

Onnie sipped her tea quietly before asking Kushima, *Is that where your library was?*

Kushima seemed hesitant, and Onnie forced herself to keep a poker face.

That, I think, is one of those questions we'd best speak of later. And within said Library.

Understood.

"Onnie?" Mal said, drawing her attention to him.

"Hmm?"

"Could you, um, make me some tea?" the feline's eyes glanced away.

"Of course," Onnie put down her cup and scratched under his chin before steeping some of the Keeper's tea in the small bowl that she always brought with the tea set, especially for Mal.

"So, then, what about the prophecy?" Onnie asked while she brewed. "Can I assume that was the catalyst for your nomination, First Keeper?"

"Close," Dany said with a proud grin. "Good guess."

Agreed, it was at the end of my life as a human Keeper, not the beginning.

"Before the First Keeper became the entity she is today, a magical being spoke the prophecy and...well...." Dany hesitated.

I cannot be of my own blood, as it were.

Onnie set the bowl near Mal and then poured herself another cup while she processed aloud. "Ah. They extrapolated that by that logic, there would at least be a *second* Keeper."

Precisely.

Logically, Onnie knew her next question, but after her previous night's conversation about Marco, she hesitated even to ask. Kushima must have realized what she'd been thinking, though, and offered the information herself.

However, my child was not fit for the role. So, it went to another.

"Makes sense," Dany chirped. "Tory wasn't Keeper before you,

Onnie."

"True."

Though her mother had wanted to become the Keeper, she was evidently not the right fit for what Kushima needed.

I needed you, daughter of my blood. Though, for the short time she was here, I enjoyed watching young Tory run between my shelves.

Onnie smiled at the genuine fondness that Kushima had for her mom, and once more, she was reminded that she needed to find the rogue guardian so life could carry on as it should. She missed her family.

Having finished his tea, Mal relocated himself into Onnie's lap and bonked his head into her chin.

Cat, you okay? Gabe asked along their Bond.

Yes, sorry.

You sure?

Yes. Dany and the First Keeper were telling me how Keepers were created, and...it's just sad.

Alright. If you're sure.

Thanks, Gabe.

Love you.

Onnie smiled and snuggled Mal.

Love you, too.

She'd been mistaken in her thinking. She didn't miss her family. She missed *part* of her family. There were multiple people with her in Alku, and while all of them were focused on stopping Jakob, they were more than enough.

"Wait," Onnie said suddenly, making Dany jump.

"What?" she said, clutching her chest.

"What about the Custos regni? Where does it fit into all of this?"

"It's the recorded history of the Keepers," Mal said while pulling one of Onnie's hands to his belly for pets with his front paws.

"Think of it like a diary. Each Keeper is added to it, and a summary of their time is recorded. Though, it's more just a formality now, I think."

Yes, realistically, most of these books in here are. I no longer need to guide my Keeper to find that which they need. I can relay what I know directly to Onnie.

"Convenient," Onnie smiled. "Feels a bit like cheating, though."

Dany chuffed, "Take what you can get, Onnie. Gods knows you'll have enough other challenges during your reign."

"Ug, don't call it that. Makes me feel like a dictator or something."

"Whatever you say, ma'am," Mal teased, and Onnie switched from petting to tickling him.

"Why do you do that, by the way?" Onnie asked but noticed Dany and Mal's confused expressions. "Sorry. Why do you make god plural? I noticed Gabe does, too."

Dany's face fell a bit, and Onnie immediately regretted her question. "You don't have to—"

Dany shook her head, "It's fine. Short answer is because Abbot raised us like that." She smiled fondly as her eyes went somewhere distant. "This world has many gods. Not just one. While Gabe and I may follow one religion or another, we still acknowledge that others exist."

"Are...are gods real then, too?" Onnie asked.

"In a way," Dany shrugged.

What you might think of as a god or, rather, what society does, doesn't matter. Someone's belief in them makes them real to that individual.

"Abbot would say, 'Your god or someone else's, it doesn't matter. They are all real to the people who believe in them.'" Dany snorted, "Then he'd add, 'Besides, when asking for help, why limit yourself to just one god when you can ask them all?'"

Onnie stared at Dany for a few seconds before they both erupted in laughter.

"Old man sure had his own sass," Mal said through his own belly laugh.

"I guess he's got a point. Oh, First Keeper?"

Yes?

Um, can I ask about the other planes Stephan mentioned? Onnie checked privately along their Bond.

You may.

"Someone mentioned other planes of existence to me the other day. Anything you can elaborate on?" Onnie asked.

Sure, but it's relatively simple in its complexity. We...well, you are on one plane, but it's not the only one.

"And you're...not?" Dany asked, evidently also catching the First Keeper's phrasing.

"The void," Onnie stated.

Correct. Technically, the void is a separate plane from yours. The Bond and I reside on that plane.

"Well, that's cool," Dany said with a grin. "I had no idea."

Kushima laughed. *I'm glad I was actually able to teach you something.*

Dany scoffed, "Not to sound too much like Mal, but shush. You teach me something all the time. Even if it's via Onnie."

Onnie beamed at her best friend and couldn't stifle her cough when the magnitude of Kushima's happiness pressed on Onnie's chest.

"So, since the Bond is a one-to-one with our plane, does that mean there are others that overlap?" Onnie asked, shifting Mal off her lap so she could lean forward and rub her temples. Everything she'd learned was making her head stuffy as she tried to file it all and not miss a detail.

"Sounds like?" Dany shrugged.

For the most part, yes. There are a few that have slipped out of the stack, as it were, over eternity, but generally speaking, most are lined up neatly like pages in a book.

Onnie got to her feet and paced the small space a few times. She faintly heard Dany talking to either Mal or the First Keeper in the background, but she ignored them.

If the void was a different plane than hers, then what was happening when she projected a visual representation of herself into it? Did that mean she'd moved to that plane? Just her mind, or maybe she was straddling the two of them. The possibilities were endless, and she felt her cheeks begin to hurt from smiling.

"Onnie!" Dany shouted, making her jump.

"Whoops," Onnie blushed and sat back in her chair.

"Damn girl," Mal said, "wish I had that amount of focus."

Onnie leaned over and booped the tip of his nose with her own. "You do."

"With what?"

"Food." Onnie, Dany, and Kushima said in unison and then began laughing.

Mal's grin went wide like the Cheshire Cat. "Hmm, what's for dinner?" he asked before joining in with their laughter.

Chapter 28: Friendly Fire

April 2022 - Alku | Gabriel Vansand

Gabe was standing off to one side in the school's gym, watching Onnie in the center of the room. Her eyes were closed, but she didn't seem to be paying much attention to either him or Dany, who was opposite him, evaluating their Keeper.

"Focus, Cat!" Gabe snapped and threw a tennis ball across the room directly at Onnie.

Her eyes popped open, and she winced, but before the ball made contact with her, there was a flash of light, and it was deflected and flew off in another direction.

"Hey! What was that for?"

"You weren't paying attention," Gabe smirked and threw another ball, this time at Dany.

"Ah!" Dany shouted, ducked, and covered her head, but as before, a flash of light deflected it away. "Gabe!" Dany screeched at him as she stood back up, hands fisted on her hips.

"What? Don't trust your best friend to save you?"

Dany glared at him, and Onnie picked up a nearby ball and tried to throw it back at him, but he saw it from the corner of his eye and sidestepped it easily.

"Too easy, Cat. I saw you pick it up. Get creative. Try to do it without moving next time."

Onnie cocked her head to the side as she processed his suggestion, but her eyes widened quickly, and her face lit up.

"Good idea!"

When an evil smile crept into her lips, he rolled his eyes. He just had to open his mouth. A second later, another ball shot at him from its stationary position on the floor next to her, and he barely managed to dodge this one.

"Better!"

He was about to praise her but was cut short by a ball smacking him in the back of the head. Both women erupted in giggles, and he had to admit it was pretty funny and chuckled right along with them.

"Alright, troublemakers. If you've got time to laugh, you've got time for scenario training." The pair groaned, and he smirked wickedly as he crossed his arms and shook his head. "Nope, you made your beds."

"You suck," Dany bemoaned as she walked over to Onnie's side.

He shrugged, "Someone has to be the villain."

Onnie narrowed her eyes at him and smirked. "You're having way too much fun with this."

"I sure am. Ready?" he asked once Dany was at Onnie's side.

"Yup," Onnie said.

"Ug," Dany added.

Gabe took a deep breath and relayed instructions audibly to Onnie and mentally only to Dany.

Her right. Grab three.

Dany dashed over to where he said to and snatched three balls from the floor.

One at her, then me, hide the third. Then distract her. Throw more, bump into her, get in her way. Whatever you can think of.

Will do.

Dany did as instructed and threw one tennis ball at Onnie and then chucked the second she held as hard as she could at him. Onnie deflected the projectile that was aimed toward her with ease. While Onnie was focused on defense, Dany ran past her, only a few inches from her face. He saw Onnie blink a few times and try to regain her focus.

"Retaliate!" Gabe shouted as the second ball Dany had thrown was on its way straight for him. At the last second, it bounced off a shield and flew off to the side. Before it touched the floor, Onnie shot it and the first ball back at Dany, who was now picking up ammunition on the far side of the room.

"Block!"

Onnie winced, but just before the first ball she'd just thrown was about to hit Dany, a golden shield flashed around her, and both balls bounced off of it and rolled away.

Damn, Gabe. She's not touched a single ball.

What did you expect?

Dany chuckled, making Gabe smile.

I'll distract her, sneak up behind her with the practice sword.

Got it, Dany said, even her mental voice breathing heavily from running around the room and throwing things.

He bent down, pulled a few more balls from the basket at his feet, and threw four rapid fire at opposite directions in the room, keeping wide of where Dany was sneaking around.

"Block the first and third. Send the fourth back!"

"I," Onnie said as the first ball bounced off a shield before it hit the wall.

"Really," the second ball was ignored, and the third bounced off a shield covering a stack of mats.

"Hate you," the fourth ball stopped its trajectory mid-air and zoomed back towards him, making him duck, but he still felt the air displacement as it whizzed by him.

When he looked back up, Onnie was bent over and had braced herself on her knees while she breathed heavily. He saw Dany wasn't quite ready, so he snagged one more ball and threw it at Onnie.

"Block, then return."

Her head snapped up at his voice, the ball nearly to her by the time she saw it, but just before he was about to feel incredibly guilty, it bounced off the glowing shield and was flung off into a far corner of the gym before it shifted direction in mid-air and sailed back toward him. This time, it smacked into his thigh, and he gasped at the impact of it. Damn, she packed a punch when she wanted to, and with him and Dany, he knew Onnie still had kid gloves on.

"Seriously, Gabe, you are both sadist and masochist," Onnie said with a grin, obviously proud of herself.

Gabe pointedly ignored Dany, who was now directly behind Onnie with her arm pulled back to swing the foam sword at Onnie's midsection. He looked down at a ball near his feet, knowing that his face would give away Dany's actions if he continued watching her.

"Ooof!" Dany grunted.

He looked up and saw that Onnie hadn't moved, turned, or even looked behind herself, but she'd raised one hand and caught the sword, a shield wrapped around her hand like a glove. The full strength of the impact was seemingly nullified. The glow pulsed and surrounded the sword blade and her palm, but she merely smirked.

"Nice try," she said and dropped the shield.

The sword and Dany stumbled forward until Onnie caught her using the Bond before she fully fell over.

"Damn, girl. How'd you know?" Dany asked and regained her balance as Gabe walked over to join them.

"I had my eyes closed and was trying to breathe. I slipped into the void to watch the Bond while I was vulnerable and saw you coming. When I opened my eyes, I just kind of…kept the Bonds up. So each time I blinked, it was there." Onnie scrunched her face, "Actually, that doesn't make any sense."

"Holy shit, really?" Dany said, grinning and basically dancing in place.

"Yeah, it was like when my eyes were open, I saw like normal, but every time my eyes closed, even for a second, the Bond showed up. It kind of flickered like an old-fashioned projector."

Gabe wrapped his arms around the genuinely remarkable human before him and kissed the top of her head.

"Good job, Cat."

She pinched his side but then hugged him back.

You're amazing, he said and sent his feelings of pride along their Bond to her.

Honestly, I'm not sure how I did it initially, but it felt like...instinct.

Nothing wrong with that. Now, we just need to practice it.

Onnie groaned, and Dany raised one eyebrow at them. "No more. Not tonight?" Onnie said, muffled in his sweatshirt.

"No, not tonight." He pulled away from her to place his hands on her cheeks and quickly kissed her lips. "You did good."

"Hey!" Dany whined. "What about me? I did good, too!"

Gabe laughed and ruffled his sister's hair, earning himself a glare and a swing of the practice sword that he parried with his forearm.

"You did good too, Dany."

Mal appeared on a nearby pile of mats and yawned. "What did I miss?"

Gabe, Onnie, and Dany looked at each other, and then Dany said, *I'll get the balls!*

Gabe watched as Mal's eyes widened, and then he relocated, their mental laughter following him to wherever he went into hiding.

Chapter 29: Coordinated Deception

May 2022 - Alku | Onnie Moore

Onnie was seated at Abbot's desk in the shop, reading an extremely old book with yellowing pages, when she realized she'd just read the same page twice. She blinked a few times, but before she could read it for the third time, Dany groaned from the couch, and Onnie looked up to see what was wrong.

"My brain hurts," Dany said, pressing her fingertips to her temples and rubbing small circles. "How long have we been sitting here?"

"Like, eight hours," Mal replied through a yawn from his place in front of the fire on a pile of blankets.

"Wait, really?" Onnie said, tapping her phone and checking the time. "Damn, you're right. These candles Xayn made are miracle workers." Onnie stared at one of the sconces across the room where new candles had been placed a few days prior.

"I'm glad he did that," Dany smiled fondly. "Elaric suggested it on a whim and was pretty shocked to hear Xayn agree to make some."

"Really?"

Dany nodded. "Most green witches stick to small talismans, tinctures, and stuff like that. Xayn's extremely rare in that aspect."

"Huh, neat. Didn't realize. I'll have to ask him more about it when I see him."

Onnie sneezed unexpectedly, and Dany jumped at the suddenness of it.

"Sorry, must be the dust," Onnie sniffled.

Dany nodded and then shifted so she sat sideways against the back of the couch, looking at Onnie, the desk positioned behind the couch. "I'm hungry."

"We should be, considering the time. Cafe?" Onnie leaned back in her chair far enough that her back cracked.

"Fine with me," Dany unburdened herself from the two dozen books she'd become surrounded by and got to her feet.

Onnie reached for her Bond with Elaric, brushed it gently, and waited for his acknowledgment as she walked over to Mal. "Mal, you coming with us, or am I bringing you back something?"

"I'll stay here. Lock up, though. I don't want to deal with customers." The feline tucked his paws beneath himself and snuggled up tighter.

"As if," Dany said, walking over to poke him playfully. "When do *you* deal with customers?"

Onnie snorted, but then she felt Elaric's brush along their Bond, indicating he was safe to talk.

Hey, Onnie. What's up?

Dany and I are going to the Day Night Cafe to grab some lunch. Anything you need from us?

Onnie stuck her phone into her pocket as she wandered to the front of the shop, leaving Dany and Mal to their friendly ribbing of one another.

Good timing, actually. He's getting antsy for progress. I'll come eavesdrop. Mind warning Vanessa and Sam?

Sure, anything you need specifically?

"I'm seeing if anyone else wants to join us," Onnie said, implying that someone was Elaric.

"Good idea."

Onnie stopped at the shop's coat rack and then bundled up while she waited for Dany to catch up.

Back in a bit, Kushima.

Enjoy your lunch.

Dany grabbed her coat and stepped onto the sidewalk while Onnie locked the door behind them and hung a small laminated sign on the door. The words, *Will return shortly*, and the shop's phone number were the only things printed on it, and she figured if someone wanted to leave her a message, they could.

Onnie looped her arm into Dany's and whispered, "Warn Vanessa and Sam that we're coming."

Dany nodded once and pulled out her phone to make a call just as Elaric answered Onnie.

Not really, but stay away from the prophecy, I think. I get the feeling he's...too interested in it right now.

Gottcha. See you soon. We just left.

Onnie felt Elaric pull away from their Bond, and she gave Dany the side eye as she finished her call.

Dany had told a few key people around Alku about Elaric's form and what to do if they saw him. Everyone was being careful not to reveal too much information, just in case someone slipped up, but it helped create situations they could set up in advance to suit Elaric's needs. Sam, Vanessa, Marco, and Stephan knew that if they called before their meal, Elaric would be close behind, and they should turn a blind eye to anything possibly odd.

After learning about Elaric's interaction with Elanor the day Harry had first left the bookshop, they realized that genuine reactions were helpful, but sometimes they just needed people to ignore Elaric's sleaze-ball character. When he had told Onnie of Elanor's response to him cursing out the Keeper on the day he'd first joined the rogue, she'd giggled at the frail-looking woman's vigor. They'd later informed her of who had been so rude, and after a hearty laugh, she nodded and began to play her part as the town's patient zero of gossip beautifully.

"Leaving now, Sam. Thanks." When Dany hung up, she grinned. "Sam's working today, and he's going to spoil your cat."

Onnie snorted, "I'm sure he will. What this time?"

"He said they got in fresh tuna. It's supposed to be for tonight, but he snuck some out to make Mal sashimi."

Onnie rolled her eyes, acting not required. "I swear, one day, he might not be able to fit through the shop's door with the inflated ego he's growing."

"Tell me about it," Dany laughed and then abruptly shivered.

They were crossing into City Center Park, and the clear sky, while beautiful, always carried with it a bit of a bite. Once they were through the trees and into the park entirely, Onnie listened to the soft whisper of leaves above her and Dany and the quiet crunch sounds of their shoes. A few birds flew past them as they traversed the obscured footpath, and everything felt calm and at rest within the garden space.

Alku had a magic about it that Onnie had begun to notice more and more each day and it was clear that the town was more sentient than everyone gave it credit for. When trouble brewed, animals hid, and the wind died. If everything was calm and peaceful, people milled about with smiles, and flowers bloomed that should still be sleeping. Even when Abbot had died, the town grew grey and lifeless, as if it were mourning along with everyone else. Onnie would bet her lake house that Alku's out of season weather wasn't being caused by global warming.

"Wanna talk about it?" Dany asked, and Onnie looked up at her with a questioning frown. "You're ruminating. I can feel it."

"Oh," Onnie's frown retreated, and she shrugged. "Nothing much. I was enjoying the calm."

Dany snorted, "Yeah, we probably should while we have the chance, I guess."

They finished the rest of their short walk quietly and enjoyed the tail end of winter all around them. Once they exited the park and crossed the street, Sam awaited them outside the Day Night Cafe in an oversized puffer coat and a beanie.

"You look like your coat is trying to eat you," Onnie teased and hugged the day walker, who was more air than human at that moment.

"Yeah, and it's winning," Dany added and playfully punched his arm, the coat sinking in and her fist never even reaching his body.

"Hey, the calendar might say May, but damn if it's not still cold this year."

"Can't argue with that, though your coat does look a bit overkill."

The three of them removed their jackets and hung them on hooks just inside the double doors.

Sam snickered, "Sure as shit's warm, though."

"Oy," Dany replied distractedly as she quickly scanned the room for Elaric. Onnie did the same, and when she locked eyes with Dany, they silently agreed he hadn't arrived yet.

"Let's get you two some food then."

Sam went deeper into the warm cafe and to the counter stocked with sandwiches, anti-pastas, and baked goods by day and shifted to a fully stocked bar after dark. Both of them followed Sam away from the store's door, and they were nearly at the counter when Onnie started coughing. Dany turned back to look at her with a raised eyebrow.

"Fine..." Onnie said through a few coughs. "I think...too much dust earlier...."

Sam frowned, "Tea for you then. With honey and lemon."

Onnie nodded and rubbed her neck. The sudden cough had caught her off guard, and now her throat burned.

"Please."

"Go sit," Dany said, indicating to a table along the side of the cafe that would leave room for Elaric but give them all a bit of privacy from the rest of the diners. "I'll order."

Her throat tickled again, so Onnie nodded and did as she was told.

Before Dany had even ordered, the young woman with a crush on Sam hurried over with a pot of hot water, a mug with honey, and a lemon already in it. She carefully set them on the table and stepped back.

"I didn't hear which tea you wanted, but I already put in the honey and lemon for you. I hope that's alright?" The woman had spoken quickly, her nervousness plainly affecting her speed, and she realized and looked away.

"That's perfect, thank you. I have my own with me."

"Oh," the woman smiled, "alright. I added the same amount my Uncle uses. Let me know if you need more or a refill of anything later."

Onnie returned her smile as she dug through her bag without looking down. "I will. Thank you."

With a small tip forward, the young woman bowed and scurried back to Sam and Dany.

I really will never get used to that, Kushima, Onnie said while she finished prepping her tea.

And what would that be?

People bowing to me.

Kushima laughed softly, and Onnie rolled her eyes. *Are you laughing at me?*

Yes and no. I only laugh because I remember saying something similar in my past.

Oh? Onnie hadn't had the chance to talk to Kushima much about the First Keeper's human life, but Onnie was painfully curious.

Yes. It wasn't until the end of my life that it began to happen, but it always made me...uncomfortable.

With her tea made and steeped, Onnie sipped it with her eyes closed. The hot water with the extra honey coated her throat, and she instantly felt better.

Why only at the end?

Ah, because it wasn't until near the end of my time that I was anything more than a human.

Would you tell me about it? I'd like to know more about your life. If you're alright with that, of course.

Yes, though that's quite a long story and one too lengthy for this afternoon.

Onnie smiled into her mug. *Thank you.*

A cold draft blew against the back of Onnie's neck when someone entered the cafe, and she didn't need to turn around to know it was Elaric.

He's here, Onnie told Dany and Kushima at the same time.

Neither replied, and Onnie didn't acknowledge the newcomer at all. Instead, she topped off her tea, another slight cough escaping before she could choke it down.

Crap, I really hope I'm not catching a cold.

Hm, yes, that would certainly be inconvenient.

Dany grinned as she approached their table, a carry-out bag in one hand and a mug of something steaming in her other. Once she set it on the table, Onnie could smell the spices and breathed in deeply.

"That smells amazing."

"Doesn't it?" Dany said, taking a seat. "You're welcome to try some."

Onnie shook her head, "No, better not. I'm not feeling very well, and I don't want to chance getting you sick."

Dany stowed the bag safely under her chair and tipped her head to the side. "Really? That was fast."

"Well, I don't feel sick, but better safe than sorry." Onnie leaned over Dany's cup and breathed in the fragrant steam. "I'll just live vicariously."

They both laughed as Elaric walked past them and up to the counter, and Onnie watched as Sam shooed off the young woman in their direction and began to take Elaric's order himself. After a minute in the kitchen, the woman came to swap the personal-sized teapot on their table with a fresh one.

"Ah," Onnie cleared her throat. "Sorry. Um, I don't think we've actually ever met. I'm Onnie, though I'll hold off shaking your hand until next time."

"Wait, you've never met Genevieve before?" Dany said quickly, looking between them. "Shit, I'm sorry, I didn't realize."

"Ah, yeah, not actually introduced," Genevieve looked down at her shoes. "I know who you are, though. Of course. Keeper."

"Nope," Onnie corrected and smiled at the young woman when she looked at her in confusion. "I'm just Onnie."

Dany sniggered, "Yeah. Call her Keeper at your own risk."

Genevieve blushed, but Sam waved her back to the counter before she could argue. She took Onnie's empty teapot and left with another slight bow.

"Thanks for that, Dany."

"Course, I know you hate it."

Onnie nodded and glanced over to the counter as Elaric collected his lunch and walked away. They didn't make eye contact, and Onnie sighed inwardly.

Guess we better get this over with, she said to Dany.

"Are you still angry at Gabe and Mal?" Dany said, initiating their conversation.

"Yeah, though it's complicated considering the...relationship. Obviously."

"Well, yeah, not to mention you all live together." Dany sat back in her chair and crossed her arms over her chest. "That can't make it very easy to get some space."

Onnie laughed, but it turned into a cough, and she saw Dany frown. "Tell me about it. For just one night, I think I want to be *just* Onnie again."

Dany didn't get a chance to respond as Sam walked over and delivered their meals, but Onnie could tell the woman had an opinion she wanted to share.

"Enjoy, you two. Come say goodbye before you leave," he smiled and left them to their food and deception.

They ate silently for a few minutes as they paid the debts from their earlier focus at Abbot's. When Onnie sneezed a minute later, Dany's eyes went wide.

"Alright, that's it. I'm calling Xayn."

Before Onnie had swallowed and could argue, Dany had done just that.

"There. I texted him."

"Why?" Onnie finally managed to ask, the bite of food she swallowed scratching her inflamed throat on the way down.

"You're clearly getting sick. I asked him to bring you one of his tonics."

"You didn't have to do that. Rest, tea, and—"

Dany's phone vibrated, cutting Onnie off, and her best friend grinned at the screen. "He'll meet us at your house in an hour."

"Fine."

Onnie really was starting to feel worse and didn't have the energy to argue. She hadn't been sick in a while and, truthfully, could use a day in bed with comfort foods and no lingering threats of annihilating the world of magic.

"Thank you. Both."

Dany waved the air before her to dismiss Onnie's thanks as unneeded as she chewed.

Hey, you two, Onnie said to Gabe, Mal, and included Dany.

What's up, Cat?

Dany and I are at the Day Night Cafe, and I'm not feeling well, so—

What? What's wrong? Gabe's voice switched to his Guardian tone in an instant.

She's got the sniffles and a bit of a cough, Dany said. *I texted Xayn.*

I was just giving you the heads-up, but I'm fine. Really.

I'll come home early, Cat.

Gabe, Dany said with a slight laugh. *She's not dying. Finish your classes, and I'll keep an eye on her. Between Mal, Xayn, and me, Onnie will be fine.*

Onnie giggled as she could feel the turmoil within Gabe as he struggled to choose between his two responsibilities.

We're supposed to be fighting anyways, Onnie added and was relieved when that seemed to calm him down.

She's got a point, man. Leave it to us, Mal said.

Fine, but...text me, Gabe added, and Onnie felt him press on their Bond, his frustration and sadness over their current situation like a rolling wave.

Promise, Onnie said, and all of them retreated from the conversation.

"Worry wort," Dany said hushed, and Onnie coughed again after trying to stifle a laugh.

"Finish eating, and we can go. You need to get in bed."

Dany paused, and Onnie saw her eyes twinkle. That now familiar spark of mischief Onnie had learned meant that the woman was scheming something. Before she could ask what it was that time, Dany spoke.

"Besides, what would happen if another roach showed up while you were sick? It's difficult enough for you to control your growing powers, and when Keepers get sick, there's weird shit that happens."

What are you planning? Onnie asked with narrowed eyes.

Roll with it.

"What...weird shit?" Onnie asked tentatively.

Dany snorted. "Well, there was this one time when Abbot was sick," Dany paused to think for a second. "I think Gabe and I were like...ten and twelve? Anyway, he had stayed out too late in the rain helping someone with something, and the next day, he had a cold. Abbot being Abbot," Dany smiled, and Onnie smirked, "he went into the shop anyway. It was a mess when Gabe and I got there after school."

"Physically?" Onnie asked.

"Yeah," Dany giggled. "He'd taken over-the-counter cold medicine, and his brain was so foggy that he couldn't feel the shop when she told him where things were. Books were everywhere. A copy of IT by Steven King was in the phonics section, Dracula was with the romance novels, and there was a book about mechanites in the computer science section."

Onnie smirked, "Are you kidding?" before adding to Kushima, *Is this true?*

The woman only replied with a laugh.

"Nope, completely true. Rebecca was furious. Running around the shop after him like a mother picking up toys behind her toddler.

Scolding him the entire time, too." Dany laughed and then looked into her lap and got quiet.

"I miss him too, Dany," Onnie said softly.

After a few seconds, Dany nodded. "Yeah." She sniffled and then cleared her throat. "My point is. You need rest. So hurry up and finish, and we can get you home and into bed."

Onnie sighed but wearily obeyed. When she sneezed a second time, her eyes rolled at Dany's crossed arms and satisfied smile of being right.

Onnie snuggled deeper into the blankets on her bed and listened to Dany and Xayn discussing her prognosis as if she weren't beside them.

"Do you think it's just a cold?" Dany asked while Xayn pulled bottles and jars from his backpack.

"I'm not a doctor, Dany," Xayn grinned before looking over at Onnie, "but looks like one to me, for what little that's worth."

Onnie smiled and mouthed a quick thank you to him behind Dany's back. The woman was overreacting, and Onnie was grateful not to be the only one who saw it.

"Fine, if you're sure," Dany said and sat on the bed at Onnie's feet.

"I'll give you a few of these tonics. They're nutrients mostly." He placed a few green glass bottles of liquid on the nightstand. "This one," he held up a larger, blue-glass one, "will help you sleep if needed. There are two doses here for someone your size, so keep that in mind."

"You mean pocket-sized?" Dany teased.

"Excuse me," Onnie said softly, "I prefer fun-sized."

Xayn snorted and shook his head, "And I prefer to plead the fifth." He zipped up his bag and looked back at Onnie. "Stay in bed, though. Whatever this is, bedrest will only help, not hurt."

"Thanks, Xayn," Onnie said smiling. "For the house call, too."

He shrugged, "No big. I brought in some things for Mrs. Radclif. Just a day early, so don't worry about it."

Onnie knew he was trying to make her feel better and appreciated the effort. "Tell her I said hello?"

"Will do."

"Come on. I'll walk you out." Dany got to her feet and followed him out of the bedroom, but not before she glared over her shoulder at Onnie. "You. Stay."

Onnie's eyes widened, and she nodded, earning herself a laugh from her friends as they left.

Are they overreacting? Onnie asked Kushima.

What do you mean?

Is what Dany said earlier about Abbot true? Was he really...dangerous or something?

Yes and no. It's not that you will be out of control or hurt anyone, but just like anyone else, sickness clouds the mind, and you have more to obscure than others. That's all. Knowing Dany, she's probably exaggerating because she's concerned, young one. Let her show her love for you in that way, as there's no harm in it.

You're right. Of course, Onnie chuckled as Dany reentered the room.

"Talking to the First Keeper?"

"Yeah. Xayn gone?" Onnie shifted to get more comfortable under the blankets.

"Yup. Why don't you get some sleep, and I'll stay in the living room for a bit. Mal's in the library also, so call if you need us." Dany patted Onnie's ankle through the comforter.

"Alright. Thanks, Dany."

"Duh," the woman grinned and then left the room again.

Alright, you win, Onnie said to Kushima, who merely laughed.

Onnie closed her eyes and tried to slow her breathing so she could sleep, but just before she'd succumbed, Elaric brushed their Bond.

Elaric, you alright?

Yes, but I have an idea if you have a second to talk.

Um, yes? But I may fall asleep on you.

Well, that answers question one—you really are sick.

I am, she answered, her forehead wrinkling. *Why?*

I think I know a way we can use it, but if you're genuinely sick, I don't want to bother you. Would you be willing to lend me, Mal? I can talk to him while you sleep.

Up to him, but I don't see why not. Where do you want him to meet you?

Wayward Clearing.

Got it. I'll send him now.

Thanks, Onnie. Enjoy your rest.

Onnie smiled and switched her focus to Mal.

Hey, can you do me a favor?

"Sure, what's up?" Mal asked from beside her.

She chuffed weakly, sleep nearly fully having clawed her under. "Go meet Elaric in Wayward Clearing. He wants to plan something."

"On it, boss. Back in a jiff."

"Okay...." Onnie said with a slur and then turned herself over to sleep.

Young one....

Onnie thought she heard Kushima's voice but didn't have the energy to reply. She was sleeping, and that was the only thing on her mind at that moment.

Keeper.

At the use of her title, Onnie mentally groaned and shook off what lethargy she could. Her body ached, and her head felt full of cement.

What's wrong?

Nothing, but we need to talk. Gabriel and Mal are at the shop, and they asked me to wake you since they couldn't get through the fog of sleep along your Bond.

Onnie further pulled herself awake and blinked a few times in the darkened bedroom before pulling herself to sit up.

Are they alright?

Yes, it seems like they've spoken with Elaric and have a plan, but they wanted to warn you first. Can you speak with them now?

Onnie tried to reach for her Bond with Gabe first, and though she could see it and feel him, it seemed like she wasn't quite able to talk along it.

It's...slippery? Like I can't quite feel it between my fingers.

Kushima was quiet for a moment, and Onnie began to feel anxious. If she wasn't able to talk to Gabe and Mal, what about—

Young one, take a breath. It's alright.

But, I can't—

Onnie, everything is fine. It's simply your illness. I promise you it isn't permanent. Call for Dany now, and then you and I can talk to the others.

"Hey, Dany?" Onnie said with a raised voice, and it cracked.

A few seconds later, Onnie heard Dany jogging down the hallway, and she flung the door open, light spilling into the room, panic filling her features.

"Why are you shouting at me? What's wrong?"

"Water?"

Dany disappeared from the doorway and, after thirty seconds, returned and handed Onnie a water bottle. The cool water felt amazing, and she nearly emptied it in one go. She wiped her mouth on her sleeve and recapped it.

"Sorry. I didn't mean to worry you. Apparently, I'm a bit sicker than we thought. The First Keeper is the only person I can use the Bond to speak with."

"Wait, what!" Dany shrieked, and it made Onnie wince as her ears rang and her head pounded. "Sorry, should we be concerned?"

"She said no. Just a symptom, but Gabe and Mal are at the shop and tried to reach me and asked her to wake me up when they couldn't."

"Wait, Gabe can talk to her still?" Dany pouted, her feelings of being left out extremely apparent, and Onnie heard Kushima laugh.

"No, I imagine they are talking to the ceiling."

They are.

Onnie smiled, "The First Keeper confirmed it."

Dany snorted, her pout receding. "Damn, that must be amusing to watch."

It is.

"She said it is," Onnie grinned and then finished her remaining water.

"Okay, so why aren't they just calling you?"

They tried, but I believe your phone is on silent, and Dany wasn't picking up.

"Oh shit, where's my phone?" Onnie dug around the blankets. "And yours?"

"Mine's in my bag, why? Did they try to call me?" Dany handed Onnie her phone but glanced at it before handing it over. "Ah. Alright, I get it."

Onnie winced, "How bad?" She looked down and saw nearly twenty missed calls from Gabe. "Oops."

The phone began to ring again, the screen flashing Gabe's caller ID, and Onnie answered and put it on speakerphone immediately.

"Sorry!" Onnie and Dany said in unison and then laughed.

"I swear, Cat, if you weren't sick," Gabe said, but his voice was more amused than angry.

"It was on silent," Onnie frowned. "I wasn't ignoring you on purpose."

"What's your excuse?" Gabe said, and Mal laughed from somewhere beside him.

"Who, me?" Dany asked innocently, and Onnie had to stifle a laugh.

"Forget it," Gabe said in mock annoyance. "Look, Mal talked to Elaric. He wants to use the fact that you're sick and we're all on the outs to stage a roach confrontation."

"Alright. What's the plan?" Onnie said, eyes locking with Dany, who nodded.

"Here's what we were thinking," Mal said and began to lay out the coming night's activities.

Chapter 30: A Miscalculation

May 2022 - Alku | Onnie Moore

Onnie stood in her front entryway wrapped in a blanket, desperately trying not to shiver and worry Dany.

"I know, Onnie, but I don't mind," Dany said outside the front door. "I'll make Gabe and Mal stay at my place tonight."

"You sure?" Onnie asked before quickly turning her head to sneeze away from Dany.

"One hundred percent. Now, you get back inside. I'll grab you some soup and return as soon as possible. Maybe...thirty minutes?"

Onnie nodded and sniffled. "Okay."

"Go," Dany shooed, and once she saw Onnie closing the door, she walked down the front path.

Kushima, she's gone.

I'll let Mal know.

Onnie looked down at the shoes resting beside a bench in the house's entryway and groaned. Another sneeze snuck up on her, but she gritted her teeth and ignored how crummy she felt.

I'm going to put on a few more layers. Then I'll make tea and head to the dock.

She shrugged off her warm blanket and plopped it on the bench. There was a pair of knee-high leather boots lined with fake fur sitting against the wall, and she tugged them on and then pulled her coat off the hook and bundled up. She nearly waddled her way into the kitchen to brew her drink and couldn't help but laugh at the marshmallow version of herself.

I shouldn't have teased Sam. I'd kill for his coat right now.

Kushima laughed softly along their Bond, and Onnie managed a weak smile.

Before Dany had left, she'd put a kettle on to boil, and just as Onnie entered the kitchen, its shrill song began to play. The sound made her ears ring, and she shook her head and quickly pulled it off of the base. Considering how many cups of Keeper's Tea Onnie had made over the many months, she could effortlessly steep it to her desired strength without much thought, which was a good thing since she felt blurry.

Be careful, young one. We don't want to truly give the enemy a real chance at hurting you.

I know I'm...well, not fine, but it'll be okay.

Now that she had an extra twenty pounds of clothing on her back and a thermos of warm tea in her hand, Onnie exited the house via the back door and drug a chair to the end of the dock.

What are the others doing?

Gabriel is pacing and mumbling about how much he doesn't like this plan, and Mal is sassing him.

Onnie snorted her tea and coughed, her lungs and throat taking the opportunity to put in their two cents. It took Onnie longer than she'd like to admit to stop and regain her breath.

Okay, maybe this wasn't the best idea, she conceded.

Kushima sighed. *Unfortunately, I think we're too far past the point of backing out.*

I agree. Onnie groaned, rested her head against the back of the chair, and closed her eyes. *Let's get this over with.*

Gabriel Vansand

When Gabe's cell phone rang, he answered quickly. "Dany, what's going on?"

"You two need to stay at my house tonight. I'll stay with Onnie, but she's...she's still angry, and I think that, on top of her being sick, is a little too much for her right now."

His sister's calm voice wasn't as reassuring as usual, and he clenched his fists. Even though he knew this was all part of their plan, he hated it, and Mal had to flex his claws on Gabe's calf to remind him of their current reality.

"Fine."

"I'm on my way to pick up soup for her from the Day Night Cafe. Do you want me to stop by and give you my spare keys?"

"No."

Mal flexed his claws again, and Gabe glared down at the furball.

"No, thank you. I have my set. Just...get back to Cat quickly."

"I will, Gabe. I promise. She'll be fine."

"Call me later," Gabe choked out, then hung up and looked down at Mal.

"It will be fine, man."

"Let's just do this quickly. We need to get to Dany's so we can leave." Gabe grabbed his coat and looked up at the shop's ceiling. "You good to handle lights and lock up?"

The lights began to click off one by one, starting at the deepest part of the shop and heading toward him and Mal at the front door.

"Thank you. Please, keep her safe, First Keeper." Gabe said before holding the door for Mal and leading them both into the chilled air and the direction of Dany's cottage.

Onnie Moore

"Hello, Keeper."

Onnie jumped, her eyes popping open and immediately searching for the voice she recognized as Elaric's when he was in his Harry form.

Shit, I fell asleep.

"Who are you?" she managed to say before the cold air invaded her lungs and ripped a fresh coughing attack from her weak body. Harry didn't answer her initially, and she glanced around, looking for him.

"Just...a disgruntled customer," he said, his voice wavering for a second.

Onnie pulled herself to her feet and reached for the railing. She stumbled but caught herself at the last moment, and she saw movement from the corner of her eye as Harry emerged from the shrubbery on the far side of the backyard.

"What do you want?" she coughed out, her knuckles white on the wood.

"I—" Harry's face was one of concern, and Onnie nodded as slightly as she could, and he continued. "I'm here for information."

"Information?"

"Yes, you see," Harry walked a bit closer, "there's someone who you *really* shouldn't have pissed off."

Onnie cocked her head to the side, and the world blurred, and she quickly righted herself, and it thankfully receded.

"Ah, I see. You work for the rogue, then. Another roach."

A few coughs cut her last words short, taking all her confidence from her declaration.

Harry laughed as his eyes darted around the area. "Let's just say he and I have a mutual goal in mind. But more to the point," he took a few more steps closer to her. "Where's your guard dog?"

"Do you mean my *Guardian?*" Onnie asked, stepping back from him and further toward the water.

Kushima, how far is Dany? I'm....

I know. She's nearly back and I'll inform Mal and Gabe of the situation.

"Whatever you want to call that cocky bastard, sure. You seem awfully lonesome out here. Not to mention...."

Harry's eyes softened a fraction, and Onnie would have bet her life that Elaric was trying to reach her down their Bond. She only prayed he wouldn't need his powers unbound while she was sick, or they'd be screwed.

A problem for another time. Focus, Onnie, Kushima scolded.

"You seem to be a little wobbly on your feet."

"You underestimate me...." Onnie growled. "I can still handle you on my own." She made a dramatic show of flicking her wrist to freeze him in place, and as they'd pre-arranged, he stopped in place and did his best not to move.

"I want you gone," Onnie continued. "As you can see, I'm just fine. However, I have no desire to fight you. So, I'll be merciful, and you can leave."

A wave of fatigue washed over Onnie, and she bit her cheek, forcing herself to remain upright. Right on time, she saw Dany open the back door, her eyes wide with shock.

Onnie returned her attention to Harry. "This is your last chance."

With another fake gesture, she flicked her wrist, but the movement was a bit too exaggerated, and she stumbled backward and tripped over her boot.

"Onnie!" Dany shouted, running at a full sprint from the house.

Shit, this is going to suck, Onnie said and closed her eyes.

Onnie! Kushima called as Onnie felt her face hit the dock, and the world went black.

Gabriel Vansand

"We shouldn't have let her do this," Gabe said quietly.

Onnie was on his lap, and they were on the couch in front of the fire after she'd collapsed in the middle of their fake altercation with Elaric.

"She wasn't that bad when I left. I swear, Gabe. I would have stopped her if she looked like that."

Dany sat in the chair opposite him, and her head rested in her palms, her anguish evident in her entire body.

"We know, Dany," Mal said from where he was lying over Onnie's feet. "How's Elaric?"

"Not sure. He looked terrified when I ran past him. I could see it in his posture." She looked up, and Gabe frowned at her guilty expression. "He was two seconds from breaking his cover and rushing to her himself. If I hadn't been there, I'm sure he would have."

Gabe sighed but nodded. "I'm sure he would have."

Onnie coughed softly in her sleep, and Gabe wrapped her tighter in the blanket and pulled her closer to his core.

When Dany returned to the house and went out to the back deck as planned, she was supposed to scare Harry off, which would be the end of it. Except Onnie's condition had apparently gotten much worse in the short time she'd been alone. Instead of running off their mock assailant, Dany had seen Onnie's pale, shaking body trip and nearly fall into the lake. Luckily, Onnie had only a bruised cheek and a few splinters.

"Has she warmed up?" Dany asked, her voice quiet and nearly a whisper.

"Dany," Gabe said sternly. "Stop it. It's not your fault."

His sister sighed but nodded and got to her feet. "I'll make tea. Want any?"

She still wouldn't look at him, and Gabe glanced at Mal.

Try to convince her? Gabe asked.

Mal looked up at Dany and raised his paw. "Actually, I think I could use some Keeper's tea, but make Gabe's and yours an Irish Coffee." The cat got to his feet and carefully stepped around Onnie's legs. "I'll come help."

"Okay," Dany said and shuffled out of the room behind the feline.

Thanks, man.

No problem. I'll talk to her.

Gabe smiled wearily but looked down at the strongest and most fragile woman he'd ever known.

"Just once, Cat, think about yourself first. Please."

He leaned forward, resting his cheek on her fevered forehead, and closed his eyes. Hopefully, whatever she and Elaric had talked about would be worth it, though Gabe wasn't sure that was a reachable bar.

A few minutes later, Dany and Mal returned to the living room, a tray in his sister's hand with three steaming drinks and a plate of snacks. When she looked down at Onnie after handing Gabe his glass, her face was filled with more concern than guilt, and he owed the sassy feline.

"Thanks, Dany," he said and sipped the warm, alcoholic drink and closed his eyes. "Damn, been a long time since we've had these."

Mal jumped back up to the couch but carefully walked over to the table and began to drink from his bowl filled with magenta tea.

"Yeah. Was before Onnie got here, I think." Dany retook her chair and stuck her lip into her drink's whipped cream.

"Probably because everyone has drunk nothing but this tea for months," Mal said between slurps.

"Not wrong," Gabe smirked. "Not much room for anything else."

"Do you...." Dany said but stopped mid-thought.

"What's on your mind, Dany?" Gabe asked and saw Mal cock his head to the side in shared confusion.

"Don't take this the wrong way, but...do you ever regret it?"

"Regret what?"

He was pretty sure his sister meant Onnie, his Guardian role, all of it, but he didn't want to jump to conclusions.

"Sometimes I wonder if it would have been better if Onnie hadn't come to Alku."

"Dany?" Mal asked and walked his way over to sit on the table in front of her.

"I mean for her...not us. I don't know what I would...."

"Hey, Dany?" Gabe said gently, and he waited until his sister finally looked at him. "Every second of every day," he answered truthfully and then looked back at the woman he loved in his lap. Sick, injured, and cut off from her powers.

"If there were a way that I could save her all the pain and struggle, I would do it. Even if that meant...even if that meant I'd lose her."

Gabe swallowed roughly, but then he couldn't suppress his smile. "Then I remember who I'm talking about." He looked up at Dany, whose expression was a mix of wide-eyed shock and concern. "If she even heard us talking about this, she'd kick our asses."

Dany snorted and laughed reflexively. "You're not wrong."

"Dany," Mal said and pressed his paw on her knee. "Trust me when I say this: Onnie is better off in Alku, even with everything happening. She belongs here. With us."

His sister sniffled and scratched under Mal's chin, and Gabe hid his frown behind his drink.

This really shook her, Gabe said to Mal.

Yeah....

Onnie shifted again, and Gabe carefully placed his cup on the table beside the couch. "She's warmed up. I'm going to put her in bed."

"Need help?"

He got to his feet in the least jostling way he could manage. "Nope. Won't take me more than a minute. I'll be right back." He stared down at his sister. "Don't. Leave."

To his relief, she chuckled and shook her head. "Couldn't force me out now, Gabe."

"Good," he grinned. "Back in a minute."

He made his steps as soft as his massive body would let him, carefully brought Onnie into their bedroom, and tucked her into the soft blankets. He brushed her hair back from her cheek and frowned when he saw a bruise forming.

Even in her sleep, she leaned into his palm, and he softly kissed her forehead and whispered, "I'm a selfish man, Cat. I'm grateful every day that you are my partner and Keeper. Even on days like this."

He left her to sleep and heal with one more kiss on her uninjured cheek.

Chapter 31: The Slip Up

June 2022 - Alku | Onnie Moore

Onnie and Dany sat on the edge of the dock, feet dangling in the water below them. Mal was beside Onnie, grooming himself and occasionally chasing a stray leaf on the wind. Gabe was also nearby, thumbing through a martial arts book in Abbot's old chair.

The four of them were enjoying one of the first sunny and warm days in Alku's extremely late spring. It also helped that the rogue had been quiet lately. Elaric had been dissuading him from attacking, as Harry built a network of spies around Onnie, and Elanor fed them false information.

"It's been two months, Onnie. When can he come home?" Dany asked, staring out onto the lake.

"You know it's not up to Cat," Gabe defended Onnie.

"She's right, Gabe. It's time Elaric pulls out, or we make our move. I know how much he wants his shifting back, and we've already learned enough about Jakob that I think we're ready."

"What does he think?" Gabe asked.

Dany twirled a stick between her fingers. "It's been increasingly difficult for him to keep the rogue from making him attack us and stick with information gathering. He's also worried he may be close to being compromised."

"Let me see if he can come for dinner at the shop. She'll provide him cover, and I can unbind his powers for the night. It's been weeks since the last time. He deserves it." Onnie smiled at Dany, "You do too."

"Thanks. While I love the man, his undercover form is not my taste."

Behind them, Gabe dropped his book on the deck. "Did my sister just say the L word?"

Dany blushed crimson and kicked water at her brother, who shielded himself with the book he'd retrieved from the floor at the same time that Onnie relocated the book from Gabe's hands to her own.

"Be nice to my books, Gabe," she teased.

"But really, Dany, I didn't know things were so serious," Gabe said, walking over and sitting down beside her.

"Well, I haven't told him, but yeah, I think I do."

Dany was glowing, and Onnie loved seeing her best friend's expression. She was even more happy that Dany had found Elaric during all of the crap they were dealing with.

"I'm happy for you, Dany," Onnie shoulder bumped her.

Mal slipped in between them and sat down. "Yeah, it's about time you figured it out."

Dany laughed and shoved the cat off of the dock and into the water. He disappeared before he hit the water and relocated to the other side of Onnie.

"Bitch," he hissed.

"You deserved it," Onnie said, shoving him off again, to which he relocated to over by Gabe this time.

"I won't save you, man," he said, ruffling the cat's fur. After a minute or two, Gabe lifted Mal into his lap. "Actually, I think I will protect you."

Onnie snorted. *Cheater,* she said to Mal, who merely smiled at her with his toothed grin.

Onnie closed her eyes, followed her Bond to Elaric's, and saw his undercover form pulsing strongly. She gently tugged on it, their signal that she needed to speak with him, and he immediately dropped his mental walls.

I'm in town. It's safe. What's up?

Come to the shop tonight. I'll unbind. Signal when you're ready. We're making our move.

Elaric pulled away again, and she knew he'd received the message.

Onnie opened her eyes. "He'll meet us tonight."

"Perfect," Dany said with a grin. "Now, what's our plan?"

"Let's talk tonight, I'm warm."

Onnie stood, pulling her long t-shirt over her head, exposing her black one-piece before she dove into the lake. Water splashed onto the dock, and Mal wasn't fast enough to move this time. He and Gabe sat dripping and scowling at her when she surfaced. Dany nearly choked on her laughter but followed Onnie's lead, drenching the boys for a second time when she, too, jumped into the water.

It didn't take long for Gabe to start kicking water at Dany and fighting back.

Eventually, Onnie left the siblings to frolic in the water, and she went back inside to change into dry clothes. Mal padded along behind her, scowling the entire way and grumbling under his breath.

"Shush Mal, you had fun, and you know it." She scooped her furry friend into her arms and nuzzled him with her nose. "You do need a bath now, though." When he looked offended, she added, "Like with soap. Come on, I'll give you a quick one, and you can help me plan."

"No way," he shook his head.

Tell him he smells, Onnie said to Kushima.

You smell.

And you suck, Mal replied. "Fine, but only if you promise to use the vanilla stuff and not to tell Gabe that I asked for it."

"Oh, you like that shampoo," Onnie giggled.

"It makes my fur soft," he purred, rubbing his damp head under her chin.

"You goof, I promise I won't tell him." Onnie kissed his head and dropped him on the bathroom counter. "Let me get the water warm."

"So, what are you thinking you want to do about Elaric?" Mal asked.

Let's talk here, Onnie said to him and the First Keeper. *I'd like her opinion also.*

That's fair, Mal nodded.

Okay, so let me talk this out, Onnie said, multi-tasking as she readied Mal's bath. *We've learned a lot in the last few months. My powers have grown, too. So, what's in our arsenal?*

You can see far more Bonds than others in the past and with increased details. You can freeze people and, in a sense, time and displace objects. Mal answered, licking his paw.

You have become highly skilled at manipulating the Bond and the Bonds that others have with the world around them, the First Keeper added.

I can rip souls from people's physical form and project a shield of energy to protect those near me.

Mal dipped his paw into the soapy tub of water. *Which comes with a downside. The shield knocks you out for a few hours, depending on its size, and can destroy the shop, and freezing more than just one or two people is not something you can actually control.*

Right, Onnie nodded, soaping up a washcloth and massaging Mal's back.

You've come far, Keeper. Do not doubt that, Kushima said and pushed pride along their Bond. *Don't forget you can also talk to me, and your ritual work has improved.*

True, but Dany is the mastermind behind the rituals.

Onnie absentmindedly sudsed up Mal and gave him plenty of rubs and scratches as she thought of possible solutions.

What if we set a ritual where I project myself into it, and we lure the rogue to it?

Nope, Mal shook his head. *There's no telling if the rogue can manipulate projections or not. Gabe would never go for it. What about letting him capture me and using me as bait?*

Mal... Onnie laughed. *You could just relocate. He'd never fall for it. Damn.*

The three of them fell silent as Onnie finished rinsing Mal and pulled the drain plug. She held open her arms, a towel draped between them, and Mal relocated into it. She floofed his fur and dried him off, giving him a good squeeze, snug, and kiss on the tip of his nose.

"Alright, you, out. I need to shower too, and then you and I can run to the shop. There's a book I want to find."

"You got it, girl," Mal winked, leaving her alone in the bathroom. *Thanks for the bath, Onnie. Love you.*

Anytime, Mal, and love you, too.

Onnie shook her head and smiled as she undressed and got into the shower.

He's ridiculous, Kushima.

That he is, but he certainly keeps me entertained.

Elaric Rickson

Two hours after Onnie had contacted him, Elaric stood in his Harry form in the rogue's lair above Alku.

"Boss, they have something in the works. I don't know what it is, but they've been overly active. The Keeper was seen at the nymphs multiple times yesterday, and your daughter—"

"She's no daughter of mine," the cloaked figure hissed.

"Apologies," Harry lowered his head and looked at his feet. "The Sister of Light has been seen carrying stacks of books with magical titles to and from the library to the bookshop, where she sits there pouring over them for hours at a time."

"And what of the Guardian and the Link?"

Elaric leaned on the large wooden table in the center of the room and pointed to the school on the large map that rested there.

"He's quite formidable looking, but rumor has it there's trouble in paradise, and he and the Link have been seen fighting with the Keeper on multiple occasions. If we were to strike when there is dissension in the ranks, we might be able to separate one of them from the pack."

"Be very careful with what you choose to say next," the robed figure said slowly and methodically.

"I—" Harry stuttered and then froze, clapping his mouth closed like a carp. "My apologies, Sir. I did not mean to imply that I knew better than you at what we should do."

"I! WHAT I SHOULD DO!" The rogue bellowed at Elaric and crushed the air around him with a gesture of his hand.

Harry gasped, and Elaric tried not to drop his mental shields as the rogue battered and buffeted his mind in his anger.

"DON'T THINK THAT BECAUSE YOU ARE STILL LIVING THAT YOU HAVE A STAKE IN THIS!"

Elaric searched out his connection with Onnie, and seconds before he pressed against it, he fell to the floor gasping.

"Get out of my sight, pestilence," the rogue spat and turned his back on Harry.

Harry scrambled to his feet and stumbled as quickly as his legs would carry him out of the stone cave and into the wilderness of Alku. Once outside, he reconnected with Onnie as he traveled to a nearby shelter he used when he needed to change his form. Onnie released his powers, and he quickly shifted into a young hiker and picked up the camping backpack he had stowed nearby as a prop.

He made his way down the mountainside and into town, stopping to pick up a coffee and connect with Elanor while he waited. The nymph had become quite the contact for him and was a crucial spy in his operation for the Keeper. Elanor knew everyone and precisely who could keep a secret and who couldn't help themselves and gossip. The older woman was a miracle worker.

As he neared the bookshop, his foot slipped, and he caught himself on the curb before he hit the ground. When he stood up, his ankle was sore, and he limped slightly, frowning at his clumsiness. He shook it off and entered the bookshop where Onnie stood waiting in the front room for him.

"Hey, Onnie."

"Everyone is in the study. Feel free to change in the backroom and join us." She walked around the counter and hugged him tightly. "It's good to see you, Elaric."

"It's good to see you too," he kissed her cheek and slipped off his hiking backpack. "I'll catch up."

She nodded, "I'll send Dany up."

"Thanks," he grinned, and Onnie left him alone. He tucked his backpack out of sight in the backroom and shifted to his preferred form, pulling out clothes and shaking the wrinkles out of them before changing into them.

"Elaric!"

Dany shouted before she jumped into his arms. She kissed him passionately and hugged him tightly, her legs wrapped around his waist and arms around his neck.

"Hey baby," he kissed her cheek again. "I can't tell you how good it is to see you."

"I think I know," she slipped back to the floor and straightened his shirt on his shoulders. "I ruffled you," she apologized.

"Ruffle me anytime," he teased.

Dany playfully smacked his arm and then looped hers through it, leading the way to Abbot's study and the rest of the group. Gabe stood and shook Elaric's hand before clapping him on the back, and Mal rubbed his ankles and then jumped up to sit on Dany's lap when she sat down on the couch.

"Glad you're safe," Onnie smiled, poured him a cup of tea, and passed it over with a heaping helping of lasagna. "Eat up while we talk strategy."

"Thanks," he sipped the tea and immediately felt better, meaning it had to be one of Xayn's. "Do you have a plan already brewing, or are we starting from scratch?"

"A bit of both," Onnie started. "Right now, I think the best course of action is to draw the rogue out and see how we can get him out of his hidey-hole and onto a level, or even skewed in our direction, playing field."

Elaric swallowed a big bite and held up his finger. "That's going to be difficult," he said around a swig of tea. "In all the months I've been undercover, he's never once left his cave that I know of. He works purely through his roaches, and if he wants to see outside the base, he will use others' vision through some bizarre ritual."

Dany shivered beside him, and he squeezed her knee in reassurance.

"Don't worry. They have to consent to the ritual. He can't just hijack your brain."

"Good," she shivered again. "Was Dad always this creepy?" she asked Gabe.

"Don't call him that," he snapped before apologizing to her. "I don't know."

"What about the day he spooked me outside Elanor's?"

Elaric shook his head, "Projection."

"Damn. Okay, so we have to give him something good enough to leave his hole for. For real."

"Exactly," Elaric nodded.

"You know him best," Gabe said. "What would draw him out?"

"I'm not sure. I'd say the Keeper, but you're always out and about in Alku, and he doesn't make a move, and I'm not sure why.

Dany rubbed her temples. "If I had to guess, I'd say he's afraid. I think he knows how powerful you are and how powerful we are together."

Elaric's chest warmed at their acceptance of him into their group only a few months prior. Now he couldn't imagine not being part of it.

"Oh, I forgot. I told him of the escalating tension in the ranks before I left today. He nearly killed me for daring to assume that it was *our* plan, not his." Elaric rolled his eyes, "Drama queen."

"Are you alright?" Dany asked with a shaky voice.

"Yeah, he did this thing where he squeezed the air around me until I couldn't breathe."

"That's why you were poking at our Bond earlier," Onnie stated.

"Yeah, but he released me, so I stopped."

"He's insane," Dany said, looking down at Mal as she stroked one of his ears.

"I think he may be heading in that direction," Elaric nodded. "In the last few weeks, he's become increasingly erratic and unpredictable."

"I wonder what's tipping him over the edge?" Gabe said, scratching his chin.

"I don't think he needs much, honestly," Elaric scoffed. "The man, if you can call him that anymore—"

"What does that mean," Onnie cut him off.

"Huh?" Elaric said with knit brows. "Oh, I don't know anything for sure because he never shows his face, but I'm not sure he's fully human anymore. I get the feeling he might have," he paused to think of the right word. "Changed? Not to mention, at the very least, he seems to be far too young for how old he really is."

Onnie cocked her head to the side and looked at the ceiling. He smiled when he realized she was probably talking to the First Keeper. Sure enough, a few minutes later, she refocused on him.

"We need to know what he's done. How is he not human? What is he? That's the information we can use to determine how he's vulnerable."

"How are you going to find that out?" Dany asked skeptically. "You said Elaric didn't have to go back."

"I did," Onnie nodded. "We will figure out a way that doesn't involve Elaric."

Elaric turned and looked at Dany, taking her hand in his. "Dany, he suspects nothing. I can go back. I want to go back. I'll be fine."

"No," she yanked her hand from his, "you just finished telling us how he nearly killed you. Next time, he might just do that!"

"I don't think he will. I'm the best roach he's got."

"You really want to do this?"

She got to her feet, and he hadn't expected her to get as angry as she was. Upset, sure, but not…angry.

"You want to go back? Make this sacrifice, potentially die?"

"Dany," he said stiffly. "Why don't we go somewhere else to talk about this."

"No, I think I've heard enough." Dany turned to focus on Onnie and Gabe. "I'll see you both later. I have to go to the library."

"Dany," Onnie tried, but Dany raised her hand to silence her.

"I know. I'll call you in a few hours."

With that, Dany stormed out of the study, and a few minutes later, Onnie said, "She's gone."

"I hate that this upsets her so much." Elaric leaned forward and put his head in his hands. "I wish there was an easier way."

"Dany's grown quite fond of you, Elaric," Mal said, speaking up for the first time since the conversation started.

They all stared at Elaric, and he sighed. "The feeling's mutual, but I wonder if that was a mistake."

"What do you mean?" Onnie asked, her brows wrinkled in confusion, not anger, thankfully.

Elaric sighed and rubbed his eyes. "I'm not sure. Was I being selfish?"

"If you're implying that you should have kept your distance from her, it's a little late for that now," Gabe said with a frown, and Onnie placed her palm on his forearm.

Elaric nodded and, after a minute, got to his feet with a wince. His ankle was starting to get stiff.

"I'll talk with you later. I need…a walk."

The three of them nodded at him, and he wandered to the front of the shop and out onto the street once more. Dany had left quickly, and Elaric pulled his phone from his pocket.

Are you alright? Do you need anything?

When she didn't reply right away, he groaned. He needed to talk to Marco. He sent a quick text that he was back for the night, headed home, and then slipped his phone back into his pocket before heading towards the Day Night Cafe.

The air was still chilled but not nearly as piercing as it had been the past few months, and he inhaled the fresh air as deeply as he could. The cave smell had started making him feel ill, and he was slightly worried that the stench would be permanently in his nostrils for the rest of his life. There was only so much rancid blood one person could take. Or at least there should be. The rogue guardian was most certainly not human at this point just based off of that data point alone.

Elaric shook the memories of the cave, thoughts of the rogue, and his undercover mission from his mind and focused on the city around him. The gas street lamps crackled, and he smiled at their nostalgia as he approached the lights of the Day Night Cafe.

His phone vibrated, and he saw Dany had responded.

I'm fine. Going to see Abbot and then home. Thank you.

It was clear she was upset, but it hadn't taken him long to learn that Dany would talk when she was ready. She knew he was there if she wanted to, but he had to wait for now.

Exiting City Center Park, he tucked his phone away again and jogged across the street and up to the restaurant.

Stephan greeted him at the door, having recognized his current form.

"He's upstairs."

"Thanks," Elaric tried to step past him, but Stephan stopped him.

"Be careful, Elaric." Stephan's face was uncharacteristically stiff, even for the sanguiste, and Elaric hesitated. "There's…something changing. It's in the air tonight."

Elaric's stomach knotted, and he managed a robotic nod before Stephan let him continue inside. In the kitchen, Elaric quickly slipped into the apartment hallway and up the stairs. Right before his hand touched the doorknob, it opened, and Marco stood before him. His eyes were sallow, his slender figure even more slight than usual, but his eyes sparkled. The contrast was stark, and Elaric quickly shifted his emotions so Marco wouldn't notice.

"Hey, Marco," he smiled and stepped into the man's open arms.

Chapter 32: Unhinged

June 2022 - Alku | Onnie Moore

Onnie jumped as the front door slammed, and she nearly dropped her phone.

"Well, where is she?" Gabe stormed into the living room.

"Thank you, Elanor. I'll let you know when we've found her." Onnie glared at Gabe and hung up.

"She's not here either, dude," Elaric shook his head, looking up from his phone where he'd been texting Sam.

Gabe paced the room furiously while he pulled on his hair with one hand, the other clenched at his side. In his daze, he bumped into a table and knocked it over, the books atop it scattering across the floor.

"Damn it!" Gabe shouted.

"That isn't helping, Gabe," Onnie said, getting up from the couch to pick up the books.

He spun to look at her, and his lips pulled into a snarl unlike any she'd ever seen on the caring man's face.

"How can you be so calm!"

Onnie glared at him and pressed on their Bond in warning, making him wince, but he quickly shrugged it off.

"She's your best friend, and she's been missing for nearly twenty-four hours!"

Onnie forced herself not to sigh in frustration at Gabe's understandable but unhelpful anger. Of course, she was freaking out that Dany was missing. Alku wasn't that big, and Dany wouldn't just leave without saying anything to a single person. Even thinking about it made Onnie's stomach knot, but that wouldn't help, so she continued to ignore it.

"It's because she's my best friend that I can be so calm. Or at least I can try to be."

She needed to be careful. She had no idea what Gabe was like, truly angry, but they were clearly wobbling on that tightrope.

Dude, watch it. You're out of control, Mal said along their Bonds.

Gabe glanced at the mirror in the entryway. His eyes shined crystal blue, showing he was barely holding it together, and when he looked back at her, Onnie knew hers mirrored his coloring. She may not be acting like she was out of control, but she was also barely holding it together. When she glanced at Elaric and saw him with his head in his hands, she knew he wasn't much better.

"How did we let this happen? He must have her." Gabe resumed his pacing in place, entirely ignoring the table he'd toppled, and then stopped and looked at Onnie. "That's the only answer."

"Do you really think your father would hurt her, Gabe?" Onnie asked, genuinely curious. She had her own opinions, but Gabe and Dany were his children, no matter what they said.

"Don't call him that!" Gabe hissed through his teeth.

I guess that answered that question, Onnie said to Kushima.

Mal, did you find anything at the cemetery? Onnie asked.

Elaric nodded and got to his feet. "Gabe's right. He said basically the same thing to me yesterday before I left. He sees both of them as obstacles in his path to power. If he truly has Dany, she doesn't have much time."

"STOP SAYING THAT!" Gabe shouted. His chest was heaving as he began to hyperventilate.

No, nothing, Mal replied.

Elaric glanced at her and then back to Gabe. *Onnie, we need to get him to calm down.*

I know, I understand the fear, but he's wasting time.

Onnie knew his sister was the most important person in the world to him, and knowing that she may be in the hands of the monster that had turned his back on them and everything they stood for, he was right to be worried. They had to find Dany, but his panic wouldn't get that done faster.

"Gabe..." Onnie called to him. "Gabe...." When he didn't answer, Elaric took a few steps toward him, and she sighed and then raised her voice. "Gabriel...."

GUARDIAN! She shouted in his head.

"*WHAT!*"

He roared both out loud and via their Bond with such strength that Onnie stumbled backward in pain, tripping on the couch and landing on it roughly. Elaric doubled over, clutching his torso with a groan.

Gabe must have realized the instant he'd made a mistake, and his eyes went wide the split second before Onnie pushed on his Bond and flung him across the room and away from them. He slammed into the wall and slumped to the floor. When he looked up and into her eyes, she looked for remorse but saw nothing. His mind wasn't there anymore.

She barely grazed their Bond and hissed as a searing pain spiked behind her eyes. Her Guardian's rationality was gone. In its place was raw anger and no thought.

Onnie erected walls around his mind and Bond, and then Gabe slumped over, his eyes closed and body unmoving, save for his shallow breath.

"Onnie!" Mal scolded and appeared on the coffee table in front of her. "Why did you do that?"

"Mal, you felt the anger he just flooded our Bond with. Right now, he's doing more harm than good. He needs to take a break."

"What did you do?" Elaric asked, standing up and shaking his head to clear the pain fog.

"She trapped him in his portion of their Bond."

"You can do that?" Elaric asked.

"Kind of?" Onnie rubbed her temples. "I didn't exactly do it on purpose, but I had to do something. I couldn't chance him incapacitating one of us or, worse, Dany. Even though I can't reach her, I don't know anything past that, and I refuse to lose that link to her. So, I erected mental walls around his consciousness and shut him in. He's pretty much sleeping."

Elaric looked at Gabe and frowned. "Well, I can't argue with that."

Onnie groaned and pulled herself to her feet. "We need to find Dany and fast. The longer I keep him locked up, the madder he'll be."

"And the more vulnerable you will be, Keeper." Mal added, following her into the kitchen. "A Keeper shouldn't be without their Guardian."

Maldwyn is correct, Kushima added. *You need to release young Gabe from his prison.*

"I can't let him out yet. He's too unstable, and it's not a prison. I'd never do that."

Elaric followed her into the kitchen and snorted, "Talking to yourself again, Keeper."

Onnie laughed and made them both a cup of tea. "The shop, actually, but I figured it was also relevant here. She wants me to let out Gabe, but I think we need to try to find Dany first. Can I ask you for some help?"

"Of course, anything." Elaric pulled leftover lasagna from the fridge and slid it across the counter towards her. "You need to eat. You're a bit pale."

"Thanks," Onnie grabbed a fork and dug into the cold pasta dish. "I have a feeling that I'm gonna need it."

"So, what's the plan?" Mal asked, jumping on the counter and taking a bite of her lasagna from the end of her fork.

"First Keeper, I have an idea. Tell me if you think this is feasible," Onnie said to all three of them.

"We've already proven that the Bond leaves a residue on others if I connect with them. Example being when I showed Marco Elaric's Bond. Yes, they already have their own Bond, but I didn't use that. I used my own as a conduit."

"I meant to ask about that. I assume that's what I felt when I first went in?" Elaric asked.

"Yes."

"What's the point, Onnie?" Mal prodded.

She glared at him. "My point is that once those connections are made, there's always a residue left behind. What if that residue isn't just between people?"

"Meaning people and objects...." Elaric's face brightened, and he smiled. "You are thinking of a breadcrumb trail."

Onnie grinned. "I am. First Keeper?"

Your manipulation of the Bond is certainly advanced, and after your solution for the souls, I don't doubt your ability.

But?

But Dany has never left Alku. Her Bond will be on nearly every piece of it if not all of it.

"Gonna share with the class?" Mal said, and Elaric sniggered.

"Sorry. Yeah. She brought up a good point. Dany's Bond will be everywhere." Onnie groaned and pillowed her head on her arms.

Mal chuffed, "Yeah. She's worse than the cotton trees."

How do I narrow it down? I wonder if the glow dims over time or something.

"Wait, Mal, you're right," Elaric said, and Onnie lifted her head to look at him.

"It does happen. You don't have to sound so shocked," Mal bemoaned.

Onnie snorted.

"What happens to the cotton a few days later?" Elaric asked with a grin.

I believe you two were thinking similarly, Kushima said, and the final link connected in Onnie's mind.

"We were just saying that, actually."

"Yes," Elaric agreed. "Think of the cotton on a car. It may settle on it for a few moments, but it can't hold on to it and gets blown away."

"What if the Bond threads can't linger on objects as long since there's no consciousness to hold on to it." *Like the souls in the fire!* Onnie added to Kushima.

I believe it's worth a try.

"Alright, Elaric, you said she stopped by the mausoleum before going home last night?"

"That's what she said she would do, yes."

"Then that's where we start. Then, once we've located her, we can wake Gabe and get her."

"What do you need from me?" Elaric asked.

"Well, right now, I am down a Guardian, and I need someone to watch my back."

"I can do that, and Mal will be there, too. Eat up, and we'll go."

Mal nibbled more lasagna, and Onnie ruffled his fur.

"He meant me, you pig."

Thirty minutes later, Onnie was leaning against the plinth Abbot rested atop. Mal was in her arms, and Elaric was standing guard nearby.

Onnie had her eyes closed and was focused on her breathing. She slowly pulled at Dany's Bond, entwined with her own, and located a matching bright spot beside her.

"She was here," Onnie said and heard Elaric's sound of acknowledgment.

Onnie followed the stray bits of Bond as they wound around the room and eventually left.

"Elaric, I need to step outside," Onnie said with her eyes closed still.

Elaric's Bond grew nearer, and she smiled when he rushed to her side and held one of her forearms. "Let me help."

She nodded and let him lead her, even though she could see utilizing the Bond nearly as well as if she used her eyes. Just differently.

They exited the stone building, and Onnie continued to follow the path of the threads, leading their group back into the hedge maze.

"She left when she was finished," Onnie informed as they kept walking.

She's a special woman. I enjoyed watching her grow up. I can't stand to think what her horrible father is doing to her, Kushima said.

We don't know if he has her, Onnie corrected but then turned a corner and gasped.

"What?" Elaric said, tensing at her side.

"Onnie?" Mal said from above her, presumably on Elaric's shoulder.

Don't we? Look closer, young one. Her Bond is damaged.

Onnie mentally lifted Dany's Bond thread to examine it closer, and Kushima was right. Dany's strand wasn't pure purple anymore. Instead, there were dim threads that rippled and snaked within it.

Onnie opened her eyes and felt them flair blue.

"Elaric, can we see his mountain from here?" She asked urgently.

"Yes, it's that one."

Elaric indicated to one of the prominent peaks overlooking the town, and she re-closed her eyes to look at it utilizing the Bond. Onnie sorted through the residues around the mountain, all bloodier than the last, until she finally found a small glimmer of Dany's among them. There was no reason for Dany to be on that mountain.

Onnie's eyes snapped open. "I found her. We were right. The rogue has her."

"His cave?" Elaric asked, and Onnie nodded. "When do we leave?" Elaric released her arm and started pacing.

"Elaric, wait. There's something else."

"What?" He turned to look at her and stiffened. "What else is there, Onnie?"

"She's hurt, Elaric."

"How bad?"

Onnie looked to her feet. "It...well, I found dim sections of her Bond. If I had to guess...it looks like she's been tortured."

Elaric resumed his pacing, fuming and clenching his fists. After a few minutes, he turned and faced Onnie. "We need to get Gabe. He'll never forgive us if something happened to her and he wasn't around to try and save her."

"You're right, and we need to get to the cave. Give me a second, and I'll release Gabe."

Onnie closed her eyes and felt along her Bond with Gabe. She felt for the walls she'd raised around him and slowly lowered them. His grogginess slipped away, and his confusion began to settle in.

Gabe, we found Dany. We need your help. Meet Elaric and me at the mausoleum. Hurry. I'm sending Mal to you to fill you in on what we've learned.

Alright, and Cat...I'm sorry.

Forget it. I'd have done the same.

I can't lose her, Cat.

We'll save her, Gabe.

She opened her eyes. "Mal, can you go update Gabe? When he's ready, I'll come get you both."

"Got it," Mal said and disappeared.

"Let's go back inside to wait," Elaric suggested, and they both returned to the mausoleum.

Elaric Rickson

"I think I should go back," Elaric said while he paced awkwardly.

"I think it's our only option," Gabe agreed. "We need more information."

"And you can't rush in guns a' blazing, or he might just kill her," Mal added.

"Thanks, Mal," Gabe rolled his eyes. "Helping."

"Gabe..." Onnie growled out, and Gabe raised his hands in

surrender.

"I think you're right, Elaric. Let me rebind your powers, and you can go back, see where Dany is, how she is, and then report back. Just get in, get the info, and get out. Screw your cover at that point. We will be right there, ready to storm in with you."

"Got it." Elaric shifted his form back to Harry, rolled the ankle of his limping leg, and frowned.

"What's wrong?" Onnie asked.

"I slipped yesterday, and my ankle's a bit sore. It's nothing."

"You sure? I can get you a salve or something," Onnie asked, concerned.

"Yeah, I'm good. Let's get this over with. I want Dany home."

Gabe nodded with a grunt. "We will head back to the house and wait there for your signal."

"See you soon," he said, exiting the mausoleum and heading up the mountain.

As he neared the rogue's base, he felt Onnie bind his powers, and he shivered. He had a bad feeling that he couldn't shake and really hoped it was just in reference to what they were already dealing with. As he got closer and closer to the cave, his ankle started to hurt significantly more, and he cursed himself for being stubborn and not taking what Onnie had offered. He needed to be at the top of his game if he was going to save Dany. He knew the Keeper and her Guardian were on standby when he needed them, but he planned on going in, getting Dany, and getting her out. She'd suffered enough, and he would put a stop to it.

"You're late," Jakob hissed from under his hood when Harry limped into the main chamber.

"Apologies Sir, I was caught up with an issue involving my bitch ex-wife." Harry bowed low, "I am once again at your service."

"Good." The rogue tucked his sleeves into one another and walked to a rusting wooden door on the other side of the room. "Come with me. I have an assignment for you."

The pit in Elaric's stomach got deeper, and he had to force himself to breathe normally, the effort causing him to shake slightly. Jakob led him through the door into a darkened room that smelled of copper and stagnant water. Once inside, the door swung shut behind them, and candles along the perimeter of the walls roared to life. Suspended by her wrists over a pit with no end below her was Dany. Blood rolled down her arms and legs, dripping off one foot's toes and into the abyss below her. Her head was slumped, and her shoulders looked near to dislocation. Elaric stopped in his tracks and couldn't hide his intake of breath when he saw the woman he loved in such a state.

"I had Gemini bring you a gift, pet," the rogue said with a smile in his voice.

"I see," Elaric choked out.

"You know who she is," the rogue stated.

"Your daughter."

A loud crack broke the silence, and Harry's head whipped away from the rogue, his hands never moving, but instead, the air slapping Harry's face.

"The Head Sister. She is a close friend of the Keeper. You know this."

"I do."

"She is expendable, but she may have information we can use before we are rid of her."

Elaric tried to evaluate quickly, going over his options in his head. Go along with the madman and get Dany alone and save her, or try to take the rogue now and spare Dany more pain, though possibly causing her more if he failed.

"Understood."

"I want you to torture her until you get everything she knows," the rogue turned back to the only exit from the room.

"Sir."

"Fail me, and you will be hanging in her place," he said before exiting the room.

Elaric walked around the pit and examined Dany as best as

possible from his vantage point. "Dany," he hissed. "Dany, can you hear me?" When she didn't answer, he started to panic.

"She probably can't hear you, shifter," Gemini said from behind him.

Elaric spun, and he immediately pulled on his Bond. Onnie released his powers in an instant and spoke, *Elaric! What's going on?*

Dany's been tortured. You were right. I can't get her out myself, but Gemini knows who I am.

"Why can't she hear me?" Elaric asked.

"The room's been warded. No one outside can hear us, and that," she pointed to Dany, "passed out after our games last night. She's been out cold ever since."

Onnie, the room's warded, unsure how since we can talk, so it must be specific.

Got it. We're on our way. Mal, relocate and do some recon. Three seconds—

Onnie, it won't matter. I can't get past the wards, Mal said, cutting her off.

"What did you do to her?" Elaric growled and refocused.

"What I was told to do." Gemini circled him, trailing her finger over his chest to his shoulders and across his back. "Learn intel about the Keeper and her friends. Wanna know what I learned?" She leaned on his shoulder and whispered in his ear, "Nothing." She stepped back and laughed, curdling Elaric's stomach.

"How do you know I'm a shifter?"

"Your limp," she nodded towards his feet. "Oh, and sorry about the little shove yesterday, but I had to test my theory, so I worked a little magic with the Master's help, and bing bang, boom, your limp in all your forms is the same. You really should learn to act better."

Elaric growled and dove at the woman, his hands clasping her around the throat, squeezing until he was ripped from her and pinned against the far wall.

"TRAITOR!" the rogue bellowed, now in the small chamber with them. "I should rip your innards out and use them to further torture your little lover here." Jakob sent a wave of magic towards Dany, slapping her across the face and waking her from her pain-induced sleep. Her head lolled, and when her eyes finally met Harry's, they went wide in shock.

"Elaric," she groaned.

"Yes, dearest daughter," Jakob spat. "I now have two for the price of one, and all it took was a little bit of magic. Next, I will have your Keeper and that Guardian of hers."

Onnie Moore

"Gabe, you need to calm down," Onnie said, pulling at Gabe's shirt front. "You'll do her no good barging in there without a plan."

"He has my sister, Onnie, and now you're saying he knows what Elaric is!" He bellowed, brushing past her and rushing to the front door of their house.

"I'm sorry," Onnie said before freezing Gabe in place and walking over to stand in front of him. "I'm sorry I had to do that."

"You gave her no choice, my man," Mal said from atop a small table nearby. "Stop acting like an animal."

"Gabe, we have to have a plan. If we don't, there's no way we will save them. Just give me a moment to think." Onnie paced in front of him and started planning aloud, her shoulders tight and her nails tapping against one another with each step.

"Option one, we go in, all wild magic, and rescue them, or perhaps losing them both and each other in the process, or maybe win. Option two is to come up with a plan. But what's the plan, Onnie...come on." She paced for another few minutes, her nails the only sound in the silent room.

"Wait," she stopped and looked at Gabe. "That's it. *You* go in there, guns blazing. He'll wonder why we aren't both there, giving me time to slip in unnoticed and get them out."

"If the wards don't interfere," Mal added.

Onnie, let me out. Now. Gabe growled along their Bond, his anger pulsating toward her with every word he spoke.

She sighed and released him. Gabe stumbled at the abrupt use of his limbs again as he knocked into the front door.

"Do that again, and you won't like the consequences, Keeper." Gabe threatened.

Mal hissed and scratched Gabe's arm. "Watch it, man. She's still our Keeper."

"If I lose my sister, I will never forgive you," Gabe hissed at her, ignoring Mal entirely. Then he turned and walked out of the house, slamming the door as he did.

"Gabe?" Onnie asked in a small voice. "Mal?" she said, looking down at her friend.

"Don't worry. He's just scared, but I do think we are on our own now."

"I think so too, but for how long?" Onnie whispered into the empty house, Gabe's tires squealing out of the driveway as a last goodbye.

Kushima?

I know, young one.

"What do we do now?" Onnie said, squatting down and pulling Mal into her arms.

"Make that the plan, I guess," Mal said, and head bonked her chin. "We follow him, use his *incredible* rage as a diversion, and get them out.

Gabriel will do the right thing, young one. Though he may be acting on emotions at the moment, he's an intelligent man and a devoted Guardian. Trust him.

I know. I do. I just….

"Let's go, Keeper," Mal said and then licked her nose.

"You're both right," Onnie got to her feet.

Elaric, Gabe's on his way. I'm right behind him.

Chapter 33: It Takes Two to Tango

June 2022 - Alku | Gabriel Vansand

"Father! Get out here and face me. One Guardian to another!" Gabe shouted up the side of the mountain that, thanks to Elaric, he knew was the entrance to his father's stereotypical evil villain lair. A light rain had begun to fall, and the sky had gone darker as Gabe had hiked up the mountain.

"I know you have Dany, and I know you have Elaric. Give them to me, and I'll let you live." No one answered him, and he growled, "I swear if you hurt her—"

"You'll what? Sic your precious Keeper after me?" a deep voice boomed over the small clearing.

"Do you see my Keeper," Gabe spit out. "I'm here for Dany. Fuck my Keeper and what she wants. I want my sister back."

"My, my," his father's voice came from behind him, shivers coursing up Gabe's back at the familiarity of it, but within it was a hint of something twisted. "How things have changed. When last we met, you protected your dear Keeper. Now you take her calling and her being and curse upon it. What has changed, my son?"

"Don't call me son, and don't pretend to care. Give me Dany and her stupid boyfriend, and we will be out of your hair forever. I will take her far from Alku, and you can go after your stupid vengeance in peace. I won't interfere."

"What a sweet offer you have for me. Were I stupid enough to believe your lies, it would be an offer too good to be true."

"I tell no lies. Give me Dany, and you can have the Keeper." Gabe took a step towards where the rogue's voice was coming from. "In fact. I can tell you she's on her way here right now. All you have to do is reach out and grab what you've always wanted."

"TRAP!" The rogue bellowed, and the wind howled up around Gabe. Trees bent and snapped, dust flurries swirled in the air, and the sky darkened even further. "You think I can be so easily tricked!"

"I see you are easily blinded," Gabe said, crossing his arms. "Blinded by your hate. You can't see past me and who you think I am and see what's right in front of you. Fine. I'll go get Dany myself." Gabe turned, walked over to the hidden stone door in the mountain, and flicked the lock. "Yeah, I knew about that. I didn't have to give you the Keeper to get in and get Dany. I didn't even have to let you know I was here, but I did. Think about that. I'm getting my sister."

Elaric Rickson

Elaric knew the plan, but the plan never included him joining Dany in the torture. The torture wasn't the problem. He'd gladly taken all of it if it meant Dany was safe, but that wasn't how it was going. Gemini got off on torture, and he'd learned that during his short time undercover. Judging by how Dany looked, Gemini had let loose overnight. His girlfriend's head lolled to the side, blood dribbling down her torso, head, and from her lips. He knew she was alive, but he also knew enough to see that she was in bad shape.

With Gemini out of the room, Elaric's eyes traced every inch of his prison, looking for a way out. After a few minutes, he had to admit that his best shot was the pit below him. They might survive the fall if he could somehow lower the chains holding him and Dany aloft. Just as he started swinging his body to gain the momentum he needed to shake the chains and maybe kick the loop on the wall, the chamber door slammed open, and Gabe stood in the doorway.

"Dude, am I glad to see you," Elaric said, stopping his efforts.

"We need to hurry, and I need to get you and Dany out. Now." Gabe said, rushing over to the loop of chains and carefully starting to unwind Elaric's first.

"No, get Dany. I'm fine."

Gabe switched to the other chain and carefully unwound the line. He lowered Dany and tied off the chain again before reaching over the pit to pull her towards him. Elaric watched as he lay her on the floor and gently tapped her cheek.

"Dany, Dany, wake up. We need to go. Dany, you need to open your eyes."

After a few seconds, her eyes fluttered open and finally focused on Gabe, tears bursting forth once they did. Elaric watched as her brother embraced her and rocked her in the safety of his arms. All three of them froze when they heard the giggling laughter of Gemini approaching them.

"Gabe, you have to hurry, take Dany and get out. There's no telling what Gemini will do if she finds you both still here."

"I won't leave you," Dany blubbered.

"Dany," both men said at the same time.

Ignore her. Go, Elaric said to Gabe.

"No!" She replied forcefully, but her body started to shake from the pain she was in.

"Dany be reasonable," Elaric said. "We only have a minute until she gets here, and I won't let her hurt you anymore."

"I won't leave you."

"Dany, I agree with Elaric. We will come back for him," Gabe said, scooping his sister into his arms.

"Gabe, I swear, if you walk out of here without him, I will never forgive you."

"I'm sorry, we don't have time to argue," Gabe nodded to Elaric and turned to the chamber door.

"Gabriel!" Dany screamed.

"Dany, quiet!" he snapped. "We only have a small window of time. We are leaving."

"Fine, but tell me how."

"How what?"

Dany leveled her gaze at her brother. "How we are able to walk out of here free and clear."

"I made a deal," Gabe answered.

"What deal?" Elaric asked with trepidation.

"Dany for Onnie," Gabe said, stiffening.

Elaric froze and watched as rage filled Dany, and she started kicking and screaming.

"Good luck, my friend," Gabe said to Elaric before the chamber door opened, a dark silhouette in its frame.

Elaric watched as Dany and Gabe stood, frozen in place. Jakob was in the doorway, his hands characteristically tucked in his sleeves and his hood up, obscuring his features. Behind him, Gemini was bouncing on one foot and clapping her hands.

"Oh look, Master, they freed themselves. Does that mean I get to torture them some more?" She slipped past the rogue, slid beside Gabriel, and rubbed against his free side. "I like this one. He's handsome."

The rogue held his palm up and beckoned her back to his side, "We'll see, pet. Right now, we need to prepare our guests for when the Keeper arrives."

"Onnie will never come here," Dany said shakily against Gabe's chest.

"How could she not, daughter mine," the rogue sneered. "When all her friends are here, besides, didn't your brother tell you what he's done?"

"He would never—" Dany started but was interrupted by a loud rumbling from the pit Elaric was still hanging over.

The rogue cackled, and Gemini started bouncing on her toes again. "Master, Master, is it them?"

Elaric saw Gabe shift his sister in his arms to a more secure position on his shoulder and tense up as if he were ready to run.

With a flick of his wrist, the rogue stepped further into the chamber, pulled Dany and Gabe apart, and flung each into the walls opposite of Elaric. He winced when he heard their heads crack against the carved rock and the breath burst from their lungs. Dany nearly passed out from the pain, and Gabe gritted his teeth.

"Let us go. You have what you want. The Keeper is on her way, and you have your traitor," he nodded to Elaric.

The rogue returned his hands to his sleeves and began pacing the small room, circling Elaric and the chasm-like hole below him.

"You think that is all I want? No, my son, I want much more than that. I want to watch as Abbot's soul writhes in pain in the afterlife, his precious protege and darling Sister crushed under the weight of evil. His granddaughter, slaughtered with the very powers he tried to keep from me, and his coveted bookshop burned to ash. Torn from this earth like the boil it is. Magic should not be locked up, granted to only a select few, but instead, free to all for use, regardless of purpose."

"Magic is free, you moron," Elaric blurted, trying to draw attention away from the others. "To those with a soul and a conscience willing to use it for good. This world already has enough evil within—" The breath left Elaric's lungs as he felt the familiar squeeze of the rogue's powers wrapped around him.

"Silence, traitor," the rogue bellowed.

The grip around Elaric's neck was released after a few more seconds, and he gasped for breath. Dany's eyes found his, and he tried to tell her how much he loved her with his eyes, but he knew they could never tell the whole story.

I still can't get past the wards, Onnie, Mal told her and Elaric.

Shit. Fine, I'll try to relocate them home once I get inside. If not, I will get them out of the room first. I'm almost there, Elaric. Hang on.

Onnie, I have an idea, but I need you to do something for me.

Anything.

Tell Dany and Marco....

Elaric, don't.

It's too late, Elaric whispered to his friend as he slipped his last hand free from his bindings. *There's no other way. On my mark, freeze the rogue, and I will do the rest.*

Elaric, there are other ways.

Onnie. Please. For Dany.

Onnie didn't respond, but he felt her surrender in her silence.

When he refocused on what was happening in front of him, the rogue stood before Gabe, ranting about his desire for power. Gemini was slowly pushing her fingers into Dany's wounds and twisting. Dany's muffled screams rang through the echo chamber and pierced his heart. Not thirty seconds later, Onnie stepped into the chamber doorway and froze Gemini in place.

"That's enough," Onnie whispered, her eyes blazing blue.

I can't relocate inside either. I'll need to get them out first, Onnie said to Elaric and Mal.

The rogue turned to face the Keeper, and his soft laugh turned into a full cackle, his breath flickering the nearby candle flames. "Well, well, Keeper, how nice of you to finally join us."

"Call off your bitch, or I will throw her into the pit."

The rogue turned only his head to look at Gemini, and then she seemed to vibrate in place before she was entirely free of Onnie's powers.

She shook her head and glowered at the Keeper, "Who are you calling a bitch? You *froze* me."

"You hurt my friend," Onnie stated and then ignored the minion. "Rogue, release all three of them, and I promise I will leave your soul intact."

For a moment, Elaric thought he might do it, but then Jakob sniggered.

Onnie took the opportunity to hurl a small rock at his head, its speed closer to a bullet than a toss, but the split second before it would have impacted his skull, it stopped mid-air.

"Oh, how cute," the rogue hissed. "You'll have to do better than that, Keeper of Prophecy."

Onnie growled, and Elaric watched as the sand and small pebbles on the ground began to vibrate. Cracks started to appear on the stone floor and quickly spread around the rogue. He merely laughed and disappeared just as a part of the floor chunked off and fell into the pit Elaric still hung over. When the rogue reappeared, he was behind Onnie.

All three tried to call out to her, but the rogue crushed the wind from their lungs, and none made a sound. They didn't need to, though. The blue of Onnie's eyes had increased, and she disappeared, a dagger hovering where her heart would have been.

"Look who's cute now," Onnie said as she reappeared, standing before Elaric, her back to him.

The rogue made a deep guttural sound, and Onnie threw back her head and cackled like a mad woman.

Elaric, make sure you're ready, she said only to him.

"You think I'm so weak as to allow you to stab me in the back?"

The rogue slipped his hands into his sleeves, the dagger along with it. "Perhaps not." The sneer on his face made Elaric shiver, and his instincts told him something was coming. "Then again, you think I'm foolish enough not to realize that who stands before me is not the Keeper of Prophecy," Elaric's stomach sank, "but merely a projection."

With the last word, Elaric closed his eyes, the dagger the rogue had used earlier flying through the air and straight into Onnie's stomach. Were she truly there. Instead, it passed through her projection and buried itself in Elaric's thigh.

As Elaric hissed in pain but refused to give the vile man the satisfaction of him crying out, Onnie appeared behind the rogue once more, stepping through the doorway. One after the other, she sent rocks and debris at him. Nothing pierced him, and nothing distracted him. Yet, she continued on. The whizzing of stones through the air was deafening, the dust making it hard to see, but from where he was behind the rogue, Elaric could tell she'd still not hit him. What she had done though, was force Jakob to step back a few feet, and he was nearly in a place where Elaric could act.

I'm sorry, Elaric, I can't get past— Onnie said in his head, even her mental voice sounding out of breath.

It's alright, I understand, he responded.

"STOP!" The rogue bellowed, and the onslaught was halted, everything hanging in the air for a heartbeat or two before dropping to the floor with a clatter. "I am done with your games!"

A roar rose from the well beneath Elaric, followed by a dark mist. It wound its way around him before pushing on the dagger in his thigh. Then it swirled over to Dany and did the same to her wounds. The instant she screamed, the room went white.

A shrill screeching noise pierced through Dany's cries, and as quickly as it had started, both sounds stopped. The white light that had filled the room flashed out, and when he looked at Onnie, she held the dark smoke within her fist. It coiled around her hand like a snake, and Elaric couldn't tell if it was trying to free itself or had been tamed.

"I told you to release them. I warned you," Onnie's eyes flashed white and then back to blue as she took one step nearer to the rogue.

You don't have to do this, Elaric, she said, their eyes connecting for only long enough that his heart ached.

Look after them both. Marco especially, he will have…no one now.

Onnie closed her eyes and gritted her teeth, and when they opened, her unshed tears were gone, and in their place was a fierce determination that Elaric found reassuring.

"You've given me no choice."

With that, she sent the black mist flying back to its master like an arrow.

Elaric wished he could have seen the look on the rogue's face because it must have been fantastic. Jakob stumbled back as he tried to avoid the misty projectile, which put him right within Elaric's reach, giving him his opening.

Elaric whispered under his breath, "*Become of my blood,*" and he felt his blood begin to shift and shimmer, the sigil scratched into his hip and colored with Marco's blood now activated.

"Now!" Elaric shouted as he freed his chains from the loop above him and swung them over his head and around the rogue's throat just as Onnie froze the man in place. Elaric's body slammed against the inside wall of the well, and he saw stars. Then he felt the chains slacken. The last thing he saw before total darkness was the rogue's body plummeting over the edge and following him down into the darkness.

Onnie Moore

It all happened so fast that Onnie nearly missed the window Elaric granted her with his sacrifice. As she watched her friend fall into the unknown abyss, Dany's screams snapped her out of her remorse. Onnie froze the remaining three people in the room and closed her eyes to focus on Elaric.

Elaric! I'll bring you back up!

No! Not...yet....

She could hear him struggling, and she watched his energy vibrating along their Bond for a few seconds before she felt it shift and begin to change. Then it went out.

Elaric! Onnie shouted along their Bond, but his voice did not respond. *Elaric! Elaric!*

After a few minutes of shouting and straining her ears for any hint of him, she sighed and rubbed her eyes.

When she opened them, she turned to look at her best friend and her Guardian. Though both were frozen, both had an unmistakable look of anguish in their eyes.

Mal, I need you.

In a split second, the feline walked through the doorway, his head bowed low. "I'll go with them."

"Thank you."

"Will you be alright?" Mal asked, and Onnie felt Kushima echo his sentiment along their Bond.

"Yes, don't worry about me. I'll be quick here and meet you at the house later."

Mal nodded, then she used the Bond to move Dany and Gabe into the hallway and then she relocated all three of them to their living room.

They are safely away, Onnie, Kushima confirmed.

Onnie nodded and turned to Gemini, who now wore a wide-eyed look of terror.

"What is your name?" Onnie asked, freeing the girl's head from her magical bindings.

"YOU KILLED HIM!" Gemini shouted.

Onnie refroze the girl and walked towards her with more calm than she truly felt.

"Listen here. I will give you one more chance to answer my questions. Yes, I killed the rogue, or rather, a dear friend did, and in doing so, he sacrificed his life. Now, I have a family grieving for their loss, a community missing a vital piece of itself, and a burden of guilt to carry with me every day for the rest of my life."

Onnie took a deep breath.

"All I want to know is what your name is. I'd like to help you." She unfroze the girl's head a second time but cut her off before she could speak. "You have one last chance. Answer my questions, and I will help you get your life back, end it, or do anything else I can in my power that you want. Continue to be difficult, and I will end your existence here and now, as I should anyway, just for hurting Dany."

Gemini narrowed her gaze at Onnie for a minute and eventually opened her mouth before closing it again.

"Gemini."

"Your real name."

After a few minutes, Gemini sighed but answered truthfully.

"Ana. Anastasia."

"Better. Now, where are you from?" Onnie asked, settling herself on the stone lip of the well and trying not to look at it.

"Arizona."

"Huh," Onnie huffed, "Long way from home. How'd you get here?"

"I ran away." Something like remorse flashed in Ana's eyes before quickly being quashed.

"Why?"

"None of your business," the girl snapped.

"You're correct. It is not." Onnie stood again. "How old are you?"

"Twenty-two."

"Your real age, please," Onnie rolled her eyes. Ana looked at the floor and mumbled something Onnie couldn't quite catch. "Hmm?"

"Seventeen."

"Thank you. I am going to release you now, but be warned, I am trusting you, and I only give trust freely once."

Ana nodded her head, and after being released, she rolled her shoulders out.

"Why are you trusting me?"

"Come on, let's go for a walk. This place is creeping me out."

Onnie led the way, not worried at all about the young woman at her back. The fight was taken out of Onnie, and reality had started settling in.

Chapter 34: Futures Uncertain

June 2022 - Alku | Onnie Moore

Onnie led Ana out of the cave and into the forest that wrapped around Alku like a comforting blanket. Both of them squinted from the sudden change in light even though the sky was a deep shade of grey and rain fell around them. The young girl hissed in pain on top of her wince, and Onnie looked sidelong at her.

"What's wrong?"

"It's bright," the girl mumbled and then looked away.

Onnie sat on a nearby rock, looking as relaxed and approachable as possible. "Would you like me to help make the pain go away?"

The young woman shifted her weight from one foot to the other, clearly uncomfortable, but her internal struggle between fear and pain seemed to be leaning in pain's favor.

"Alright, let me explain." Much to Onnie's relief, Ana looked at her. "What that man did to you is in your veins, and it's acting like a poison. Between it and whatever he's been drugging you with, or you've been willingly consuming, it's killing your body. I can help you, but you will have to trust me."

Ana looked like she was considering it, her dirty forehead knit together, and she nibbled on her lower lip.

"Will it hurt?"

"I will do my best to make it as painless as possible. I swear."

"Um…" Ana hesitated one more minute before nodding. "I know I have no right, but…."

"Ask."

"Can you make me forget?"

That was the last thing Onnie expected her to say, and her breath caught.

You've finally found one who chose the other option, Kushima said, and Onnie nearly broke into tears.

She stood from her seat on the rock, walked over to Ana, and smiled. "I can, and I'm *so* glad you asked. Are you ready?"

Ana swallowed hard, took a deep breath, and then squeezed her eyes closed. "Yes."

She's a strong one, Kushima said.

I will save her, Onnie said, gently placing her hands on either side of Ana's head, resting over her temples.

"I'll begin. Goodbye, Gemini," Onnie said as the young girl's silent tears began to flow.

Onnie finished pulling the drugs, darkness, and memories from Ana's body and put her to sleep, resting her gently in a nearby tuft of grass beneath a dense tree. The girl would need a lot of it, along with food and affection, but for now, sleep would help her the most.

With Ana taken care of, Onnie took a few minutes to take some deep breaths and clear the nausea and chills from her body that always followed when she interacted with whatever evil Jakob had used to infect people. She focused on the crisp mountain air, and the sounds in the trees around her.

Once she felt better she looked down at her hand, flexed it, and winced. The skin was raw and pink from where the shadow beast had wrapped around her.

Are you alright? Kushima asked.

Yes. It'll heal. Onnie squeezed her eyes shut. *I will be given that chance.*

Onnie....

She took a deep breath and reopened her eyes. *Come on. I want to do some recon in his creepy ass base before we leave.*

Kushima sighed but dropped it. *Do you think this wise to do alone?*

Course not, but I have you. Besides, what other option have I got right now?

I don't like it, but...I cannot argue. Be quick.

Onnie approached the wall of the mountain, finding the place that Elaric had described earlier that day. Her heart constricted as she replayed their conversation from mere hours earlier in her head. Everything had changed so quickly.

Focus, young one, here is not the place to grieve.

Onnie shook the memory from her head. Kushima was right, and Onnie refocused on triggering the hidden mechanical lock and sliding the stone aside. When she'd rushed in earlier, everything around her had flashed by in a blur, with her focus solely on reaching the others. Now, as she stepped into the dark, wet, and cramped entry tunnel, she began to shiver and couldn't stop.

Kushima, can you feel this? Onnie asked, rubbing her upper arms to fight the cold.

I can. Continue on, young one. You need to do this quickly but stay on your guard.

Onnie took a deep breath and regretted it immediately as her chest was filled with moss and mold. She coughed and wheezed but covered her mouth and nose with one arm and continued into the next room. This one was much larger than the claustrophobic entrance, but it wasn't much different other than the size. Cloudy water oozed from the cracks in the rock ceiling, and moss crept over everything not touched regularly. She almost felt like she'd fallen into an algae-covered lake.

The room had three branching paths, and she knew one would lead her back to the room with the well, which she would refrain from going into ever again if she could help it. The other two paths led off in what looked to be parallel directions to each other. Without any context, she decided to go down the left path first, the smell of the air that flowed from it just a touch less foul.

The hallway between the two rooms was very short, only a few meters, and when she reached the end of it, she stepped into a vast open space full of light.

"Holy shit," Onnie said aloud before adding, *Kushima, can you see this?*

I cannot.

Here, let me try this. You have got to see this.

Onnie closed her eyes and viewed the world around her via the Bonds. After quickly confirming no threats were nearby, she felt safe to enter the void for a minute or two. She dimmed her view of the Bonds and instead pictured the void as it truly was in its endless black.

I've been wanting to try this.

She tried to imagine the room she'd just seen as an image floating within the void. Much like when she projected herself, she hypothesized that maybe she could project other things.

Oh my, Kushima said with a gasp, and Onnie grinned.

Floating in front of her in the void was a hazy image of the room she was standing in, and from the angle she was witnessing it. The stone walls were chiseled and sharp, and the ceiling was carved out of the rock by what looked like crude tools. In the center of the room was a large table with rickety wooden stools at various intervals. The floor was covered in muck and the stains of old blood, the smell of the copper threatening to choke her without her arm covering her mouth and nose.

None of that mattered.

The part she wanted Kushima to see was the glass. Across the room, a wall was made, floor to ceiling, of clear glass panes. Light streamed through it and into the dark, diseased space, flecks of dust and other matter she didn't want to think about floating in the putrid air. Outside the window was the sky, mountains, trees, and below them, Alku.

She knew where they were relative to the town, but being so high above the city, seeing the small buildings, the lake, and the forests surrounding them and keeping them safe, she was awestruck.

I…. Kushima began but quickly trailed off.

Onnie opened her eyes and crossed the room to get a closer look. *I know.*

She stepped over puddles of varying degrees of darkness and chose to ignore them. When she reached the glass, she tried to mimic what she'd done in the void, except without having to close her eyes. After a minute of trying and failing, she nearly gave up until Kushima spoke once more.

Onnie, it's spectacular.

I agree. Onnie's lips curled in a small smile, although it did not reach her eyes, which glowed blue in the glass's reflection. *I wish it weren't in a place like this. The others would love this.*

Perhaps someday, Kushima said, and Onnie swallowed roughly. *Not for one of us.*

They stared out over Alku for a few more minutes until Kushima gently prodded Onnie to return to their investigation. Having seen all that was in this room, she went to exit from where she'd come in and saw a second door tucked off in the corner. The instant she touched the door, she recoiled, pulling her hand back and shaking it to rid herself of the feeling it had given her.

Do not do that again, Kushima warned.

Agreed. What the hell is in that room?

Nothing good, young one. Leave it for now and finish the second room. You're losing the sun, and we've lingered long enough.

Onnie agreed and rushed back to the center room. Kushima, being spooked by something, had Onnie on the edge of panic, and she couldn't shake the feeling from her fingertips from when she touched that door. It was complex, like the slithering of a snake mixed with the burning of fire and the sting of ice. She shivered again and tentatively touched the last door with the tip of her pointer finger. When nothing happened, she pushed it open and gagged.

A small pallet of moldy grasses sat in one corner, a shoddy stool on the opposite side, and a few rats scurried away from the light creeping in.

"Good gods, no wonder—" Onnie stopped. *No sense thinking about it now, is there?*

There is not. You've helped the young woman escape from here. Let's do the same. It's time to go.

Onnie retreated to the main room and headed back to the entry, but before she did, she looked over her shoulder to the remaining hallway, knowing it led to the room with the well.

I'm so so sorry, Elaric. She squeezed her eyes and her heart shut and returned to the woods.

I'm coming home. I have the girl with me. Do not fight me on this. She isn't a threat anymore, Onnie told Mal and Gabe.

Understood, Mal replied, and Gabe remained silent.

Onnie relocated her and Ana to the library at home and nestled the girl in the blankets in front of the fireplace. Mal appeared at her side and went to sniff the sleeping woman.

"You've removed it all," Mal stated.

"I have. She's just a normal seventeen-year-old now with no memory of what she's done or endured."

"I'll watch over her," Mal said, settling beside her on the blanket. He glanced at her hand, "Onnie, your hand."

"It's fine. It'll heal."

Then she nodded, ending the discussion, and left to check on Dany, pulling her phone from her pocket as she went.

"Oh, fuck."

Onnie? Mal said, hearing her from the library.

I have to go. I'll be at the Day Night Cafe.

Mal was silent a minute before he replied. *I'll get Xayn and handle Dany and Gabe. Go. I'll ask for something for your hand, too.*

Thank you, Mal, Onnie said before she relocated outside Marco's door.

She raised her hand to knock, but he flung it open an inch before her fist hit the wood.

"Where is he!"

Marco's eyes were dilated and nearly black, and Onnie shivered Involuntarily.

"Can we go inside?" she said more bravely than she felt.

"Answer my question," Marco's voice said forcefully.

All of the day's events came crashing down, and Onnie quickly put up her mental walls as her eyes filled with tears. Marco went blurry, and she felt her knees give out, but she never hit the floor. Her body shook, and she couldn't stop. Her shoulders heaved, and she was struggling to breathe. Marco was all but forgotten as she let go of everything.

It will be okay, my dear, Kushima said, the only one Onnie hadn't cut off.

How!? This is my fault, Kushima.

No, young one.

Onnie sniffled and wiped the tears from her eyes, and when she looked up, she was no longer in Marco's doorway but seated on his couch with him kneeling in front of her, his head resting on her knees. When she quieted, he opened his eyes, no longer dilated but bloodshot, and they matched his blotchy face.

She looked around and saw the clock and that an hour had passed. "Oh, my god, Marco, I'm so sorry. What happen—"

Marco shook his head and squeezed her knees gently.

"I'm sorry. I nearly lost control, and I think it was too much for you. Keeper or not, at the end of the day, you are a human, and I am a sanguiste. Your body gave out, and your emotions flooded the space. I moved you in here and let you," he squeezed his eyes closed before he continued, "grieve."

Onnie leaned forward and hugged Marco as tightly as she could. She hugged him for her guilt. She hugged him for Dany's shared sadness. She hugged him for Gabe's regret. She hugged him for Elaric's last wish.

Marco returned her embrace, and it was her turn to hold him while he cried, but not for long.

Kushima was the one who broke their sadness. *Keeper,* was all she said, and Onnie's eyes snapped open at her rare use of her title.

What happened? Onnie pulled away from Marco, who looked confused but didn't ask anything.

Come to my library. Bring Marco.

Kushima said nothing more, and Onnie blinked a few times before wiping her tears away with one of her shirt sleeves and then used the other to dry Marco's.

"I need you to come with me."

"Where?" he asked with more curiosity than hesitancy as he got to his feet and helped her to hers.

"My shop. Something happened, and I need you to come with me." Onnie needed to be careful. She didn't know what was happening, but the last thing she wanted to do was to get Marco's hopes up for nothing.

Marco nodded. "I'll go. What—"

Before he could finish his thought, Onnie had relocated them to Abbot's study within the shop. Marco coughed and clutched his chest as the lights came on around them.

"What the hell was…."

Mal, I'm going into the First Keeper's Library. Marco's with me. I don't know how long I'll be, but….

Do what you need to, was all her Link said, and she breathed a sigh of relief.

"Sorry, I don't want to waste any time. It will pass. Can you walk?" Onnie held his forearm and led him to the First Keeper's Library door in the corner of the room. Marco managed to nod, and he let her lead him, but she paused when they reached the door.

"Don't panic."

Before he had the time to react, Onnie yanked the door open, pulled him through, and closed it behind them.

"For the love of gods, Onnie!" Marco screeched, and considering he couldn't see the door and probably thought she was trying to smash him into a solid brick wall, she wasn't offended by his shock and distrust.

Onnie winced. "I'm sorry, but there's one more."

She held up her hand to silence him and closed her eyes, focusing on calling Kushima into her semi-physical form. When Onnie heard Marco's breath hiss, she opened her eyes and raised her hand for Kushima to match her palm.

"Hello, my friend."

Thank you for coming, Keeper.

Kushima nodded to her and then approached Marco, whose eyes widened, and he was suddenly kneeling before her.

"It's an honor, First Keeper," he said with his head bowed, and Onnie snorted at his formality and familiarity.

"So…um, you know each other then?" Onnie asked reflexively.

I do not want your bow. Stand. We have work to do. Kushima's voice was terse, and Onnie hadn't heard her so clipped before.

Onnie walked to Marco's side, pulling him to his feet only because he let her.

"You heard the woman. Get up." Onnie chuckled and forced him into a chair, his resistance slight. "Few ground rules," Onnie looked at Kushima, who nodded. "This place does not exist in the real world. We are currently in the void where the Bond resides."

Marco's jaw dropped. "How? Is that why your eyes are blue?"

"Too long. I'll explain later, but yes. For now, I need you to do something for me," she looked at Kushima, again, "for us."

"Anything."

Do not tell anyone of this place, seeing me, talking with me, or any of what happens within here.

"That includes Gabe, Mal, and Dany," Onnie added.

Marco looked from Kushima to her and back once before shifting his posture in his chair, taking a deep breath, and suddenly he'd shifted back into the guarded Marco she knew. Formal, controlled, and slightly old-fashioned.

"Consider it done."

Onnie chuckled. "That was easy. I'll explain it all later, but I think she has something to talk to you about. She requested I bring you."

"Oh," Marco shifted in his chair, "alright, what can I do—"

What did you do to Elaric?

Onnie's eyes snapped to Kushima's face, and Marco stuttered. "I— I'm not sure what—"

Kushima held up her hand to silence him. *Let me rephrase. You gave something to Elaric. What was it?*

Marco looked confused for a minute before Onnie saw his face light up, and he must have realized what Kushima was referring to.

"Are you telling me he activated it, and *that's* what I felt earlier."

I believe so.

Marco paled and dropped his head between his knees to drag in deep breaths while Onnie stood there, mouth flapping like a guppy.

"Someone want to inform me what's going on?"

Marco looked up at Kushima and nodded, still recovering.

Kushima turned to Onnie and smiled. *I believe Marco here saved Elaric's life.*

Onnie jumped backward on her heels. "What the hell? That's not possible. I felt it. His Bond, it...it faded. It's gone."

No, young one. Tell me exactly what you saw.

It was Onnie's turn to sink into a chair, and she rubbed her eyes roughly.

"It was normal, and then it began to dim," she tried to dig through her memories, the adrenaline at the time hiding the truth from her now. "Wait! It flickered. Like it was changing, then it went out."

She looked up at Kushima's smile and over to Marco, who had silent tears on his cheeks.

Kushima turned to Marco once more. *You've done well, Marco. Would you explain to us what you two did?*

Marco nodded. "Before E left, he asked me for a favor. I was worried he—" he cleared his throat. "I was worried he wouldn't come home. He promised he would, and I think he was trying to make me feel better, but he asked me to help him create a blood link."

Onnie tilted her head to the side in a very Mal-like gesture. "What's that? Why don't I know what that is?"

"It's not something spoken of outside sanguiste kind. Even that E knew of it was an anomaly."

"Alright, so what is a blood link?"

"Sanguiste create other sanguistes by swapping blood with a dying human—standard human-vampire myth stuff. A blood link is different. A sanguiste carves their unique mark into the flesh of a non-sanguiste and fills the wound with their own blood."

Onnie's face scrunched up, and she shivered. "Ug, so like a blood-ink stick and poke tattoo?"

Kushima laughed, and Marco's eyebrows raised. "Actually, yes."

"Okay, keep going. Sorry." Onnie shut her mouth and tried to listen more than interrupt.

"The mark heals, and a scar is left behind with the blood remaining just below the surface. It's inert at that stage, but once the barer recites the activation phrase, the blood of the sanguiste is pulled into the body, and they begin to mix."

"But that doesn't turn them into a sanguiste," Onnie stated.

Correct. The blood link is only a one-way transfer of essence.

Marco nodded. "Once the blood is converted, the two beings are linked, and the non-sanguiste has a temporary evolution into a sanguiste and some of the benefits and changes."

"So…Elaric was basically a sanguiste when he fell?"

Yes, and I'd bet the transformation was completed before he found out what was at the bottom of his drop.

Onnie stood and began to pace the worn cobblestone. Her brain was going super speed, and she needed to get the extra energy out.

"So, if Elaric gained sanguiste traits, what does that mean?" She talked to herself, and Marco and Kushima didn't interrupt her verbal processing. "He could feed on blood or emotions. Okay, not helpful. He would get the aura reading, predatory traits, and immortality. But none of those would help."

She paused for a second before continuing her pacing and outward thought stream. "I'd like to assume immortality would help, but sanguiste *can* be killed, and his Bond did dim after I saw it change, so it's likely that it wasn't able to save him."

You are missing something, Onnie, Kushima said with amusement in her voice.

"Well, yeah. I know that," Onnie quipped, putting her fists on her hips.

Think about his Bond changing. What did it actually do?

Onnie groaned at Kushima's blatant attempt to lead her to the answer she already knew.

"It shimmered and then…changed. It looked completely different. Almost as if it was another pers..on..s…." Her eyes snapped open, and she jumped. "Marco! His Bond. It looked like yours!"

Correct, young one.

"So, what does that get us?" Marco asked hesitantly.

Onnie rushed over, pulled a chair beside him, and plopped herself in it. "Remember when I came over and let you feel Elaric via the Bond?"

"Yes…."

"I used a piece of your Bond to do that." Onnie knew she was grinning like an idiot, but she didn't care.

"Onnie, I'm sorry, I don't follow."

Marco seemed frustrated, and Onnie couldn't blame him.

"Alright. Let me start from the beginning. For months, I've been ripping the souls of the rogue's minions from their bodies."

Marco's eyes went wide, then dilated.

Calm, it's not as you think, Kushima cooed.

"They were given many chances for a new life, but when they refused, we were disposing of them. In the beginning…but the rogue would regain their souls and…well, you can imagine."

Marco recoiled.

"Exactly, so I've been keeping them safe instead. We can cover that later, but right now, back to Elaric. When I connected you two, I saw what your Bond looked like, and more importantly, I saw what your Bond *together* looked like at the point where it connected."

"Okay, so…you what? Know what his new Bond should look like?"

"Exactly!" Onnie shrieked. "I bound Elaric's powers, meaning they were connected to me while barely tethered to him, but they still were. We hadn't fully removed our connection yet."

"Wait, so is he still there? His Bond, I mean. Our Bond," Marco rubbed his eyes. "Oh, you know what I'm trying to say."

Onnie closed her eyes, entered the void, and brought into view the Bonds in the room near her.

Marco, I can see yours. She gently tugged on it and heard him gasp. *Sorry, proving a point.*

She looked at her Bonds and found the thread connecting her to Elaric. It was dark and it reminded her of Abbot's except even more… empty.

Because of the Keeper aspect, he's not truly gone.

Understood, Onnie replied to just Kushima, then switched back to the three of them. *My Bond with Elaric is dark, which means exactly what you think, Marco, but don't panic yet.*

Alright? Marco's mental voice said skeptically.

Good, this will make it much easier to do this part. I want your permission to use a piece of your Bond.

I told you, anything. Do it.

Onnie was relieved to hear the resolve in Marco's voice, and she began right away.

I'll talk through it as I go. First, I will pick through your Bond fibers and see if I can find the ones that lead to Elaric.

Wouldn't they also be dark? Marco asked.

Indeed, Kushima answered while Onnie worked. *They would, indeed. From his original Bond.*

Ah, Marco replied, *but his new Bond, the changed one, is different.*

Correct, Onnie said, *and if I can find that one, I can see if it, too, is dark.*

As Onnie searched Marco's Bond, she couldn't help but feel hopeful, and she just prayed it wasn't a false hope.

Please, let this work… she thought as she searched.

Have faith, young one.

I trust you, Keeper, Marco added, both contributing to her focus and determination.

Okay, not this one, not this one. Still no, nope. Wait….

She felt Marco hold his breath as she pulled a single strand from his Bond that looked different than the others.

Oh, my gods, I found it.

And…. Marco asked quietly.

Marco, it's not dim! He's here. He's still here!

Onnie watched as Marco's Bond with Elaric flared, nearly blinding her.

Marco, I'm going to take this thread and tie it to myself as well, alright? I'll explain what that means later.

He nodded, Onnie, Kushima answered for him.

Onnie quickly finished her task and left the void to find Marco hugging her tightly while Kushima smiled nearby.

You've done beautifully, Keeper, Kushima said, her eyes glittering with pride.

Chapter 35: Moving On

June 2022 - Alku | Gabriel Vansand

It had been three days since Elaric died.

They had been the longest three days of Gabe's life. In the aftermath of their confrontation with Jakob, Gabe and Dany were relocated home, where Dany proceeded to fall unconscious on the floor. Gabe carried his sister to his bed and waited for her to wake, which is where he still was, sitting beside her because Dany had yet to open her eyes.

Gabe could hear Onnie in the hallway talking to the roach—Ana. He corrected himself with a visible reaction to the thoughts in his head. A few hours after Elaric and the rogue had plunged over the side and into the pit, Onnie had returned to their home, Gemini in tow. Only now, her name was Ana, and she had no idea who they were. Onnie had worked her magic, restored the young woman to her former self, and taken away the horrible memories of her time with the man who'd abused her.

Mal told him to trust Ana. Even worse, Onnie let the girl sleep in the library while she healed. Then Onnie disappeared for hours with Marco before coming home and collapsing in fatigue.

Gabe was trying to be understanding, but to be fair, he wasn't trying very hard. Not that he cared. Dany was his first priority. He reached out and gripped his sister's cold hand, his larger, calloused one dwarfing her slender one.

"Dany, I need you to wake up. I know you're hurting, but so are we. We need you, Dany. Please, come back to me." He rested his head on the side of her bed and closed his eyes.

He felt Onnie before he heard her enter the room. Their Bond vibrated slightly as she tested their connection and probed his current mood. He must have been locking his emotions away enough because a few seconds later, she quietly opened his bedroom door and came to stand beside him.

"Gabe."

He grunted his response, not opening his eyes or lifting his head.

"Can I have a moment with Dany? Besides, I think you need a break." Onnie ran her fingers through his hair, and he felt some tension drain from his shoulders. Even when he was angry at the woman, she had power over him like no other he'd ever met.

"Sure," he said, lifting his head. "I'll grab a water."

He kissed his sister's hand, placed it back beside her, and stood to leave. Onnie gently took his forearm in her hand and looked up into his eyes.

"She'll make it through this, Gabe, I promise."

He made some generic sound at her and left the room. Halfway down the hall, Mal appeared by his side and matched his pace with his.

"She's right, Gabe. Dany's a tough chick. She'll wake up soon."

Once again, Gabe grunted in response as he walked into the kitchen. He froze when he saw Gemi—Ana sitting at the kitchen counter, a stack of magazines around her and Onnie's clothes on her back.

"Settling in, I see."

The girl startled with a squeak. "Sheesh, you shouldn't sneak up on people like that." She smiled at him, and he forced his face to remain impassive. "I am, thank you for asking. I like it here. Onnie is so nice, and I like talking to her. Later, we are going to go into the town and get coffee."

Gabe growled, and Mal not so subtly reached up and clawed his calf.

"How...nice," Gabe grumbled between clenched teeth.

How quickly Onnie replaced his sister with her abuser. He felt Onnie reading their Bond again, and he closed himself off to her. Part of him wanted to yell and scream at her, but the other part of him, the part that still relaxed at her touch, knew she was just being herself. Selfless and honorable. Ana had done nothing wrong. She was not Gemini, which meant that Onnie would help her. Just like a Keeper should. It was him who needed to get over his prejudices.

He looked at the young woman, grabbed a water bottle off the counter, and walked back to his room. He'd get over his prejudices after Dany was awake.

Halfway down the hallway, he heard crying and recognized Onnie's voice. He leaned his back against the wall next to his door and crossed his arms, not intending to listen but unable to ignore the sound of his girlfriend's tears.

"I'm so sorry, Dany. Really, I am. I told him not to do it. I'd find another way, but that man is so stubborn. There was no talking him out of it. It was all his idea, and when I couldn't come up with anything better, I had to admit he had the only option."

Gabe rubbed his eyes. Onnie had told him about her conversation with Elaric minutes before his death, he couldn't fault the man for wanting to protect his sister, but he wished they'd asked him for input too. He may have been able to help. Now, here he was, resenting a dead guy because Gabe was the one picking up the pieces of his shattered sister.

Onnie's sobs were broken by murmurs that Gabe couldn't quite make out, but then her voice rose again.

"I know you think he betrayed you, all of us, but he didn't. He never would. He's nothing like your father, and you know that. Can you really believe I would allow him into my family if he were? He loves you, and he would do anything to protect you. He did."

Gabe's brows furrowed as he heard more muttering from within his room.

"You know that's a lie!" Onnie shouted, and before Gabe realized it, he was barreling through the door and pulling Onnie away from his sister.

"What did you do to her?" he demanded.

Onnie's face was streaked with tears, her brow creased, and her eyes closed. "Dany, you have to trust me. We all agreed. We just needed to get you out of the room, but I..." Onnie cried, unphased by his outburst.

When Dany started mumbling behind him, Gabe instantly dropped Onnie's arm and was at his sister's side.

"Dany?"

"You know they're talking along the Bond, man," Mal said from where he now sat at the foot of the bed. "They're ignoring you or blocking you out."

"That means Dany can hear Cat?" Gabe said, looking between the two women.

"Yes. They are talking. Onnie's only talking out loud so *you* can hear her."

"Does that mean Dany's not just sleeping?" Gabe was confused.

Mal rolled his eyes at Gabe and licked his paw. "Do you really need to ask that? She's sleeping, but she's also healing her mind. Xayn may be able to mend her body, but Onnie can help mend her heart."

Gabe collapsed back into the chair beside the bed and buried his head in the blankets beside his sister.

"Just talk to him, Dany. He's your brother."

Gabe looked back at Mal and tilted his head. "Mal...."

Mal walked over to him and gently bit his arm. "Come on, man, let's take a walk, and I can tell you what I know."

After a few more seconds of hesitation, Mal bit him again, and Gabe got to his feet.

"Fine, but tell me everything."

"Never anything but my man," Mal said, leading the way out of the bedroom.

Onnie Moore

Once Onnie felt Gabe and Mal leave the house, she broke her connection with Dany and opened her eyes. Dany was still practically lifeless and barely breathing, but some color had returned to her cheeks.

She's returning, young one.

Thanks for your help. I think hearing what happened from you convinced her.

Anytime.

"Dany, I'll be in the kitchen when you're ready. My room has clothes, and you're welcome to anything you find. Take a shower, too, if you'd like. Ana and I are the only ones home, and I'll make sure she doesn't bother you." Onnie paused before adding, "And thank you for allowing her to stay. I know how hard that must be for you."

Dany didn't respond, but Onnie knew she'd been heard. Onnie checked her Bond with Gabe as she left the room, pulling the door shut quietly behind her and making her way into the kitchen. Gabe was still a mess of emotions. He was angry, sad, and confused, but it felt like Mal might be making progress with her Guardian.

"Hey, Onnie!" Ana said, jumping up from her stool at the counter and running over to her. "Look what I found in this magazine!" She shoved the book under Onnie's nose and giggled. "It's a recipe for a triple berry pie. I saw you had bushes out by the lake. Can we try making one?"

Onnie smiled and gently tugged on one of the girl's pigtail braids. "That's a wonderful plan, and you know who would be a good person to ask for baking tips?"

"Who?"

"Rosalie from the coffee shop, she's their master baker, and I have never eaten anything that she's made that wasn't outstanding."

"Can we go!?" Ana asked, nearly jumping up and down.

Onnie laughed and nodded. "Yes, of course, but I think Dany may want to go with us."

"Dany!" the girl shouted. "She's awake?"

"She will be, but let's give her some privacy and some time to return to feeling like herself. Okay?"

"I'm so excited to meet her! She sounds awesome."

Onnie laughed and made her way to the fridge, pulling out a pitcher of iced tea and pouring three big glasses before handing one to the girl.

"That's an understatement, but yes, you'll love her."

Ana sipped her tea as she walked back to her stool and pile of magazines, already looking at other recipes. Onnie's heart warmed at the girl's progress in just three short days. She was already starting to put weight back on and regain some luster to her hair and skin. The sallow and haunted look she used to have from the drugs and mind control was gone and replaced with enthusiasm for life.

Onnie hadn't pressed the young woman for her reasons for running away from home, but cleansing her memories had told Onnie enough. Ana was better off with a fresh start, and since she turned eighteen in a little over a month, she was old enough to live with her decision. So, Onnie had pulled the drug addiction from her body, removed the memories from her time with the rogue, and replaced them with generic and happy ones. If Ana thought too hard about her time with Jakob, she wouldn't quite be able to remember, but she'd have a good feeling about the time. It was a very similar response to how Outsiders viewed Alku once they left.

The difference between Gemini and Ana was night and day, and Onnie knew the young woman had a bright future ahead of her.

"Onnie?" Dany's small voice came from the hallway, and Onnie placed her cup on the counter and went to help her friend.

"You okay?" she asked, reaching for one of Dany's arms and helping her walk into the kitchen. To her friend's credit, she didn't even flinch when she saw Ana but smiled and made her way to the stool beside her.

"Hi, I'm Dany."

Ana fetched a glass of tea and passed it over to her. "I know. You're all anyone has talked about since I got here. How are you feeling?"

Dany sipped her tea and sighed. "Much better now. Thank you for the tea. How are you settling into Alku?"

Onnie watched as the two women made casual conversation back and forth like old friends. She was proud of Dany. Granted, Ana looked and acted nothing like Gemini. Still, the fact that her friend could see past all of that after the horrors she'd endured was a testament to her character.

Mal, Dany is up and about, and she's doing fine.

Has she met Ana yet?

Yup, they are chatting like long-lost sisters. Nothing to worry about here. Dany listened carefully when I explained the situation, and even though I worried, she's doing perfectly.

Good, I'll tell Gabe. When can we come home? This man is running me into the ground.

Onnie laughed out loud and switched back to her inner conversation with Mal. *What are you two doing?*

First, he made me run with him to the school, and now he wants to practice sparring and then go running again. The man is a machine, girl.

Oh, hush Mal, the workout is good for you. You'll be fine. Come home when you want, though I may take the girls to coffee. Ana wants to meet Rosalie.

Mal's contented purr vibrated down their Bond. *Yum, Rosalie. If you go, will you bring me back some of her butter biscuits? You know how much I love those.*

Onnie shook her head and switched her focus to Dany and Ana, who were now rifling through magazines and ooh-ing and ahh-ing over various desserts.

"You two up for a trip to the coffee shop to see Rosalie?"

Dany practically whimpered, and Ana and Onnie stopped and stared at her. Red colored Dany's cheeks and she giggled.

"Sorry I haven't eaten in days, and one of Rosalie's scones may just undo me, but yes, I'm up for it."

"Yess!" Ana hissed, "I'll go start the car!" With that, she dashed off to grab Onnie's keys from the hook by the door.

"Energetic, isn't she?" Dany said with a smile.

"You have no idea," Onnie laughed and put the tea back in the fridge. "She's made so much progress over the last few days. It's remarkable." Onnie paused and carefully searched her friend's eyes. "As have you. How are you doing with all of this, honestly?"

Dany shrugged. "I know it wasn't her fault. I mean, it will take a while for the nightmares to stop, but I know that wasn't Ana, especially now that I've met her. I think I'll be fine. She seems like a bright young woman."

"She is. I'm not sure of all the details in her past, but from what I did see, I'm glad it's behind her. The world is brighter with her in it."

Dany nodded and stood up. "I'm ready when you are, though I am a bit wobbly."

"I think that's why Ana offered to drive," Onnie smiled and took her friend's arm. "You are still a bit pale, and I don't think you're ready for a walk quite yet, though I'm sure Gabe will be ready to have his sparring partner back. I know Mal will happily relinquish the title."

Dany stiffened, and Onnie sighed.

"I know you're still angry—"

"I'm not angry at him, Onnie. I feel betrayed. He went behind my back, and thanks to his plan," she practically hissed the words, "Elaric is dead. Even if you believe there was no way he would ever sacrifice you to save me...."

"Dany," Onnie warned.

"I'm not so sure anymore."

It was clear that Onnie and the others couldn't help Dany anymore. She would have to learn to trust her brother again on her own, but sadness still welled inside Onnie for the damaged family she now had around her. Gabe's presence flowed along their Bond, and though she knew he was trying to reassure her, she felt him searching her for clues about Dany's well being at the same time.

"I'll leave it to you two to figure out, but I'm here if you need me."

Dany squeezed Onnie's hand and smiled slightly. "I know you are. Thank you. I think I just need time."

"And time you shall have, but first," Onnie grinned, "Scones!"

Dany laughed a deep belly laugh, and Onnie had never heard anything more beautiful in her life.

Chapter 36: Comfort

June 2022 - Alku | Onnie Moore

Onnie stood in the mausoleum where her grandfather and some of the Keepers before him were memorialized. She wore black and the face of a grieving friend, but inside, she was full of hope that only two others knew of.

I hate lying to them, Kushima.

I know you do, but this is for the best.

Onnie sighed. *I know it is. There's no guarantee I'll ever find his soul or be able to get him back, but when I see Dany....*

I know.

Are you able to talk to Grandfather, Kushima?

When she didn't answer right away, Onnie smiled to herself. *I'm sorry, that wasn't a fair question. Can I ask, if you can, please tell him what's happening to Elaric if he doesn't already know the details? I don't want him to worry or be in the dark like the others.*

Kushima still didn't respond, and Onnie didn't press it further.

You should rejoin the others, Onnie.

Yeah, I guess I can't hide forever. Onnie bent and kissed her Grandfather's stone forehead. "I'll fix this. I swear it," she whispered before she turned and left the beautiful building.

Onnie moved past the remaining mourners, the headstones, and the giant trees and shrubs that made the town's burial grounds more of a park than the home of the dead. The Keeper's Mausoleum was at the center of a hedge maze, and there was a section outside and nearby that was set aside for the families of Keepers, which was where she had placed Elaric's tombstone. A rock without a body beneath it. A facade. Just like the face she wore.

She approached the grave, and Dany was still where she'd left her. Kneeling in the grass before the stone, her black skirts splayed around her. Her pale Pacific Northwest skin was in stark contrast to her clothing and hair, which was also a deep black.

Onnie slowed as she approached and gently pushed on Dany's Bond so she wasn't startled. *No rush. Just wanted you to know I was here.*

Dany nodded but didn't look her way, so Onnie settled herself nearby under a tree and closed her eyes. She opened herself to see the Bonds around her and smiled at the glowing rainbow she'd grown accustomed to seeing the past year.

After weaving a piece of her Bond with Marco's, Onnie could see a slight flicker of people's aura when she looked at them. No Bond connection required. She looked at Dany a few feet away and, as she'd expected, she saw what she'd come to learn was sadness. Onnie carefully looked at the other people around her. Most were also blue. Once again, not a surprise considering her current location.

She wasn't entirely used to this new ability, and if she tried to focus on anyone for longer than a few minutes or look closer than a cursory glance, she found her head started to hurt.

Probably because this is not a typical ability a Keeper should have, Kushima said, vocalizing what Onnie'd been thinking.

Probably. I'm not sure if it's something I should get used to anyway. I might lose it once I remove my connection to Marco anyway.

It's possible, but for now, I think you should continue to learn to use it as if you were going to be able to keep it. Perhaps you'll be pleasantly surprised.

Onnie snorted. *Yeah, cuz that happens often.*

You never know. You did get Ana.

True.

As if summoned, Onnie watched the young woman's Bond come from further in the cemetery and sit down beside her. Onnie opened her eyes and smiled at her.

"Did I wake you up?" Ana asked since she was now an average, ignorant human. An Outsider once more.

Onnie shook her head. "It's alright. Where've you been?"

The young woman picked a blade of grass from beside her and twirled it between her fingers. "Nowhere. I just walked around."

Seeing her solemn expression and fidgeting reminded Onnie not to forget Ana was only a mere seventeen years old and still had a lot of growing up to do.

"Have you ever been to a cemetery before?" Ana nodded but didn't say anything more, so Onnie dropped it.

After a few minutes, Ana looked at Dany and pulled one of Onnie's arms into herself as if she were a security blanket.

"Onnie, will Dany be alright?"

Onnie scooched herself closer. "She will be, but it's going to take time."

"She loved him, didn't she?"

"She still does," Onnie said with a smile.

Ana's eyes were far away, but she turned her head to the ground and mumbled. "I wish I'd have gotten to meet him, too."

Onnie's heart constricted with the love and pain the young woman beside her was feeling. Her compassion for one she'd never met starkly contrasted with the horror she'd been forced to become.

"I've no doubt he'd have liked you," Onnie said genuinely. "You both have a sort of…free spirit to yourselves that I think you'd have had in common."

"Really?"

"Mm hm," Onnie said with a nod. "You also have a large heart, Ana, and care about those around you, even if you've just met them. Elaric did as well."

Ana smiled and leaned her head against Onnie's, and they stayed like that for a while. Eventually, a shadow crept over them both, and they looked up to see Dany standing above them. Her cheeks were tear-stained, and her eyes were bloodshot, but to Onnie's relief, she was smiling.

"Look at you two, napping in the shade," she feigned anger and put her fists on her hips. "Without me?"

"Nope," Ana said before grabbing one of Dany's hands and pulling her to sit between them, "we were waiting for you."

Dany looked at Onnie, and fresh tears formed in her eyes, but she put her arms around Ana and pulled her into a side hug.

"Is that so," she sniffled, "then I'm sorry to have kept you waiting so long."

No matter how long, Dany, I will always be here, Onnie said and squeezed her best friend's free hand, who squeezed it back and sniffled.

Onnie entered the Day Night Cafe and found that Marco wasn't at the front podium. Not that she was expecting him to be there anyway. Nor did it matter. She wasn't there to see him.

Stephan emerged from the kitchen, and when he saw her, he smiled, though it was the most guarded she'd ever seen him. He quickly crossed the room, turned her around, and ushered her back onto the sidewalk.

"Apologies, Keeper, would you mind walking?" he asked once they were adequately away from the restaurant's doors.

"Only if you stop calling me Keeper," she scowled.

Stephan looked away, and Onnie's heart sank.

Kushima...he, he blames me.

I do not think that's the case, young one.

Stephan sighed. "Come on, Onnie. Let's walk through the park."

She nodded and watched her feet as they crossed the cobbled street together and stepped into the park. Once they were past a few trees, Stephan spoke.

"I do not blame you, Onnie."

She couldn't help but snigger. Now that she knew firsthand how a sanguiste's aura reading worked, it was apparent his mind reading was more aura than mind.

"I'm simply concerned. For all of you," he stopped and looked down at her. "Not just Marco."

She looked away. His dark eyes felt like they saw right through her, and Onnie found it harder to lie to Stephan than the others.

"Focus on Marco. He's who I'm most worried about," Onnie said quietly.

Stephan sat on a nearby bench. "Onnie, I was here that night."

She quietly sat beside him, and he leaned forward and rested his elbows on his knees.

"Marco is not mine by blood, but we've been together a long time. The four of us. We see him as family, but to Marco, family isn't a word with comforting connotations."

"Birds of a feather, I guess," Onnie said quietly.

"Marco is very old, Onnie. He's spent the last one thousand years perfecting his control over his instincts. Now, even when he slips up, a fraction of his control is all he drops." Stephan took a deep breath. "When you came to see Marco that night, he nearly released it all."

Onnie's head whipped around, and she knew she must look possessed with her wide eyes and rapid pulse. "What?"

"I was downstairs, and I felt it the moment he let go. It was only for a few seconds, but it was enough."

She looked out into the dark of the park's trees. "I don't remember. All I remember was trying not to...break, but I failed, and then I fell, but when I came back around, we were on the couch."

Stephan nodded. "Yes. Those few seconds were enough to overwhelm you, and your body collapsed. Marco understood and regained his composure. All of it happened before you had a chance to hit the floor."

"You saw?"

"I did. I told you, the instant he let go, I was at the bottom of the stairs." Stephan smiled, and Onnie was surprised to find his aura was filled with pride. "He didn't need me, though. He had you."

"But it was my fault that he...."

"No, Onnie. His grief was his own and no fault of yours, but when he saw what he was doing to you, that mattered more to him than his grief."

"Then what happened?"

"Marco took you inside, and I returned to the cafe and closed for the night."

"Wait, you did?" Onnie said, surprised.

Stephan chuffed, "Yes, but considering you didn't use the doors when you left, I can see why you missed it."

Onnie felt her blood drain from her face.

"I won't ask, Onnie. Though, I will add I'm here if you need anything, even if it's to talk. I only mentioned it because I wanted to thank you."

"Why?"

"Son or not, blood or not, Marco is mine, and I will protect him until the day the demon reclaims my soul, but that night...you were able to do what no one else could, and I will be eternally grateful for that."

Kushima?

Yes, young one?

I...I don't want the others....

I'll close off your Bonds, daughter mine. It will be alright.

She felt when Kushima put walls around her Bonds, and Onnie understood why. Stephan must have noticed something had changed, too, because he shifted, and she was pulled into his arms as she finally released her grief.

"I'm sorry, I'm so sorry," she cried into his coat. "I should have been stronger. I—"

"Quiet, Onnie," Stephan said softly. "None of this is your fault, and no one blames you. Least of all, Marco and I'd wager Dany doesn't either."

Onnie's shoulders shook, and she barely understood what Stephan was saying, but it didn't matter. She could still see his aura, and the gratitude and pride he was feeling became her lifeline. No matter how hard she cried, no one called her, spoke in her head, or tried to push their emotions on hers and cover them up.

Stephan and Kushima were letting her cry as Onnie. Not as the Keeper.

Which was exactly what she needed.

Chapter 37: In Loving Memory

June 2022 - Alku | Onnie Moore

"Thank you for everything, Onnie," Ana said as she hugged her tightly.

"You are more than welcome." Onnie grasped the young woman's hands and smiled at her. "You and Rosalie are going to get along great. You'll love working with her, and her house is more than large enough for the two of you."

"I'm excited!" Ana said, jumping up and down a bit in place. "You'll come to visit, right?"

"Of course, we will," Dany said from behind them as she came up and wrapped her arm over Ana's shoulders. "You're not leaving Alku, and it's a small town. You'll never get rid of us."

Onnie beamed at her best friend and then leaned over and picked up the duffel bag that carried all of the trinkets and clothes Ana had accumulated over the past few weeks.

"You better get going."

Ana took the bag and hugged Onnie and Dany one more time before placing her hand on the bookshop's doorknob and turning for one more small wave. Then she was gone.

Onnie shook her head, returned to the front counter, and popped herself up to sit on it.

"So, what's the plan for today?" she asked Dany, who leaned on the front counter on her elbows.

"I was going to go visit Elaric's grave, actually." Dany looked down and traced a splotch on the marble counter top.

"I think that's a great idea. Would you like company or solitude?" Onnie asked, aware of her friend's mood shift.

Dany didn't answer at first, but after a minute, she cleared her throat. "Solitude today, if you don't mind."

Onnie jumped off the counter and walked into the back room of the shop. "Not at all, I completely understand. Would you mind taking something with you, though?"

She walked over to the delicate tea table and removed a small box from beneath it. Quickly and quietly, she pulled an amber stone from the box and dropped it into a vase of flowers, shifting the stems to hide it from view. Elsi had spelled the stone to act as a beacon for Elaric's soul to latch on to. Dany would bring it to the grave, hidden among the blooms and her intense emotions would fill the stone, helping it to grow brighter the more time she spent with it, at least, in theory. If Elaric did find his way back to them, Onnie had used Marco's Bond to assist with binding Elaric's to the stone until they could get to him.

"I wanted to bring these to him, but I am happy to leave you to it if you wouldn't mind."

Dany's eyes softened when Onnie emerged from the room and passed her the vase.

"Of course. I'm not sure he was much of a flower guy, but he'd appreciate the sentiment."

"Thanks, Dany," Onnie hugged her and walked her to the shop door. "You coming for dinner?"

"Yeah, it'll be quiet without Ana."

"I know."

"I'll call you when I'm done at the cemetery."

Onnie nodded, "Oh, and if you get a chance, say hi to Grandpa, please."

Dany rolled her eyes and stepped into the sun, "Duh." She waved one more time and was off.

Onnie closed the shop door and waved at a patron browsing the romance novels as she passed them before heading back up to the counter and into the back room. She flopped onto the couch and sighed before pulling her phone from her pocket and texting Marco.

It's done.

When she saw that the message had been read, she put her phone away, knowing there would be no reply.

Gabriel Vansand

He couldn't take it anymore.

Gabe had never gone more than a day without speaking to his sister, and the past few weeks had been complete hell.

Dany was furious with him over their plan to pretend to hand Onnie over to the rogue. She wouldn't speak to him, look at him, or be in the same room with him.

He'd had enough.

Today, he would make her talk to him. They were all each other had left, and he was done being shut out by the person he loved most in the world.

Where is she, Cat?

Gabe, you know I won't do that to her.

I'm not asking. Tell me. I'm done with this. I'll behave, I promise, tell me where she is.

She's going to see Abbot, Onnie answered, and then he felt her sigh.

Thank you.

Before he could say anything else, Onnie blocked their connection in what he could only describe as a mental huff.

Gabe grabbed his car keys from his nightstand and slipped on his running shoes before heading out the door and over to the cemetery. He put soft music on in his car and rolled down the windows, letting the sun and slight breeze invade his space and put his mind at ease. He knew he'd need to confront Dany calmly, but his adrenalin was so high that he had trouble taking deep, relaxing breaths.

After the short drive, he finally arrived at the cemetery and pulled his car into the space next to Dany's. He rested his hand on her hood, and when it came away the same ambient temperature as the air, he knew she'd been here a while. That was better. She'd have had time to grieve, and he wouldn't intrude quite as much. He hoped.

Gabe shoved his hands into his pockets and slowly walked up the grassy hill to the crest overlooking Alku's only cemetery. He took a deep breath to steady himself when he reached the top. His chest warmed, and he knew Abbot was close by, and he hoped the old man was approving of his next conversation. Abbot hated it when his family was at odds with one another, but he was also fiercely protective of Dany, and Gabe knew confronting his sister on his terms, not hers, would hurt her no matter what he did.

A special section of the cemetery was dedicated to the Keepers' relatives, and Onnie had a tombstone installed for Elaric in a place of honor. Gabe could see Dany kneeling at Elaric's grave, her back to the faraway hill he was perched upon.

Gabe swallowed hard and calmed himself more before descending the hill and heading into the hedge maze that guarded the Keeper's graves. As he walked, his mind shifted to memories of him and Dany as little kids running throughout the maze while Abbot was in the mausoleum paying his respects. They'd picked flowers for crowns, tried to climb the unclimbable hedges, and even tried to dig under one once.

He turned a corner, and the mausoleum came into view. He remembered the day they'd come here to bind Elaric's powers.

He sighed.

From the very first day, everything Andrew, Harry, Elaric, or whoever he'd shifted to for the day, did was for others. He came back to Alku for Abbot. He bound his powers to help Onnie. And at the very end, he gave his life for Dany.

Gabe owed him everything.

His pacing slowed as he stepped nearer to the family portion of the cemetery, and Dany came into view. Next to her was a vase of flowers and an old paperback book. As he approached his sister, he made sure to rustle the leaves so he didn't scare her on top of intruding. He knew at once when she realized it was him. Her shoulders tensed, and her spine went rigid.

"Leave Gabriel. You don't deserve to be here," Dany said, her voice severe and clipped.

He knew that.

"Dany, I just want to talk," Gabe stopped behind her and waited.

Dany pressed a kiss to her fingertips and brushed Elaric's engraved name before slowly getting to her feet and turning to face him.

"I don't have anything to say to you, Gabriel. Just go."

Gabe shook his head and rocked on his heels. "Nope, not until we fix this. Abbot must be rolling in his grave to know we've—"

"Are you serious?" Dany burst out. "You think he'd be worried because we're not talking? Oh, yeah, that would be his biggest concern. Not that his granddaughter's Guardian tried to sell her out to the largest threat Alku has seen since Charles the Malicious!" Dany scoffed. "You're delusional, Gabriel."

"Dany, that's not what happened."

"Isn't it?"

"No."

"Sure. Right. It's not like you didn't have a perfect role model or anyth—"

"Dany!" Gabe snapped. "Don't you dare."

"Truth hurts?"

Gabe took a deep breath and ran his fingers through his hair roughly. Shouting at Dany wouldn't get them anywhere. "Do you really see me like him?"

"No."

Gabe nodded and exhaled in relief.

"Worse. Jakob abandoned his Keeper. You sacrificed yours."

His stomach sank and he looked away. Dany was right, at least from her perspective. It had looked like that from her view and no matter how many times he, Onnie, or Mal tried to explain it, Dany saw what she saw.

"Dany, you're my sister, what was I supposed to do?"

"How about anything but that, Gabriel?"

"Stop calling me that," he said flatly.

"What? Gabriel? It's your name," Dany crossed her arms and rolled her eyes.

"You never call me that unless I'm in trouble. I hate that you're using it now, and it slips from your mouth so easily."

"I AM MAD AT YOU!" Dany bellowed, hands fisted at her sides, heat creeping up her cheeks. "YOU LIED! You put all of us in danger, sacrificed the woman you love for nothing, and in the process, you got the man I loved killed. YOU did this, Gabriel," Dany pointed roughly to Elaric's headstone. "You. No one else. If you hadn't come charging in alone, none of this would have happened, and Elaric would still be here." Dany's breath caught on the last word, and tears welled in her eyes.

"Dany..." Gabe said, taking a step forward.

"Stay away from me," she said, stepping back and holding out her palm.

"You'll forgive the woman who tortured you but can't forgive me?"

"She didn't have a choice!" Dany hiccuped. "You did. Besides, I didn't forgive the woman who tortured me. Onnie erased her. Ana is not Gemini."

With the last word, Dany shivered, and Gabe was astounded by how much Dany believed what she was saying. She did see them as two different people. She got over it, and he needed to as well.

"We have to get past this. What can I do? How can I prove to you that I would *never* have turned Cat over to Jakob. That I'm nothing like him."

"That's not the point, Gabe," Dany sighed and rubbed her eyes.

He watched as Dany struggled to force down her grief and anger and he remained quiet and gave her the space to do so. Nearly a minute later, she sniffled.

"I know you wouldn't have," she finally said in a small voice. "The point is you didn't trust us enough to tell us your plan, and when it went south, Elaric paid the price for your temper and rashness."

Gabe didn't have anything else to say. His sister was right. It was his fault. He walked past her, knelt next to his friend's grave, and closed his eyes.

"You're right. I'm sorry," he whispered to his sister before offering a silent prayer and apology to his friend.

Gabe felt Abbot's warm soul brush past him again, and this time, Onnie's reassurance joined it along their Bond. He sat in the grass, bowed his head, talked to Elaric, and prayed silently to the gods. He wasn't sure how long he sat there, but at some point, Dany had joined him cross-legged, Mal sleeping in her lap while she petted him. Gabe's knees had fallen asleep, and he lowered himself to sit next to Dany and rested his head on her shoulder. When she didn't pull away, he smiled.

"I'm sorry, Dany, you were right," he said softly, his voice that of a child rather than a Guardian and grown man.

"I know, but I'm sorry, too. I shouldn't have been so hard on you. I know you must also miss him."

Dany continued stroking Mal, but she laughed when he purred, stretched, and then disappeared.

"Guess he was done."

Gabe chuckled. "Cat probably called him or something." He put an arm around his sister and kissed her temple. "I love you, Dany. Am I forgiven?"

"Love you, too, Gabe," Dany said, snuggling closer into his side. "Thank you for coming to get me. That day, and this one."

"Never won't," Gabe said with a small squeeze of her shoulders.

Epilogue

July 2022 - Alku | Elaric Rickson

He knew the moment the chain caught his quarry, and his life was forfeit. Elaric tugged with all his might, and the rogue came tumbling over the edge of the well and down towards him. The darkness took over within a second, but Marco's elevated sight made it so Elaric saw each and every brick and rock they tumbled past. The woosh of the wind in his ears tried to deafen him as he tumbled deeper and deeper.

After a few seconds, he heard the rogue break out from Onnie's control, and he began to struggle against the chain around his neck. Elaric pulled the vile man closer to him and shifted his form into a large, burly man he'd once personified. The rogue could no longer struggle against the headlock Elaric had him in, and they continued to plummet.

Elaric felt as they neared the bottom and what would ultimately be his final resting place. He braced for the impact and wordlessly said goodbye to those he loved.

Then he felt nothing.

His body never hit the bottom, and Jakob was no longer in his hold.

"I don't think so, shifter. You will live to see the downfall of your precious Keeper and her friends," a voice hissed in the dark.

In an instant, Elaric felt more pain than he ever thought possible. His body was ripped apart and put back together a thousand times, and eventually, he lost all sense of time. Pain pierced his skull as if a red-hot poker was slammed through his eye sockets. He felt his bones crack, his lungs pierced by his ribs, and his nails ripped from their beds.

At some point, Elaric went numb, the torture still ongoing, but his mind shut itself away as a protective instinct.

When he was able to look around during the few seconds that his body was whole, he realized he was hovering in the air above a basin of water. As he was forced to shift into each of his forms, one after the other, he couldn't help but think his blood link with Marco was why he wasn't dead yet. If that was the case, maybe he'd made a mistake in requesting it, and death would have been better.

"Do not think of anything besides your anguish!" the rogue shouted before crushing Elaric's windpipe. "I want you to *feel* every second of our time together. I want you to beg for death."

Elaric's throat was released, and he involuntarily sucked in a huge gasp of air, but before he had recovered, he began to shift into forms he'd never taken before.

He was Dany, Gabe, the young girl in town who wouldn't speak, and then he was Marco.

"STOP!"

Elaric screamed into the darkness, sobs breaking from his chest and pounding in his ears. The rogue cackled, and Elaric continued to shift into additional impossibilities—bird, spider, snake, rat, cat, horse, cow, and so on.

"You will feel the pain of one thousand lifetimes before I am through with you, shifter," the rogue laughed again, his sickening cackle echoing up the small chamber walls. "Then I will shift you into the form I desire and lock you in it. You will live forever, doing nothing with your life but watching everyone around you die."

Elaric screamed until his throat was raw, and when he thought he couldn't scream anymore, the pain vanished entirely. His ears rang, and he squeezed his eyes shut even though he was already wrapped in darkness.

"I will have to keep you close, though. I want you to see every drop of pain I inflict on those you love."

Elaric could feel Jakob pacing around him, circling him like a hawk's latest prey.

"First, I will start with the Guardian. I will slowly break every bone in his body, and you will watch as he screams out in agony with each snap. Then I will leave him alive to watch as I strip the flesh and magic from his Keeper's body, inch by inch, until she is nothing but a bloody mass, devoid of magic and barely hanging on to life."

Elaric could feel Jakob's hot, rancid breath on his cheek.

"Then I will start with Dany. I will lock her up and keep her alive," he laughed, "for you, of course. She will be a wonderful test subject for my new magic and those of my followers. Whenever she is near death, I will bring her back from the beyond and start again. Slowly, you will watch everyone you love die, all while being powerless to stop it. What do you think of that, shifter?"

Elaric roared with rage, a roar of the most wounded soul. He screamed with so much soul that he felt it tear. His feet began to tingle and then further up his body until all he could hear in his head was the sound of his own heart beating.

Then, it stopped.

Once again, Elaric felt nothing, but his eyesight was crystal clear, and there was no more pain. Instead, he was staring down at the rogue.

"Impossible!" the man roared. "How did you do it?" The man looked frantically around the room. "Transmogromorph or human, neither has that much strength nor power."

Elaric looked down and saw a lifeless body, unmoving, lying in the mud and muck.

"Where are you? Show yourself!" the rogue bellowed. "Is this some final trick of your precious Keeper? No mortal can rip their soul from their body. It's impossible!"

The rogue continued to howl with rage, but Elaric blocked him out. Instead, he looked skyward and willed his incorporeal form up the shaft he'd recently fallen down and back to the world he knew and the family he loved.

Now, he just hoped that Onnie had a trick up her sleeve.

Eliza Leone

Eliza Leone is an author from the Pacific Northwest who specializes is chronicling the stories of her imaginary friends. As a kid, you could find her on the playground with a few kids acting out the stories they'd made up. When she got older and discovered there were entire worlds hidden within the pages of endless books, chances are her nose was in one. Over time, Friday nights were reserved for bookstore runs with her mother and together, they'd resupply for a week of adventures.

Writing had always been a far off dream, her ability to spell and do that grammar thing correctly, severely lacking. It wasn't until her mid-twenties that she decided if she was only writing it for herself, then no one would care about her lack of proper punctuation. Ten years and over a dozen books later, her family, human and fiction, convinced her to finally share her stories with the world.

From short stories and micro-fiction to the entire urban fantasy universe of Alku and its people, Eliza can't wait for you to giggle, sob, and throw your book across the room with her. Just...please don't throw the e-readers.

You can find Eliza Leone on: Instagram @ElizaLeone_author, Twitter @ELeone_author, and at ElizaLeone.com.

Leave feedback, read exclusive bonus content, and support this project at www.campfirewriting.com/explore/ElizaLeone

www.ingramcontent.com/pod-product-compliance
Lightning Source LLC
Chambersburg PA
CBHW060215030726
47499CB00004B/1057